Praise for the work

Schuss

This is an absolutely charming first-love, new-adult romance between characters that I had already bonded with. Seeing how they have grown and matured in the four years is a treat and watching the two struggle with their feelings for each other just melted my heart... *Schuss* could be read as a standalone novel, but honestly, I think you should read both books together. They are wonderful stories, and I highly recommend them.

-Betty H., *NetGalley*

E. J. Noyes has this way of writing characters that you get completely absorbed into. When we were left with the Gemma and Stacey cliffhanger in *Gold*, I was hoping we'd get their story and it was phenomenal.

-Les Bereading, *NetGalley*

If I Don't Ask

If I Don't Ask adds a profound depth to Sabine and Rebecca's story, and slots in perfectly with what we already knew about the characters and their motivations.

-Kaylee K., *NetGalley*

Overall, another winner by E. J. Noyes. An absolute pleasure to read. 5 stars.

-*Lez Review Books*

If I Don't Ask was just the right mix of old familiarity and exciting newness. It was a lot of fun reading about Rebecca's feelings during the early years of their relationship. This book is one of the many reasons that I will read anything that E. J.

Noyes writes in the future, it is a guaranteed hit. Her work is consistently good, characters always entertaining and full of heart. I'm definitely a reader for life.

-Ashlee G., NetGalley

Go Around

Noyes excels at writing both romance and intrigue and it shows in this book. Her characters might as well be real they are so well-written. I'm a pretty big fan of second-chance love stories, and I love the way this one is done. You get the angst you expect from the two women trying to get past the pain of their separation and work their way back to being a couple in love. The outside forces that had a role in their breakup are still around and have to be dealt with. Add in a nasty bad guy (or guys) who are physically and psychologically stalking Elise and you get a tale full of danger, excitement, intrigue, and romance. I also love the Easter egg the author included for her book *Alone*. I actually laughed out loud at that little scene. E. J. Noyes' works always get my highest praise and recommendation, and this novel is no different. You really need to read this book.

-Betty H., NetGalley

In *Go Around*, E. J. Noyes has dipped her toes in the second chance romance pool and was masterful in blending angst, enduring love and suspense in it. The chemistry and dynamics between the pair were thick and palpable but what stood out for me throughout the book was the type of love everyone wished they had; fierce and protective, grounded in loyalty, passionate yet to be able to just be when you are with the other. Noyes also made Bennet, Avery's dog another highlight for me. He was the tension breaker and a giant darling.

-Nutmeg, NetGalley

Pas de deux

Pas de deux doesn't disappoint: the writing is excellent, the pace is ideal, the characters are layered and, yes, relatable, including the secondary characters, from Caitlyn's groom Wren, to Addie's friend Teresa and, of course, Dewey the horse. One of the many things I loved in this book is the way the MCs deal with problems. They do this very adult and very rare-in-lesfic thing: they talk to each other. This book is proof that miscommunication isn't required for drama. Neither is a breakup. Well-fleshed characters with very human hang-ups bring all the angst and drama necessary. It's all the more interesting here as *Pas de deux* is part enemies-to-lovers romance, part second chance, depending on whose point of view is playing.

-*Les Rêveur*

This story is not the traditional enemies-to-lovers romance, and I love that. Noyes really puts emphasis on how skewed memories can become as you get older, and how an experience may appear different to another person who had the exact same one. Even if you are unfamiliar with dressage, Noyes' writing is still spot-on and delivers the same compelling, fun, and intriguing story with loveable characters of both the two-legged and four-legged kind. This love letter to a sport she obviously has a passion for is so evident and I felt honored to have her share her passion with me and every reader who picks it up. If you love horses, enemies-to-lovers, or even just Noyes' stories in general, this one will definitely be a favorite on your list.

-*The Lesbian Review*

This romance hit two main tropes. For one main character this is a second chance romance, for the other character, this is an enemies to lovers romance. I loved the two different sides of how the character saw things and I think it gave the book a little zip that caught my attention from the beginning. I was very happy that while this was first person, the POV is actually from both main characters. It was perfect for this book especially since both mains can't even agree on their past. Seeing how each character thought and why, was the right choice for this romantic story. As long as you are a fan of horses, or at least are okay with them, then I would absolutely recommend this one. Noyes writes really well and makes smart choices so that is why she is one of the best.

-Lex Kent's Reviews, *goodreads*

Reaping the Benefits

The story is quite eccentric with its paranormal context but in fact is a pure romance at heart with a nice dose of humor. The book is written in third person, from the point of view of both protagonists, which is not common for Noyes, but it is executed perfectly. With all main elements done well, this makes an awesome read which I could easily recommend to all romance fans.

-Pin's Reviews, *goodreads*

I've read many love stories that entertain the idea of soul mates, but this one does something even more interesting. This one explores the depth of love and its ability to transcend death. This story plays with the idea that love has no limits or boundaries. Its exploration provides a unique setting for this heartfelt romantic tale. At its core it remains a romance. The love story between Jane and Morgan is tender and sweet. It's so cleverly and delightfully done; I've never read anything quite like it before. Noyes possesses the ability to see a story where others don't and turn that into something unique and captivating. She uses rich storytelling and engaging characters to enthrall and delight us.

It's fresh and original. It's everything you crave when you want to dig into a great romance. I highly recommend it.

-Deb M., *NetGalley*

I'm spectacularly smitten with Death, to be specific with E. J. Noyes' personification of death as Cici La Morte in this new and most wondrous book. Cici is not one of the main characters but she is the fulcrum about which the whole plot rotates. She simultaneously operates as a beautiful symbol of our fascination with the theme of death and loss, and as a comedic but wise Greek chorus guiding Morgan through the internal conflict threatening to tear her very soul apart. All of E. J. Noyes' previous books have had emotionally charged first-person narrative, so I was curious how her switch to writing in the third person would play out here, but it really works. Despite many lighthearted and genuinely funny moments I found that this book not only had E. J. Noyes' signature ability to make me cry, but also fascinating ideas and philosophies about grief, loss, and hope.

-Orlando J., *NetGalley*

If you're looking for a lesbian romance, but with a twist of something different, I recommend *Reaping the Benefits*. It's sweet, sexy, and fun.

-*The Lesbian Review*

If the Shoe Fits

When we pick up an E. J. Noyes book we expect intensity, characters with issues (circumstantial and/or internal), and a romance that builds believably. Considering this is *Ask, Tell* #3 we expected all of the above layered with epic seriousness. We were pleasantly surprised and totally floored by the humor in addition to what was already expected!

-*Best Lesfic Reviews*

Alone

E. J. Noyes is easily one of the most gifted writers pulling us into whatever world she creates making us live and feel every emotion with her characters. Definitely, loudly, vehemently recommended.

-Reviewer@Large, *NetGalley*

Alone is an absolutely stunning book. This book is not a 5-star, it is well above that. You don't see books like this one very often. Truly a treasure and one that will stay with you long after the final page.

-Tiff's Reviews, *goodreads*

There are only a handful of authors that I will drop everything to read as soon as a new book comes out, and Noyes is at the top of that list. It seems no matter what Noyes writes she doesn't disappoint. I will eagerly be waiting for whatever she writes next.

-Lex Kent's Reviews, *goodreads*

There are only a few books out there so compelling they seem to take control of you and force you to read them as quickly as possible. You can't put them down. You just want the world to go away and leave you alone until you can finish this story. *Alone* by E. J. Noyes is that book for me. This novel is absolutely wonderful.

-Betty H., *NetGalley*

Not only is this easily one of the best books of 2019, but it has worked its way onto my personal all-time top 10 list. There is not one formulaic thing going on, and it's "unputdownable."

-Karen C., *NetGalley*

I cannot give this anything more than five stars, but damn I wish I could. I would give it 15.

-Carolyn M., *NetGalley*

Ask Me Again

Not every story needs a sequel. *Ask, Tell* demanded it, and Noyes delivers in spectacular fashion. Sabine and Rebecca show us their fortitude and their strength in their love for each other...Thank you, Noyes, for giving us a great story, a great series, and amazing women that teach us the best things in life are worth fighting for.

There really is only one way to tell this story, and Noyes executes it perfectly. She gives us events from the first-person perspective. However, she alternates each chapter between Sabine's point of view and Rebecca's point of view. You're able to get the full perspective of their inner feelings and turmoil they hide from one another. In addition, you're able to get the complete picture of the unconditional love Sabine and Rebecca have for each other. It's this little light of love that propels the reader to keep going and hope these women will finally reach the end of the darkness.

-The Lesbian Review

Gold

This is Noyes' third book, and her writing just keeps getting better and better with each release. She gives us such amazing characters that are easy for anyone to relate to. And she makes them so endearing that you can't help but want them to overcome the past and move forward toward their happily ever after.

-The Lesbian Review

This book is exactly the way I wish romance authors would get back to writing romance. This is what I want to read. If you are a Noyes fan, get this book. If you are a romance fan, get this book. I didn't even talk about the skiing... if you are a skiing fan, get this book.

-Lex Kent's Reviews, *goodreads*

Turbulence

Wow… and when I say 'wow' I mean… WOW. After the author's debut novel *Ask, Tell* got to my list of best books of 2017, I was wondering if that was just a fluke. Fortunately for us lesfic readers, now it's confirmed: E. J. Noyes CAN write. Not only that, she can write different genres… Written in first person from Isabelle's point of view, the reader gets into her headspace with all her insecurities, struggles, and character traits. Alongside Isabelle, we discover Audrey's personality, her life story and, most importantly, her feelings. Throughout the book, Ms. Noyes pushes us down a roller coaster of emotions as we accompany Isabelle in her journey of self-discovery. In the process, we laugh, suffer, and enjoy the ride.

-Gaby, *goodreads*

The entire story just flowed from the first page! E. J. Noyes did a superb job of bringing out Isabelle's and Audrey's personalities, faults, erratic emotions, and the burning passion they shared. The chemistry between both women was so palpable! I felt as though the writer drizzled every word she wrote with love, combustible desire, and intense longing.

-*The Lesbian Review*

Ask, Tell

This is a book with everything I love about top quality lesbian fiction: a fantastic romance between two wonderful women I can relate to, a location that really made me think again about something I thought I knew well, and brilliant pacing and scene-setting. I cannot recommend this novel highly enough.

-*Rainbow Book Reviews*

Noyes totally blew my mind from the first sentence. I went in timidly, and I came away awaiting her next release with bated breath. I really love how Noyes is able to get below the surface of the DADT legislation. She really captures the longing, the heartbreak, and especially the isolation that LGBTQ soldiers had to endure because the alternative was being deemed unfit to serve by their own government. I applaud Noyes for getting to the heart of the matter and giving a very important representation of what living and serving under this legislation truly meant for LGBTQ men and women of service.

-*The Lesbian Review*

E. J. Noyes was able to deliver on so many levels… This book is going to take you on a roller-coaster ride of ups and downs that you won't expect but it's so unbelievably worth it.

-*Les Rêveur*

Noyes clearly undertook a mammoth amount of research. I was totally engrossed. I'm not usually a reader of romance novels, but this one gripped me. The personal growth of the main character, the rich development of her fabulous best friend, Mitch, and the well-handled tension between Sabine and her love interest were all fantastic. This one definitely deserves five stars.

-*CELEStial books Reviews*

INTEGRITY

BOOK ONE
IN THE
HALCYON DIVISION SERIES

E. J. NOYES

Other Bella Books by E. J. Noyes

Ask, Tell
Turbulence
Gold
Ask Me Again
Alone
If the Shoe Fits
Reaping the Benefits
Pas de deux
Go Around
If I Don't Ask
Schuss

About the Author

E. J. Noyes is an Australian transplanted to New Zealand, which may be the awesomest thing to happen to her. She lives with her wife, a needy cat and too many plants (and is planning on getting more plants). When not indulging in her love of reading and writing, E. J. argues with her hair and pretends to be good at things.

INTEGRITY

BOOK ONE
IN THE
HALCYON DIVISION SERIES

E. J. NOYES

BELLA
BOOKS

2023

Bella Books, Inc.
P.O. Box 10543
Tallahassee, FL 32302

Printed in the United States of America on acid-free paper.

First Edition - 2023

Editor: Cath Walker
Cover Designer: Heather Honeywell

ISBN: 978-1-64247-465-7

Acknowledgments

This story went through many evolutions, a lot of hair-pulling, and a massive dose of imposter syndrome because I'd never tackled a plot that had so many moving pieces before. As a person who doesn't plan her novels, it was a daunting task, but the result is something I'm incredibly proud of, and I hope you follow Lexie and Sophia through the rest of their journey in the Halcyon Division series.

Kate – I mean, yeah, your insight and all that is amazing, but what I'm most grateful for is that you always give me the most important thing of yours—your time.

Claire, we changed it up this time! Thanks for the alpha read, pal. Hopefully this iteration is a little more polished.

Abby, thanks for the crash course in yoga poses.

I'm so thankful to Rrrose, who told me straight-up that the whole basis for the plot I'd written in my first draft would never fly in the intelligence world, forcing me to rewrite pretty much the whole thing. Welcome to pantser woes. But I think this book, and the series, is far better for the change brought about by your insight.

I cannot express the enormity of my gratitude to Betsy, who responded to my plaintive (and vague) wail on Twitter and went above and beyond to help me make Lexie's world sound authentic. Betsy, thank you for your expertise, your kindness, and your time, especially when I snuck up on you again with what was supposed to just be questions, then threw this at you at the 11th hour to read for me.

Cath, plot fixer extraordinaire! We took a bit of a different (and quicker) path than usual, but we did it! Thank you for prioritising this one for me at such a busy time of year.

Linda, Jessica, Bella Books Behind-the-Scenes Friends. You're all awesome and work so hard. And, Jessica? You were right about the timing of these ones; glad you saw it when I was still all gung-ho, flex, I can do three in a year! Spoiler alert: I now know I totally couldn't have.

Pheebs – this was a whinge-fest, I know. But guess what! There's two more (at least!) to come in this series that'll be equally as whingy until I fall in love with what I've written as much as I fell in love with you. In sickness, health, and spousal author woes, right?

Author's Note

It's fiction.

CHAPTER ONE

The day I received the call that would change my life, and not in a good infomercial promise kind of way

When the VoIP phone on my desk rang, I had to excavate the infrequently used handset from under a pile of paper. An early-morning call from an asset. Exciting. I set aside the taskings I was reading and brought up a blank document ready for notes. As I typed the date, time, and incoming number from the digital screen, I started the recording function, double-checked the encryption, and answered the call not with my usual crisp "Lexie Martin" but with a bland "Hello?"

"Ellen, hello," said a man in accented English.

Ellen… Nobody had called me that in months. One of the first things I'd had drilled into me during my initial training was never give my real name to an asset. I'd had a thing for Ellen Ripley from the *Alien* movies. It'd been a logical choice.

I smiled at the sound of the voice. "Hadim." I had no idea if Hadim was his real name either, but it was way down the list of things important to our working relationship. "How are you? It's been some time."

Almost a year, but that was generally how our contact was. Sporadic. We'd first met in the Middle Eastern region almost ten years earlier, when I was an Ops Officer instead of an Analyst, and my job was more about collection rather than analysis. Back then I spent a lot of time moving around the world instead of just from my apartment to my cubicle and back again each day. I'd been talent-spotting and recruiting female assets—men often forgot their women overheard things—and Hadim had approached me after his wife mentioned I'd been speaking with her. After the usual period of suspicion and vetting, he'd quickly proven his usefulness and loyalty to me. Or perhaps more accurately, his loyalty to my country's money. In all the years we'd been working together, he'd never once passed me bad intel—and he would only pass it to me, even though I'd left fieldwork behind five and a half years ago.

"I'm as well as I can expect, and you?" Behind his voice was the background drone of cars and people, which meant he was in his city apartment overlooking the marketplace. I could picture the hot, noisy space with its distinctive sights, scents, and sounds, and had a sudden urge to go back there and slowly browse through the almost-overwhelming amount of offerings, to find something for dinner, something to wear, something to give as a gift.

"About the same as the last time we spoke. Are you safe?" My question had a dual meaning: safe both physically, and with his communication channels.

"Yes."

"Good, I'm glad to hear it." Dispensing with further unnecessary formality, I asked, "What can I help you with?"

"Five nights ago there was an incident. A squad of Red Wolves attacked a small village in the Aqtash District in Kunduz Province, up near the Afghanistan-Tajikistan border. A village comprised mostly of civilians, not insurgents. There were no survivors among the three hundred and sixty-two inhabitants. Men, women, and children."

I swallowed hard, and tried to sound casual. "Okay, and why should Red Wolves doing what they always do concern me?" Rhetorical question of course. The Red Wolves were a well-organized militia group, with rumored ties to Russia, that'd popped up almost eighteen months ago. No agency in any country had been able to determine their true nationality or loyalty, but everything they did seemed to be magically in Russia's best interests. If the shoe fits...

"Because they didn't go in with assault rifles blazing, Ellen. They used something that they should not have. Something I have *never* seen or heard of before, and something that I believe would be prohibited under the Chemical Weapons Convention."

That immediately got my attention, and sent a simultaneous surge of excitement and worry through me. There were only a few countries who were non-signatory on the CWC, and if someone had broken the treaty... I had to bite back my *fuck*. "What exactly did they use? In what form?"

"I don't know the specifics, but I believe it was airborne."

I couldn't bite this one back. "Fuck," I muttered. A new chemical weapon capable of airborne dispersion. Brilliant.

Hadim cleared his throat before I heard the long drag on his cigarette. "There is more. I am hearing a lot of chatter and everyone says the Red Wolves didn't plan this themselves, but instead were operating under a, what is it you would say? Quid... pro quo arrangement with another country."

My attention was now at attention and the tingling down my spine out in full force. "Okay. What do you have that I can take to my boss?" Hearsay was as worthless as no information at all. And this information would need to be shared with another specialized counterterrorism department, namely those who worked in WMD—Weapons of Mass Destruction—so I needed solid, actionable intelligence.

"The three Vs." Voice, video, visual. A jackpot.

"Perfect," I breathed, typing furiously. "Thank you. Is the video from Airborne, or...?"

"A body camera." He swallowed audibly. "And it is not pleasant viewing. In fact, I would say it is very *un*pleasant." Coming from Hadim, who'd been in the middle of one war or another for most of his life and would have seen some truly horrendous things, that was saying something.

Side thought: Why would a militia group film their chemical weapon attack on a group of (probably) unarmed civilians? I didn't want to sound ungrateful, but I had to ask, "You didn't come across any Airborne footage at all? That seems strange."

There was an uncomfortably long pause. "Perhaps it is. But I think the *why* of that fact is a question you will need to direct to those who operate your drones."

My gut sank to my feet at his implication. What he wasn't saying was as important as what he had said. I made a note about the pause and his careful tone. "Got it. I haven't seen anything at all about this." Even if it was being handled by another team or agency, I should have seen *something*. But there hadn't been a single bit of chatter. Any chemical weapon attack, hell even just the planning of one, should have been picked up by someone in WMD. The thought that we'd missed something made me feel trembly inside. We had eyes *everywhere*. I forced cheer into my voice, unwilling to let him hear what I felt. "You're a magician, you know that?" I would have loved to know how he managed to get body cam footage from a Russian...sorry, *stateless*, militia.

He chuckled. "Yes, you have told me that before. I have sent everything I could get to you via our usual method. Use password number fourteen to unlock the encryption on the email."

"Thank you. Check your account tomorrow and there will be something in there for your trouble."

"I appreciate that. Next time you're in my country, come find me. You still owe me a chess game for the one you abandoned to catch your flight. Dinner will be on me."

"A seven-year-delayed chess game?" I laughed, genuinely amused. "And you mean dinner is on *me*, considering I'm paying you." What he'd been paid for his intelligence could fund thousands of dinners. But he was worth every dime.

"That is true," he agreed teasingly. Hadim took another slow drag on his cigarette, and when he spoke again I could hear the hesitation. Nervousness... Unusual from him. "Ellen? I do not have a good feeling about this one. Be cautious."

The fact he'd expressed the sentiment made me pay attention. "I will. Take care, talk to you when I do."

We hung up, I saved the recording to my computer and backed it up, then put on headphones and transcribed the call, fleshing out the notes I'd made during my conversation with Hadim. Once I had a solid bare-bones document, I logged in to my assets-only account on one of the agency's private email account servers, input the *Hadim Password #14* from memory (no, it's not Hadimpassword14), and started malware scans that would stop even the sneakiest thing a hacker might try to slip through. Not that Hadim was a hacker, but inadvertently introducing a virus or worm into one of the most secure government areas would earn me a black mark on my performance evaluation.

I rolled my chair back, hitting the filing cabinet behind me, as usual. Nine thirty a.m. Tea and processed snack food time. Samuel, one of my teammates, was in our fourth floor's communal kitchen, hovering over the coffee maker like he was afraid someone would steal it from him. He glanced over his shoulder and offered a smile, then leaned over to flip the electric kettle on for me.

I returned the smile, though it took some effort given what I'd just learned. "Thanks. How's Muffin?" I pulled down the container of Oolong tea labeled "Lexie's—please don't steal!" from the cabinet. My colleagues were tea heathens, and the thought of one of the Earl Grey in a Tea Bag group butchering my Oolong made me want to cry.

"Still hates her cone of shame but seems to be healing up okay." His cat, a.k.a. Sam's most favorite thing in the world, had had an altercation with the neighborhood cat-bully. I'd been hearing about it, including comforting him when he'd thought Muffin wouldn't make it, for the past week.

"Just tell her it's the latest in cat fashion and I'm sure she'll change her mind." I peered around the tiny, dated kitchen. "Have you seen my tea infuser?"

"Dish drainer," Sam said instantly. "I emptied and rinsed it before I left work yesterday afternoon."

"Thank you, kitchen angel. You wanna get married? I'll cook, you do all the dishes."

"Mmm, tempting," he drawled, then quickly added, "but, pass. Even if we set aside the insurmountable issue of neither of us being attracted to the opposite gender, I can't stand the way you make cauliflower rice in the microwave. It's bad enough having it at work a few times a month. Not in my own home, thank you."

"Someone has to be the office microwave jerk. And it could be worse, I could be microwaving fish. You're being dramatic."

"True. But still a pass." He took his eyes off the coffee machine for a moment. "Speaking of marriage, how'd that second date go last week?"

Chemical weapons fell out of my head, warm fuzzies jumped in. "Really well. She's cute and funny and smart and she still hasn't run screaming, so I'm taking that as a good sign. I'm also taking a lot of flirty messages and calls around us trying to schedule dates as a good sign. Oh, and I should also count our third-date late-breakfast tomorrow as a good sign, right?" The sparky chemistry I felt every time I looked at, texted and talked to, or touched her, was also a very good sign.

He applauded me. "Way to go, you! Putting yourself out there. It's been...how long since you last dated?"

"Mumble-mumble-mumble years." Five years and six months, to be exact, and not even in this country. Stepping back into the dating pond was beyond weird. After filling my infuser with loose tea and dropping it into my octopus mug, I leaned against the mottled gray Formica counter. "Hey, have you seen anything coming out of Kunduz Province, or anything involving Red Wolves anywhere?"

Sam's eyebrows bounced up. "Timeframe?"

"Within the last week or so."

He stared absently into space, and after about thirty seconds, said, "Just the usual low-level chatter from Kunduz, nothing that stands out, and I don't recall any mention of Red Wolves operating at all recently. Why?"

The kettle clicked off and I carefully poured water into my mug. "I heard something this morning from a friend, something I don't like, something we should have heard about sooner. I was wondering if I'd fallen out of the loop somehow." And more than that—wondering why nobody seemed to know about this.

Samuel laugh-snorted. "As if. You're like Derek's prizewinning pet. You're the center of the loop." He nabbed a packet of Cheddar Cheese Pretzel Combos from the basket of snacks in the corner and tossed it at me.

I caught it one-handed.

After being waylaid by colleagues wanting my opinion or wanting to ask about my weekend plans—which was really just a way to segue into telling me about *their* weekend plans—I finally got back to my cubicle. The files Hadim sent were all clean—not that I'd expected anything dirty. I downloaded everything which, as usual, he'd thoughtfully labeled for me, then I filled in a payment request and emailed it to Accounts who'd wire him some money. Job done. Except for the job still to be done.

There was an audio file, a video file, and a folder full of photographs. I put on my noise-canceling headset to block out the chatter filtering over the annoyingly low "let's encourage collaboration" cube walls and cued up the audio. This first pass, I'd take no notes, just listen.

Two men. One obviously American, well-educated Boston-ish accent, authoritative. The second was Russian, his English good, accent smooth and cultured, so he wasn't a Russian roughneck. The tone between the two was casual, almost congenial, as if they were two pals talking about a sportsball match. The content of the conversation was not casual. I scrubbed back to the start and this time, as I listened, transcribed frantically.

American: The product will be delivered to the warehouse at nineteen hundred tonight, operation begins at twenty-one hundred. Do you have appropriate safety equipment?

Russian: Yes, Colonel, and my team have been instructed in how to safely handle the product.

A: Good. [Long pause – smoking?] Once we've confirmed the efficiency and efficacy, the funds will be wired to your government and the other items delivered to the drop points you requested.

R: What if it does not work? What happens to our payment?

A: It'll damned well work, if your team uses it as instructed. Any inefficiency will be on your head, and it'll be your fault the funding and equipment don't come through.

R: *Russian expletive* Red Wolves do not fail.

A: Good [Slap sound – handshake or back slap?] Then it works out for everyone, doesn't it? I'll see you at twenty-one hundred. [Laughter, like a chuckle or snicker – sounds condescending] Don't forget to bring your gas mask.

Notes: Background noise busy, mechanical/cars, no other voices detected on recording, no animal sounds detected, no echo indicating that it's indoors. Colonel – legitimate military, or backyard militia? Russian – no title or rank, feels inferior to the American?

As I listened for the third time, I read through the transcription to ensure I had it all down correctly and to confirm what I'd heard was actually what I was hearing. Yep, it seemed like it. Unfortunately. Time to flesh this out a little with the photos and video. The moment I opened the photos I really wished I didn't have to flesh it out. A tiny part of me, the part that always reacted this way when I saw how awful some humans could be, wanted to turn off my screen and pretend I'd never received Hadim's call.

Thankfully my rational brain took over. If I didn't investigate, there would be future victims of this new chemical weapon. People in another city, another province, another country. I owed it to them to get as much information as I could, so nobody else would suffer the way these civilians had. And they had suffered.

After an hour of poring over photographs and the body cam video of the…incident, I wanted to barf. To say what I was watching was disgusting, horrifying, and heartbreaking would barely scratch the surface of my emotion. Whatever they'd used to murder three hundred and sixty-two people, with no regard as to whether they were men, women, or children, acted like someone had mixed sarin and sulfur mustard and phosgene gases into one nightmare chemical agent. It was like it was designed to cause a horrible, painful, prolonged death, and nothing else.

My mouth was dry, my stomach burning with an unpleasant mix of heartburn and nausea—the horror of what I'd witnessed was taking physical form. Adding to my discomfort was the fact I'd spotted a very familiar flash of fabric in a few frames of the video. I'd need video enhancement techs to confirm, but I'd bet my last cup of Oolong that it was a US Army uniform. So the American, "Colonel," really was military, rather than a backyard militia guy? Active duty, someone retired or discharged, or worst-case for the investigation—someone who'd grabbed a uniform from a surplus store.

Time to take a break, clear my head a little, and see what my boss thought. I copied the files to a shared internal server, password-protected each one, then wandered through the hallways to his office. Derek said nothing when I knocked, simply indicated I should come in. So I did. Midfifties, fit, and with his silver-gray hair cut into a neat buzz, Derek looked exactly like what he was—an ex-military intelligence officer, as hardass as he was compassionate. We'd met when he was still in the military, and I was still wet behind the ears and trying to figure out how to exist while doing my job in a hostile area. We had become close despite our age, background, and job differences, and not long after I'd changed roles five years ago, he'd retired from military intelligence and taken up a job at the agency as my boss.

Sam was right. I was Derek's pet. But it was about more than me being very good at my job and working hard. Derek and I never talked about that day. But every now and then he would ask me, almost absently, and without context, "You okay?" I knew exactly what he meant. And I always said "Yes," because I was okay. Mostly.

"I had a call-in a few hours ago," I said, "and I want to know what you think. The files are on our shared drive, folder named LM-2022-10-14."

"What's the password?"

I told him.

Derek started a virus scan, and I gave him my best withering look, even though I knew it was just a habit, and a good one at that. He shrugged. "I don't know what you get up to on that computer of yours."

"Apparently, watching virus-laden porn all day every day," I deadpanned.

"I'm not sure when you fit that in around all the cat videos and memes."

"I'm surprised you know what a meme is. Have you been researching how to sound like a millennial?"

"You brat."

I ignored the obviousness of his statement to tell him, "Listen to the audio first."

Derek slipped his clunky, eighties-esque headset over his ears. "I'll have you know I'm very hip," he said, too loudly, and too late. He navigated through files then turned slightly away and closed his eyes.

I dropped into one of the old, badly upholstered chairs on the other side of his desk and waited, turning the intel over in my head. After over a decade in this field of work, I'd found if I relaxed and let my brain wander about as it pleased, I usually had more luck than if I tried to force connections. I kept coming back to one uneasy conclusion, though I'd never say it with any certainty until I was certain—a Russian militia group had been bribed by a member of the American military, who likely had orders from higher up the command chain, to test a new, illegal, chemical weapon on civilians. That was the top of the umbrella, and all the reasons why this was really *really* bad fell from it like raindrops.

After a few minutes Derek tugged one side of the headset from his ear and confirmed my thoughts. "I think that sounds an awful lot like an American, possibly military, coercing a militia group who we suspect are Russian to do something dirty for us or they will withhold financial packages and-or weapons or something else they would want or need." He played it again, and after finishing his second forehead-furrowed listen he looked up at me. "What else do you have?"

"Body cam footage and photos, of the test and its aftermath. Neither are very nice." I gestured. "They're on the drive. I hope you haven't eaten."

His eyebrows went up. "You know that stuff doesn't bother me."

"Don't say I didn't tell you..." I said as he started clicking through files.

"That's not nice," he said calmly once he'd finished, though his face made it clear he was bothered.

"Mmm," I agreed, thinking I'd just told him it wasn't nice and he should really listen to me. I would have said more, but his expression had made my brain drag those images from the secret hiding place I'd put them in so I didn't have to think about it. And now I was thinking about it. "Scroll to two minutes fifty-one in the video and tell me if you see anything."

Derek did as I'd told him, but said nothing. Either he hadn't seen the brief glimpse of US Army camo, or he was keeping his cards close. Probably the latter. Intelligence analysts were notoriously allergic to commitment in the workplace. I'd seen satellite images of locations of interest showing something a five-year-old would recognize as a tank, labeled "probable tank." Derek tapped his pen against the side of his neck, a thinking habit he'd had for as long as I'd known him.

"What do you think?" I asked, leaning forward expectantly.

He shook his head, pulled the headset off and dropped it on his desk among a stack of papers, two dirty coffee mugs, and so many broken pencils I'd consider him a sociopath if I didn't know him so well. "Nothing I'd commit to without further information."

Exactly the response I'd expected. "Okay, but, I mean, this is kind of a big deal, right? You'd have to imagine the White House knows that we've basically bribed a foreign entity, and not a friendly one at that, to do our dirty work in exchange for giving them aid." I smiled sweetly, and amended my statement. "Or... that's the *probable* explanation."

"Yes. So it looks like."

"Also concerning is why Russia would risk its relationship with Afghanistan in such a huge way, because this is something that'd immediately sever their already fragile diplomacy if the Afghans had the intel we do. Unless something massive is happening that nobody knows about, and the Afghan government is also involved in this." In which case, I was doubly confused. And alarmed. America plus Russia plus Afghanistan equaled...something really fucking scary. I shook the thought off. There was *no* way. Was there? Because if we'd missed this, what else had we missed?

"Whoa. Back up a step. Back up ten steps. No leaps."

"Okay, okay." I mumbled a phrase my father had often repeated at me, even before I'd started this job. "Think before you act. I got it."

"Exactly." Derek eyed me over the top of his reading glasses. "But I think you're right. This doesn't sound or look like some small-time guy acting on his own to impress his terrorist friends."

I popped double gun fingers at him. "Bingo. I'd put money on the fact someone in the White House authorized this, or at the very least, knows about it. And if that's the case then why haven't any of us been briefed about it?" It was no secret that the member organizations of the United States Intelligence Community sometimes forgot how to share amongst themselves, but still... "Or have you been briefed? Is there something I don't know about? Also, another thing I really want to know is why didn't Airborne catch anything?"

"Don't." The word was flat, completely without anger, but his meaning was clear. Accusing our government of such things was a good way to lose my security clearance and even end my career. "Dig some more, figure it out, show me some solid and workable intel on this."

"Solid? Are you shitting me, Derek? I'd say what I have now is rock." Well, maybe not rock solid but it was definitely gravel solid. You could build on gravel. "Something stinks, and even if it's not what it looks like, then we've still got a group of Russian militia illegally testing a new chemical weapon on another country's citizens. I know Russia-Afghanistan relations aren't that healthy, but still...Can I prioritize this?"

"Well, it's obviously worthy of investigation," he said dryly. "So, give me a report I can disseminate through the IC by next Thursday at the latest. And let me know if you need a team." He paused. "I have a briefing on the top floor next Friday and if this is what we think it might be then we'll need to interface with another agency or office, WMD at the very least. Always fun," he added under his breath.

I made cheerleading motions. "Yay, collaboration."

Derek hmphed. "I have to get ready for our team meeting. Don't be late today." I knew his expression—we're done for now, do your job and come back to me.

I left Derek's office, mulling over my boss's unusual apathy. No, not apathy, but almost…disinterest. His reaction was odd. Here I was with something that was one-hundred percent actionable and he was acting like I'd just told him my brother's girlfriend's hairstylist's second cousin had seen a rumor on Facebook. Maybe he had Fridayitis like the rest of us.

The one thing I did have was a gut feeling that got stronger and stronger the more I thought about what I'd seen and heard. Since I'd started this job, my gut was the one thing I never questioned. Something stank, and I needed to find the source of it even if Derek apparently had a clothespin on his nose.

It was after six by the time I'd finished the bare-bones draft of my report, and my eyes felt like I'd been pouring sand into them all afternoon. Let's see you try to shut this down now, Derek. Okay, so I was still running with nothing more than a bunch of dots that needed connecting but I could see that they *would* connect with a little more work. I'd have a relaxing weekend and be ready to continue the investigation on Monday morning when I came back into the office. I snorted to myself, because even I knew that was a lie. I'd be thinking about this until I came back after the weekend.

"This is why you don't have a social life, Lexie," I mumbled to myself. "Sorry, can't go to the movies or spend a weekend at some romantic location because my every waking hour is spent trying to stop terrorism and keep diplomatic relations stable." Yawning, I pulled off my glasses, saved everything in three locations then shut down my computer, gathered my things and left the office.

"Burning the midnight oil again?" Kevin, one of the many personnel who kept the premises secure, asked as I approached the door.

"Six p.m. oil. Not so bad." I pushed my handbag and gym bag through the portal into the scanning machine, then held up my credentials, despite him knowing exactly who I was and the fact I was exiting not entering the building.

He peered at the hand I had outstretched. "Bad enough."

I shrugged. No point in going over something we both knew—I had no life outside of work. "I missed you this morning." We'd been bantering daily since he'd started two years ago, most of which was me imparting a random fact of the day upon him. All because he'd made an offhanded comment about me being Dr. Martin, which led to me correcting that it wasn't medical, but actually a PhD in Political Science-slash-International Relations, to which he'd responded that I must be clever. So of course I had to flex my random-fact muscles. Google while eating dinner helped prepare me for our next-day fact interaction.

He pulled a face. "Had to see my cardiologist."

I paused. "Oh? Everything okay?"

"Clean bill of health."

"Good for you, glad to hear it." I passed through the human scanner arch and was halted instantly by its blaring. Should have known.

Kevin didn't blink as he asked, "Anything unusual on your person, Dr. Martin?"

I backed out and unbuckled my belt. "Sorry. New belt." I yanked it through the loops on my skirt in one smooth motion and passed it to him. "It did the same thing this morning. Looks like it's relegated to non-work wear."

I walked through again without any alarm and collected my scanned and cleared handbag, gym bag, and belt from him. "Marie Curie's laboratory notebooks are still radioactive from all her work and research into radium and stuff, even after a hundred years. They'll have to be kept in lead containers for another fifteen-hundred years. So, stay away."

"Damn, there goes my vacation plan of visiting her books… wherever the books are." It was delivered perfectly deadpan.

I laughed as I scanned my badge to activate the turnstile. "Paris. I recommend it if you ever get the chance, radioactive notebooks and all." As I pushed through the turnstile, the door ten yards ahead buzzed and clicked open, permitting my exit. "Night, Kevin."

"Have a good evening, Dr. Martin."

Doing a one-eighty to face him, I said, "You too, and enjoy your weekend. See you Monday."

I slipped outside and veered around a concrete bollard disguised as a planter, and onto the sidewalk. I'd never felt any discomfort walking around outside work at night—the entire site was well-lit, securely fenced, gated, and patrolled. Which was good, because I'd missed the shuttle that would take me to the very far corner of "Parkistan," the auxiliary parking lot farthest from my building and the only place I could find a spot that morning after arriving late thanks to a traffic accident.

After a twelve-minute powerwalk-slash-jog, I stowed my bags in the trunk of my VW EV and extracted my personal phone from its daytime resting place inside a thermal-protection lockbox secured to a bolt on the chassis. The moment I'd powered it on again, a handful of personal email alerts landed. Bill, bill, you're-due-for-a-dental-checkup email, bill, shipping notification. Boring. I couldn't even recall the last time I'd had an email from a friend. Maybe around the time Myspace was popular.

Friendships and relationships were great, but also…not. It was one thing to maintain those things when you already had them, but when you worked the hours and sometimes the locations I did—or rather, the locations I used to—it was infinitely harder. Creating new relationships was a nightmare, as I'd discovered during my sporadic attempts in the last few years to make friends and find someone to date. Or even just someone for some no-strings sex would be great. But…thanks to an epiphany a few months ago on the first anniversary of my parents' death, I'd decided to do something about my lack of personal life and signed up for a dating app. Then I'd ignored it for a month. Baby steps.

I opened up my messages, rereading the brief exchange from yesterday.

I'm really looking forward to seeing you again on Saturday.

Me too. I promise I won't forget to kiss you this time.

I smiled at the thought, and scrolled back through the flirty messages, enjoying the anticipation as I let the words sink in anew. I'd think about that promised kiss when I got home.

The drive was its usual metro hell-commute, and after a shower I drank a small glass of pinot while cooking dinner, ate dinner, then settled on the couch to read until it was an acceptable time to go to bed. I was tired but my brain was still humming with what I'd seen and heard in Hadim's files, and I lay there thinking instead of sleeping. New strategy needed. I stripped my bed and remade it with crisp clean sheets, then lit candles in my meditation room and lay on the plush carpet until my mind had shed everything unwanted. I was asleep within minutes of climbing naked under the sheets.

Asleep, until the instinctive awareness that I wasn't alone woke me from my usual dream-filled sleep. Groggy and disoriented, I lay still with my eyes closed, taking a moment to figure out where in my room the person who should not be in my room was. Near the door. Near my only exit.

I tensed, and a deep male voice said, "Oh, good, that saves me waking you."

CHAPTER TWO

Add this to the reasons why I don't like men in my bedroom

I turned on the bedside lamp, then pulled the covers up over my breasts. Probably should have covered myself *before* turning on the light. The stranger in my bedroom wore a tailored suit that hugged his muscles, so was clearly not a random hobo breaking into my apartment for some of my food and jewelry. The bulge of a holstered handgun under his armpit was an unpleasant sidenote. Mhmm, yeah…really doubtful that he wanted jewelry or a snack.

He leaned casually against the wall, like breaking into someone's house was one of his regular nighttime activities. I studied him, though even as I memorized his features—full lower lip which made his mouth seem unbalanced, mole on his left cheekbone, requisite boisterous boyhood scar on chin, brown eyes and hair, blandly accented tenor, five-eleven, obviously enjoyed the gym, maybe thirty years old—I realized how pointless it was. The fact I was seeing his face meant he didn't care about me seeing his face, which didn't bode well for me being able to make an identification once this was said and done.

The only thing I could think to say was a very clever, "Who are you? What do you want?"

He didn't answer my first question, and in a roundabout way answered my second. "Ms. Martin. I'll be brief so we can get this over with and you can come back to bed. You received intelligence regarding a minor and regrettable incident in Kunduz Province, Afghanistan. You are going to forget what you heard and saw. Please get dressed, collect your credentials and other necessities so that we can go in and debrief you regarding this intel, and then you will access the server and remove those files from any place they might be saved."

Uh…thanks for the invitation but yeah, no fucking way. If this man was from my agency, or even my government, he'd know they could easily access the secure email account that assets used to send me intel—after all, it was an agency private email server, and they could go wherever they wanted to find where I'd saved the files. I pressed the sheet harder against my breasts. "Doctor."

Both his eyebrows shot up. "What?"

"It's *Doctor* Martin. I have a PhD, which I imagine you know if you know this much about what I was doing"—a quick glance at the time told me it was just after one a.m.—"yesterday. If you're going to break into my apartment and threaten me, then it'd be nice if you could at least address me correctly." It was a pointless assertation to make at that moment, but I needed to buy myself time.

"My apologies," he drawled, laying on the fake sincerity. "*Doctor* Martin, please get up and get dressed." He moved to stand six feet from my bed, his bearing confident and commanding, yet totally relaxed, as if he knew he had the upper hand. Which he obviously did. My nudity was a great equalizer. As was the fact he had a gun, and I didn't.

"I actually don't know what specifically you're talking about. After a while all intel starts to look the same." I tightened my grip on the sheet.

He sighed, playing up his exasperation. "This isn't a game you want to play. Not with me. Now get out of bed and get dressed." Almost as an afterthought, he added a smiling, facetious, "*Please.* Unless you want me to pull you out of bed and dress you?"

"That's a solid no thanks."

"I thought as much. You have twenty seconds, and then…" He made a *you know* gesture with his hand.

My brain, previously just trundling along on This Is Not Great mode, kicked into What The Fuck? mode. The issue of what he wanted aside, whose team was he playing for? Independent agent? Foreign agent? US Government agent? Regardless, it all pointed to one thing. Not good. Really not good. "I'm not a fan of going places with people I don't know. Stranger Danger and all that. May I see some identification?"

"You may not."

"Can you at least tell me your name?"

He shook his head.

"Does the Fourth Amendment mean anything to you?"

"Please get out of bed and get dressed."

I opened my mouth to decline the invite again, but he casually moved his right hand toward the left side of his ribs. Okay then, reading you loud and clear. I swallowed, hating myself for my obvious discomfort, and tried one last thing. "I'm not the only person who knows about this."

"I'm aware, and that fact isn't relevant right now." He undid the button on his suit jacket, and reached inside. The snap of the holster clasp was deafening.

Ohh-kaayy, yep, I'd run out of time. I raised my hands, then remembered they were doing the very important job of covering my boobs and slowly brought one down to drag the sheet up over myself again. "Can I at least have some privacy to get dressed?"

He swept his arm back and half-bowed. "By all means." The fake gentleman act was incredibly annoying. After a few seconds, he averted his eyes.

I made a spinning motion with my forefinger. "Seriously. I'm naked here and you haven't even told me your name, so you don't get to sneak a peek. Can you turn around?"

He paused before slowly turning one-eighty degrees. I knew every tactical bone in his body would hate giving me even that leeway. With good reason. He probably registered the sound of me reaching under the other pillow, then the distinctive sound of the baton's extension—doesn't everyone keep a tactical baton under their pillows?—a millisecond before it connected with the back of his head and then his jaw as he turned. He stumbled forward… sideways…forward, smashing his face against the wall before he slumped facedown on the carpet.

Well, that went far better than I'd expected. Apparently I still had it. I resisted the urge to crack triumphant knuckles, and leapt out of bed. His suit jacket had pulled up, revealing handcuffs in a pouch on his belt. Good, because my sadly neglected kinky-times-drawer handcuffs wouldn't hold him, and I didn't have any heavy-duty zip ties. While kneeling on his legs, I dragged uncooperative arms behind his back and restrained him with his own handcuffs. And because I wasn't completely without a heart, I turned him onto his side so he wouldn't die of puke aspiration. And then, because I wasn't totally stupid, I took his gun, spare magazine, and the suppressor he had fitted into a slot on his holster. Handcuffs, suppressor? This guy was serious.

Fuuuuck. Fuck! Fuckfuckfuck. Fuckity fuck.

Okay okay, think. Think.

First things first. I needed clothes. My good friend Adrenaline focused my attention and sped up my movement. I had to work fast before I came down the other side of the adrenaline mountain and hit trembly uselessness. I dragged on underwear and bra, jeans, a tee, and a flannel shirt to turn myself into a boring, nondescript person. The guy groaned as I was tying the laces on my Doc Martens. I grabbed my worn leather duffel and empty laptop backpack from the top shelf in the closet.

I'd packed like this before, given less than ten minutes warning that I had to move, and it was second nature. The trick was to not think, just pack on instinct. And to leave half the shit you really want to take, but that's actually useless, behind. Important things only, you can always buy your basic necessities. I opened the safe inside my closet, and stuffed its contents—flash drives, my laptop, my lockbox of "not me" IDs and prepaid Visas I hadn't needed since my last assignment overseas, and the always-kept-charged blue-cased phone I hardly used—into my Faraday backpack, which I zipped and shrugged into. Pocketknife in my front jeans pocket. I packed an assortment of clothes and shoes in record time and on a whim, stuffed in the dry-cleaning bag full of work suits and shirts that I'd collected on my way home. Plenty of room in the duffel for my personal handgun and the tactical baton which had followed me around the world and slept under countless pillows beside me, and which had finally come in handy. Less than five minutes. Not a new record, but not bad.

The guy came to and began squirming, trying unsuccessfully to free his hands. I pulled on my well-traveled Patagonia shell jacket. "Right, so it's been wonderful, but I might go now. Who's outside?"

He was silent, his eyes a mix of defiance and embarrassment. Understandable. I'd be embarrassed too if a naked woman half my size managed to disarm me. His tough-guy act might have been more convincing if not for his watering eyes and the blood running from his obviously broken nose, over his lips and down his chin. That was going to require medical attention for him. And new bedroom carpet for me. Oh…and a wall repair too. Oops.

"Come on, I know you're not alone. I won't tell them you told me, and I really don't want to have to shoot you in the leg to make this look convincing. So, who's outside and where?"

"Just one on the front entrance," he mumbled, bloody spittle spraying from his mouth. "Silver car across the street."

"Thank you. I assume they'll come up here when you don't return with me, so…good luck. I'll put the key to those cuffs in my freezer so your friend can release you when they get up here. Please lock the front door when you leave." I put my work and personal phones in my pockets and offered an automatic and totally stupid wave goodbye. I received snarly lips in response.

Right, time to get the hell out of Dodge.

I tossed the cuffs key into the freezer, hidden behind frozen meals, ice cream, and bags of frozen vegetables. Gun, gun, gun. What to do with his? I didn't need it, I had mine. I quickly broke down the firearm, thumbing ammo from both magazines onto the floor and tossing gun parts around the living room. That should slow him down further once his partner freed him. After locking the front door and pocketing my keys, I took the elevator down to the parking garage and slipped out the back door. From across the street, his partner could see the exit of the underground garage and given the things they knew, they would also know my car.

I wanted to sprint away from my building, but forced myself to walk slowly, calmly. My skin crawled and my neck felt tight with the sensation someone was behind me and about to tackle or nab me. I kept to the side of the sidewalk farthest from the street, just walking, nothing to see here. I needed somewhere safe for the rest of the night, and a hotel was the obvious choice. Then tomorrow… tomorrow…I…had no fucking idea what I was going to do. Call Derek? Wait, no, should I call Derek now?

I shut that thought right down. Given there were only two people at work who knew about Hadim's call and the files I'd received—me and Derek—calling Derek to have a freakout about the fact someone had broken into my house and threatened me for said files did not feel like a good idea. Because logically, he was the simplest route for whoever was in my bedroom to have known about it.

Oh hi, Derek, sorry about the early-morning call, but there's a guy in my bedroom, hahaha yeah I know, that hasn't happened since my dad last tucked me in when I was ten, but this one wasn't there to read me a story, and about that intel I said felt icky, well it seems I was right, and you know how only you and me knew about it, well…I gotta ask—did you send a goon to my house to threaten me?

No way could I make that call. At least not yet. Not until I was safe. I'd trusted Derek with my life, literally, and the thought he'd known about this capture attempt made me feel sick. *Possibly* known. Like my dad used to say, never make something a certainty until you're certain it's certain. But if it looks like a duck etcetera. I shook the thought out. Think about that later. For now, get safe, make sure the intel is safe and then figure out the next step.

Strolling the brightly lit streets, I tried to look like a woman who'd just randomly packed her bags and decided to leave home for a walk to spend the night at her girlfriend's house. At one thirty in the morning. Totally normal. Totally not someone fleeing a possibly murderous intruder who might work for a government, country unspecified. Or who might be a solo operator. Either way, not great. The adrenaline that had been so helpful before now had my skin twitching, and every approaching car was someone coming for me. By the fourth car, I was almost running and had to force myself to slow down so as to not draw attention to myself.

I needed to get inside, safe, away from eyes both human and electronic. As I walked, I Googled hotels, filtered by twenty-four-hour check-in, and within five minutes was inside an Uber and on my way to a place on the edge of town. It was only when I was safely upstairs in a room behind locks and chains that I took a full breath.

I dumped everything on the bed and pulled out my laptop. My first priority was to secure what I'd received from Hadim so Thuggy McHousebreaker and his friends couldn't wipe it from existence. Clearly, it was valuable, and I couldn't risk them getting rid of the evidence of...something I wasn't sure of yet. But I *was* sure it was important. I'd known that before my middle-of-the-night visitor had woken me up, and now I was utterly certain there was more to it than I'd first imagined.

Despite being on an unsecured Internet connection, my laptop was as secure as it could be. And I wouldn't be long, just a quick login via the portal to grab what I wanted, then out again. If someone who'd break into an apartment and threaten the occupant wanted this intel, then it was up to me to keep those files safe.

It took a few seconds to connect through my VPN routing service and bounce via California to sneak through cyberspace and into the encrypted portal we used when working in the field. As soon as I entered my credentials, I was met with a simple message. Not the big red flashing animation that movies and television always show to make sure the audience immediately understands that the protagonist is screwed, but a boring: *Incorrect Password, Portal Access Denied.*

I spluttered, groaned, and finally managed a raging, "Oh they did not. Bastards!" How had they locked me out already? A rhetorical question of course. They'd probably put a cyberwall around everything of mine before bringing me in. Correction— before trying to bring me in.

I tried again in case my 2:27 a.m. brain was simply being stupid. Nope. Same again. I closed down all browsers and my VPN, disconnected then reconnected to the Internet and VPN before routing through Sydney, Australia because why not. Once I'd connected, I navigated to the encrypted login page again. Only this time I didn't enter AEMARTIN but SCGORDON and Sam's password of ILoVeMuFfIn54321*. I'm not even joking, and best not to ask how I knew it. The number of people working in one of the securest government departments who had passwords like password123 or 012345678910 or even their names was astounding.

Nope again. Okay. Relax, and think. So they've closed down *all* secure external access. The timing was beyond suspicious, and my good friend Logic pointed out that it was because of me. I took the laptop offline, calmly closed it, and wandered into the bathroom to puke in the sink. Adrenaline's great. Until it isn't. I ate a couple of the mints I'd grabbed from the bowl at the front desk and stared around the room, trying to figure out my next move. My next move was more staring and trying to figure out my next move.

Knowing mindless tasks would help me refocus, I unpacked my hastily thrown-together bag, set the dry cleaning flat on the bed, used my emergency handbag charger to top up my personal phone, then neatly repacked my duffel. There, just like a person on vacation. A working vacation. Thanking myself for having the foresight to grab my handbag, I rummaged for my headphones and the travel kit of toiletries I always kept in there. Years of travel, lost luggage, and working odd hours had taught me that keeping spare necessities in easy-to-access places was a smart idea.

My stomach rumbled, demanding sustenance to fuel thought—I always got hungry if I happened to be awake in the middle of the night. Time to raid the room for overpriced snacks. Once I'd cleaned out the chips and chocolate, I flopped backward on the bed, covered my mouth with both hands and blew out a long breath that whistled through my fingers.

Okay. These were the things I knew…

One of my trusted sources had given me intel about an American pushing a suspected Russian militia group to use a new and illegal chemical weapon on foreign civilians. I had come by this information through acceptable and reliable channels. My boss knew about this incident. An unpleasant man had tried to threaten and coerce naked me into a, forgetting what I knew, and b, going into the office to wipe the files from the servers even though they were capable of finding the files and pressing Delete themselves. My agency had initiated a lockdown of those servers. Oh, and this was a fabulous hotel bed. Pity I wouldn't get to sleep in it.

I took a moment to run over everything again. Yes, that was pretty much all of it. So, what's the logical conclusion here? I drew in a deep breath and let it out again as I unbuttoned and unzipped my jeans, kicking out of them while I unfastened my bra and Houdini-ed it through the arms of my tee. I cleared some space to lie flat on my back with my legs up against the wall. Eyes closed. Deep, slow breaths. Elongated breathing…slow breathing… Thinking of nothing but my breaths, pushing the negativity and anxiety out on each long exhalation. After fifty inhale-exhales, the stress had abated somewhat, but the anxiety of someone breaking into my house, my safe space, remained.

Crawling across the soft carpet to a spot with nothing nearby, I relaxed into Child's Pose and focused on feeling my fingers and forehead in the carpet, the sensation of my big toes touching, my breath moving in and out through my lungs and around my body. I was safe here, safe in my body, my mind. Breathing in and out. The grounding pose slowly soothed the anxiety, and I stayed with it until all the intrusive thoughts had left my brain. I sloughed away more tension and negative energy with Sun Salutations and rolling through Bridge Poses until my body and brain felt like my own again.

I walked slowly back and forth across the room, concentrating on my footfalls, the swing of my arms, the sensation of my breathing sustaining my body. The mindfulness had eased my upset, brought some clarity. There really was only one logical conclusion. There was something in those files, or some*one* more likely, that had the power to cause a national scandal or an international diplomatic nightmare. The chemical weapon incident would be spun as us protecting our assets, and they'd argue semantics to wriggle out of it, so there *had* to be more. Using Russian militia against their tentative allies made no sense, especially not when you added our government trying to forge—mmph—ties with Russia to make that happen.

Don't force it. Let it come to you.

But it wouldn't.

I lowered myself to the floor and went through twenty slow pushups. The connection with my body and the movement cleared my mind again. Okay, so now we've established you don't know what's going on with this intel, let's figure out what you're going to do next.

More pacing. More pushups. More yoga.

You are in possession of intel that a potentially negative player wants—not ideal. You don't know who you can trust—bad. You have a stupid need to always work for the greater good—noble, but sometimes annoying. So, what are your options, Lexie? Call Derek and explain what's happening, despite having the awful and sickening feeling he might be involved, and if he's involved, then this might end up somewhere it shouldn't, or more likely…end up nowhere. Bypass him and try to go higher up the chain? Bypass my agency altogether and make a call on the blue-cased cell phone?

Every scenario I went through felt like a dead end. And who knew what would happen to Hadim's intel. My trusty gut said it would magically go away, that nobody would ever know, nobody would ever be held accountable. And that meant this chemical weapon could be used again. And that was unacceptable. Unthinkable. Yeah, maybe I needed to use the blue phone...

The distinctive app ringtone of the phone I hardly used made me jump, partly because I'd *just* been thinking about using it and was freaked out that they might somehow know my thoughts. I blew a raspberry at that ridiculous notion. Not answering was never an option and the timing of a call on this phone couldn't be coincidental. I inhaled a steadying breath and answered with a calm, "Yes?"

The man I knew intimately, yet didn't know at all, said simply, "Halcyon has been mobilized. The Protocol is now in effect." I'd never met him in person but had met some of his underlings when I'd first been recruited to the department he headed—Halcyon Division—just a few months before I started my job at the agency. We all referred to him as Lennon. I had no idea if that was his surname, a code name, or just that he loved the Beatles.

I dropped down onto the edge of the bed. "Confirm."

Lennon puffed a cigar, or I'd always assumed cigars because who puffed cigarettes? "Quite the conundrum you seem to have found yourself in," he said conversationally.

"Yes, it is," I agreed. "Care to enlighten me?"

"There's not much I can tell you yet, except the man who came to visit you is not with us."

Well, that was something, I supposed. Not that the thought had even occurred to me. I didn't bother asking how Halcyon knew about my nighttime visitor. Halcyon's job was to know everything. "Do you know who it is?"

"We've discerned that they were there under instruction from the top."

The top as in the head of my agency? Or the top as in the President of the United States? Either way, fuck. I expressed that exact sentiment in a hiss.

Lennon hmmed. "Your coming into possession of that intel forced their hand, and one of the Halcyon agents in the White House took note and contacted me. I've just been briefed by them, and this is multi-level issue, both a high-level national and international security threat, as well as having the potential to cause a scandal in the Oval Office, with far-reaching implications throughout government. I need you to unravel it, and quickly. The very integrity of the institution who governs us depends on the Protocol's success."

"The institution who governs us. I think there's a name for that. Hang on...like...our *government*?" Stress made me snarky.

Lennon ignored my tone. "Yes."

A horrible icky nausea sensation filled my throat. "Understood. But I don't have the files, obviously, and they've shut down offsite access to the servers. And now I *really* don't think going back to the office is a good idea." An image of me waltzing into the building, only to run smack-bang into two dozen assault-rifle-carrying beefcakes in suits, flitted into my head. No thanks. "I need you to get those files for me if you want me to figure it out."

"We can't do that. Halcyon has also been locked out, even our agent in the White House who has the highest clearance. You need to find a way to locate and secure the intel before it disappears. I suggest utilizing Scott."

Bianca "Bink" Scott could, and did, get anywhere in cyberspace, even deleted places. "Okay," I sighed. Sure, Lennon could have contacted Bink, or someone else equally as talented, and retrieved the files himself, allocated a team to work on this. But I knew why he didn't, why it was all on me. The agents of Halcyon tended to operate solo, rather than in teams like at my "real job." Less chance of mass exposure, easier to fly under the radar. And I was already involved, already had a head start. Plus, I was just really fucking good at my job.

"Alexandra." He stressed each syllable of my full name. "This is a priority-one task. The safety and secrecy of the information is paramount, more important even than you peeling back the layers to see what's inside. And once you have the files, you *must* keep them secure. The Protocol cannot be enacted if this intel is lost, so I suggest you lie low while you figure it out."

Well that was a contradictory set of instructions if I'd ever heard them. "Just to be clear, you're asking me to hide, as in disappear hide, and also dig deeper with this?"

"Yes. And of course, if you can't connect the dots, someone else will be able to, but we can't do that if we don't have those files."

I bristled a little at the insinuation that I might not be able to unravel the threads of Hadim's information. "It may be difficult to maintain my security clearance within the agency if I'm doing as you've asked." Running away after being told by an unknown intruder, who I now knew was sent by the White House, to scrub all traces of some intelligence from accessible places, while I still knew about said intelligence, looked more than a little suspicious. Add sneaking into secure government servers to grab files, well…I may as well handcuff and fire myself.

"Then that's the price to be paid," he said bluntly.

This really was some serious shit. I inhaled slowly. "Am I in danger?"

"Yes. But not your life. And if you have to sacrifice your position within the agency, then so be it. You won't be the first to do so in service of your country."

Goodbye, lovely government pension. Sigh. "Will I have your assistance?" I already knew I'd be on my own, but I'd meant, "When the dust has settled."

"I'm not sure. That may risk exposing you as Halcyon."

"Then I'll be claiming deep-tissue massage and a million pints of ice cream to help manage my stress."

He chuckled. "Please do."

"I'll need a secure laptop and phones, some funds, and new IDs for accommodation and all that. I've already used my overseas ops ID to check in to this hotel."

"Done. It'll all be in the storage facility by eight a.m."

"Thank you." I cleared my throat. "Who is it? Who's responsible?" My questions were little more than gossipy curiosity.

"I can't tell you that."

"But do you know? It'd make my job a lot easier if I know who I'm supposed to be tying this to, what angle I'm supposed to be looking at."

"Yes, I know who the target is. And perhaps it *would* make your job easier, but it would also narrow your focus. And I need every single piece of information you can uncover about this, unbiased and broad. This is perhaps the most important clean-up Halcyon has been tasked with to date. Stay safe, do good work. I'll be in touch."

As usual, the call ended without a goodbye from either of us. Calmly, I placed the phone back into my backpack. What an interesting and unexpected turn of events. And…I was even more confused.

Now, I know what you're thinking, and I *know* what this looks like. But I promise I'm not a spy, I'm not a double agent, I'm not a triple agent. I'm a patriotic American. Beyond patriotic. A diligent US Government employee—twice, actually! But alas, only once the benefits, because my second salary is hidden in an offshore account, where it does nothing but gather large amounts of interest ready for my very comfortable retirement.

Let's get this out of the way so you'll stick with me without hissing "Filthy traitor spy!" under your breath. I'm part of Halcyon Division, a hidden bipartisan-founded government organization, known to only a few high-ranking government officials, that has members inside all America's intelligence-gathering offices and certain high-clearance civilian operations. CliffsNotes version—Halcyon is kind of like an anti-virus program running permanently in the background of the highest level of national politics. Halcyon keeps an eye on the people running our country, ensuring they aren't working in a way that compromises our national security, or diplomatic ties. And if they are, those corrupt or compromised-by-foreign-entities leaders are removed. Intelligence is awesome.

Sooo…basically, I'd learned something that was going to help remove someone from Washington. And given my nighttime visitor, we weren't just talking about a John Doe from Congress—this was someone right up the top of the ladder, someone important. Of course, I didn't know what I knew yet, and I had to unravel this mess while somehow trying to keep my analyst job, where I not only worked legitimately in intelligence, but like other Halcyon agents, funneled pertinent intel to the Division.

Finding out what Lennon was alluding to was really going to make keeping my agency job difficult—running was really suspicious, especially after my nighttime visit. But I *was* going to find out. Because my number one priority, the thing I held above everything else, was protecting the security of our interests at home and abroad. At all costs. Maybe even at the cost of myself.

I exhaled loudly. It was a lot easier to feel good about what I had to do—break into a secure government server, take classified intel, work with it offsite—when I came to terms with the fact I was probably going to jail when this was done. But I'd have protected my country from an attack from within.

Right. Time to pretend I was a spy. I shot off an encrypted email to Bink to say I needed an urgent meet, and an encrypted, encoded response landed less than five minutes later. It only took a few minutes to decrypt and decode using our usual keys. An address in Tampa. Airports were too risky, too many eyes. I'd have to drive.

I found a pair of nail scissors in my toiletries bag and, leaning over the sink, cut my shoulder-blade-length dirty-blond hair to an inch above my shoulders. It would make me look like a different person to those who didn't know me well, especially if I shunned my usual ponytails and French twists and left my hair down. If Lennon wanted me to hide, then I'd do every damned thing I could to stay hidden.

CHAPTER THREE

Woman + her unruly kids = safety, but not enjoyment

The moment I looked into the front desk clerk's eyes I knew I'd made a mistake. When, what, and where this mistake had been made was something I couldn't quite pinpoint at nine a.m. with a brain fogged by less than an hour of uneasy sleep after the shitfight that had been the past twenty-four hours. Not to brag, but I was excellent at reading people, and this guy was hiding something. He was trying desperately to smother it, but guilt seeped from the reedy young man like the remnants of a four-day bender.

A quick sweep of the lobby's other occupants told me I was in no immediate danger. The only others present were a couple in their seventies having an argument about whether to drive or take the bus to the museum, and a woman who looked like she was regretting producing each of the three young children causing low-level mayhem around her.

Of course, those were the people I could see. It was the ones I couldn't see that worried me. I made eye contact with the clerk and wondered just how much I was worth. At least a hundred bucks. Anything less would be insulting, considering my late-night visitor and his threats about the intel I now knew to be of the highest priority. I tossed the room key on the desk. "Checking out."

He forced a bright smile. "How was your stay?"

Terrible, actually, but not for any reasons that I'd use to give your hotel a one-star rating on Tripadvisor. But give it time—betraying a guest's privacy was definitely grounds for a bad review, even if someone had flashed a government badge at you. "Fine, thank you."

"I'm very pleased to hear that." He tapped a few keys and the printer to his right spat out a sheet of paper. He passed it to me, along with a pen. "If you'll just sign here, please."

I resisted the urge to write *Screw you, asshole* on the signature line, and quickly scrawled *Candy Apple xo*. Smiling, I stole his pen, thanked him with a solid dose of passive aggression, and bent to collect my battered leather duffel from the floor. It was as I was laughing to myself about Candy Apple that I made the connection to exactly how I'd been found. Not through my Internet browser or attempts to access my files—I always hid myself impeccably online. Not my work phone—I'd turned it off and removed the SIM card in the car on my way to the hotel. I'd always had all trip location data services disabled in my Uber account and without a legal reason, whoever was trying to find me couldn't subpoena my account records from Uber, especially not this quickly. My private phone was private. Not by a credit card or ID with my real name on it, because I'd used a prepaid Visa and my overseas ops ID to check in to the hotel.

My overseas ops ID...with a name known to the agency. I hadn't even thought they'd track that. So stupid. They'd probably called every hotel within a twenty-mile radius of my apartment to ask if someone with the name Alexandra Martin or Ellen Jackson had checked in around two a.m.

I shook off my annoyance at my own carelessness. It wasn't helpful now. New focus—get away from them. Again. Once I knew who and where they were, of course. I sorted and discarded options until I came up with three choices. I could either stroll boldly and stupidly straight out the front door and probably right into the waiting hands of whomever they'd sent this time. I could go to the ground-floor ladies' room and out of the window I knew was there from my reconnaissance when I arrived, and which they would probably also know about from their own site survey. Or...I could pick up some human insurance.

Making an obvious scene in public—especially now in the age of everyone-has-a-cell-phone-recording—with possible public collateral damage was generally a no-no. Clandestine snatch-and-grab was more their style, as confirmed by the attempted events of last night. Keeping myself in the public eye and in close proximity to people seemed like the best of a bunch of shitty options until I could find a not-shitty option. After another visual sweep of the lobby, I did some easy math.

Woman plus kids equals safety.

The maybe-I-shouldn't-have-had-kids woman was still trying to wrangle her offspring. It looked like trying to herd hyperactive puppies while holding a leaking sack of flour, and I decided she would be more amenable to an offer of help than arguing septuagenarians. I pulled the embossed gold band from my right ring finger and shifted it to my left hand. Voilà! I just got married. After a few adjustments to my luggage configuration, I approached the family, and when the mother turned to see who was daring to interrupt her horrible mayhem, changed my voice to a high-pitched below-the-Mason-Dixon drawl, adding an A-Grade friendly smile for good measure. "Excuse me, hi. I am so sorry to butt in, but y'all sure look like you could use a hand."

She opened her mouth but before she could decline, I barreled on, "I have five-year-old twins at home and you have the exact expression I feel like I have whenever I leave the house with them. I'm happy to help out if you need it."

She sized me up and I knew exactly what she saw, because it was what I wanted her to see. Late thirties, upper middle-class businesswoman glad to get out of the suit she carried in the dry-cleaning bag slung over her arm, on a business trip but on her way home to an imaginary loving husband and fake twins.

The woman exhaled, her face relaxing. "If you wouldn't mind, I'd be so grateful."

"Not at all. Who can I help with?" I squared the backpack on my shoulders, slung the duffel strap across my body, and rearranged my handbag and dry-cleaning bag to free up an arm for a child.

"This guy, thank you." She handed me the toddler—yuk—and got to work on the girl and boy.

"What's his name?" I asked, resisting the urge to hold the squirming, fussing child at arm's length like he was something radioactive. Instead, I held him close even as he arched his back to get out of my grasp. Bouncing him and patting his leg seemed to settle him fractionally. People watching has its advantages, even if it's just to learn something like how to calm a small human.

"Fennec," she offered distractedly before bending down again to deal with the other two. A no-nonsense mom finger moved between the girl and boy. "Maverick, Arcadia, I swear if you don't stop this behavior right this instant there will be no birthday party next month."

I—Okay then. I turned slightly away so I could check the doors again, and kept up with my child bouncing and patting, and juggling bags routine. Fennec scrabbled for my hair and as best I could, I moved my head out of the way without seeming like what I really wanted to do was drop the dribbling germ bundle. Pat, bounce, pat, bounce. "So your name's Fennec, huh? You're going to be a big-eared Fennec Fox when you grow up?" I glanced around, assuring myself that a, the space was still safe and b, that his mother wasn't paying attention to us. She wasn't—too busy trying to convince her other two offspring to behave like actual humans. I walked away a few feet, lowered my voice to baby-soothing, and gave it to Fennec straight. "Just so you know, I have a low tolerance for bad behavior *and* I know a lot of ways to make people do what I want, so probably best you be quiet and stop this squirmy stuff or I might have to get radical. Catch my drift?"

I had no idea if it was the tone or if the baby had somehow realized that he was going to be in trouble if he didn't behave, but he went still, staring at me with huge brown eyes. Spit dribbled from the edge of his mouth and without warning he burst into giggles, blowing a spit bubble. Gross. I stared at the now borderline-manic child, fighting to keep the disgust from my face. Were giggling spit-bubble-blowing babies better than screamy squirmy ones?

The woman looked at her happily babbling child in my arms and for the first time since I'd approached her, she smiled. "You're a miracle worker."

I turned on a smile of my own. "Aw, thanks. Just deployed a little charm." And maybe some threats to your kid. Who knew what'd actually worked. With a tilt of my chin I indicated the front doors. "Where are you headed? Do you need a hand getting them into their car seats?"

"Home. Our house had to be fumigated, so last night was a hotel adventure, wasn't it, guys?" The older two looked like it had been anything but an adventure for them. "My husband had to leave for a round of golf about an hour ago," she said, and I caught the hint of annoyance, probably that he'd left her to deal with the kids on her own. "And if you wouldn't mind, I'd love a little help. Fennec really seems taken with you."

Oh dear. Just what I didn't need. An adoring child. Another smile, more forced than the first. "Absolutely, anything I can do to help."

She grasped the handle of her suitcase in one hand, and a hand of each twin in her other. And here I was thinking my kid-bag juggling skills were epic. She paused. "I'm so sorry, my manners seem to have departed me this morning." The woman dropped the suitcase handle and placed that hand on her chest, as if I might be unsure to whom she was referring. "I'm Helen." Helen grabbed the suitcase again and started walking, dragging case and kids all in one smooth motion.

I rushed to keep up and hoped my jiggling didn't turn the gurgling toddler into a puking toddler. For some reason I couldn't fathom, maybe it was fatigue or the fact I just really wanted to trust *somebody*, I told her the truth. "I'm Alexandra."

"Nice to meet you. My car's just in the lot out front."

"Great." The moment I stepped outside, I glanced slowly around the parking lot and to the street beyond. Ah, there you are. The black SUV with its darkly tinted windows, parked four spaces from the front door, stuck out like a sore thumb. Remind me to send a copy of *How to Not be Conspicuous 101* to these guys. Both the SUV's front doors opened a foot. I stared, raising my eyebrows. You guys really want to do this now when I have a baby in my arms and am with this woman and two other kids? With all those people on the sidewalk just over there? The doors closed again. Yeah, I didn't think so.

Helen peered around the lot. "Where's your car?"

"Back home in Charleston," I lied easily. Though lying and manipulation for the greater good had always been easy for me, I actually didn't enjoy it. "And no rental. I always try to use public transport when I fly for work. Makes me feel better about those... whatchamacallits"—I pretended to think—"emissions. I'll just take

Metro to the airport or something. Do you know where the nearest station is?"

I could see her cogs turning. Mercifully, Helen was a nice human, albeit someone with questionable choices in child names, and had stepped right through the doorway of opportunity I'd just opened for her. "Well, I can give you a ride. There's a station not far from our house."

I put some extra gushiness into my response. "Really? Oh my, that would be so helpful. I'd really appreciate it. My flight leaves in three hours and I will be up the creek if I miss it. I promised the kids I'd take them to the movies this afternoon."

She beamed. "It's my pleasure. Us moms have to stick together, right?"

"Right!" I agreed as cheerfully as I could manage.

I helped her get the kids into their booster seats, and fobbed off my ignorance of how the numerous belts and buckles worked by telling Helen I'd rather she got her kids belted in just how she liked. My duffel and dry-cleaning bag went into the back, but I kept my handbag on my lap and the backpack wedged between my feet with my hand tangled in and wrapped around a strap.

In the side mirror, I spotted the black SUV pull out and slip onto the tail of the car behind us. I'd expected nothing less. While Helen drove, I leaned back in the seat and tried to look nonchalant and relaxed while I was scanning the road in front of us and the view in the side mirror every few seconds and thinking about how I was going to get free once I got to the Metro station. I just needed to get to Florida and figure this out. Because if I didn't, then maybe I'd get fired from two jobs instead of just one.

During the drive I learned Helen, aged thirty-two, had married her childhood sweetheart and was pregnant again with a second set of twins. I said a silent prayer for her sanity and for the new children who would probably be named Pharaoh and Alabaster. I did my duty as doting babysitter, leaning around from the passenger seat to talk to the kids, while trying not to act like I didn't want to slap the boy—I still didn't know which one was Maverick and which one was Arcadia—for kicking my seat.

The drive took just under twenty minutes and I directed Helen to drop me a block over from the station—no need to fight the traffic of drop-offs and pick-ups, I'd said cheerfully...or give SUV a firm idea of where I was going. The moment Helen came to an abrupt stop, she popped the trunk of her soccer mom van. I leaned forward and put my backpack on, tightly clipping the chest strap. A wrist squeeze and dialing of drawl up to an eight helped complete my picture of gratitude. "Helen, thank you so much. You truly are an angel in disguise. Now if you'll excuse me, I have to run so I don't miss my flight." I turned around and narrowed my eyes at all three kids, and said a cheery, "Bye, guys! Behave yourselves!" before slipping out of the car, grabbing my things from the back, and booking it into the crowd to lose myself.

Well, that whole experience certainly cemented the fact I never wanted to reproduce. I made a quick perimeter check. Black SUV was five cars back, stuck in traffic. Nobody was jumping out of the vehicle, which meant they probably hadn't seen me get out. They'd soon notice I was no longer in the passenger seat and leave Helen to backtrack and find where I'd parted ways with her. Helen and her unruly crew of kids would be fine, which alleviated my mild case of guilt at putting her between me and them.

Nobody in the crowd pinged my suspicion radar and my tension went from a 15 down to a 14.75. Waiting for the crossing signal so I could disappear into the safety of the underground station, I turned on my personal cell phone to search for a rental car company. Seconds after I'd opened the browser, the phone started ringing, startling me so much I almost stepped into oncoming traffic. Great, what a way to die after everything I'd evaded since last night.

The number on my screen was known and not problematic. I debated answering, ran at light speed through the pros and cons, and came up with one very large pro. *If* I could make it work. Very big if. They'd left me alone when I'd been with Helen and her harem of horrors, so all I needed was a perma-Helen who wasn't Helen because if I had to spend any more time with Helen I'd probably just turn myself in. Charm and Persuasion—I really need you right now. I took a deep breath, and answered with a cheerful, "Lexie speaking."

"Lexie, hi, it's Sophia?" It sounded like a question, as if she wasn't sure who she really was.

Imagining her expression made me smile. I knew who she was. Sophia Flores—thirty-nine, website and graphic designer, youngest of three kids—was fun and funny, kind and thoughtful, somehow both forceful yet sweetly timid, with a tantalizing hint of dirty girl simmering under the surface of her almost girl-next-door persona. Oh, and did I mention cute? She was really cute.

Despite the fact I was fleeing, not for my life but for my freedom, it wasn't hard to be enthusiastic. "Sophia! Hey, how are you?"

"I'm good. Really good. So, uh, just checking in but I thought today was the day we were having breakfast then maybe a movie or something after? I'm already at the café but now I'm wondering if I got my days mixed up because you're not here. Is everything okay?" There was both steel and shyness in her voice.

Of course I'd forgotten, or I would have rescheduled the date we'd confirmed by text just a few days ago. The date I'd been really looking forward to. But scheduling my love life had been pushed out of my brain-space in favor of other, more urgent things—like figuring out who wanted Hadim's intel so badly they'd break into my house in the middle of the night and threaten me for it. I forced some extra ditzy contriteness into my response. "Oh, dammit. I'm late."

She laughed. "Yeah, twenty minutes."

"Right." I peered left and right then jogged across the street before the signal changed. "I'm *so* sorry."

"It's fine." There was a slight pause. "But, listen, if you've changed your mind about a third date then that's totally fine. I mean, I thought things were going amazingly and we've got some great chemistry, but if you don't feel the same, then obviously it's okay. But I'd kind of like to know if I've been ghosted or not." She was trying to sound cheery and nonchalant, but I could hear trepidation underneath the words. The trepidation was good. It meant she hoped she hadn't been ghosted, she wanted to spend time with me. I needed that.

"Ghosted?" I laughed genuinely. Oh, if only you knew, Sophia. "Not at all. My hellish week has bled into a hellish weekend and everything has run away from me, including time. I'm sorry, please forgive me." I took in my location, did a little mental math. "I know you've already waited twenty, but do you mind waiting another ten or fifteen minutes? I get it if you want to reschedule, or…just call it off altogether, but I'd *really* like to see you today. I've been looking forward to it all week." It felt nice to tell some truths in amongst the lies and half-truths of the morning.

There was a long pause and I could imagine her debating whether or not she should teach me a lesson about punctuality. Apparently and thankfully, she decided that she'd enjoyed our other dates as much as I had, and wanted this one. "No, it's fine. I can wait. You're my only plan for today."

My tension eased by another 0.25 points. "Fabulous. Again, I'm so sorry." I added a touch of seduction when I murmured, "I promise I'll make it up to you. See you soon."

There was anticipation in her quiet, "Looking forward to it."

We ended the call, and I slumped against a light pole.

Shit. Okay, priority number one: find something to wear that might actually keep this woman attracted to you. Looking frantically up and down the street, I spotted a clothing store that might have what I needed. Five minutes later I'd swapped outfits in the change room, finger-combed my hair, and hastily applied impulse counter-purchase mascara and eyeliner that, combined, cost more than the new top I'd just bought—but *were* totally organic, vegan, animal-testing free and probably rescued cats from trees in their free time. I was ready for breakfast. Almost. I folded my dry-cleaning bag into my duffel to ensure my handgun was covered and out of sight.

I'd just exited the store when my phone rang again, this time with a call through a communications app, rather than a regular cellular network call. Dammit. Yeah, my private number was private, but one person at work had it for emergencies. Derek. Despite the sick uneasiness that'd filled me when I saw that name, I still answered. "Yes?" While lying awake at five this morning, I'd decided I'd trust him. For now. Maybe that had been a mistake.

"Martin, what the hell is going on? Where are you? I've spent hours already this morning on multiple calls from multiple people about you. Care to tell me why people are interrupting my Saturday morning to tell me they suspect you've stolen intelligence?"

Stolen? I hadn't stolen a damned thing. Not yet, anyway… The alarm I'd been keeping a lid on started to bubble up and boil over. I fought to keep my voice calm. "They're wrong and that's all I can tell you now. I'm not comfortable speaking about it here."

He sighed. "Whatever's going on, I need to know about it. Meet me at the office in an hour." His voice softened. "You know you can talk to me."

"No chance."

"Okay," Derek said evenly. "Meet me anywhere then. You name the place and time."

"See my previous response. Feel free to go to my apartment and have a look at the mess in my bedroom if you need a reason why I'm not ready to meet anyone right now."

I hung up on his response. I didn't have time for this. I had a woman to win over.

CHAPTER FOUR

Flirting for Dummies

Sophia either had excellent awareness of her surroundings or had lucked out with a table that had a good view of the entry without being right by it. I stood outside the café, out of her direct line of sight, and took a few moments to watch the patrons obliviously absorbed in phones or food, or dexterously both. Except for Sophia. She cupped a mug tightly in both hands, her gaze fixed intently on the door as if she could force me to appear just by staring.

Unlike our other two dates where she'd worn her hair up, now the thick dark waves were settled on top of her bare shoulders and cascading down between her shoulder blades. I wanted to trail my fingers lightly over the skin of her shoulders and gently push her hair aside, and could easily imagine how soft her hair would feel against my cheek if I bent to kiss the curve of her neck, lick the—

Yeah, this is really not the time to be horny. Or actually, maybe it was…

A driver blared their horn right behind me, and I startled, spinning around just in time to see rude hand gestures exchanged between a cyclist and driver. Slow clap for Lexie. Standing outside staring goofily at a woman and leaving yourself completely exposed.

Good thing Lennon hadn't just seen that or I definitely wouldn't be getting a bonus this year.

I shook myself off and refocused on the task at hand, though calling it a *task* sucked some of the fun out of it. I mean, it was a date, sure, but also…the fate of the country might depend on whether or not I could make it a really good date. I quickly tidied myself and checked nothing was amiss. Everything fine, looking good, except… Oops, that could have been awkward. I swapped the ring from my left ring finger back to my right. World's quickest divorce.

When Sophia leaned down to rummage in the handbag nestled between her feet, I pushed through the door and picked my way through the two-thirds-full café toward her. I was surprised by the sudden surge of excited nerves as I approached. It wasn't nerves about what I had to do. It was nerves because I was genuinely attracted to her and wanted that attraction reciprocated. After a deep inhalation, I quietly said, "Sophia." She looked up instantly, her mouth curving into a smile. I held my free hand out and adjusted my tone to contrite with a touch of appreciation. "Please forgive me for keeping you waiting, and then waiting again. You look amazing, and I'm an idiot."

Still smiling, Sophia took my hand in hers and I allowed myself a moment of indulgence in the smooth warmth of her skin as we held eye contact. Her eyes moved to the duffel in my hand then to the backpack securely clipped across my chest before coming back up to meet my gaze. Totally deadpan, she asked, "Did I miss the memo about bringing my worldly possessions to the date? I mean, I know the whole U-Haul joke, but maybe we should talk about this." Her voice was low and melodic with an edge of huskiness, and from the moment I'd first heard it I'd thought of lazy mornings in bed. I forced myself to concentrate on her, not the fluttering feeling in my stomach. The smile turned to a grin, offering me a view of the gap between her top front teeth, which gave her a slightly cheeky, naughty air. Its appearance had the same effect on me as it had during our previous dates—smitten. So smitten.

Laughing, I leaned down and after a quick pause to check her reaction—receptive—kissed her cheek, right near the edge of her mouth. I made sure to linger. "If I ask you to move in with me, you'll definitely know about it." I paused a moment to let my words sink in, then blurted a Helen-borrowed reason with a little elaboration, hopefully to lay the foundations for later. "My apartment is being fumigated, and I totally forgot about it. The company just turned up this morning and I had ten minutes to grab some things. I still need to find a hotel for tonight, and my car's in the shop so I've had to Uber and Metro everywhere." I turned on my most charming smile. "I'm *so* sorry, I know I've just thrown a bunch of excuses at you, but everything has piled on these past few days and I'm still playing catch-up."

Sophia's expression softened and she reached for my hand again. "Oh god, no no, don't worry about it. Sounds like you've had a horrible couple of days." She lightly squeezed, her fingers brushing against my palm. "Are you okay?"

She was such a sweetheart. I pushed aside a pang of guilt—guilt for what I was going to do, and guilt that I was taking time to enjoy my personal life when my professional life was a metaphorical ticking bomb.

I settled in the free chair, shuffling closer to her. My bags went to the floor, the backpack wedged securely between my feet. "It sure has been a hectic few days, and yes, I'm okay. Thank you for asking." Okay-ish. It's all relative, isn't it? Waving aside the fake inconveniences, I said, "But anyway, enough about me. It's so great to see you again, and you really do look incredible. That dress…" I fanned myself. It wasn't an idle compliment; she did look incredible. Since our first date, I'd thought about her often, her mental appearances a pleasurable intrusion into otherwise mundane days. But now I was with her, I realized I wanted more than just mental appearances.

"Thank you." Her cheeks pinked as she glanced down, smoothing her hands over her thighs. She looked up again, and the intensity of her gaze made something zing between us. I'd misremembered the exact color of her eyes—a beautiful light brown that reminded me of almonds. Her eyes lingered on my breasts for a second, and I hoped I hadn't done something stupid in my haste to buy date clothes, like mis-button my shirt or leave one gaping to expose my bra.

A quick peek down confirmed I was okay and that apparently, she just wanted to look at my breasts. Fair enough. I mentally added another point to the "This might work out" column. Sophia gestured around my face. "You cut your hair. I love it. Shorter really suits you."

I ran my hand over the back of my neck, slightly alarmed by the lack of volume I found there. It was going to take some getting used to, having short hair again, though it wasn't exactly *short*. I'd had far shorter. "Ah, thank you. I just…had a whim and did it without thinking. Have you ordered?"

She raised her mug. "Just coffee."

"Great." I gently pulled the menu from under her elbow, glancing around as if pretending to look for a server. Nobody nefarious. Or rather—nobody obviously nefarious. "This one is on me."

Once we'd ordered, we picked up where we'd left off from our last date, when she'd told me all about her family, in loving detailed detail, and I'd told her barely anything about mine because there wasn't much to tell compared to the intimate unit in which she'd grown up. So when she gently probed again about my parents, I felt like I had to give her something beyond "They died almost a year and a half ago in a light plane crash, and we weren't exactly a close lovey-dovey family."

I tried to make it sound warm instead of cool and bland. "My father was a diplomat, so as a kid I lived all over the world, in a whole lot of fancy apartments. And Mom taught English wherever we were living. No siblings, cousins, aunts, or uncles." I smiled at her expression, which contained both shock and upset. "I'm what happens when two only children have an only child."

"Wow. I can't even imagine that. Where exactly is all over the world?" she asked. "I know you've traveled a lot." As had she. A shared love of travel had been one of the things that had attracted me to her right away. One of the things…

The arrival of my coffee gave me a moment of respite. Talking about myself felt foreign, uncomfortable almost. As I stirred latte foam into my coffee, I gave her an honest answer. "I was born in Washington, DC, then when I was eight months old we moved to Turkey, when I was three we went to Malaysia, and when I was five we moved to Jordan, then…well, you get the idea. Sometimes we'd come back to the States for a while between my dad's postings. Generally, every two or three years, we'd move, I'd change schools, learn enough of the new language and culture to feel comfortable. And then we'd move again."

"That sounds…tumultuous for your formative years."

"A little," I agreed. "But it gave me amazing experiences, instilled a love of travel and other cultures, and taught me how to deal with change, so…" I shrugged. Glass both half-full and half-empty.

"When did you stop moving around?"

"Once I'd finished high school in Singapore. Then I turned eighteen and was legally allowed to stop following my parents to every corner of the globe." Yeah, I'd had a bit of a weird childhood, but the experiences and exposure it had given me were incredible and I wouldn't have traded it for anything. "I came back to the States, went to college, followed in Dad's footsteps with my government job, and here I am."

"Here you are," she murmured, reaching out to stroke the back of my hand with her fingertips. "And I'm very grateful."

Thankfully our food arrived, saving me from trying—and undoubtedly failing—to think of something suave to say in response to her overt flirtation. If I'd known I'd need to utilize seduction so soon, then I would have studied *Flirting for Dummies Who Haven't Dated Much*. But despite my ineptitude, conversation flowed easily as we ate. It'd been so long since I'd done something as normal as dating, that even after a couple of easy, chemistry-laden dates with her it still felt alien, especially when I was in the middle of a minor crisis and trying not-obviously to keep an eye on my surroundings for those who didn't belong there. But Sophia was…*easy*, and she made it easier just by being what I'd discovered was her usual friendly, kind self.

Friendly, kind, *and* gorgeous. I snuck sneaky peeks at her, absorbing the strong bone structure, her soft full mouth, curved nose, expressive eyebrows. If I wasn't careful I was going to forget what I needed to do. As if she sensed me watching, Sophia paused cutting her waffle, and glanced up at me. Her smile started slowly, then her teeth skimmed her lower lip before the curve of her mouth faded, turning her expression into one of pure desire.

The look sent a slow burn of excitement through me. Spending time with her was not going to be difficult. Quite the opposite, I thought. I made a mental note to thank that agency therapist who'd suggested that I make an effort to form relationships outside work. It looked like it was going to prove far more valuable than he'd anticipated. Again, an expected surge of guilt welled up. I pushed it back down. Sophia was acceptable collateral damage. She wasn't going to lose her life, obviously, but she would undoubtedly lose her trust in me if she found out what I'd done. An unpleasant and unfortunately necessary trade-off. It wouldn't be the first time I'd given up something personal for this job.

When Sophia stopped looking at me like she wanted to have me for lunch, I picked up the conversation. "So, when we were FaceTiming on Tuesday, you said you wanted to compare continents visited. How many have you been to?" She'd had a distinctly mischievous look when she'd mentioned the "continent competition," stating she was fairly certain she was going to beat me.

"Five. You?"

"Six. Everywhere but Antarctica." Laughing at her wrinkled nose, I added, "Sorry. I win."

She exhaled a long, exaggerated breath. "Damn. Okay then. How many European countries have you visited?" Her competitive streak was adorable.

I took a minute to tally them mentally, winking when she laughed at my finger counting. "Eighteen."

"Ha! Twenty-one."

I held up my hands in defeat. "Okay okay, you got me there, fair and square." She grinned triumphantly, and the moment she moved her attention back to her plate, I peered around the café. Still nothing amiss. I relaxed down to a solid 14. "When was your last 'away' vacation?"

That pulled her up. Sophia set her knife and fork back down. "Shit. I—It's been at least four years. Maybe more? I finally took the leap in 2018 and started my own business—graphic design and website creation—and I've been building that up. Everything else took a back seat." She frowned as if she'd just had an unpleasant realization. "I used to just…*go* places on a whim, at least a few times a year, like if I had the money and the time I'd just book a trip to Thailand or Japan or Italy or something. Even for just a week or two, just to travel. And if the money wasn't there, I'd get in my car and drive across states for a few weeks, exploring. Then I'd just drive back. I love being at home, around my family, but I also get itchy feet. I guess I haven't been scratching them like I used to."

I bit my tongue on an innuendo-laden "scratching an itch" quip. "Do you prefer to travel alone or with someone?"

"With someone if I can," she said immediately, "but I've done plenty of trips solo because I had no choice. I'd rather alone than not at all."

Another opening. I jumped through it. "I've always preferred traveling with a companion." I took her left hand, turning it over to study the lines on her palm. "There's something incredible about sharing adventures with someone you...really like."

"Agreed..." Sophia curled her fingers, briefly trapping mine before she released me. She slowly turned her head until we were face-to-face, barely an inch apart. Her gaze rose from where it'd been focused on my mouth until she made eye contact with me, her gentle brown eyes holding a pleading expression. Without a word, she closed the tiny gap between us and kissed me. Just a quick, soft press of lips to mine as her fingertips traced the edge of my jaw. Though it was a chaste kiss, it still sent a tingle down my spine.

I would have deepened the kiss, except someone male cleared their throat, dragging us apart. Bastard. When I saw who it was, my mind went blank, except for one word. *Fuck*, repeated indefinitely as a scream into the void. What I wanted to say was, "How long did it take for someone to get you out of those cuffs and ouch, that broken nose looks painful, did I do that?"

Instead, I said the first bland thing that came to mind around the repeating mental expletive. "Can I help you?"

Broken Nose was apparently a better actor than thug. His expression never changed as he said in a low and almost enticing tone, "We need to talk. Why don't you come outside with me?"

Squeezing Sophia's thigh—both for my own comfort and her reassurance, I looked up at him and said conversationally, "I think you might have me mistaken for someone else." I raised my eyebrows. Also, you might notice, Broken Nose, that I have company *and* a café-worth of people around me, and some of them are starting to look our way. Goddammit. So much for the whole hiding and lying low.

He moved closer, mouth opening to speak again, but Sophia got in first, lifting herself from her chair. She raised her chin, staring him down as she quietly stated, "Dude, she said she doesn't know you. And you're interrupting us. End of story."

Broken Nose turned to her, his surprise at being challenged obvious. And genuine. He didn't know her, and the relief was so strong I almost sagged. He didn't know her. She was a safe place when I just...really *really* needed one of those. I didn't think she was...I mean, I hadn't consciously thought...but clearly the unconscious, always-alert part of me *had* thought she might somehow be involved.

I pulled Sophia back down, noting the rigidity of her body, the tightness of her arm muscle. There was a lioness inside of that sweet house-cat body.

He stared at her, looked to me, then his eyes took in the rest of the space. "My mistake. Sorry." Broken Nose backed up, turned around, and walked out of the café. I watched him cross the street and get into a blue 2018 Ford Fusion Sport. It was just him, and I wondered where his partner was. Nowhere in my sightline but that didn't mean they weren't around.

Layered on top of the panic and upset that I'd been found, yet again, was a sense of relief. My human safety bubble had worked as intended. So now I just had to be in public, or with one person in private, for the rest of time. Or at least until Hadim's intel and I were no longer associated with one another and Lennon told me it was safe to emerge. Oh, I'm actually not needy, Sophia, but just as a hypothetical question...how do you feel about being together for like, always?

Another layer jumped on top of the other emotions. Fear. So he'd left us alone now, but what happened tomorrow or the days after when the stakes got higher? Was it possible I'd be putting her in danger when they grew more frustrated and started getting bolder? My answer to my question was immediate. No. They wouldn't want an uninvolved person becoming involved. And if it came to it, I'd step in front of her. But his arrival had hammered home that I needed to flee, and soon, and I needed to do it with someone by my side.

Sophia touched my wrist, startling me. "What was that about?" she asked quietly.

I plastered a smile on my face. "No clue." I thumbed the edge of her mouth. "Guess I have a doppelgänger?"

Her eyebrows bounced. "Hot."

CHAPTER FIVE

Sometimes clumsy seduction works

I lasted another twenty minutes before the twitchiness grew too uncomfortable to ignore. Too exposed, too much time ticking away. We'd finished eating and were lingering over second and third coffees when I asked if we could go back to her place to "hang out and talk." Sophia couldn't agree fast enough, and as soon as I'd paid, she told me her apartment was just a short walk away. Excellent—no driving meant Broken Nose and Co. wouldn't know Sophia's car. Of course they'd follow us, but them knowing where she lived and how I...we would leave her place later without being noticed was a problem for Future Lexie. After a casual check of my surroundings, I took Sophia's hand, relieved when she interlaced our fingers. The Ford Fusion was nowhere in sight, which meant nothing more than it was somewhere out of sight waiting to tail me.

Sophia seemed to have forgotten about the strange intrusion into our date. Thankfully. I might have broken Broken Nose's jaw as well if he'd messed up my carefully laid plans with his ill-timed appearance. Though, I didn't really think any appearance by him would be well-timed.

We settled into a mutual silence for the fifteen-minute walk, but it wasn't an awkward one. Comfortable silences were amazing. And also gave me some time to think. I really needed to get to Florida, and I really needed her to come along with me. Well, not *her* specifically, but I needed someone, and she was a someone who I really wanted to spend more time with. It made sense to convince Sophia to accompany me. Normally I'd take a few months to build trust and rapport with a person before I started pushing them for more. But I had three completed dates, a bunch of chemistry, dozens of flirty texts, a handful of deep conversations, and…maybe three hours *max* to convince Sophia to take a road trip with me. If this didn't work, then I'd just have to go it alone and cross all my digits that I could remain hidden, because it was going to be a lot harder to keep them from taking me in when I didn't have a safety net companion.

Sophia's apartment was on the top floor of one of the newer buildings near the university. It was roomy for a two-bedroom and had a large open-plan living space backing into a kitchen that looked like an advertisement for professional cooking. I wandered around, pretending I was taking it all in. I mean, I was…but I was also memorizing the layout and entry/exit points.

I leaned over the counter to look into the kitchen. "You cook much?"

"I love cooking, but I'm pretty horrible at it. My older sister, the actual chef, got all the good cooking genes." Laughing, Sophia pulled a face. "The kitchen came with the apartment when I bought it. I like it, gives me the illusion of being able to cook."

"Ah. Well, I've been told I'm an excellent cook." Unbidden, the memory of Elaheh's praise rushed through me, washing away everything except her words, my response.

"You learned how to cook this dish so quickly. I'm surprised. And impressed."

"And I'm surprised how quickly you've learned to enjoy me being in your bed."

I stuffed the thought aside, not wanting to think of where Elaheh might be, if she even still…*was*. I'd never loved her, but in some warped way I felt responsible for her. When I turned around, Sophia's closeness surprised me. Lightly brushing my fingers over her hip, I added, "And I'm always happy to cook for people, any meal. Dinner, breakfast…" Leaving the implication hanging, I took a tiny step away, gratified when she leaned forward as if to follow.

Sophia gripped my blouse, her fingers tangling in the fabric a clear "don't move" signal. "I'm pretty partial to breakfast," she murmured. "Especially in bed."

Her words had welcome desire flowing through me. Elaheh's mental intrusion had left me feeling rattled, reminding me of how long it'd been since I'd last been intimate with a woman, and of all the events and complications surrounding our affair. I shook the past from my head, and centered myself in the present, where I desired *this* woman. I needed Sophia to trust me, to come with me, and wanting her was going to make that a whole lot easier. But not yet, not yet. Just a little more anticipation.

Even though I took a calming breath before answering, I wasn't surprised when my response came out hoarsely. "Good to know." I cleared my throat. "Maybe breakfast in bed is a…fifth date event?"

"You think you're going to get another two dates out of me?" Sophia teased.

"Yeah, I'm confident. But for now…" Time to move things along. I tugged at my blouse, raising it slightly to expose some skin. "Is it okay if I change quickly? I'm feeling a little self-conscious about this huge hollandaise stain on my top." I raised it slightly higher and peered at my stomach, absently rubbing my palm over an imaginary stain. "Actually, it's on my skin too. Would you mind if I took a shower?" My accidental sauce spill hadn't been as accidental as she might think. I know, this was turning into every bad porno ever made, but I had no time to play the long seduction game. My seduction game had had so little use in the past…let's not think about how many years, that I wasn't even sure it was working.

Sophia stared, then seemed to realize she was staring. Her head snapped up, and I caught the blush spreading up her neck as she agreed, "Of course."

Okay, maybe it *was* working.

She indicated that I should follow her into her room. "My bathroom's just through here, use whatever you need. Fresh towels are on the shelves." Sophia's eyes made another quick sweep over my body. "If you pass me your blouse, I'll put it in to soak."

"Thanks." I set my bags in the corner of the master bathroom and turned, intending to close the door partway so I could undress and pass Sophia my top.

She'd stopped by the bathroom doorway, staring at me with unabashed interest. What the heck—now or never, right? Without closing the door or moving where she couldn't see me, I pulled the blouse over my head and held it out to her. As soon as she'd taken it, I unfastened my jeans, and had slid them halfway down my thighs when Sophia nervously cleared her throat and backed out, closing the bathroom door behind her. Good. Not her closing the door, but her reaction. I leaned against the wall, hating myself for my manipulation, even as I was absolutely certain of its necessity.

Sophia's shower had a rainforest showerhead and it was a struggle to not stand in there for half an hour, using all her hot water. As the heavy-yet-soft streams of water cascaded over my head, I decided this would be a fabulous shower to have sex in. Maybe that's why she had it. Closing my eyes, I gave myself a few moments off the on-the-run clock and let my thoughts loose. They inevitably turned to a very graphic imagining of us in this shower doing delicious things to one another. Mmm yes, Plan A—Stick with Sophia—was a good idea.

After five blissful minutes, I ended with a ten-second cold-water blast then reluctantly shut off the water, dried off, and slipped into fresh underwear and bra. Right, time to put the plan into action. Wish me luck. I really should have packed better underwear, except, you know...I didn't know this was going to be my new plan.

Toweling my hair, I left the bathroom wearing nothing more than perfectly fine, but definitely not "fuck me now" underwear. Hopefully she'd ignore that fact in the face of the amount of skin I had on display. "Sophia? I can't find your deodorant. I forgot to grab some in my rush to escape being fumigated along with the roaches."

She burst into the bedroom like she'd been waiting outside for me to finish, paused, and then shuffled as if she was going to turn around but didn't want it to be conspicuous. With her chin raised, she slid past me, carefully not touching my bare skin, and into the bathroom.

"So, you...work out, huh," she said offhandedly as she reached into the bathroom cabinet.

"Mhmm. I always make it a priority in my schedule. Partly because of work, partly for my mental health, partly because I really like food, and partly because I'd like to be prepared in case some thug breaks into my apartment in the middle of the night." I bit back my smirk. No, really.

"Ah. You look…really good. Um, fit and strong." She passed me the deodorant, very purposefully staring at the sink while I sprayed my armpits. "I should go to the gym more. I'd like to lose some pounds, but…" Her smiling shrug was the epitome of "But meh, effort."

I passed the can back. "Yeah? For what it's worth, I like the way you look, a whole lot." Sophia was gorgeous—luscious and feminine, and I honestly hoped I'd have a chance to enjoy her body. Multiple times.

She turned around to face me fully, offering a blushing, quiet, "I'm pleased."

"I'm pleased you're pleased."

Sophia apparently lost the battle with her willpower, her gaze straying downward, lingering on my breasts before pausing on my torso. Her forehead wrinkled and it was obvious from her expression that she desperately wanted to ask. I decided to answer the unasked question to save her the embarrassment. Brushing my hands down my stomach, I felt the familiar scars. "I was involved in a work incident overseas, a little over five years ago. Someone I was meeting had been followed by, uh, the 'bad guys,' and it went south from there. Luckily, the people I work with are very good at their job and I got away with just these few little scrapes." There. Nicely underplayed. I fought the urge to fidget. I got away. But not everyone did.

Her eyes stayed on my torso, intensely focused on the long surgical scar that went from just above my navel and hooked around my ribs, and the six inch-long scars that were peppered in random spots over my belly and ribs. Finally, she lifted her eyes to find mine. "What exactly were you doing to get those?" She asked the question neutrally, as if she had to work at moderating her emotion.

"Just my job." I paused, debated, and gave her something truthful but not dangerous. She needed some truth and so did I— constant lies were unsustainable, especially when I needed her to stick with me, needed her to *want* to stick with me. The answer was an easy enough truth. I'd already told her I worked for the government, so now I elaborated, "I work in intelligence."

Sophia's eyes widened so much they seemed almost cartoonish. "You're a spy?"

Leaning in, I offered an exaggerated conspiratorial wink. "If I was, I wouldn't tell you." At her uncertain smile, I added, "But no, I am definitely not a spy. I'm an analyst, I evaluate and investigate information I receive from various sources, then prepare reports so the policymakers can utilize it for the good of the country. That's the simple, public-knowledge version of course. It's kind of like… investigative journalism."

Sophia exhaled loudly. "That sounds important."

"Yes, it is." I paused, feeling like a gung-ho weirdo. "It keeps people safe, and that's important to me."

She didn't ask which agency I worked for, or for some gory exciting details of my job. Instead, she said, eyebrows creasing together in thought, "Oh my god. I just realized…Is this weird?"

"Is what weird?"

"*Me.* Me being an espionage-thriller groupie. I *swear* I had no idea what your job was, obviously."

Smiling, I reassured her, "I know you didn't. And no, it's anything but weird. I saw your hobbies in your profile and it made me laugh. So ironic." Loves travel, good food and wine, brainteasers and puzzles, Nancy Drew afficionado, longing for a Jane Bond.

"I feel like an idiot. This is so embarrassing."

"Don't worry about it. It's perfect."

She raised an eyebrow. "How's that?"

"Because my hobbies happen to include gorgeous computer nerds who like to travel. It's a perfect match."

"Looks like it," Sophia teased. Then she sobered. "I don't remember anything about a situation involving American sp—uh, *intelligence* people in the last five years."

"No, you wouldn't. We tend not to advertise where we're operating or how our military works. Especially not missions like that."

She worried her lower lip with her teeth, and her eyes held nothing but naked truth. "So you might have been killed?"

I shrugged. "Possibly?" The idea had never concerned me, that I'd be nothing more than a footnote in a report, an unnamed carved star on the Wall of Honor that honored those lost in the line of duty. The thought of not being missed had no impact on my psyche. What bothered me, what kept me up with existential thoughts into the small hours, was not leaving a mark, not changing the world before I died. That very thought had been what'd had me falling over myself to sign on the dotted line when Halcyon had approached me.

"I don't like that." Sophia's tentative fingers brushed my stomach, along the edge of the long surgical scar, without actually touching the sensitive skin. "I might never have met you," she whispered.

The simplicity of her statement stirred me and the touch of her fingertips sent a flood of goose bumps over my skin. "Sophia?" The raw huskiness in that word surprised me and I had to swallow before I could continue, "I've been thinking about kissing you, *really* kissing you, ever since you texted me the photo of you eating a pear." She didn't move away and I ran my thumb along her lower lip, indulging myself in its soft fullness. "And I've wanted to take you to bed pretty much from the moment I saw you walking into the coffee shop on our first date. You are the stuff of wet dreams. I'm sorry if that's too forward, or soon, but…it's the truth."

She blushed as she had earlier in the café when I'd complimented her dress, the slow spread of pink fanning out and down from her cheeks. Her lips turned upward in a knowing smile before she answered, her voice almost as low and husky as mine when I'd admitted how much I wanted her. "I promised you a kiss, didn't I?" she mused. "And that interrupted one in the café doesn't count."

"Yes…you did promise me that." I dipped my head, paused, and when she moved closer I finished what I'd started by kissing her. She was warm, gentle, and surprisingly tender considering her tongue was doing something pretty spine-tingling as it played against mine. I wrapped my arms around her waist, pulling her tightly against me.

Oh yes, this was the better of my two options for a number of reasons. Not only because of the absolute pleasure, but I hoped my assessment of Sophia was correct, that she would want to spend time with me after we'd been intimate. Option two was force her to come along and wait until Stockholm Syndrome kicked in. And that was an unpleasurable, time-consuming, and all-around-shitty option, and one I'd never be able to stomach.

This was the part of my job I'd never liked. The untruths and manipulation—that they rarely realized was happening—to get people to do what I needed them to. Necessary but still not nice. Using sex like this wasn't something I'd ever done before, though I knew it was sometimes a tool used by people who sent my team information. I'd often marveled and admired those assets for doing anything necessary to get what they needed. Clinical and detached were not natural parts of my temperament—I'd had to learn those traits.

That detachment frayed somewhat when Sophia's hands went to my waist, her palms caressing the skin above my panties. Thumbs dipped under the waistband and stayed there as her fingers massaged my hips. She pulled me closer in a gesture surprising in its forcefulness. "I'm not usually like this," she breathed, tonguing my ear.

My stomach tightened at that touch of her tongue. "Like what?" I asked. "Sexy as hell?"

She laughed. "No, forward."

"Me either," I said truthfully. I'd known right away on our first coffee date that I wanted to sleep with her, but I'd always thought I'd let her initiate it.

"I mean, I'd imagined this happening but not right now." She kissed my neck, softly nipping my skin until I shuddered, and she apologized by kissing the spot she'd just bitten.

I put an inch of space between us, immediately regretting it. "We don't have to. I mean I *want* to, so much, but if it's too soon then we can wait." Despite knowing this was the quickest way to what I needed, I wasn't a creep. If she said no, then I would never force her. I'd just figure something else out. I always did. A small, not work-related part of my brain chimed in to tell me emphatically that it really, really wanted Sophia Flores to come in my mouth. My arousal spiked. Thanks. Just what I needed when I was trying to keep some part of myself alert.

Her fingers tightened on my waist. "I don't want to wait. And honestly? If we keep seeing each other, I don't know how much longer I'd be able to resist…this."

Well that was a nice ego inflation. I dipped my head, lingered close to her mouth and lightly slicked my tongue over her lower lip. "Me either. So, uh, this is my obligatory everything's okay and safe disclaimer before we go further."

The smile quirking the edge of her mouth made me want to kiss her again, so I did, just as she murmured, "Oh, yes. Me too."

"Great." I let my fingers dip down to the small of her back. She was so warm, so tantalizing, that my hands drifted lower to cup her ass. "And that's a yes to sleeping with me, like…right now?"

"It is. Emphatically."

"Mmm, good," I purred. "Sophia?"

Her hands fluttered over my neck and her answer was a breathy, "Yes?"

I knelt in front of her and lightly trailed my hands up her legs until they were under her dress. Slowly, I pulled her panties down to her ankles, then helped her lift each foot so I could remove the fabric entirely. "I told you I love this dress. But I think I'm going to like what's underneath it even more…"

CHAPTER SIX

Manipulation is shitty pillow talk

Despite my responsibilities to Halcyon and the fact I was seriously short on time, I wanted nothing more than to slow down and enjoy Sophia. It had been far too long since I'd been intimate with another woman, and she had an insatiable desire to connect. To please and ask for pleasure. I'd surrendered to her as she'd pressed me to the mattress, pushed my thighs apart, and kissed and licked her way down my body until her mouth was buried in my arousal.

Sophia intuited exactly what I needed, her hands and lips and tongue skillfully working in synchronicity until I climaxed in a white-hot flash of pleasure. I'd forgotten that kind of climax existed, the intensity of someone else drawing out my orgasm. Then it'd been my turn to reciprocate, and I'd almost quivered with the anticipation of having her. She was soft and delicious, responsive, warm and pliant under my lips and hands, and for those too-short minutes, I'd thought of nothing except the simplicity of intimacy.

We lay tangled in Sophia's sheets, me on my back and her against me with a leg slung over my thighs. And now I was still, the niggling anxiety returned. I tried to stifle it for just a few minutes more so I could enjoy this, enjoy her. But my reality refused to be pushed aside. I had to move. As much as I wanted to, I couldn't stay here, couldn't cocoon myself in her apartment, in her bed, for the weekend then saunter back into the office on Monday like nothing had happened. Dammit, I wouldn't get to tell Sam how my date had gone.

Sophia propped herself up on an elbow. "What are you thinking about?" she murmured.

"Nothing important," I said automatically. Just boring shit like national security. Diplomacy. Potential world wars. Mass murder. Government duplicity. Smiling, I added, "Just reliving the past hour…"

"Mmm. I have a feeling I'll be reliving that quite a bit in the coming days," she said, her voice low and lazy with residual pleasure.

I traced the rainbow Care Bear tattoo on the underside of her wrist, then brought her hand to my mouth and kissed her palm. Time for the thing I didn't really want to do. I pushed myself up on the pillows and casually asked, "When do you want to meet up again? I'm going out of town for a week or two, so it'll have to be when I get back." I slowly brushed my hand up the inside of her thigh, enjoying the way her muscles tightened at my touch. "Of course, I'm making a huge assumption that you want to meet up again."

Sophia tried to cover her disappointment before it showed, and failed utterly. "Oh. Shit. And of course I want to meet up again. I want to meet up many agains."

The temptation of her bare skin was too hard to resist and I drew my fingertips up her belly and between her breasts. This touch was made sweeter for the fact it was all me, all my desire, and nothing to do with what I was trying to accomplish. "You could always come with me," I said, still stroking. "I need to take a short work trip, drive down to see someone in Florida, then I've taken some vacation time after. We could take a road trip together, get away from this cool weather for a few days, spend some time at the beach? I'd love to see you in, and out of, a bikini."

Her eyebrows dipped. "That's a long road trip, and isn't your car in the shop?"

Dammit, caught me. "Work is paying for a rental car. And it's only thirteen, fourteen hours of driving. We *could* do it in a day if we had no distractions." I kissed her, long and deep, insinuating exactly what distractions I meant.

"Mmm. But why not just fly?"

"Residual pandemic flight paranoia," I answered, hoping it would be enough of an explanation.

"Can't you just call or Zoom this person?"

I laughed at her obvious, logical reasoning. Of course I could, if I lived in a simple world. "No, I need to collect something that's too delicate to ship to me. Until they figure out a way to transfer solid objects through cyberspace, Zoom just won't cut it." I lightly ran my thumb along her cheekbone.

Sophia's forehead furrowed and she exhaled a soft musing sound. I could see pros and cons clicking against each other as she decided whether or not to take my offer, and I kept my expression deliberately neutral, not wanting to show how desperate I was for her to come with me. She pulled a face. "I have some client projects I'm working on. Website design waits for nobody."

This was an easy fix. "Then bring your laptop with you, like I am. Part work trip, remember?" I trailed my fingers over her hip. "You know, once I'm done we could go down to Miami, charter a small boat and hop to the Bahamas for a few days."

Her entire body relaxed, as if she'd simply ceased thinking about the things that were worrying her, and made the choice to do what she wanted to do rather than what she felt she *should* do. Lucky her. She leaned over and kissed me. "You know what? Fuck it. Yes. Let's do it. It's been way too long since I took a spontaneous trip. Didn't I literally just say at breakfast that I've been letting building my business get in the way of all that? My business is built. I want to *go* somewhere. I want an adventure."

Relief made me feel giddy. I had a safety net. For a short while at least. "Fabulous. It'll be an adventure indeed."

Smiling, she eyed me. "Have you ever done this before?"

"Gone on a trip with a woman I've only known for a month? No, never."

"Me either, but it doesn't feel wrong, so it must be right." What wonderfully simple logic. "I'll let my pickleball teammate know she has to find a sub for next week's game."

"Fantastic. But, uh, what's picketball?"

Laughing, she corrected me, "*Pickle*ball. Like tennis and Ping-Pong and badminton all in one. I'm excellent at it. Not as good as I am at Eye Spy though, so prepare for an ass-kicking."

She was so adorably dorky that I had to kiss her again. Kissing her could get addictive. "Well, shit," I murmured. "I'm screwed."

"If you're lucky," she drawled, rolling me over and settling on top of me.

I exhaled a moan as her thigh slid between mine. Being with her was not going to be a hardship at all. But… I made a show of looking at my watch. "If we're going to have an epic Eye Spy battle, we should probably get on the road."

"Now?" Sophia grabbed my wrist to check the time. Almost two p.m.

"No time like the present and all that. If we leave now we can be in North Carolina for the night. Dinner's on me." I kissed her lingeringly—bad idea—then carefully extracted myself from underneath her and rolled out of bed. "Breakfast tomorrow is on you."

She flopped onto her stomach and stared at me as if she couldn't believe I'd chosen starting a road trip over more time in bed. Both eyebrows rose slowly. "Didn't you offer to cook breakfast for me?"

"I did. Except hotels don't exactly lend themselves to great cooking experiences. But when you stay over at my house for that fifth date…"

"I'm going to hold you to that."

"I really hope you do," I said seriously.

While she showered, I dressed, checked Google maps of the area, peeked out the window for spooky SUVs and freaky Ford Fusions—none in sight—and ordered a cab. No Uber, just in case that'd been how they'd found me last night. Derek had messaged four times, each with varying stages of *WTF, Martin?* And Lennon's message on the blue phone was a simple: *Everything is arranged.*

Sophia was still in the shower, so I wandered around the neat apartment, quietly opening drawers to borrow a few things that might come in handy later, and sporadically peering out of the window to see if we suddenly had company. If we did, they were somewhere inconspicuous. When I heard the water shut off, I strolled back into her bedroom and sat on the bed.

Wearing nothing but a towel, Sophia pulled a small hard-shell suitcase from the high shelf in her closet and dropped it onto the bed beside me. "How long do you think we'll be gone?"

I deliberately didn't answer. I had no idea. "We'll be in Florida late tomorrow and I should only need three or four days to do what I have to do there, and then we can drive back slow or fast." Shrugging, I added, "Or, if you want to, we can keep driving, go wherever. Let's just see where the mood takes us."

Sophia laughed and began to pull clothing from her closet. "Like a regular Thelma and Louise."

I forced a smile. "Something like that. But with a far better ending for us." Hopefully.

"Phew." She dressed quickly then just as quickly began sorting clothes for our trip. She held up three pairs of shoes and discarded a pair of heels before packing the sneakers and ankle boots. "How much vacation time have you taken?"

"A few weeks." Should probably tell my boss that. Maybe. I was pretty sure Derek got the vibe that I wasn't coming in next week. I stood and moved to lean against the wall, trying to appear casual and not like I was so desperate to get out of the city I wanted to just throw her over my shoulder and go. "Are you going to let your family or someone know who you're with?"

Sophia folded two pairs of jeans into her suitcase. "Mhmm. I need someone to feed my fish, so I'll tell my sister where I'm going, and make her come around to take care of them. She lives nearby, so she won't complain too much."

"Excellent. I've ordered a cab. It'll be here in twenty minutes." If they were here, they'd be watching her parking garage, and them seeing us drive out was an invitation to run her plates and figure out who she was. They'd discover her identity eventually, but I wanted to delay that as long as I could. Renting a car would leave a license imprint—either my real or "fake" one, but only at my point of origin. They wouldn't know my destination. Best of a bunch of bad solutions.

"What for?"

"To take us to the rental car place, so you don't have to leave your car there, which is weird and unnecessary. I couldn't remember your address, so we have to walk a minute to the street name I *did* remember." I didn't want to get into a car outside her building. As we'd walked, I'd noticed a path along the side of her apartment complex which my map-check confirmed met the street behind it. Perfect spot to slip away.

"Oh, sure. No problem. We can still split the driving, right?"

"Of course. And tell you what—you can be in charge of music and I promise I won't even complain." After a beat I qualified, "Unless it's country music."

She grinned, and kissed me lightly. "Then I'm afraid you're going to be doing a bit of complaining."

"Shit," I deadpanned. As she laughed and walked into her bathroom I called after her, "That was *not* in your dating site profile!"

* * *

"What's this?" Sophia asked, craning her neck to peer out the window as I made a sharp right-hand turn.

"Just grabbing a few things," I said airily as I pulled the Nissan Rogue into a storage rental place on the outskirts of town. "Clothes and stuff I keep in storage rather than clogging up my closets. Saves me buying things just for this trip." I crossed my fingers that she wouldn't ask why I hadn't packed for a road trip when leaving my "fumigated" apartment. There were so many pinprick holes in my story. I needed to close them before they tore wide open.

The old, rundown complex was empty save for an older gentleman and a middle-aged woman who were rummaging in open storage units and didn't seem interested in anything other than their stuff. I parked near the entry, left the engine running, and leaned over and kissed Sophia. "I'll just be a minute."

Halcyon's unit was around the corner and as I walked across the cracked tarmac, unease made my stomach churn. What if this was a trap? I shook off the thought. This was Halcyon's storage unit, one nobody except Halcyon agents knew about. Nobody was coming for me here. Despite my self-reassurance, I still couldn't shake my ingrained uneasiness. There was nothing inside except a bag on the oil-stained concrete floor. I checked the contents of the duffel. As requested: a secure laptop, two driver licenses and passports with not my name on them, cash and prepaid Visa cards, a couple of untraceable credit cards, some electronics, three new boxed cell phones, another handgun and some ammunition. Everything one might need for a casual day of espionage. I double-checked the names I'd be using: Jessica Beaumont and Elizabeth Whitney. How wonderfully WASPy. I left the gun and ammo. I had a gun and two guns was too many guns.

I put my hand up to drive the first leg. Sophia, I discovered, suffered car sickness, and the best way she'd found to combat it was talking as distraction. Or so she said. I was beginning to realize that talking was just part of her, and rather than being annoyed by the noise and her expectation of interaction, I found myself enjoying the engagement. It made a nice break from constant vigilance.

"What about motion sickness pills?" I asked after the first half hour of her inane, but adorable, chattering.

"They make me sleepy."

"Ah, well we wouldn't want that."

"Mmm." An alert on her phone cut short any further response. Her snorted laugh prompted me to ask, "What's up?"

Sophia waved her phone. "Just my sister. She thinks I'm crazy for going on a road trip with someone I hardly know."

Oh, don't derail us now, sibling. "Do you think you're crazy?" I glanced at Sophia.

She smiled. "No."

"Would it make her feel better if you sent her a picture of my license? Would it make *you* feel better?"

"No. Would it make you feel better?"

Yes and no. Yes, her family would know who I was in case things went south. No, her family would know for sure who I was. "I don't need to feel better," I said. "I feel great."

"Me too."

"Is she worried I'm going to get you stuck in a landslide or trapped by an earthquake or something?"

She raised a dubious eyebrow. "In Florida?"

"You never know."

"Getting trapped by a natural disaster is a morbid thought," Sophia said.

"Think of all the things we could do while waiting to be rescued. Card games, board games, learn to salsa dance, sex on every available surface…"

Sophia inhaled sharply. "They say it's a great way to get to know someone," she said on her exhalation.

"Playing board games?" I teased.

She shot me a look that would have been withering, if not for the smile that followed. "No, sex."

"I agree." The prospect of spending an isolated week with Sophia, doing little but making love…fucking…sleeping together, started a slow roll of excitement through me. Another time perhaps. If I made it out of this. I cleared my throat.

Sophia twisted sideways and drew her legs up so she was like a small bundle of human snuggled on the car seat. She let her head fall against the headrest, and I sensed her watching me as I drove, her fingers tapping irregularly on her knee.

"What?" I finally asked after a minute of her quiet study.

"I just…don't quite know what to make of you."

I set cruise control, made sure I wasn't about to drive into anyone while doing seventy miles per hour, and glanced over at her. "What do you mean?"

Sophia gestured vaguely. "You're a total contradiction. Our dates, the conversations, our time in bed earlier, showed me you're impulsive and funny, charming and sexy. Irreverent," she added, drawing the word out into a teasing kind of observation. "But then now, you're quiet and watchful, almost cautious. And I'm wondering where all the other parts of you are when you turn into *this* person."

"Maybe I'm just a safe driver and that's where the quiet and watchful and cautious comes into play," I said.

"Maybe," she mused.

I let the silence stretch as I thought about how to best answer her. "All the other parts of me are still in here. Nobody can partition off bits of themselves to become a completely different person, can they?" Laughing, I said, "What's that saying? An enigma wrapped in a puzzle wrapped in a…ah, shit, I can't remember the next bit." I quickly checked my mirrors. Still all clear. "Isn't everyone a little like that? A mix of things to make up the whole?"

"I guess. But I don't know anyone who's such a mix of so many different things the way you seem to be. Things that feel like they should conflict, but when you show them to me, they fit so perfectly together. And all those things are all wrapped up in that hot, thoughtful, sensitive bundle."

"I feel like you're complimenting me," I said dryly. The compliment felt amazing, and made me realize just how long it'd been since I'd received a personal compliment. Hearing "You're good at your job" was great, but yeah...

She grinned. "I am."

"Thank you." I squeezed the wheel hard, twisted my hands back until the leather creaked. "I suppose I am a mix. Changing schools so much, it was easy to see the best way to fit in was to be outgoing and funny, so I guess that's who I evolved into. But my work makes me careful and serious, so some of that has leached into my personality. It's a balance between all aspects of myself."

"Balance," she said slowly, like she was examining the word.

"Mhmm." I looked over at her again. "You know why my agency, and all our other government agencies, work so well?" At her headshake, I told her, "Because we're all different. Some of us are superrr serious, like what you see in television or movies. Then some are quiet. Some are gregarious. Some are irreverent. You get the idea. Having a mesh of different personalities means we all approach a task in a different way and that gets results. What one person focuses on, another may miss and vice versa. We have shared core skills and personality traits but other than that, none of us are alike. But we complement each other. Like a relationship."

"Balance *is* a good basis for a relationship," she murmured.

I laughed to hide the heat that had flooded me at her implication of a relationship between us. She was doing a good job of hiding her thoughts, unless you were someone like me who was trained to look beyond just words. "Well, we do spend a lot of time together at work, so I suppose that's one way of looking at it."

"I've always liked that thought, the idea of people balancing each other's strengths and weaknesses in a relationship." She reached over and hooked her fingers in the waistband of my jeans.

The way she'd talked about balance, about what she wanted in a way that was both confident and wistful, then tucked her fingers so casually inside my jeans to connect us without being overbearing, stuck in my head for the rest of the drive. And she kept her fingers in my waistband almost the whole time.

Even after stopping for groceries and other necessities, we made good time, and it was a little after seven thirty when I pulled into a twenty-four-hour motor inn Sophia had found. The place seemed to be in good shape and I left Sophia in the car while I went in to grab us a room. Despite knowing how careful I'd been, how vigilant, the fact I'd seen nobody, I couldn't shake the unease that we were being tailed. Sometimes paranoia is good, sometimes it's incredibly unhelpful and annoying. But nothing stood out, no coincidences, nothing suspicious. If someone *was* tailing us, they were so excellent at their job that they were practically invisible and deserved to find me just for that.

Bored middle-aged-man clerk had apparently had a slow day, and perked up when I walked in. He made a show of pointing out all the best places in town to eat and where I could buy groceries and alcohol. Provisioned with keys and a bunch of useless maps and brochures, which I dumped in the trash just outside the door, I went back to Sophia. She sat with legs raised so her sock-clad feet were up against the glove compartment, absorbed in a game on her phone.

I opened the driver's door and leaned in. "Why don't you wait here, and I'll check for bugs before we take our bags in. Bedbugs," I quickly amended. I didn't actually expect anything to be in the room, but I hadn't made it this far by being reckless.

"Sure," she said amicably.

I climbed in to kneel on the seat so I could kiss her then hopped out and grabbed the frequency-detecting device from Halcyon's duffel in the trunk, slipping it into the back pocket of my jeans. Our room was on the second floor, a typical midrange hotel room, with clean-smelling sheets and a surprisingly clean bathroom. A quick visual check showed nothing out of the ordinary. Good start. I unplugged the small fridge and television and started my sweep. Nothing, nothing, nothing. Huzzah. A quick investigation of the rest of the room and mattresses confirmed there were no bugs, insect or electronic, of any kind in the room.

The first thing Sophia said when I escorted her through the door was, "Two beds?"

I froze. "Uh, yeah? I wasn't sure...um, where we were given the situation, and...yeah." Laughing, I tried again. "Sorry, that was quite possibly the most inarticulate thing I've ever said. What I meant was, I didn't want to assume. It's one thing to sleep together but I didn't know about *sleeping* together." I set my bags down beside one of the two chairs hugging the small table.

"Right. Well I'm fine with it if you are. I can always use a warm body." Apparently my expression gave away my amusement, and she tossed a pillow at me before clarifying, "I'm a cold sleeper. And I already know that you run hot."

"I sure do." Sharing a bed not only went against my instincts from a lifetime of no serious relationships, but my love of sprawling across the bed in my sleep. "Happy to oblige then. You pick the bed. I'll take the side closest to the door." It made every tactical instinct I'd instilled in myself over the years sound alarm bells, but if anyone came through the door it would be me first, always.

While Sophia busied herself making the hotel room more homey by hanging clothes and setting out personal things, which I discovered were her e-reader and laptop, I took my duffel into the cramped bathroom under the pretense of unpacking toiletries. I clipped my handgun holster to my belt and covered it with my loose hoodie. The moment I did it, I felt like an idiot in an action movie, like a gun was actually going to stop them from grabbing me if they were here. I was sure they weren't here, but my instincts had unfortunately been wrong before.

When I emerged, Sophia was sprawled on the bed farthest from the door, staring up at the ceiling, but she rolled onto her side to watch me stow my bags in the closet without unpacking anything else. "Hungry?" she asked.

"Starving. But first, I need to get some ice and check we got everything from the car. Lock the door behind me, and don't open it unless you see it's me and only me."

She frowned. "You're not taking a key?"

"I'll probably lose it between here and the ice machine, so it's safer this way." No key meant nobody could take it from me and get to her if I was gone. I smiled to soften what I'd just said. I had to be careful not to frighten her unnecessarily. This was the finest of fine lines, and I wondered if I would be able to make her wary enough to be safe but not so wary that she felt scared. I kissed her, lingering until she relaxed. "Can never be too careful, especially in strange cities. I won't be long, and when I get back we can order dinner. Your choice."

She nodded and I left the hotel room, waiting beside the closed door until I'd heard her engage the chain, before I walked away.

The closest ice machine was on the ground floor and I took the internal stairway instead of the elevator, jogging down to try to ease some of the discomfort in my body. I needed to run, to stretch, to make my body move so it could be useful.

I slipped around to the dedicated smoker's area, which was mercifully empty. For now. Set back from the road and hidden from view, it was as good a place as any to make a call. A few deep breaths settled my nerves, and gave me some time to think of what I wanted to say. *Hey, so, did you betray me?* Solid start.

I would have preferred to be using a secure landline to make calls, but Signal with its end-to-end encryption was as good as I could do under the circumstances. Derek answered the call on the second ring. "Martin, what the *fuck* are you doing? I'm up to my ass in shit because of this and you are too. Where are you? I want you back here yesterday."

I kept my voice low, chin tucked into my chest to afford me another layer of privacy. "Derek, listen. I haven't done anything wrong, but something *is* wrong. I think this thing with the Red Wolves is bigger than I first thought. I don't know if you actually went to my place like I told you to, but someone broke into my apartment while I was asleep, and threatened me about it."

He grunted a sound of surprise and when he spoke again, some of the frustration had fallen out of his voice. "Go on."

I still didn't know how much I could trust him, and the feeling of being without his support was awful. But…basic details weren't harmful. And maybe he'd show his hand. Leaning against the brick façade, I murmured, "He demanded I go with him to the office where I'd show him all I had, we'd have a nice little chat, and then I'd delete everything and forget about it. No ID, no real explanation. Just a gun and an attitude. He followed me the next day and tried again, showing off the broken nose I gave him."

"Why not call me?"

"Because I panicked, okay? How would you feel if a thug broke into your apartment while you were sleeping, *naked* I might add, to threaten you for doing your job? A job that already had my spidey senses tingling." I inhaled a deep breath of cool air. "And given there were only two people in that office who knew about this, can you see why maybe I was a little cautious about calling you?" I was still cautious but I needed answers, even if that meant periodically exposing myself.

"I'm wounded," he said flatly. "What happened to trust?"

"Tell me you wouldn't think the same thing I did under the circumstances."

He mmphed. "I've reached out to you, so why don't you come in and we can work through this. I guarantee you my protection."

"I can't," I whispered.

"Then you know what this looks like, don't you?"

"I do." Naughty naughty intelligence stealy.

As if reading my mind, he asked, "Did you take this home with you?"

"Of course not!" I spluttered. "Why the hell would I?" Even if I'd thought it was something that needed protecting, I'd *never* just slip a flash drive in my pocket and try to get it past the security checkpoints, though I knew there *were* ways if someone was serious about taking something offsite. I almost wished I had, because it would make this a lot easier.

"Then why can't you come in?"

"Because I just can't." During the drive, I'd thought long and hard about how I'd explain myself and the fact I wasn't turning myself in for debrief as directed. I'd been given an order by people whose authority was greater than the agency's, and I had to follow it. But of course I couldn't say that. It's never just easy. "I know what this looks like, even though it absolutely is *not*. I'm not dirty, I'm not a rogue agent, I'm not a foreign agent. I've done nothing wrong, but I got scared last night, okay? And because I know what it looks like I can't come back unless I have something to bargain with. My bargaining chip is answers."

"Answers? You don't mean…"

"Yes." I took a deep breath, and went on before he could start yelling at me. "Can you at least admit that this is sketchy? The nighttime visitor? The threats? My gut tells me this is big, Derek. Bigger than an illegal chemical weapon test."

"I've always trusted your gut," he said begrudgingly.

"Thank you. I just…I think this intel is going to disappear. And that can't happen. I'm not going to let it happen."

"Martin, I'm hearing what you're saying, but that's not your call to make." Derek's voice grew very quiet and calm. Forced calm. That really was the worst kind of calm. I said a prayer for his blood pressure. "I cannot express strongly enough how much of a bad idea this is. Working this outside of the building? I don't even know what to say. You're going to risk everything—your security clearance, your job, and maybe even your freedom. For what?"

"For the truth. I'm being *very* careful. I know what I'm doing. I'd have thought some faith in me was within your abilities."

"I do have faith in you, but what I think is irrelevant. I don't make the rules. They could string you up for this. If you stop what you're doing and come in now, I can help you."

I ignored him. "I need honesty. Did you know anything about that thug that broke into my house last night and then followed me this morning?" And could still be following me.

"No," he said immediately.

"Well, I suppose that's something. I appreciate that. I have to go." I heard his frustrated "Martin!" as I hung up.

It was only when I was a few feet from our room that I realized I hadn't gotten any damned ice.

CHAPTER SEVEN

I don't believe in coincidences

Sophia was apparently safety-minded or good at taking suggestions. After I knocked, she jokingly asked through the closed door if I was reeeeally alone, and then cracked the door open to the end of the straining chain. "I'm not sure I can trust you," she said after I assured her I was definitely alone.

"And why's that?"

"Would *you* trust a strange woman at your door?"

"Well, that depends"—I held up the ice bucket that I'd run back down to fill—"if she'd brought ice for the whiskey or not. And considering yes, I have brought ice, I deem myself trustworthy."

The door closed on her grin and then opened again to an even wider grin. She tugged me inside and then locked and chained the door behind me. I kicked off my boots while Sophia took the ice bucket to the small kitchenette and began fixing drinks for us to enjoy before dinner.

This social charade was so unfamiliar. My brain was begging me to make what I knew would be an awful cup of tea from the Oolong tea bags I'd bought, then spend some time trying to connect mental dots. But first, food and acting like a normal person instead of ignoring the woman I'd begged to accompany me. I leaned against the short side of the L-shaped kitchenette counter. "Did you decide what you wanted for dinner?"

Her face seeped apology. "Sorry, I already ordered and paid. Mexican. The reviews of a nearby place were really good and they had vegetarian *pozole*, so I just went ahead. I'm so hungry." Her expression turned sheepish as she rambled, "I know, I should have checked before ordering, but I remembered you talking about the pinto bean pozole *verde* you had when you were in Mexico, so…"

"You remembered that?" It'd been the briefest passing comment nestled within a conversation about favorite foods on our first date. She'd admitted to loving Mexican, growing up with her paternal grandparents' cooking, then in the next breath had laughed and said that I shouldn't tell them but she also ate "the bad Mexican food"—said with a wavering, elderly Spanish accent—like Taco Bell, as much as she could.

Her eyebrows rose fleetingly as she passed me a glass with ice and two fingers of whiskey in it. "Of course I remembered."

"What else did you get?"

"*Enmoladas de plátano macho*—plantain enmoladas—and *arroz con vegetales*. Oh, and chips and guac, and *elotes*." She shrugged shyly. "All vegetarian for you. I thought we could just share?"

Her Spanish was so sexy, I made a mental note to ask her to speak it for me again. "How do you know I'm a vegetarian?" I knew I hadn't mentioned it yet.

"I wasn't one-hundred percent sure, but I took an educated guess. We've had three dates that involved food in some capacity, and you've ordered vegetarian each time. And that conversation about favorite foods? Every one of yours was vegetarian. Plus…" She smirked. "I don't know anyone who would choose pinto beans over pork for pozole, unless they didn't eat meat."

"You're sweet. And right."

She winked. "I'm an excellent detective."

"Nancy Drew would be proud," I agreed.

"Technically, I graduated beyond Nancy Drew when I was a teenager, but I still credit her with my mystery and detective fiction-loving roots. Now it's Miss Marple and Sherlock Holmes."

"Ah. No wonder you found me out." Smiling, I gestured vaguely toward the table. "I don't mind if you eat meat, though. But I thought I was paying for dinner."

Sophia shrugged, seeming unconcerned. "So you pay tomorrow, it'll all work out. You paid for the hotel tonight," she pointed out.

"Hotels and food are technically a work expense, because this is partially a work trip. So all the accommodation is on me. Or, on work more accurately." There, that should get us around the problem of her using a traceable credit card like a breadcrumb trail left at hotels on our way.

She laughed. "Ah, the truth comes out. Your 'I'll buy dinner tonight' is actually 'I'll pass it off as a work expense.'"

I grinned. "Caught me. When did you order for?"

"Be here in…" She checked her phone. "About fifteen minutes."

Enough time to get cleaned up after the drive. "Perfect. I'm going to take a shower before dinner." I dangled an invitation, something to remind her that I wanted her here. "Do you want to join me?"

"I do." The faintest flush spread over her cheeks. "But one of us should probably wait in case the food is early."

"Good point."

She sipped from her glass, swirled it to settle the ice, then casually added, "And if I'm going to fuck you in the shower, I don't want to worry about being interrupted."

"I—" I blinked hard, trying to figure out if I'd heard what I thought I'd heard. Studying her face, I decided she really had just said that. Her expression was casual salaciousness, as if dropping something like that on me was no big deal. It was a *huge* deal. She was the most incredible mix of gentle and sultry, turning from one to the other on a dime. Seemed she had a certain kind of balance too… Knowing that she wanted me was not only a boost for my battered romantic ego but made me feel better about dragging her along with me. I cleared my throat. "Well, thinking about that is going to make my shower a little more interesting." I pulled my shirt off and folded it into one of the garbage bags we'd bought for dirty laundry.

"I hope it's going to be thinking only." The words were confident but her expression was cautious, almost hopeful, as if she didn't believe I would wait for her.

"Given how you blew my mind in bed earlier, anything but you is going to be a letdown. So, yes. Thinking only." I shucked out of my jeans.

Sophia's eyes roamed slowly down then up my body. "Good. Because I have plans for you after dinner."

I inhaled slowly to calm myself before answering, "I look forward to that." After a quick glance at the door, I said, "Just uh, make sure it's really a food delivery when they knock, okay?"

"What else would it be?"

"The bogeyman," I joked.

I left the bathroom door cracked open and my gun folded inside a towel, just in case, while I showered. I took a few extra minutes under the spray, trying to drum out some of my tension with the feeble press of the water. Dinner arrived as I was pulling on underwear, and I positioned myself where I could see the door to our room through the cracked bathroom door. Innocuous early-twenties delivery driver, extremely grateful for his large tip. Not a thug with a broken nose and frustration at his inability to grab me.

When I came out of the bathroom I found Sophia had set everything out onto the small table, including a beer each. I stashed my dirty-clothes bag and gun in my duffel, nothing out of the ordinary here. If she wondered why I was screwing around with my bags so much, she didn't question it. I could only hope she kept up with the not-questioning because it would make this a whole lot easier.

Sophia started pulling lids off containers, releasing heavenly wafts of food aromas. "You're not afraid of a little heat, are you?"

"Not at all. Heat, spice, lay it all on me." I settled in one of the chairs and twisted the tops off both beers. "Every time I was stationed overseas, the running joke was if I was missing they could always find me at the market, enjoying the food stalls or buying spices. I always managed to persuade some woman to teach me how to cook their local dishes." I was about to keep blathering, to tell her about the hours I'd spent huddled over small braziers or portable gas stoves learning to make *samaroq*, *golpi*, and *ashak*, among other wonderful things, at Elaheh's instruction. But it would give away too much, more than what I could tell Sophia.

But I wanted to tell her, wanted to share even though I knew I never could. Sharing was what normal people who were dating did. But my life wasn't normal. So I made myself smile and picked up my spoon to try the pozole. Sophia watched me as I ate the first mouthful, her expression expectant as if my enjoyment, or not, of the food was her personal mission. Her tongue flashed out to wet her lower lip. "Good?"

"Yeah," I managed once my taste buds had stopped rejoicing. "If the pozole I had the last time I was in Mexico was a ten, this is an easy seven." When I offered my spoon, Sophia hesitated for a moment, so I spooned some pozole and held it up. "We've already shared cooties."

Smiling, Sophia held her hair back over her shoulder and carefully leaned in to take the mouthful. "Mmm." She settled back in her seat and turned her beer around before raising it to her lips for a long drink. "If that's your version of a seven, then Mom's pozole is a fifteen. She took learning to cook Dad's cultural cuisine very seriously, and *abuela* was all too happy to teach her. I think she'd make a pretty awesome veggie pozole if she tried."

"Okay, well, if that's true, please introduce us posthaste." In the next heartbeat I realized exactly what I'd just implied and tried to reel it back. "I mean, you know what I mean."

"I do. And I would like you to meet them, eventually, but not after three dates and one day of road tripping." She grinned. "I think that might be just a little too soon to do the 'bring you home to the parents' gig." Sophia used the side of her fork to cut up enmolada.

"How did your parents meet?"

Sophia chewed and swallowed, covering her mouth as she laughed. "This is going to sound like the start of a romance movie, but he saved her from drowning. She was vacationing down at Kings Beach on Lake Tahoe and *grossly* overestimated her basically nonexistent swimming abilities. My dad dragged her out of the water, and stayed with her until she was okay. According to my mom, he was so handsome and gentlemanly and the perfect mix of confident and shy that she fell in love with him right there." She smiled fondly. "I have to admit, he's a pretty handsome guy. When he was younger, he looked like a Latino Clark Gable, mustache and all."

"That's really sweet. So it was love...to the rescue?"

She laughed as I apologized for my awful pun. "Pretty much."

"You said he served during the Vietnam War? Did he meet your mom before or after the war?"

"Just before the draft lottery, and she waited for him to come home. I think he was one of the guys who were excited to get picked. Said he thought it might change their minds."

I frowned. "What do you mean? Change whose mind about what?"

She slowly sipped her beer. "Mexican American guy in the military—he thought it'd give him some status I suppose, and that if he did well it'd change people's opinions. He came here with his parents from Morelos when he was just a baby, but he's often said he sometimes feels like people look at him like he's illegal. My maternal grandparents also weren't thrilled at Mom's choice of fiancé, and he was desperate to show them he was worthy of her."

"Did he"—I air-quoted—"do well?"

"As well as a man of his ethnicity could." The unspoken implication was clear, despite her neutral tone and expression.

"And did they stop being assholes?"

Sophia smiled. "The other Army guys, mostly no. My maternal grandparents, yes. I think they found it hard to hold on to their horror about Mom marrying someone 'different' when they realized what a good man he is. Grandchildren helped too. By the time I came along I think they'd forgotten about everything except having him enfolded in the family. I was really cute."

"You still are." I ate the spoonful of pozole I'd scooped up. "Among other things."

The dinner I'd wanted to rush through so I could work somehow turned leisurely. Our conversation meandered pleasantly, mostly about Sophia's family which sounded large and loud and loving. Family always felt like an odd concept to me. My parents were…fine. Adequate would probably be the best way to describe them. I'd never felt I lacked for material things, nor did I feel I got everything I ever asked for. They were the picture of moderation, even with affection, and when they died, the only thing I'd really felt was empty.

By the time we were done eating and talking I felt more relaxed and comfortable than I'd have thought possible, especially considering the circumstances. "You're in charge of finding dinner every night. Seriously. I'll just hand over the cash and you can pick the place." I finished my beer, trying to cool the pleasant lingering heat in my mouth. "That was fantastic."

"Glad you enjoyed it." We tidied up the remnants of the meal, and Sophia held up the bottle of whiskey.

I shook my head. "I'm good, thanks. I'm going to make a cup of tea."

She poured herself another half inch then capped the bottle and pushed it away. The kettle boiled surprisingly quickly and, grimacing at what I knew was sure to be a horrible cup of tea, I dropped a tea bag into the mug of hot water and carried it back to where Sophia sat on the couch, one leg up and the other tucked under her butt. She watched me approach and just before I sat down, asked, "Did you find a roach in that mug?"

"Hmm? Oh, no. It's just..." I held the mug aloft to prevent spillage, though judging by the smell it wouldn't be the worst thing in the world to lose some of this tea. "I'm a tea snob," I sighed. "I never used to be, but working overseas where tea is incredible turned me into a tea lover and gave me really specific tastes. And it's a ritual, making tea and then drinking it. It's always calming, helps me clear my mind. And I left my tea stash and infuser and whatnot at home, and tea bags just don't feel right. They definitely don't taste right." Wrinkling my nose, I stared into the mug. "I'm just being precious."

"I don't think it's precious. When you like things a certain way then that's how you like them. Precision, not preciousness."

"You really are Ms. Glass Half Full, aren't you?"

"Me? No, I think I'm a good mix of full and empty." She smiled. "Maybe it's you who's bringing out the optimism in me."

"I think it's just you." The tea was nowhere near ready, but best to check early so I knew if it was a lost cause or not. I cautiously tasted the brew. Oh god, it was as awful as it smelled. Musty and weak and who did quality testing on this?

Sophia laughed. "Judging by your face that really isn't how you like it."

"Not at all. Not even close." I leaned down to set the mug on the floor by my bare feet. Even having it in my line of sight was too much. "I think it's more a psychological thing than anything. My job is so intense and focused and it's easy to put myself into a bubble where I'm just doing the same thing every day, where I get into a headspace where I feel like it's my routine that makes everything work so well. Especially when I was overseas where *everything* feels different. Something familiar can make or break how you cope."

There was a long pause as she sipped her whiskey. "When you go overseas for work, is it…in, um, hostile areas?" she asked quietly.

"Sometimes. I go where I'm needed to gather information. *Went* where I was needed," I amended. "I changed job focus after the"—I gestured to my stomach, making sweeping motions—"event. It's been a while since I left my cozy cubicle."

She tried not to, but she looked to my belly. "I have a hard time picturing you doing things in war zones like, fighting and all that."

"Really? Why's that?" I flexed. "I mean, look at these biceps. Made for being in *war zones*," I said teasingly. After dropping my arm I reminded her, "And I was never fighting. I'm not in the military, remember?"

"No it's not that." Her fingertip traced the line of my bicep down to my elbow, and I suppressed a shudder. "You're right," she murmured, "these are some capable arms. It's just that you're quiet and funny, sensitive, sweet, and when I imagine what it's like over there I can't put the pieces together. You don't seem like you should be there."

An unexpected sensation of embarrassment flooded through me and I fought to stop myself blushing. "Well yeah, I am all of those things." I winked. "And honestly, I'm not sure anyone should be there."

She seemed to turn the idea over in her head. "Will you have to go overseas for work again?"

"Maybe. Maybe not." Definitely not. After the event I was no longer medically cleared for fieldwork, and I had no desire to push psych so I could return to my old job.

"You know, every time you're evasive about your job, you make me insanely curious about it." Thankfully her tone was light and teasing, not annoyed.

I held up my hands, palms toward her. "I'm sorry. I'm not trying to be coy about it." I bent down for the mug, not to drink tea, oh no no, but because I needed something to fidget with. "I really don't have anyone outside of work, Sophia. Friends or whatever, definitely not family. People I can talk to, I mean. Aside from colleagues, the main people I converse with are grocery store cashiers and sometimes waitstaff if I make myself go out for dinner so I'm not staring at my apartment walls every night. I'm just trying to get used to this."

Sophia reached out to rest her hand on my knee, her fingertips lightly stroking through my jeans. "What's *this* exactly?" The way she asked the question made me sure she knew, but wanted the verbal confirmation.

"Conversation that's personal. Sharing information when my job makes me cautious about such things. Someone wanting to know about *me* instead of just details that are related to work. That sort of thing."

She held my gaze. "I want to know everything, Lexie. Everything you want to, or can, tell me that is."

I wanted to tell her everything, though of course that would never happen. I could share the basics of my government job, yet at the same time withhold all information about my role in Halcyon. My situation wasn't unusual—intelligence agency employees routinely kept secrets from their family, and agents within Halcyon had families or significant others and managed to keep them unaware of their secondary role. But I really didn't like lying. A professional liar who didn't like lying. Ironic.

Uncomfortable and embarrassed by my lack of basic social skills, and unable to stand the smell of the tea any longer, I got up and poured the liquid down the sink. With my back still to Sophia to hide what felt like blushing cheeks, I said, "I'd like to try to get to Tampa by dinner tomorrow. How are you with early mornings?"

"Depends. Define early."

I turned around. "Leave by six a.m.?"

She blinked. "Then I suppose I need to go to sleep right now. After I fulfill those plans I said I had for you…"

After she had indeed fulfilled her plans, and then some, Sophia had promptly fallen asleep. She'd been out like a light for forty minutes when I decided she wouldn't wake up if I left, and slipped out of bed. I took my handgun, laptops, and a notepad and pen into the bathroom, closed the door and left the light off so as to not disturb Sophia, who thankfully remained fast asleep, sprawled in the middle of the bed. She'd started neatly on one side then slowly spread across the mattress as if she were liquid. Coupled with my own tendency to sleep sprawl, we were going to end up sleeping on top of each other.

I sat on the closed toilet lid with my feet up on the edge of the bath and the laptop I'd brought from home on my knees. I'd use this machine for dirty tasks which required accessing the Internet. It would be a few days until I had access to Hadim's files, assuming I *could* get access to them again, and until then I wanted to get more information.

After weighing up the good and bad, I decided it was worth the risk to go digging. I hid myself in London via my VPN, logged in to one of my throwaway email accounts for Ellen Jackson, deleted spam—how the hell they got this address I'd never know—and emailed Hadim.

Need more information.

Not in office.

Please provide a number for me to call you.

-Ellen

It would be late morning where he was and I knew he spent his mornings doing what he deemed administrative tasks, so he should be near a device to receive the email. It took less than two minutes to receive a response, and the moment I saw *Mail Delivery Failure* in the subject line, my stomach dropped.

A message that you sent could not be delivered to one or more of its recipients. This is a permanent error.

As calmly as I could I cleared my browsing history and passwords, closed down the browser and disconnected from the Internet. Fuck.

I knew Hadim well enough to know he would never willingly cancel an email account, especially not one he had as a line of communication with those for whom he did work. So there was only one explanation. Well, three, technically. One: I'd typed in the email address wrongly, which I knew I hadn't. Two: There was an issue with the email provider which, given it was a major one, was less than likely. Three: Someone had closed down the account— someone probably connected to Broken Nose.

My ever-trusty gut said option three was the best bet.

But why?

If they knew Hadim was my primary contact for this intel, wouldn't they want to monitor any subsequent communication between us? Another possibility that hadn't been immediately obvious popped into my brain. Four: Hadim deactivated the email account himself. And there was only one reason I could think of for him doing that.

He wanted to warn me.

Thanks for the warning, and don't worry, friend—I'm all over it and totally aware that someone doesn't want me to know what I know. It would have been really nice to talk to Lennon, but I didn't want to risk Sophia waking and overhearing me. Flying solo it was.

I spent an hour typing up everything I remembered about Hadim's intel, and my thoughts about it, until a jaw-splitting yawn reminded me how late it was. How early was more accurate. There was nothing more I could do. I needed some sleep or I was going to be utterly useless. Everything in balance, blah blah. Tomorrow we'd be in Tampa and I could start getting everything I needed to move forward. Hopefully. Though the room was dark there was enough muted light from streetlights persisting through thin hotel curtains to see without turning on any lights. I made sure everything was secure before stashing my equipment away again. Despite climbing back into the bed with all the stealth of a spy, Sophia woke when I raised the covers to slip in.

"Whatareyoudoing?" she slurred.

"Couldn't sleep." After staring at the screen in the darkness my eyes felt like they were made of crushed glass. I closed them, desperate to ease the grittiness.

"Mmm." Sophia rolled over, sleepily fumbling for me. "Time's it?"

"Early."

"You're wearing glasses," she mumbled as her fingers brushed my face.

"I was reading." That was a first, going to bed wearing glasses. One point to stress and fatigue. I set my frames on the bedside table. "Go back to sleep, sweetheart." I pulled her closer and Sophia snuggled into me, pressing her warm feet against my cold calves.

CHAPTER EIGHT

Sociopaths can be useful friends, once you stop worrying about them murdering you

Sophia crawled to the end of the bed and stared down at me. "What on earth is this?"

I glanced over without stopping my bicycle crunches. "This is me enjoying the morning."

"Enjoying?" Her sleep-rough voice cracked on the second syllable. "God, I count myself lucky if I manage to work out a few days a week. It's Sunday. Do you do this *every* morning?"

"Mhmm, get up, do yoga or meditate, then go straight to the gym at work. Blood moving equals good thinking." I smiled at her from my position on the floor before rolling over for another set of pushups. "Can I take it from your horrified expression that you don't enjoy mornings?"

"Oh no, I love mornings. But I prefer an 'ease into it with slow coffee and breakfast and raging at the news' kind of morning, instead of a 'leap out of bed a fully functioning human' kind. Why do you think I suggested late breakfast for our date yesterday?" She settled so her arms hung over the end of the bed, her chin resting on the bedspread. "When do you eat breakfast if you yoga as soon as you wake up, then go straight to work and into workouts?"

I lowered my upper body into a plank. "I shower at work then eat breakfast at my desk while I read my emails."

"Oh nooo," she whispered. "That's not relaxing at all. I work from home and it's one of my rules that my workspace is for working only. When and where do you relax? Tell me you relax," Sophia pleaded.

"Of course I relax," I said. And I did, when things weren't so insane. "At home after work with TV or a book. I like cooking, a long run on the weekend, yoga and meditation. Every now and then, I go out for dinner or to a movie." By myself... I lowered myself to the carpet, rolled onto my back and started stretching, relishing the sensation of muscles unfurling. I made eye contact with Sophia. "Sex is also good for clearing mind and body, but that hasn't been part of my routine for quite some time."

Her eyebrows shot upward. "Really? I would never have guessed it." She rested her elbow on the bed to prop her chin in a palm. "Maybe we can add it back into your routine. I'd hate to think of you not being at your best because you're missing out on *that*."

"Maybe we can," I agreed. I'd had more sex in the last twenty-four hours than in the twenty-four months prior, and I still wanted more.

"But not until I've had coffee," she declared. Sophia pushed herself up and side-rolled off the bed. She crouched down to kiss me then continued to the bathroom.

I watched her walk away, and wondered yet again if it was wrong of me to drag her into this. Turning to the side, I crossed one leg over the other to stretch my lower back and glutes, and ran through all my options. Again. It was "wrong" because she didn't know the deeper implications behind this trip. It was "wrong" because I wasn't being entirely truthful. But Sophia's company would help me achieve an outcome that was essential for national security and more, which meant it was right and I needed to make peace with my decision. It was so much easier to justify your actions when you ignored all the gray lingering around a black-or-white choice.

We left once Sophia had raged at the news from overnight, downed the coffee I made for her like it was life-giving, and we'd both taken separate showers. As I made my way to the car after checking us out of the hotel, I found her in the driver's seat. Instead of settling in the passenger seat, I hovered by the driver's side door.

Sophia lowered the window, smiling up at me like butter wouldn't melt in her beautiful mouth.

"What's this?" I asked. "I thought I'd drive the first segment today."

"Judging by the time you crawled back to bed, you hardly slept. Then you got up before the sun to play Workout Barbie when you should have been resting. So, I'm driving."

"But—"

Still smiling, she held up a hand. "No no, this is where you don't argue. Plus, I don't get car sick when I drive, so you can have a break from my talking." She eyed me. "And maybe sleep a little."

"Sleep." The idea, when applied to me in a car, seemed foreign. Add to that the fact I really needed to be alert and on the lookout for anyone who'd managed to find us, a little nap while she drove wasn't in the cards. "Hmm. I doubt it." I leaned into the window to kiss her. "And I like your talking."

She smiled. "I like that you like it."

Sophia taught me more car-trip games, like Apocalypse Meal, as in what would you eat if it was your last meal before a nuclear apocalypse (me, my mom's broccoli cheddar soup with her homemade French bread; Sophia, the most expensive steak and lobster she could get her hands on), 20 Questions, and Fortunately/ Unfortunately which had me almost peeing with laughter.

And the whole time we played and talked, I was profiling her— which felt awful, because it was awful—filing away these snippets of information in case I needed them later. But…wasn't getting to know someone romantically kind of the same thing, where you tried to learn as much as you could about them so you could establish a connection? Black and white. And a little bit of gray.

After an hour and a half, we stopped at a small café in Fayetteville for breakfast, sliding into one of the window booths overlooking the parking lot where I could keep an eye on cars entering and exiting. Nothing out of the ordinary that I could see, and my tension eased by one point. If they kept this up, my anxiety levels might get below a ten sometime this week. Being with Sophia made it easy to forget that I was fleeing from people who wanted to…well, not kill me, but who definitely wanted me under lock and guard, instead of out in the free world figuring this out. I added "worrying about letting my guard down with her" to my list of stresses.

Sophia good-naturedly declined my invitation to drive until our next break, and as she reversed out of the parking space—I really needed to teach her that reversing in so you could leave quickly was a better idea—I pushed the passenger seat right back so I could stretch my legs. The two espressos I'd had with breakfast weren't working their magic as I'd hoped and I fought fatigue like a kid fighting naptime.

I couldn't fall asleep in the car, even though I couldn't see anyone tailing us. I couldn't leave her to drive on her own when this wasn't even her fight. And I…couldn't…I…couldn't… My eyes drooped, head lolled, and when I realized what I was doing, I pushed myself upright. Scrubbing both hands over my face, I shook my head then angled the air vents so they were blasting wake-up air in my face. "I need to stay awake," I said, even though Sophia hadn't asked about my sudden movement.

"Why?"

So I can make sure nobody is following us, of course. "To keep you company, help you stay awake. Play more road-trip games, sing more songs and…stuff. You didn't sleep much more than I did."

Sophia eased to a stop at a red light and turned to me, eyebrows raised above her sunglasses. "I woke up three times and you weren't in bed. Which leads me to believe you were awake reading between one and four. I slept plenty more than you did."

"I'm equipped to run on little to no sleep."

She snorted. "Sure thing, cyborg." Her voice softened. "I know I probably shouldn't point this out after only a few dates, but you look a little worn down. You may as well get some rest while I'm driving." She reached over and stroked my thigh, murmuring, "I've got you."

"Blunt honesty this early in the dating game? I'll take it." I took her hand, curling my fingers around hers. "I won't sleep, but thanks."

When I startled awake, I checked the mirrors, then the time. Shit. Almost four hours gone. "Where are we?" I mumbled, pushing myself up in the seat. Must be alert. Must check…things? My body was heavy, felt almost intoxicated with that awful just-woken dragged-out-of-sleep sensation, and for a moment I panicked that I'd been drugged. As the feeling flooded back to my brain and body,

I realized I'd just completely zonked out. I'd need to work on that, because passing out asleep during the day was a no-go.

Sophia tugged out the earbud from the ear closest to me and glanced at the GPS screen. "About five hours outside of Tampa."

We'd made good time—she'd make a great getaway driver. Technically, she was a getaway driver. "I'm so sorry." I won't sleep, my ass. "You've done so much driving. How long did my promise to stay awake last?"

Laughing, she extracted the other earbud and dropped them both into the center console. "About fifteen minutes and then you were out like a light. Didn't even wake when I stopped for more coffee and snacks."

"Shit, really?" Now that was dumb and dangerous.

"Mhmm." She pointed a thumb to the back seat. There's a few fresh muffins back there, and also an iced coffee in the cooler bag if you want."

"I think I'm going to need ten iced coffees." I stretched my arms and legs forward to loosen up, then reached over for the drink. "Do you need me to take over?"

She looked at me, her grin slightly maniacal as she begged, "Please."

Sophia exited the interstate and stopped at a gas station so we could refuel, stretch, and pee. I stifled a yawn as I pulled back out onto 95. "Anything exciting happen while I was dead to the world?"

"Passed a pretty epic four-car pileup, said nope to a hitchhiker, and listened to three full episodes of my podcast."

"Sorry I missed all that." I dug my fingers into one of the hard knots that'd taken up residence in my shoulders. God I needed a massage. When all this was over I was booking myself in for a weeklong relaxation package. In the Maldives. And you'd better believe I was going to expense it to Halcyon.

Sophia reached over and slipped her hand underneath mine. "Oh god, your shoulders are like steel."

I tried to make a joke, but the sensation of her massaging my tense muscles had turned me to incoherent goo. Eventually I managed, "You should feel the rest of me."

"I already have, but I intend to do so again." She pushed her fingertips into my muscle, murmuring an apology when I yelped. After a softer stroke, Sophia withdrew her hand. "But at the hotel tonight. For now, less massage and more driving concentration before you veer off the road because I'm touching you."

I mumbled my reluctant agreement and returned my focus to the next five hours of driving.

The rest of our journey went much as it had before I'd so rudely fallen asleep. My anxiety and anticipation built steadily as we approached Tampa, and by the time we rolled into town just after five p.m., I was about ready to climb out of my skin. Sophia found us a hotel and after a quick bug-bug check, we freshened up, then left again so I could meet my contact. What a great and relaxing vacation I'd dragged Sophia on. Once I'd finished my Halcyon task, I was going to find us a five-star hotel in the Bahamas and make it up to her for treating her like a safety blanket. Assuming I was still around, of course. I had to keep assuming. Assuming kept me going.

As we drove out into the burbs, Sophia didn't ask what was so urgent that I'd made a two-day road trip, but I got the feeling I wouldn't be able to put her off for too much longer. My contact, Bink, had apparently decided the best disguise was hiding in plain sight. Looking at the two-story house shaded in the pinky-orange-sandy rendered façade common in Florida, with a tightly mown front lawn and tasteful holiday decorations adorning the exterior, you'd never know that nestled inside was enough tech and brainpower to bring down ten governments. And Bink lived and worked alone.

I'd met Bink early in my government career when we'd both been working at the same overseas posting. I was an Ops Officer and they were a contractor tasked with getting us anything we needed from the web. We'd clicked immediately. Well, as much as a regular person—me—could click with a borderline or maybe not-so-borderline sociopath—Bink. Ex-naval intelligence turned contractor, computer genius, actually all-round general genius, Bink could hack their way into pretty much anything. And had, because they'd helped design half of the systems currently in use in the most secure places in the world. Now they freelanced, mostly for law enforcement to help catch "sick fuckers" as they'd once told me, and peeked into what they pleased, whenever they pleased, to help show government agencies and branches, and private companies where their weaknesses were.

Bink was one of the few people who rated highly on my trust scale. Their odd code of ethics meant they were fiercely loyal to those who paid. I buzzed and held up a prepaid Visa card to the doorbell camera, counting in my head. Exactly forty-seven seconds after I'd buzzed—Bink had a thing for prime numbers—the door opened. Huge blue eyes behind horn-rimmed glasses dominated a blankly staring face.

I held the Visa between two fingers, hand outstretched. "Two hundred to get in the door, more later."

The stare morphed into a smirk. "Keep talking dirty to me. Come in." They opened the door, but didn't move out of the way. Bink was the exact opposite of every stereotypical hacker in the movies. No punks or cigarettes or drugs or booze here. Sober and a dedicated vegan, Bink was petite but wiry, sported a neat, short brunette bob with straight bangs, and was never without thick-framed glasses. They reminded me of the cartoon character Daria, even down to the low, deadpan drawl. "Been a while. I'd like to say I've missed you but honestly, I haven't thought about you."

"Neither." I gestured to Sophia behind me. "Friend of mine. I vouch for her." Before we'd left the car, I'd explained in a vague way that the person we were about to see was a little paranoid.

"Good." Bink raised their chin, red-rimmed eyes studying Sophia. Clearly they'd been up for a few days if the twitchy fatigue was any indicator.

Sophia's manners won, and she offered a hand. "Hi, I'm—"

"No!" Both Bink's hands went out, palms facing Sophia. "No identity here. I don't want to know who you are, what your pet's name is, or whether you prefer chocolate or vanilla ice cream."

If Sophia was fazed by Bink's abruptness, she didn't show it. "Actually, I don't like ice cream."

I turned to her. "You…what? How can you not like ice cream?"

"Hurts my teeth." She grinned, showing those beautiful teeth in a cheery smile.

I lowered my voice. "I'm starting to rethink this relationship."

Sophia's eyes widened, and if we'd had more time and we were alone, I might have backpedaled and reworded what I'd just said. But I didn't. Because either way, in the scheme of things, the exact nuance of language I used to describe us didn't matter. Did it?

Bink cleared their throat. "Are we going to do whatever it is you're here to do, or do I have to keep watching this mating ritual?"

"Right, sorry." I turned back to Sophia and gestured to the L-shaped leather couch taking up a decent percentage of Bink's living room. "I won't be long. Will you be okay to wait here by yourself for a few minutes?"

"Sure, no problem," she said amicably.

Bink held eye contact with Sophia then pointed to the bookshelves that filled each wall of the living room. "Read a book."

I wasn't sure if it was a command, or an invitation for Sophia to look at their collection. Bink didn't have a television and as far as I knew, had never had one. They made a *come with me* gesture and walked off down the hallway, leaving me to follow.

I flashed Sophia what I hoped was an encouraging and apologetic smile, and jogged after Bink. They led me upstairs, opened a door at the top of the staircase, then gestured for me to step into the huge room that was basically the entire top floor of the house. Bink closed and locked the door behind us. They'd done that the first night I'd met them in an out-of-the-way overseas installation too, only back then they'd pulled out a flick knife, held it up and told me, "If any of those Army pricks come after you, tell me and I'll cut their balls off." And I'd nodded and squeaked out "Okay" while trying not to look like I was going to pee myself because I'd thought this stranger was about to gut me. I still had no idea what had made them form an instant, protective attachment to me, but I didn't question it. Bink was someone you wanted on your side. Hack the securest databases in the world or castrate a creep, it was all the same to them.

Bink folded their arms over their chest. "What do you need?"

Once I was sure I wasn't going to lean on something important, I rested my hip against the edge of a desk. "I find myself cast adrift and I need access to some files of mine at work, and also military databases." Crossing my arms over my waist, I hugged myself. Bink's tech rooms were always freezing but they never seemed bothered.

"Slipping through the government's back doors. It'll cost you."

"It always does." Shrugging, I added, "It'll be a cakewalk for you. Not like you haven't already done it. And probably twice already this month."

"It's more like a muffinwalk," they drawled. If I hadn't known better, I'd have actually thought they smiled. "Where am I going?"

I gave them the specifics of where to find Hadim's files. "It's possible someone has moved them to a more secure location so if you have to go digging, then please do. I need these files. Could not be higher priority."

Both Bink's eyebrows raised fractionally. "Am I leaving them there once I have copies?"

"Yes." The agency couldn't know I'd been in there. Or rather, that my proxy had been. "I'll also need the US Army personnel database, active members only for now, with searchability by name, age, rank etcetera." I was confident enough in my uniform identification to narrow it to that branch of our military. "Male only. It's possible I'll need other military branches and even civilian later. Possibly international. Possibly retired service members."

My hunch was that the American was a current member of one of our armed forces, not just some backyard cowboy pretending to be a colonel in his little militia. And given Derek had agreed, I'd decided that was where I'd start. The authorization for something like what had happened with the Red Wolves wouldn't have passed through unsecured, amateur channels. Even if it had, I could think of no organized militia within the States that had the kind of clout and cash needed to get something like this off the ground.

"Shouldn't be too hard. Leave your machine with me." Bink held out a hand, fingers wiggling, for my backpack.

I gripped the strap tighter. "I can't."

Their eyebrows shot up as if electrified. "Tease. I can't believe you'd dangle a treasure chest in front of me and then snatch it away."

"Sorry."

"Liar. Do you want access on your machine or will you come back and work here?"

"Mine. I need to be mobile. And it's sensitive," I reiterated. I trusted Bink implicitly. Before they'd been honorably discharged, they had held the highest security clearance. The fact they now used their skills to hack into the databases they'd had an oath to protect was a weird sort of irony. But they understood the importance of secrets. And having been paid for a job, Bink never stepped over a line they hadn't been asked to. I knew they'd done work for Halcyon before—hence why Lennon suggested I go to Bink—but I didn't know if they were part of the Division. Of course I couldn't ask, and it's not like we had a secret Halcyon handshake.

"It'll cost you again. That's a massive pain in my ass, not to mention a huge drain on my servers to download all that."

"I know." Thankfully Halcyon had left me plenty of funds.

"You're lucky I like you."

"You like how much I'm going to pay you to do the things you love doing."

"True," Bink mused. "What else?"

"Video-enhancing software. The agency has their own purpose-built program that you can probably get me. Hopefully I remember how to use it." I'd sat in on a digital enhancement training course last year, just out of interest's sake, so should be able to fumble my way through the basics.

"Like riding a bike, isn't it? Whatever it is, I'll get you a user manual," they said dryly.

"Right." I would have loved to have access to the Department of Defense's full database so I could run some vocal matching but I had to admit to myself that it was outside my skillset. As it was, manipulating video and photo with a beefed-up version of Photoshop was going to stretch me to the limit. But what I was trying to achieve wasn't for evidentiary purposes—that was up to Halcyon—and as long as I could make the illegible legible then I'd be golden.

Bink used a thumbnail to scratch the end of their nose. "What's my timeframe?"

"Two days ago. Oh! And I need a mouse so I can work more easily with the video software."

"Got it. Earliest I can have what you want is tomorrow p.m. and that's dedicating my life to it and only it. It'll likely take longer, depending on whether things are where you say they should be. Good thing I just refilled my Adderall."

"Wasn't it you who once told me sleep was for the weak?"

"I was probably trying to impress you."

"It worked." I paused, and decided to ask for one more thing, even though it made me feel like shit. "And…I also need you to peek into a civilian file, make sure everything looks legit."

"Legit how?"

"As in not fabricated. Clean. Organic." Bink would be able to find the cracks that indicated a put-together life instead of one lived organically from birth to now.

"Name?"

I paused for a second. "Sophia Flores." Saying her name made me feel like the worst human, but I couldn't shake my paranoia. And my paranoia had gotten me this far, and still alive. I gave Bink Sophia's address and DOB which I'd seen on her driver's license while I'd been snooping around her apartment.

Bink shrugged. "Easy." They'd written nothing down, but I knew I'd get exactly what I'd asked for.

"I'll wait for your call." I handed them a piece of paper with a throwaway cell phone number on it.

They stared at the digits. "This isn't your usual number." They peered up at me. "Why do I suddenly get the feeling this job is something really naughty?" Bink's smile was feral. "Can't wait."

CHAPTER NINE

I wouldn't tell your boss about this

I'd been working almost nonstop since we'd returned from visiting Bink yesterday evening, trying to find ways to connect dots I couldn't even see yet, just for something to do, just in case something twigged. Until I had the intel, I was flailing around in the dark. It was futile to hope that writing out all the details I had, and spitballing theories would send a lightning bolt of "aha!" from the sky, but I was terrible at being idle.

Sophia had been antsy since we'd come back from breakfast—staring at her laptop, wandering aimlessly around the hotel room, flopping onto the bed, turning on the TV and then changing channels like someone deathly allergic to every show she saw before jumping up again. She'd been enthusiastic when I'd woken her up by going down on her, but her good mood faded the longer we stayed in the room. Understandable. We'd taken a quick walk along the beach after dinner yesterday, ducked out for breakfast this morning, but other than those few outings, it'd been nothing but four walls. I'd promised her cays, and instead was giving her captivity.

I paused typing and glanced over to where she'd finally settled at the other end of the table with her laptop. She was hammering the keys like she hated the thing, mumbling to herself.

"Do you want to take a walk and get some lunch?" I asked, even though the last thing I felt like doing was leaving the hotel, exposing ourselves. But I was starting to run out of excuses to stall her, and convince her that inside was way better than outside. Sex only got me so far, and I wasn't an inventive enough lover to keep her in bed for days.

Sophia's expression turned instantly from meh to hopeful. "Can we? I mean, we *can* just order in if you want…but, air would be nice."

I saved my document of unconnected dots and unproductive postulation and closed the clean—a.k.a. offline work only—laptop. "Let me take a peek outside and see what the weather is doing." And see if anyone who shouldn't be there was there. "I don't see why we can't get some fresh air." Staying inside would have been preferable, but it was clear she was suffering some serious cabin fever. If this was how she felt after one day, then I was going to have to work hard to manage her feelings and expectations for the rest of this trip. I stood up and as I passed her, leaned down and kissed her temple. "I'm sorry, this is shitty for you. I just got totally absorbed in what I'm doing."

"It shouldn't be shitty," she huffed out. "I mean, sometimes I spend days locked away at my desk when I'm focused on a project. But for some stupid reason now, I'm so bored that being inside is just making me apathetic and cranky."

I cracked the curtain and took a look out into the real world. "True, but at home you can come and go as you please, do whatever you want to break up your time." There was nothing outside that jumped out at me—no strange cars or people milling about—and hope surged at the thought they'd given up once we'd left Sophia's. Or maybe they were still trying to locate me, or had decided to go with a new, sneakier tactic. My gut said it was probably one of the latter two options.

"Yeahhh," she mumbled in a tone that made me think of a kid scuffing their foot. "I think not having any real work to do isn't helping. I can't proceed with my current jobs until I get client approval or feedback, so I'm just twiddling my thumbs."

I quickly weighed Pros—air, sunlight, food, Sophia happy and no longer making me dizzy with her pacing; versus Cons—leaving the safety of four walls, possibly being out when Bink contacted me to tell me they'd finished my job and having to waste time coming back for the car. Pros, four. Cons, two. I pulled the curtain back into place. "Let's go out for an hour or so, get some food and some air."

Sophia brightened immediately. "Really? Are you sure it's fine? I know you're waiting on a call from your…friend."

Fine was at the very edges of what it was, but we'd manage. We'd managed to this point. We'd manage past this point. "Mhmm, of course," I said brightly. "Let's do it." As I secured both laptops in my backpack, I hoped I hadn't just made a stupid mistake. Another stupid mistake.

Sophia's declaration of a desperate burger urge had us wandering down the street in search of a suitable burger joint. I pointed to the familiar logo looming above the buildings about three hundred meters away. "McDonald's?"

She turned to me, her mouth open in horror. "You're kidding, right? That's not…I can't even…shame on you." Sophia playfully slapped my arm. "Just when you think you're getting to know a person."

I slid an arm around her waist and turned her slightly away from the street. Nuzzling her neck, I took a quick look around and when I was certain I could afford a few moments of relaxation, kissed her. She had one hand jammed between us, and she played with the fabric of my hoodie as she opened her mouth, her tongue lazily stroking mine. Reluctantly, I pulled away from the kiss, but remained close. "I think you know me pretty well by now. I'm not exactly a deep well of hidden personality." Hidden other stuff, sure, but not hidden personality traits. "And as for the things you don't know, we've got time."

"Time," she mused. "I like the sound of that." Sophia dropped down off her tiptoes and indicated a restaurant across the street. Beast Burger. "Check that place out to make sure they've got a suitable veggie option?"

"Sounds good." I had a sudden desire to get burgers and a mountain of fries and take them to the beach. Sit and eat and talk and laugh like a regular couple not worrying about anything, just be together. I forced the intrusive thought out. It wasn't helpful to be thinking of wishes and dreams right now.

I elbowed the crossing signal button and winced at the movement. My shoulders still felt like someone had clamped a monster truck claw around them. Yay, stress. I moved the backpack strap to the side and started trying to work out a knot. Sophia pushed my hand aside and squeezed my shoulder. "Remind me to give you another massage when we get back to the hotel."

"That's one thing I will never forget to remind you about. Naked?" The massage she'd promised while we'd been driving yesterday had turned into so much more, and the thought of another long session of lovemaking made my stomach dance with excitement.

"Is there any other kind?"

Laughing, I said, "I meant, will you be naked too?"

"Depends on how nicely you ask me," she said, a smile twitching her lips.

"Oh I'll ask very nicely."

"Good." The signal turned green and we strolled across the street. Sophia hopped up onto the sidewalk like a kid jumping puddles. "What's going to happen when we get home?" she asked.

The question had come completely out of the blue and it took me a moment to process. "What do you mean?"

"Well, we haven't really had a conventional start to dating. I was thinking last night how much I'm enjoying this road trip, just *being* with you. And then I thought about what it'd be like to keep being with you when we got home. Without the road trip."

Pulling her to a stop outside Beast Burger, I took both her hands. "I'd like to keep seeing you, I know that for sure. I think I've realized I like this dating gig. It's just…" There was no way I could tell her what might happen when we went home. "Sometimes I'm not around. Sometimes I get caught up working late. My job might send me away for a little while when I get back. Or they might not. I really don't know. But I'll try to always tell you what I can, if I'm going to be away, even if I can't tell you where I'll be." A roundabout way to tell her that I might suddenly disappear, but not because I wanted to.

"That works for me. I get that you can't share a lot about your work but being frozen out of the things you *can* share, the things that aren't part of your job, isn't going to work for me." There was no nastiness in the statement, simply fact. "I really like you, Lexie, and I'm willing to meet in the middle, or even more over on your side for some things, as long as you're willing to meet a little more on my side for other things. I've learned that some stuff I just can't compromise on."

I doubted she really knew what sort of compromise being in my life would mean. "I get that. Secrecy has been part of my life for so long that sometimes I forget not everything should be kept secret." Shrugging, I smiled. "You'll just have to tell me what you need, and I'll do my best."

Her face softened, and she couldn't have looked more pleased if she tried. "I'll do that. Now come on." Sophia dragged me toward the door. "Let's check out the menu. Standing out here with the smell from inside is making me even hungrier."

The third time I saw him I knew it wasn't a coincidence. He'd been sitting at a bus stop not far from the hotel, then inside Beast Burger eating fries at a table by the window, and now he was thirty feet away, staring inside a store window like he really wanted that skirt and blouse. My first thought was a bunch of expletives. My second thought was to wonder how he'd found me when every trace of tracking they could use was gone from my life. Except… maybe one.

After the breakfast intrusion on Saturday, I'd been sure they'd figure out who Sophia was, and now I had no doubt they were tracking her phone or email. My annoyance stretched for the stratosphere. They had no right. Well, okay, they had every right but it was still wrong. I gave myself a mental wrist slap. I'd dragged her into this mess and it was my fault they were now tracking her and, by extension, me, intruding upon her privacy.

Sophia squeezed my hand. "Is something wrong?"

"Nope. Just want to get back to the hotel and go into a food coma. That burger was intense." I smiled down at her. "Then hopefully I'll get what I need from my person and we can start doing some of those fun road trip things I promised you, before we head home. Like get our asses into some bikinis."

Her forehead wrinkled. "You okay? You seem kind of wired about something."

I weighed up lies and truths and decided on a soft truth, which would make it easier to get her away if she understood why I was pushing it. "That guy looking in the window over there, I've seen him a few times today." I shook my head, feigning exasperation with myself. "I'm just being paranoid after that idiot at breakfast on Saturday. It's probably nothing."

She moved as if she was going to look at him, but I held her more firmly, kissing her neck as I murmured, "First rule of spy camp? Don't let someone following you know that you know you're being followed."

"I thought you weren't a spy."

I laughed. "No, I'm not. But I *have* been to spy camp." I deliberately kept myself between the street and her, wrapping a protective arm around her waist. Turning her away from the reflective shop mirrors, I quietly said, "It's fine, I promise."

"It doesn't feel fine."

I paused for a few moments before agreeing, "No, it doesn't. It feels weird."

"Lexie…" Sophia's tongue swept along her lower lip. "Is there something you're not telling me?"

I almost laughed at the innocence of the question. If only she knew. Smiling in an attempt to ease her tension, I said, "Yes, but it's better you don't know for now."

"Are we in danger? Is it drugs? I'm okay with lots of things, but not drugs."

"Absolutely not," I said instantly. "No drugs, not now, not ever. Nothing illegal. Upstanding government employee, remember? And no, I don't think we're in danger." I squeezed her hip and gently persuaded her to walk with me. "So, what's this website you're working on? The one you're waiting for the client to approve something so you can proceed?"

"Um, life coaching."

"Sounds interesting. Are you doing the whole thing from scratch like all the graphics and everything?"

"I am, yep." Her eyes darted to the side then forward again.

"Nice. I can't imagine having those sorts of skills or the creativity. Did you like your burger?"

"I did." After a beat she seemed to twig to the game. "How was yours?"

I grinned widely. "Cheesy."

She smiled back at me, but hers was tight and forced. "That's a good trait for a cheeseburger."

"My thoughts exactly. And it was pretty good for a fake meat burger. Sometimes that stuff is so dry." We paused at a set of lights and after punching the crossing signal, I shuffled to her left, the side he was on. In my periphery I could see him keeping up his fake window shopping, still about thirty feet away from us. He liked shoes too apparently. "We're going to cross the street here, and duck into that boutique over there. When we get inside, you're going to take your hair out of that adorable high ponytail and leave it down, and I'm going to buy you a new shirt."

"Lex—"

"It'll be a nice shirt, promise. Then you'll go out the back and keep walking toward the hotel. I'll go out the front, and I'll catch you up after I figure out what's going on." I pressed the hotel keycard into her pocket. "When I knock, check the peephole and if I don't say anything, then don't let me in."

"What if you don't come back?" she said, her voice barely a whisper.

"That's very unlikely." I kissed her quickly, rethought and went back for a longer, deeper kiss. "You owe me a naked massage. Don't think you're getting out of it that easily."

A flash of unease darkened her face before she nodded. We crossed the street and I opened the boutique door for her, quickly scanning the space. Oh, that was a nice little black dress. Some other time. I snagged a pale blue linen button-down shirt from the rack, checked the size and took it to the counter. "Just this one, please."

The saleswoman, a midforties brunette whose expression made ice look warm, looked me up and down. I felt like Julia Roberts in *Pretty Woman* as her pursed-lips gaze lingered on me. Fine. I sighed, took a few steps to my right and nabbed the great and stupidly priced black dress from the rack. "And I'll take the dress too." God I hoped it looked good on me.

She rang up the purchases, and seemed surprised when I handed over a not-in-my-real-name credit card to pay and it wasn't declined. I gave her my best fake with underlying *fuck you* smile. "Where's the change room?"

A dismissive forefinger raise. "Through there."

I led Sophia past the change rooms to the storage room which was certain to have a delivery entrance out back. And it sure did. "Here you go, new threads." I pulled the tag off the shirt and passed the garment to Sophia. She slipped into it without a word then loosened her hair from its ponytail to fall free and wild around her shoulders. God she was gorgeous and god this was the worst time to be thinking that. I handed her my new dress. "Can you please take this back for me as well?"

Her gaze was utterly disbelieving as she offered a drawn out, "Surrre."

"Great, thanks." Noting the expression, I tried to ease some of her distress. "Don't worry. It feels weird, but I'm sure it's nothing. I just have to be sure. Trained to be cautious is all. I'll see you soon, okay?"

"You promise?" She asked it as if she knew she had no right but had decided to just blurt it out anyway.

"Promise," I said, though I had no right to give her that word either, no matter how much I wanted to. Jokingly, I added, "That dress was *really* expensive, there's no way I'm not collecting it. Now, just walk back to the hotel normally, like you've been out to lunch and to buy a nice dress and are taking it home. It'll be fine, you'll be safe. I just want to make sure I'm not being paranoid." I knew I wasn't, but it was the easiest explanation.

"But what about you?" Sophia asked, so quietly that I wasn't sure I'd heard her. But the wide-eyed expression would have been enough to telegraph her fear even if she'd said nothing.

Instead of answering, I kissed her again, lingering longer than I should have, then after a quick check outside to satisfy myself she'd be okay leaving, I pressed her through the back door.

Ice Queen looked up from her screen as I came back, eyebrows raised as she seemed to take in the fact I was alone. She looked me over, but said nothing. Verbally at least. Her expression said it all.

I jerked a thumb behind myself. "My friend was feeling a little queasy so I shoved her out the back door so she didn't puke in your change room. Must be this frigid air-conditioning." I leaned on the counter and pointed to the security monitor that was not-so-well-hidden under the counter behind her. "Check your cameras and you'll see nothing's stolen. But what a nice assumption for you to make." I slapped my palms lightly on the counter, spun as snootily as I could in Doc Martens, and left the store.

Game on.

Across the street, my stalker was pretending not to watch the door to the boutique. I strode confidently down the street in the opposite direction Sophia had gone, peered in windows, paused to thoughtfully tap my chin and generally made a very good show of pretending to be a woman trying to find her sister a birthday gift.

We played cat and mouse for five minutes, him creeping closer while trying to appear like he was doing the exact opposite of that, and me keeping well out of his reach. I got a good look at him when he crossed the street and was nearly mown down by a passing car. Idiot. He was just a baby, obviously still wet behind the ears if his surveillance technique was anything to go by. That pulled me up. Why would they send a newbie? Unless new inept guy was a decoy and someone very capable, perhaps someone still nursing a broken nose and bruised ego, was waiting in the wings.

I doubled down on my surveillance of the surroundings. Aside from Newbie, nobody stood out, though of course that was the point of undercover surveillance. I managed to lose him for a few minutes by slipping in the front and out the back of a few stores, but after my third store in-and-out, he popped up even closer. Sophia should be safely back at the hotel now, so I could stop with my distraction. Time to get serious. Time to become the cat.

The department store across the street was my best bet for getting what I needed to elude him. I inserted myself into a crowd entering the glass front doors and beelined for the well-known chain store where I bought a gray slouch beanie, a backpack in camo pattern, and a bright red hoodie—a fashion clashing nightmare. I used a self-checkout, then threaded my way through the streams of people entering and exiting the store on their way to the food court. Newbie wasn't in sight. I pushed into a ladies' room to change and stuff my gray hoodie and old backpack into the new backpack, and was out again in a minute. It took thirty seconds to spot him.

He stood near the front door, sipping a drink in a huge cup, casually staring around like he was waiting for his girlfriend to come back. It was easy to loop around behind him. "Boo," I whispered in his ear as I pressed my handgun into the small of his back.

He tensed, free hand going to his waist. I jammed the gun harder into his kidney. "No, no, not a great idea. So many people around. Put your hands down."

He let his hand fall. Adjusting my position slightly, I turned us away from the door and eyes and reached for the gun on his waist, tugging it from its holster. Mine now. I thumb-checked the safety was on and slipped the gun into the waistband of my jeans at the small of my back, pulling the hoodie down to cover it. I took the drink from his hand—the naïve idiot should have thrown it at me and used my surprise to grab me—and tossed the cup in the nearest trash can. "Time to walk," I said, nudging him forward. Thankfully everyone was too absorbed in shopping and eating to have seen what I'd done.

Newbie wore a loose jacket, which made it easier to hide my mini-kidnapping. I threaded my left arm through his right and pressed into him as if we were just an in-love couple taking a stroll through a department store. With my right arm flat across my front I could tuck my hand into my unzipped hoodie to keep the gun against his side. I really did not want to have to shoot him in the…uh…come on, anatomy classes…liver, but fair's fair in the game of assholes stalking me.

His movements were tense and jerky and I shook his arm. "Relax," I said in a low, soothing voice as we exited the building. "Don't be so stiff. You've got to make it convincing. It's already going to be hard to make all these strangers believe we're together, with me being so hot and you being so…young and male."

"This is—"

I cut him off. "Shhhh, this is a no-talking zone, unless you're me or I ask you a direct question. Let's keep walking. You're parked at the McDonald's, right?" When he didn't answer, I continued, "The black tinted-window SUV stands out like a sore thumb. You guys really need to think about the image you're projecting."

He confirmed my question with a nod.

"Who do you work for?" When he didn't answer, I nudged him. "That's a question I want answered. You can speak."

He turned his head toward me, surprised etched on his face. "The same people you do."

Well that's one thing I could move from the not-certain to certain list. I had to assume he meant the government, not Halcyon.

I didn't feel better for having put one piece of the puzzle into place. "What's it going to take for you all to leave me alone?"

"You come with us for debrief and agree to stop pursuing this."

I laughed. "Debrief, right. And the rest." I nudged him again with the gun, though softer this time. "What I've done does not warrant this...treatment. Because I haven't done anything except exercise caution."

He was silent. Fine. I nudged him harder, harder than he needed, and he grunted.

"I mean it," I said. "I'm not rogue, not at all."

"That's not for me to say. I'm simply following directives," he said flatly.

My response was anything but flat. "You can tell them that I'm not coming in until I've decided I'm ready to come in. Tell them I haven't done what they think I have. I am *not* a traitor."

"And what about Sophia Flores? What does she know?"

His usage of her name confirmed my uneasy suspicion that they'd tracked me through Sophia. "If you say her name again I'm going to cut your tongue from your mouth." Wow. No idea where that had come from. *Really* not a violent person.

A hint of triumph was underneath the fear as he eyed me. I'd been so stupid, saying that. Now they knew she meant something to me. I jammed the gun into his body, pressing so hard my bicep quivered. He was going to have a nice muzzle-shaped bruise to remember me by. "She knows nothing, she's seen nothing. To her, we're just enjoying a road trip." A weird road trip. I was going to have to explain this latest adventure to her, somehow. "You don't touch her, you don't talk to her, you don't even *look* at her. And you don't track her. She's a private citizen."

He said nothing.

"Are we clear?"

A nod. It meant nothing, he may as well have just confirmed he was going to give me a million dollars and a new house. I leaned in to snarl in his ear, "I mean it. And I'm not going to tell you, or any of your pals, again. She's off-limits."

Another nudge made him nod again and this one at least seemed to be agreeable. I guided us to the sore-thumb SUV. "Here's your car, right? Give me your keys and your phone, I don't want to put my hand in your pocket. Do it slowly."

He passed them to me. No second weapon in a pants pocket? Not even a blade? Amateur.

"Thanks. Now, you're going to stand right here. I'm going to take your keys and phone and hand them to a cashier inside McDonald's. You can go in there in fifteen minutes and ask if anyone's handed in lost things to collect your belongings. Then you are going to go away. You're going to leave me, and Sophia Flores, alone. Or I'll just shoot you right here inside your car with your own gun, which is probably one of the most embarrassing things I can think of. Even more embarrassing than being outsmarted and taken captive by the person you were supposed to capture."

His jaw bunched. "Got it."

"I didn't say you could speak, but I'll let that one go." I held out my hand. "Give me five dollars."

"Why?" he asked incredulously.

"Because I want a chocolate shake."

CHAPTER TEN

Adrenaline sex is incredible and I really should have tried it earlier

I waited in the bar next to Beast Burger to make sure Newbie drove away and didn't sneak back to trap me. *Try* to trap me. After twenty minutes nursing a mediocre beer until it got warm, and thinking about my current situation and how Sophia fit into that situation, I was sure he was really gone. Or he had suddenly discovered how to be inconspicuous. Given his earlier attempt at being inconspicuous, I was sure it was the former. I was also sure he, or someone in his place, would be back. But probably not today. Hopefully not today.

I left a few dollars on the bar then slipped out the back door, earning the ire of a staff member who caught me as I was exiting. Whatever, bar staff ire was worth the safety of exiting through a different door than I'd entered. A quick look around showed nothing out of the ordinary and I clipped the chest strap of my new backpack together, stuffed my hands into my new hoodie pockets and started my casual stroll back to the hotel. My casual stroll took longer than it should have because I strolled right past the hotel, checked out the parking lots and every entrance, then looped around the two blocks on each side of the hotel.

Despite having performed recon walks like this countless times before, I couldn't shake the dread that always held the back of my neck in a vise until I was safely inside again. With my skin still crawling, I wandered as calmly as I could through the rear parking lot, noting our rental car was still there, and took the internal stairs up to our hotel room. Lights on inside. She hadn't caught a plane out of here and left me. Relief made my limbs weak.

A few seconds after I knocked, there was a flash of color behind the peephole. But no sound. I rested my forehead against the frame. "It's Lexie," I said, voice cracking. I cleared my throat. "I'm here for my massage appointment and a little black dress." I heard the chain slide back a second before the door opened. I slipped inside, almost colliding with Sophia before I slammed the door closed, locked it, and engaged the chain.

She grabbed me by the shoulders, turning me side to side as she inspected me. "You've been gone for almost two hours!" she blurted. "Fuck. I've been worrying my ass off. Why did it take so long? Are you hurt?"

I gently cupped her face, trying to calm her, and was surprised to find the touch calmed me as well. Also surprising was the sudden desperation for physical connection, needing to keep touching her, wanting her to touch me. I stroked her cheekbones with my thumbs. "Had to be certain everything's fine. Which it is," I said as easily as I could around the trembly adrenaline comedown. "And I'm also fine, not hurt at all. Why would you think I'd be hurt?"

Sophia shrugged helplessly. "Just a bad feeling." Her hands ran slowly down then up my arms as if testing I was solid and unharmed. "Are you sure you're okay? Is he gone?" Her hands slipped up to the back of my neck and she pulled my face down, urgently meeting my lips with hers.

When she finally released me from the frantic kiss, I said, "Yes, I'm sure and yes he's gone." The backpack felt like it was full of lead, my clothes and shoes uncomfortable and constricting. I slipped out of the backpack and left it by the table. "For now," I added as I began unlacing my Docs.

Her voice pitched up as she asked, "For *now*? Who the hell *was* that? What's going on, Lexie? I'm kinda freaking out here." She was doing an admirable job of trying to seem calm.

"Don't freak out. It really is okay." I inhaled slowly, trying to force down the upset that'd jumped from her to me, like a little empathy hop. I toed out of my boots. "This vacation is kind of dual purpose."

She eyed me suspiciously. "Dual purpose...how?"

While I was sitting in the bar, I'd thought about what to tell her and my words flowed smoothly. "It's part of my yearly performance evaluation, think of it like certifying that my escape and evasion training is up to scratch. I have two weeks to evade 'capture'"—I air-quoted—"anywhere in the world. I run, they follow, I hide, they find me. Or try to."

Sophia's mouth fell open. "Not *real* capture?"

"No," I said, a little too quickly. "Of course not. The easiest explanation is that every day that I'm spotted is a point in the fail column, and every day I'm not is a point in the pass column. Amass enough pass points and I've passed the evaluation."

"Oh." She relaxed instantly, and I knew my choice to tell her this story instead of a version of the truth was the right one. "But... why bring me?" A tinge of hurt crept into her voice. "Why didn't you just tell me this instead of making up a story about a road trip?"

I'd known she wouldn't just accept my explanation—no sane person would—but some part of me had hoped she wouldn't probe. Wishful thinking. My answer came easily. "It's not against the rules to tell someone, but it's also kind of frowned upon. And, I guess most importantly, persuasion is part of my job and asking you to join me was...keeping those skills sharp too." I took both her hands, relieved when she didn't snatch them away. "I'm so sorry I was duplicitous and that I didn't tell you what I'm really doing. I really, *honestly*, wanted to get to know you better and didn't want two weeks to pass without seeing you. I just thought I could take care of two birds with one stone."

"I...don't even know what to say."

"That you forgive me for not telling you at the beginning?" I said hopefully.

She glanced away, staring at some unseen spot on the wall before slowly turning back to me. "I can't believe this."

"I know. And I'm sorry, and I hope you realize why it was necessary for me. But like I said, even if it weren't for this, I *really* want to spend more time with you." The truthfulness of that statement felt like inhaling a deep breath of air. I cupped her face, dipping my head as I pulled her close to kiss her. But I didn't kiss her, didn't want to force that upon her after admitting my manipulation.

She paused, whispering, "Me too" before she closed the space between our lips. Sophia looped her arms around my neck, pressing her body into mine as she kissed me. The touch of her lips soothed my anxiety and inflamed my desire, and when she opened her mouth, deepening the kiss, I couldn't suppress my moan.

My adrenaline retreated, replaced by far more pleasurable arousal that turned my excitement into a want so desperate I almost shuddered. "Sophia…" That single word left my mouth as a hoarse plea.

"What's wrong?" she asked as her eyes searched mine.

"Nothing. Everything is right." I gave in to my desperation, gripped her by the hips, and pulled her hard against me to kiss her again. It felt like no matter how deep, how searching or scorching our kisses, I couldn't satisfy my need. I wanted to tear our clothes from our bodies, shred the fabric keeping us apart, spread her open and devour her, surrender as she devoured me. But this sudden, carnal need was new and a little frightening and I didn't want to scare her more than I already had.

I pulled away, burying my face in her neck. After a deep breath, I felt slightly more controlled. Slightly… Sophia huffed out an exhalation as I grazed her collarbone with my teeth. She reached up to hold the back of my head, her fingertips massaging as I lightly bit her neck. "Oh god," she groaned. "It's not just me? I thought—" She was cut off by my teeth, which were a little harder this time.

"You thought what?" I soothed the bite marks with my tongue, lovingly sucked the smooth skin of her neck.

"I thought maybe it wasn't appropriate to jump on you the moment you came back from something that seemed so scary." She gripped my wrist, pushing my hand downward until it was nestled on the button of her jeans, making her desires absolutely clear. "But I wanted to. I wanted…this and I was trying to ignore it because it seemed so…out of place. I don't know why it came on so fast."

"What did, baby?" I asked as I unfastened the button and slid her zip down.

"*Want*," she said, that single word so urgent it was almost choked out. She inhaled a shuddering breath as she pulled the hoodie from my shoulders and yanked it off. "I want you. So badly."

She lifted herself up on tiptoes, and I felt the hard peaks of her nipples chafing against mine. This kiss was soft at first, her lips moving with such tenderness I felt like melting. It was as if she wanted to soothe me, love me. Sophia's tongue slid over my lower lip, and when I opened my mouth to her, she groaned. The remnants of my anxiety fell away completely, leaving only one thing in its place. Lust. Fierce and unrelenting. My hands went under her top, cupping her breasts through her bra as Sophia began working at my belt.

We weren't soft and sensual with each other the way we had been when we'd made love previously. This time we tore at clothing, used teeth and nails. Our foreplay was rough and frantic, needy. She kissed me like she wanted to consume me, her teeth grazing my lower lip as her tongue stroked and teased. Her hands groped my ass, pulling me against her as I maneuvered us toward the bed. But we didn't make it there.

"Fuck me," Sophia demanded as she shimmied out of her underwear and kicked it away. "Do it hard."

I pressed her against the wall beside the kitchenette, kissing her as she guided my hand between her thighs. I pushed deeper, seeking her warmth and wetness, exhaling a moan of pleasure as I found what I wanted, what she wanted. "Oh, god, yes," I breathed. I kissed her neck, sucked the salty skin above her collarbone as my fingers circled her clitoris. She was so wet, so ready, that my fingers slipped inside her with the slightest pressure.

Sophia inhaled sharply, as if she hadn't expected me to do exactly what she'd asked me to, but her breathy "Yes" was all the consent I needed to keep fucking her. Sophia wrapped a leg around my ass, tilting her hips into me as I thrust deeply. She held on around my shoulders with her face buried in my neck, her mouth moving over my skin. "More, harder. Please, deeper," she begged, grinding against my hand.

I obliged, panting as I sank deeper into her. Sophia groaned, her whole body tensing as she rode my fingers. She exhaled with each of my thrusts, her breath and little moans of pleasure huffing out against my neck as I drove her toward her climax. I had her pinned to the wall, my body against her body, my mouth against her mouth. But if I was hurting her, she didn't complain. I bit lightly, sucked firmly, stroked deeply, and with every movement of teeth and tongue and fingers, she begged me for more. She seemed to know what I was doing, and why, as if she had the same desperation as I did. The desire to feel something outside of the rush of fear and relief. To feel something real. Something raw.

She kept begging, kept grinding, kept biting my neck, until her breathing became ragged and she sobbed and shuddered out her climax, collapsing into me. I held on to her, carefully eased myself from inside her, placing light kisses over her face, neck, shoulders, until I felt her breathing steady. My own arousal had been prickling under my skin—there, but easy enough to ignore…until Sophia licked her lips and looked up at me with unrestrained desire.

She pushed me backward across the small hotel room and down onto the bed where we fell in a mess of tangled limbs and sweat-slick skin. I rolled to settle on top, snugged between her spread legs, feeling the hot, wet remnants of our fucking against my hip. Her legs instantly came around my ass and she lifted her hip, pressing herself up into me. Then, in a move I should have been prepared for if I wasn't so focused on the building desperation between my thighs, Sophia flipped us so she was on top, straddling me.

I sat up, trying to maneuver her so I was on top again. I wanted to lie her down and spread her apart, wanted to taste her, to make her come again. But Sophia held firm, digging her knees into the bed to keep me in place. She twisted and wiggled, slid her hand between us and bent down to murmur against my ear, "Open your legs for me."

Her command made me abandon my efforts to top her again. I let my legs fall open and watched her face as I felt her hand working its way around obstacles of limbs and flesh until she found my clit. Sophia stroked firmly, adjusting to each of my reciprocal movements until her renewed arousal slicked my thighs. She kissed me hard as her other hand cupped my breast, her fingers firmly pinching my nipple until the hot, tingling sensation of pleasure slid into my stomach and lower. When I bucked my hips, Sophia slid off me and wriggled backward until she knelt between my legs. With firm hands on the inside of my thighs, Sophia spread me wide apart. She lingered without touching anywhere else, teasing me, until I begged a hoarse, breathless, "Please."

She fucked me roughly, hard and fast. And I couldn't tell if it was her adrenaline, the intensity of what had happened after lunch or if she just…wanted to punish me for putting her through this. That thought was fleeting, and I dismissed it right away—she was rough but not cruel, raw but not hurtful.

And the whole time, she watched my face as if searching for even the slightest hint that I didn't want what she was giving me. But I wanted *everything* and I begged her for it, pulled her closer, pushed up into her until my climax scorched along my nerves and I had to stifle my cries with my hand lest I frighten the neighbors in the rooms on either side.

Sophia pulled me close, rolled us until we were on our sides facing one another, and kissed me so softly that it barely registered. She kissed my cheeks, my lips again, my forehead, then pulled me against her. Stroking my hair, she murmured something I couldn't make out. But I didn't need to hear the actual words. I knew exactly what she was saying.

And it scared the shit out of me.

CHAPTER ELEVEN

Make the implausible seem plausible

I'd half-drifted to sleep, lying naked with Sophia spooned against my back. With each breath, I isolated the sensations cocooning me. Soft warm skin, the touch of her nipples against my back, the almost-tickle of her hands stroking lightly over my belly. This was… really nice, for lack of an articulate description. Snuggling after sex had never really been my thing, even with Elaheh, the longest relationship I'd ever had at just under five months. If you could call occasionally seeing each other under the guise of friendship, all-too-brief moments in bed, sneaking around and knowing you could be killed for what we were doing a *relationship*. I didn't really.

Even if Elaheh escaped her life and we'd been in America, I wasn't certain I'd have been the post-coital cuddle type with her. We didn't have that kind of relationship and if I was honest with myself, which I could be now that I was so long past that point in my life, I didn't fully trust her. Could never let my guard down the way I did with Sophia. The way I'd almost immediately felt I could.

Sophia was a safe place.

She mumbled something against the back of my shoulder, but I couldn't understand what she was trying to say. I turned my head to ask, "What was that?"

Sophia leaned over me. This time, instead of a mumble, she said quietly, almost pained, "Did I hurt you?"

It took a few moments to make the connection. She'd been rough, raw, and needy, at times all harsh teeth and nails, then other times all loving lips and tongue and hands. And I'd loved every moment of it. Wanted everything she'd done. I'd never given myself over so completely during intimacy the way I had with her. Never. I smiled and answered honestly, "No."

"Are you sure?"

I rolled over so I could see her expression, and found worry, guilt, fear. "Yes. Very sure. That's why instead of telling you 'no, stop, I don't like this,' you'll recall I was begging you to keep going in a very 'more, more, yes, fuck yes, please yes' type way. Begging you quite a lot, if I'm remembering correctly?" That exact memory sent a delicious rush of heat through me.

She went still, as if processing this information, then relaxed back down into the mattress. "I remember…" she said, a smug smile curving her mouth.

"Mmm. And if *I* recall, you asked me for the same…"

Sophia's teeth brushed her lower lip. "I did. And I'll ask for it again." She resumed stroking my skin, the softness of the touch both soothing and sweet, a counterpoint to before. I sensed the next time we made love—er, uh, fucked?—she'd be slow and gentle, wanting to show love instead of roughness. Love. An interesting concept, and one I wasn't sure she would ever, could ever, apply to me. Like and lust, sure. But I was not an easy person to love. Who could love a person they knew was never being totally honest with them?

Her tentative fingers traced around my nipple. "Did you really want me here with you for your evaluation?"

"Yes," I said honestly, even as I feared the consequences of that honesty. The elephant of how they'd tracked us filled the room. I needed to get rid of it. Smiling, I teased, "But I'm not sure it's working out so far in my favor. Professionally that is, personally it's *definitely* working out in my favor."

Her forehead crinkled in confusion as she absently stroked the backs of my hands. "What do you mean?"

I almost told her I'd never been tracked before, but that was a lie. So I went with what I knew to be the truth, speaking without accusation. I was hoping that hearing it would make her a little more amenable to toning down her phone habits if she thought it was interfering with my fake work eval. "I know I've been completely untraceable this trip. No credit cards or ID in my name, no phone with a number associated with me. I think they found me through you."

"What do you mean?" she repeated.

"Well...the guy at breakfast would have been first contact, and he saw me with you. Saw me leave with you. It would be easy enough for them to figure out who you are and track your cell phone etcetera."

Her mouth fell open. She closed it. Opened it. Closed it. Eventually she spluttered, "Oh, shit. Oh my god. Can they really do that?"

"Mhmm, and they do. Every day, for whatever reason they want, if it's for national security or law enforcement, not just some analyst and ops officer training." I hastened to add, "It'll only be your location, I swear they wouldn't listen to your calls or see your text messages or anything like that."

"Gross." As I nodded my agreement, Sophia chewed lightly on her lower lip, her emotions playing out clearly across her beautiful face. Annoyed—probably at me for deceiving her, anxious—probably because of Newbie stalking us, accepting—probably because of my gentle coaxing and reassurances. After a deep breath, she quietly asked, "It was me who made you get a fail point?"

"No," I said instantly. They would have found me with or without her, and making her feel bad wasn't on my agenda. "You're not responsible for any of this." Smiling, I drew an X over my heart. "Cross my heart."

Sophia returned my smile. "Well...what do we do then? If they know where you are?"

"Well, darling"—the endearment slipped out, and I liked how it sounded so much that I left it out in the world—"something that would help is if we adjust your phone and Internet habits to make them a little more private so they can't track you and, by extension, me so easily. Like using a messaging app that encrypts calls and texts, and using a VPN while on the Internet. And I think we should change hotels, just in case. I'm sure I lost him but I don't want to take the chance that I've been followed and that someone knows we're staying here."

"Okay, sure," she said. "Can we move closer to the beach?" It was such an innocent question, like she was still stuck in "we're vacationing" mode. Because to her, this was nothing more than a vacation.

And I didn't hesitate to answer, "Of course." Closer to the beach was in a different part of the city. Always good to change things up.

She trailed her fingers up and down between my breasts. "Will you get a promotion if you do well?"

"Most likely just a pay raise." It sounded much better than *Most likely I'll go to jail.* "Maybe a better office if I ask nicely." Office, cell. Whatever.

"Worth it then."

"That it is. But…You don't have to keep doing this, Sophia. This work thing of mine is going to get tedious for you very quickly, and having to change the way you act with your phone and stuff just to help me isn't really fair. I want you to stay with me, but you can go home whenever you want to. I'll buy you a plane ticket and take you to the airport right now, or whenever. It's your call." I desperately hoped she wouldn't want to leave, but I had to give her the choice.

She barely even hesitated before answering, "Nah." With a grin, she added, "Now I know what's going on, it's exciting, like I'm living in my very own James Bond movie. I want to help you get a good evaluation score."

"Bond is a spy," I teased. I had to tease to mask my unease. Of course it would be exciting if it wasn't real. But it was real, and it was anything but exciting. "And I'm not."

"Fiiiine," she drawled. "Like I'm living my very own intelligence analyst thing. It's…something new and interesting. I needed that. And, I really like being around you," she said, almost shyly.

I pulled her hand up to my mouth and kissed each fingertip. "I like being around you too."

We lay quietly together on the bed, fingers stroking and exploring without teasing. Her touch paused on my hip. "At least now I know why you haven't wanted to go out touristing much. I just thought you were vacation-activity adverse."

"Yeah, sorry about that," I said ruefully. "It's probably not going to get that much better, honestly…"

"As long as you don't leave me, I'm good," she murmured.

"I won't." Relieved at not having to push and goad and beg her to stay, it wasn't hard to sound cheerful. "Right. Great. Okay. Thank you."

She waved me off. "I mean, I *will* need to be not-inside sometimes. But I'll trust you to manage when you feel like it's okay to sneak out into the real world and not ruin your spy game."

"Deal." Trust. Such a dangerous thing. I wasn't sure how deep mine was for her yet, but I knew I'd never intentionally break hers in me. Smiling, I reminded her again that, "I'm not a spy."

She kissed me. "Okay then, Not-Spy."

I'd almost finished packing when the throwaway cell phone chimed a text alert. Only Bink had that number. I used my body to shield the screen from Sophia as I read the text.

It's done.

I texted back. *Thank you.* After a pause I typed three words that terrified me. *And Sophia Flores?*

Legit, and clean as a whistle. Lucky for you, considering you brought her to my house…

She was clean. She really was a safe place. The relief was so acute I almost cried. After a few deep breaths to settle my tears, I texted that I'd be there soon, then tossed the phone in my backpack. When I turned, I found Sophia's interested gaze on me. "I just have to go do something before we find a new hotel."

"Go do something as in food, beach, touristing, or…reading books?" she asked slyly. "Because the reading was an interesting experience."

"Reading," I said instantly. "And yeah, I know. I'm sorry about them steamrolling you like that, the whole 'I don't wanna know who you are, sit here and don't interact' thing. They're just…who they are. I'll be quicker than I was the first time, promise. Just collecting something to help me with the evaluation."

Sophia zipped her suitcase. "Take your time. Your friend has the new Jamie Blasser thriller. I started it the other day, so I can keep reading while you're doing whatever you're doing. Do you think I could borrow it?"

"I'll ask." Or I'd just take it on my way out.

"Thanks." Sophia's love of puzzles, thrillers, and detective-slash-espionage-slash-spy fiction made her acquiescence easy to understand. This was exciting to her, and now that I'd confirmed there was no danger it was just like stepping into her own, real-life novel. I had to make sure it always seemed like fiction, because once she learned how serious what we were doing was, she'd be gone faster than I could say "Halcyon."

"I'll just pee before we go." After shutting myself in the bathroom, I dropped onto the closed toilet lid and leaned forward to rest my face in my hands. Adrenaline and arousal—those good sensations—had fled completely, leaving me feeling drained and smothered by my own stupidity. I'd been so careless. They'd come too close. I'd promised her that what we were doing was boring and innocuous, just a road trip, but oh that's right, I forgot to mention it's actually a work practice spy tailing exercise dealio and people are following us, but it'll all be fine.

They'd found me once. They'd find me again, which meant the window I had for figuring this out had shrunk even more. And I'd barely fit through it in the first place. I estimated I had maybe four, five days before this all blew up in my face. And then what? Did I keep running and trying to work it out, hoping I'd crack it and everything would be fine? Did I tell Sophia it was over, that I'd "failed," lie to her even more and pretend I wanted her gone, just so I could keep her out of the inevitable shitstorm? Or did I just take us back home, take myself to work and walk through the doors with my hands up and a "Sorry about all of this. I wasn't as clever as I thought I was."

Giving up would be so easy. Except for Halcyon. Going in, giving up now *was not* an option. I had to make a decision and I had to make it soon. The decision was easy really. Implementing it was not going to be. Five more days and then Sophia had to go home, even if I wasn't done with what I was trying to accomplish. I couldn't have something like today happening again, or something worse if they decided to get nasty.

A rap of knuckles on the door startled me out of my spiral. "Lexie? You okay in there?"

"Yep. Sorry, just thinking." I jumped up and shoved the door open.

The moment I emerged, Sophia said, "Uh, you didn't flush. Or wash your hands." Her expression was a hilarious combo of incredulity, embarrassment, and gentle mom-ish reminder.

Smiling, I shot back, "That's because didn't pee after all. Decided I didn't need to."

Sophia stepped in behind me, hands starting on my shoulders then drifting to my waist, my ass, until she was pressed against my back with her hands settled on my stomach. She nuzzled my hair, the back of my neck, and I felt the softness of her lips against my skin. Her hug was tight, almost too tight, but the tenderness of her lips tempered her grip. It was an odd sort of desperation mixed with sweetness, as if she was trying to keep me safe and show me love all at once.

Before I could take her hands, she released me and stepped away. "Eye Spy with my little eye, something beginning with…B."

Smiling, I checked my bags and zipped them up. "Bed?"

"Nope. Amateur pick." Sophia collected her own things and gave the room a quick visual sweep.

"Blargh bedspread?" After collecting my backpack from near the door, I held the door open for her. "Backpack?"

"Nice. But no and no."

"Buick?" I asked once we'd handed back the room key and were walking to the rental car.

"There are none here."

"Okay, I give up."

"Butt. Specifically, yours." Sophia patted it.

She didn't question a quick stop to swap cars because the one we had "was making a funny noise," and I felt she probably knew it was all part of the "evaluation." As I drove the low-milage Chevy Equinox, I gave Sophia my phone to search for a hotel, giving her free rein to stay wherever she wanted. By the time I parked a few houses down from Bink's place, she'd booked us into a new home right by the beach.

Bink looked like they'd had an hour's sleep since yesterday, if that, and all of that sleep broken into five-minute clumps during the night and day. Their greeting was a grunt I think was "hello." Or maybe it was "hate-you."

Sophia waved hi, and without saying anything, went straight to the bookshelves and pulled out a novel. I followed Bink upstairs and closed and locked the door behind us. "No problems?" I asked.

"None. They'd moved those files by the way, left the clumsiest trail I've ever seen."

"Suspiciously clumsy?"

"No. Inept clumsy. Looked like they were in a hurry is all." They handed me an external hard drive and a mouse. I handed over a prepaid Visa card I'd loaded with five grand. Fair trade.

Bink fingered the plastic, turning it over and over. "There is *a lot* of fucking data in there. I didn't even get a chance to take a sneaky peek at my own government files, I was so busy getting what you needed."

I laid on the sarcasm. "Aww, I'm so sorry. Maybe next time."

"Yeah. Except I'm going to have to find a legitimate reason to go looking. You know I don't like to poke around in places I'm not wanted unless I have good reason, or permission."

"Curiosity isn't a good enough reason?"

"Unfortunately not."

I forced a smile. "Well, hopefully you won't need to do it for me again."

"For your sake, I'm relieved. For mine, I'm annoyed."

"Sorry," I said insincerely. "Hey, can my friend have one of your books?"

Bink waved dismissively. "Sure. I guess your payment just about covers a book."

"Thanks." I made a move to open the door but Bink stopped me with a hand on my arm.

"Hey," they murmured. "You know I'm not one to want details, and I don't give a fuck what people are doing unless it's hurting someone, but this doesn't feel good. You in trouble?"

I shrugged. If they were asking then it meant they already knew I was.

Thankfully Bink wasn't into prying and understood a "can't talk about it" even if it was nonverbal. They eyed me for a long moment. "What about your friend out there? What does she know?"

"Nothing," I said instantly. "She thinks I'm doing a training exercise where I evade capture and she's just along because I didn't want to get lonely." I held up the hard drive. "Now I need to think of a reason why I'm going to want to be glued to my laptops twenty-four-seven. Do you think telling her that part of the training is that I have to solve an encrypted intelligence puzzle sounds okay?"

Bink shrugged. "Works for me. You were always great at making the implausible seem plausible. And you should keep it that way."

"My bullshitting?"

"No. Her not knowing anything."

"I intend to."

"Good. Be careful with all this. I don't want to see your gorgeous face on the news."

"I always am." I grinned. "If you think I'm gorgeous, why haven't you ever made a move? All those lonely nights cooped up in the office together and sleeping in the same quarters. Geez, it could have been so much nicer."

"Because we would have killed each other," was the dry answer.

"True." I patted the hard drive. "Thanks for this, I owe you. Now forget I was here."

"I always do." They lightly gripped my shoulder and it felt almost friendly. "Come back if you need anything else. You know I'll always help you stay out of trouble."

"For a fee, right?"

"Nah, by now I owe you some freebies." Bink's gaze was measured. "So here's a freebie for you—you should fire whoever cut your hair. It looks like absolute shit."

What? I reached a tentative hand up to touch it and realized immediately that they were right. "Thanks…"

CHAPTER TWELVE

Workaholic

Driving from Bink's to our new hotel, I stuck to the speed limit like a kid doing their driving test. The last thing I wanted was to draw attention to myself with a cop pull over. I couldn't afford the time delay or the possible flag on my license...s catching the attention of a well-meaning officer. I just needed to get to the new hotel. The moment we got settled in our room I could get started on cracking the case. And by cracking the case I meant just seeing if something made sense.

And though all I wanted was to find the hotel, order in some food, drink a relaxing glass of wine and get started on the intelligence Bink had acquired for me, Sophia deserved a sit-down dinner and my full attention. Honestly, she deserved so much more than that, but it was a start. But when I suggested we stop for dinner at a restaurant on the way home, her reluctance was palpable. And strange.

"Why don't you want to grab dinner?" I asked, glancing over at her as I drove like a law-abiding citizen with absolutely nothing to hide.

"I think maybe we should just get to the hotel and have dinner there."

"Are you worried about something?"

"No, but…" She gestured to the back seat where my ever-present backpack of really important things was strapped in like a newborn baby. "Whatever is on that hard drive has to be important."

I tried for casually curious. "What makes you think that?"

Sophia turned sideways to look at me. "Because ever since you got it, you've had this expression."

"An *expression*, huh?" This time I went with teasing. "What's this expression look like?"

But Sophia wouldn't be deflected with teasing. "Like it pains you to not look at whatever is on the drive, like whatever is on it will keep the world turning and you're singlehandedly responsible for spinning the wheel."

"Interesting theory." I couldn't believe I'd let my guard down enough that she'd seen things I didn't want her to see. Or maybe she was just scarily observant and intuitive. More than I'd given her credit for. That intuition was going to help me, or ruin everything. "Well…we have to eat, and I don't know about you, but I'm feeling actual plates and cutlery instead of takeout provisions." I changed lanes and pulled into the parking lot of an Italian restaurant I'd spotted from further back while I'd been scanning for those who shouldn't be around. "Come on, let's get some dinner and we can talk." I leaned over and snagged the backpack, stuffing the small external drive into the pocket of my hoodie. It made me feel marginally better having it on my person, though if they managed to grab the backpack, they'd also manage to grab me.

The restaurant's decor gave me an immediate warm, homey feel, and I fought down a wave of nostalgia. It felt like I'd been dragged back to my childhood, back to Friday night dinners with my parents at Alberto's whenever we were living in DC, back to my unchanging order of spaghetti bolognese, a Coke, and a chocolate ice cream sundae, back to the few hours every week where my parents were focused solely on me and the inane stories I had to tell them about my week, instead of their usual distracted interactions with me.

Sophia slipped her hand into mine. "You okay?" she asked quietly.

I pushed the memory back down, smiling as I assured her, "Yeah, just thought of something." Something that stirred both pleasant and unpleasant emotions. I wondered what it would have been like to grow up with parents like Sophia's, parents who thought you were the center of their universe instead of a star at the very edge of their galaxy that they noticed every now and then.

She squeezed my fingers, but didn't say anything further.

The restaurant was about a third full, and I did the very gross thing of slipping a twenty into the hostess's hand and indicating in a low voice that a table away from everyone else would be perfect thankyouverymuch. If I was about to come clean, well...clean-ish to Sophia, the last thing I wanted was to be overheard. Nobody had looked up when we'd entered the restaurant, and upon my scan of the space, none of the patrons seemed out of place. Maybe we'd get through dinner without interruption.

Once we'd been seated, met our server, and ordered drinks and appetizers, I opened my mouth to explain...kind of, but Sophia beat me to it. In a low voice she said, "I'm starting to think your job is a lot more important than you let on." She nervously fiddled with her napkin.

"It's more involved, yes."

She glanced around the room, the movement of her eyes so quick I wouldn't have noticed if I wasn't so focused on her. Apparently she saw nothing that concerned her, if she'd even know what that concern might look like. "Can I ask you something?"

"You can ask me many somethings and I'll answer as best I can."

Sophia exhaled loudly, clearly relieved. "Thank you." She paused, and it was obvious she wanted to press forward but didn't know how. After almost a minute of our mutual silence, she said, "Your friend who gave you the hard drive. Are they part of this work evaluation?"

"In a way, yes. They're a resource. Like a hotel or car or change of clothes."

"Right. I know you said you can't tell me everything, but I'm curious. And kind of...not scared, but...weirded out by it."

I pushed down my concern. Weirded out didn't mean on the verge of bailing. She was still with me. I smiled gently at her. "Because now you've stopped to really think about it?"

"Yeah."

"Understandable. It's a little more complex than I first told you, but I didn't want to pile on any more than I had to." I kicked myself for not thinking of this before, because now it felt like a tacked-on "Oh, hey, whoops, silly me to forget this important detail." I tucked my hands between my knees, and leaned toward her. "To ramp up the stress, make the evaluation feel more 'real-world,' I have a problem to solve. Before I started, I was given an intelligence file that I have to investigate and uncover the truth from. But I don't have the usual tools I'd have if I was at work, so I have to find workarounds to solve the puzzle." I patted the backpack I kept wedged between my feet. "That's where my friend Mr. Hard Drive comes in. Utilizing people I know to get tools I need was step two in the treasure hunt." I smiled up at the server who approached with our drinks and set arancini and bruschetta on the table before he politely asked if we were ready to order entrées.

After a frantic menu skim, we ordered and once we were alone again, Sophia asked, "Why would they make you do that?"

"Because sometimes we're left out in the cold, cut off for one reason or another, but still have to produce results, so we have to improvise. It's easier to improvise if you've practiced improvisation beforehand, have set up networks of people to assist you." God, I should write a book.

She bit off an impressive mouthful of bruschetta, licking a drizzle of olive oil and balsamic from her lower lip. "When are you going to solve this puzzle?"

"Whenever I can around us having a vacation-ish time." Between the hours of midnight and five a.m.

Her grin was lopsided, like only half of her wanted to cooperate. "So, like…most of the day, the way you've been glued to your laptop so far?"

It wasn't a reproach by any means, yet I still felt the sting. But I'd told her I'd be doing work during this "vacation." A little work, I corrected myself. I cut into an arancini ball, and after eating a forkful to buy myself a moment, I said, "It'll probably be much the same as it has been 'til now—bit of work, bit of vacation, an overabundance of caution."

That made her smile. "I'd classify it as an abundance, not overabundance."

An over-overabundance, but I'd managed to keep most of it hidden from her. Guilt gnawed at my insides, again. "Sophia…" I reached over and took her free hand. "If you don't wanna spend time cooped up in a hotel for most of the day, watching me working on this, then the offer to fly home is still there. It's always on the table. No questions, no judgment. I want you to stay with me, but I'd understand if you'd had enough."

She shrugged, snuck a taste of my arancini, then scooped up one for herself. "If I go home, I'll just be working, and I can do that here, with you, which is more pleasant than being at home alone. For many reasons." The raised eyebrow conveyed exactly what reasons she was referring to.

That look twisted my insides. Being with her was so easy. And also so hard. The intimacy and our connection was incredible and unlike anything I'd ever experienced before...but it spread my concentration thin, took my focus from the big picture. "Okay then," I said. "I'm very glad you want to continue our weird little vacation-not-a-vacation."

"Me too..." Sophia loaded bruschetta onto my plate. "How long do you have? To solve your puzzle."

"Not as long as I'd like." I turned my glass around on the table, smearing the circles of condensation. "I'll have to get creative, because I can't approach it the way I would if I was at work with everything I need right at my fingertips." Good thing I was flexible. "And, I have to do it alone."

"Unfortunate. I'm excellent at that sort of thing. You know," Sophia mumbled around a mouthful of arancini. After a quick swallow, she continued, "This is quite possibly the weirdest series of dates I've ever had."

"Dates?" I almost choked. "Oh these aren't dates, trust me. When we go on dates, you'll know about it."

"We've totally had dates." Her expression was comically convincing and broke some of the tension churning inside me. "We had coffee and sweet stuff, then dinner, then our late breakfast and totally unexpected but incredible sex"—an eyebrow bounce— "then the road trip, staying in hotel rooms, more incredible but now expected sex, meeting your hard-drive person, beach visits, meals, running from that guy who was trying to get to you, beyond incredible sex, and now here we are." She gestured expansively with her fork. "Dates."

"I'd like to politely disagree. I'll give you the first three scheduled ones, but the rest of those events have just been...getting to know each other. Trust me, when I take you on a date, a real date, you'll know about it."

She feigned being taken aback. "Will I now?"

"Mhmm." All I had to do was make it out of this a free woman so I could show her exactly what I meant. "I am going to date the heck out of you." It'd come out as an attempt at wordplay but the moment I realized what I'd said, I also realized the implications of it. And that I'd meant it exactly as it had sounded.

Sophia's teeth brushed her lower lip as her eyes held mine with contact so intense I thought she might be looking into me and seeing my deepest desires, my deepest fears. Her expression softened, as if she understood exactly what she'd seen. "Lexie, I really, *really* hope you do."

Our new hotel came with the glorious auditory backdrop of crashing waves, spacious rooms, a cheerful front-desk clerk, and free buffet breakfast. Win. Henceforth, Sophia was in charge of booking all accommodation. She'd also booked us a studio room, with a small functional kitchen. After checking out the room, and declaring it clean and clean, I carried most of our stuff up the internal stairs, mentally reviewing each floor's exits on my way.

Sophia unpacked with the same loving care as always, then dragged me into the bathroom to take a long, hot shower with her. It was just that—a long, hot shower together. She soaped my body, turning me this way and that to rinse me off, gently kissing my shoulders, my back, my neck, as we stood under the spray. But that was all. Her attention felt more like loving care, rather than foreplay, and I gave in to it and let myself enjoy being cared for.

I was trying to figure out a way to tell her I wanted...*needed* to get to work on my puzzle when she told me she'd had an email from her client. "I should probably do some work," she said, in a way that made me think it wasn't actually that urgent, but she wanted to give me an excuse to work as well. Trying to act like I wasn't going insane doing nothing was apparently not going so well.

"Sure," I said calmly, though inside I was doing happy backflips. "You okay if I work too?" It was barely seven p.m., which meant I had a massive block of time in front of me where I could make some real progress with Hadim's intel before we'd have to venture out to boredom-bust tomorrow.

"Of course." She peered around the room, which, while spacious, only had one desk. And a small-ish one at that. "You want the desk or table?"

"You work wherever you need to and I'll just fit in around you." I nabbed my backpack from where I'd set it on a chair at the table in easy view. "You want the table? More room?"

"I'm making a self-help website, Lexie. You're practicing saving the world." Sophia's kiss was fleeting, but warm. "You take the table and spread out, I'll take the mini desk."

"Sure." Saving the world. A frightening concept. But perhaps not inaccurate. While Sophia got organized with her laptop and portable second monitor on the desk by the closet, I unpacked my own hardware and Bink's hard drive, setting them on the table and angling the laptops so the screens would open facing away from the middle of the room. Sophia set a glass of red by my elbow, then turned to leave. I lightly grabbed her wrist, pulling her back and kissing the butt of her palm. "Thank you."

"You're welcome." Reflexively, she glanced at the laptops, both of which showed nothing but log-in screens.

That quick glance made my stomach drop. I gestured at my laptops. "I…you can never see any of this, Sophia. And I can't talk to you about it. The test probably contains elements of real, classified intel that nobody without clearance can see." I squeezed her hands. "Do you understand? This is a nonnegotiable thing for me. If you want to stay and play superspy with me, then this is probably my only rule." Smiling to ease my school-principal lecture, I added, "Aside from always checking the coast is clear when we go outside."

"I thought you said you weren't a spy." Apparently, it'd become a joke to her and I'd decided to let her keep joking if it kept her at ease.

I grinned. "Smartass." Sobering, I reiterated in my best gentle-but-firm tone, "It's really important. Beyond important. I can't stress that enough. I'll do everything I can to keep what I'm working on out of your sight, close the laptops when I'm away. But I'm working out of my usual zone, I'm tired and stressed about not screwing this up and I just…Like, I know you would never snoop, but in case you're passing by and get the urge to take a peek. I mean, I would if I were in your shoes," I added teasingly.

A flash of unreadable emotion crossed her face. "Okay. I will. Or I mean, I won't. I promise."

"Thank you," I breathed. "Well, it's time to practice saving the world, I guess."

She raised her glass of wine in salute. "And time for me to help someone teach people to be the best versions of themselves."

I exhaled a long breath, pushing out as much tension as I could along with the air. So far, so good. End of day three of being on the run, I now had what I needed to further Halcyon's cause, and I had an incredible woman keeping me company and keeping me calm. I snuck a glance at Sophia, who'd settled at the small desk and was shimmy-dancing in her seat like she had an amazing bop playing in her head. I suppressed a wistful sigh. She was so cute. It would be so easy to fall for her. Bad idea. Not fair to her. I shook myself out, drank a slow mouthful of wine, and got to work.

Bink ran the cleanest system I knew—nothing made it to their machines unless they wanted it to—and I knew I could trust the hard drive to be free of malicious items. I downloaded Hadim's files, the reports I'd started that fateful morning, and installed the graphics manipulation software they'd extracted from the agency's servers. The laptop Halcyon had provided that I'd use to work with Hadim's files was set up with multifactor authentication to access—a very secure password, facial recognition, and my fingerprint. Nobody was getting a look inside unless they hypnotized me for my password and then cut off both my finger and…oh, gross.

Puffing out a loud breath, I tapped my fingers on the mouse as I wrestled with myself. Go hard, or go easy? I decided to ease myself back in with the photographs instead of diving into the video. Ease was a relative term—everything about this event was disgusting, shocking.

All the pictures were good quality, considering they'd most likely been taken in haste, and with a phone instead of camera. Groups of people standing around corpses, trucks, machinery. But nobody in any sort of uniform. It was civilians, white masks on faces, likely to help with stench and stop the spread of whatever had killed those people. Judging by the fluids and excretions on the ground around the corpses, I'd have thought full-body hazmat jumpsuits would also have been in order. Given the soft daylight instead of the spot-lit darkness in the body cam video, these photos had been taken hours after the video had been filmed.

I made a note to follow up on the method of dispersal, and if it was strictly contained to one form. Could the chemical make secondary transfer through bodily fluids, or was it strictly an inhalation/ingestion/absorption deal? Given I didn't know what the chemical actually was, I really needed Hadim. But the email address I had for him was burned and I had no others. Forget the movies where spies duck into Internet cafés and shoot off a dozen emails and engage in a vigorous instant-messaging conversation with zero regard for online security. If Hadim had cut ties, for whatever reason, I was adrift until he saw fit to throw me a rope again. If he saw fit.

After an hour zooming in and focusing on every area of these photos, I needed a break. Just like on Friday, I'd spotted nothing in the still images that struck me as useful—nothing to indicate where exactly it was, no identifiable faces, dead or alive, nothing to tell me exactly what had been used for this mass murder. Just horror. The photos *were* useful, part of the bigger picture, but my gut feeling was that whatever Halcyon needed had to do with the American. I saved my reports then loudly closed both laptops. I needed a break.

Sophia twisted around in her seat. "Saved the world yet?"

"Almost." I stood and walked over, stopping by the wall where I couldn't see her screens.

"You're allowed to look at my work," she laughed. "Nobody from the government is going to leap out and drag you away for seeing something you shouldn't have here."

The innocent, facetious statement made my heart trip. "No? Phew." I rested my hands on her shoulders. The website layout reminded me of a rainforest, earthy and soothing, and I let it calm me. "You drew...made all of these graphics?"

"Mhmm. All my sites are full-service. Every bit of graphical design on them is made by me."

"Wow, that's incredible. Do you like art?" It was a dumb question, but my brain was apparently incapable of creating engaging inquiries.

She smiled patiently up at me. "I do. Drawing is my jam. I started off with 'pure' art in college then moved into graphic design."

"Will you draw me something someday?"

"Sure. I'll draw you something right now." Sophia reached for the plain lined notepad to her right, and quickly sketched out something while I kneaded the tops of her shoulders. She ripped the page from the pad and held it back to me, smiling like a kindergartener handing a parent their first drawing.

I held it up proudly. She'd drawn a stick figure with a cape streaming out behind her, one hand on her hip and the other balancing the Earth like a basketball. "Wow. It's beautiful," I said earnestly. "I can see why you went into art."

"Thanks," Sophia said, fluttering her eyelashes. "It's you, Super Lexie."

"I gathered that from the SUPER LEXIE you wrote underneath it." Cupping her face gently in my palm, I leaned down and kissed her, slow and deep. Staying close, I asked, "Need anything while I'm up?"

She shook her head, smiling lazily and maybe a little wine-ily. Her gorgeous, smiling mouth was too tempting to resist, so I kissed her again.

"We both have work to do," she whispered when we broke for air.

"We do…" I agreed. And she made doing that work a little easier. Those all-too-brief moments of connection buoyed me enough to make another dive deep into human depravity. I set the drawing on the table where I could see it with the slightest turn of my head. "Super Lexie," I whispered to myself as I opened both laptops.

Before I delved into the video and audio files again, I made sure the headphones were snug in my ears. I couldn't let Sophia hear anything, even just an accidental snippet.

I didn't want to listen again.

I didn't want to look again.

But I did. I listened to the audio file and sat through that awful footage twice, suppressing the nausea that grew stronger with every minute I endured of watching innocent civilians struggling for the last minutes of their lives. Though the video was just over ten minutes long, it was so intense, so awful that it felt like watching a full-length horror film. And it was made worse by the warm hotel room lighting which added an almost disorienting feeling to the video. I remembered how I'd stupidly hoped, on that ordinary morning at the end of last week, that it would get easier with subsequent viewings. I was wrong. So wrong.

My job would be so much easier if I could somehow desensitize myself to things like this. But then…maybe I wouldn't care as much as I did. And caring about the people behind these events got results. I had a special mental compartment for horrors, but it wasn't airtight. Some of my emotion always managed to mix in. But this wasn't just about following Halcyon's directive now. I also had to follow my personal need to get to the bottom of this, to have someone held accountable, no matter the cost. To ensure this would never happen again. Stupid personal integrity.

Sophia got up to refill her wineglass, deliberately turning away each time she passed into and out of the kitchen space, even though my screens were facing the closed curtains. But I still minimized what I had on my screen before she came close. National security issues aside, this footage was not something I wanted her seeing accidentally. She didn't deserve these images seared into her consciousness.

I continued fleshing out the report I'd started on Friday, filling in gaps, expanding on things I already knew. My dialect ear was pretty good, and I was utterly certain that the American *was* American. Not Canadian. Not someone putting on an American accent.

After another two viewings of the murder…massacre…I didn't even know what to call it, I still hadn't found anything new. It was time to get some distance from it. I stepped away from the table and did a quick calisthenics workout to loosen my body, with an attentive audience of one. As I groaned into a stretch, I mumbled, "God, I want a cup of tea." I'd tossed the tea bags of doom in the trash at our previous hotel. I respected myself too much to drink that swill.

"Poor baby," Sophia sympathized. "How long do you think we'll be here?"

I popped up to my knees. "I'm not sure. A few days at least, if we're discreet. Probably gone in a week." I hoped.

"Okay. Can I please have one of your no-name prepaid Visa cards? I need to order something online. I won't use my name, or yours. And I can Venmo you to cover it."

She was learning. "Sure," I agreed. "And don't worry about it." Whatever would help keep her happy. I found her a card that would cover just about anything she wanted to purchase. "As long as you're not buying a yacht to sail around the cays, it's fine."

"Nah, just a Jet Ski."

"Cool. Make it a dual-seater."

She gave me a double thumbs-up, then turned back to her laptop.

I plonked down at the table and started the video again, blanking my mind as I looked for clues. I needed a smoking gun. All we had was the US Army uniform. The most logical answer was usually the correct one and logic dictated that the man inside this uniform was the American. I moved slowly through video frames until those seconds of camo pattern came into view. The quality of the video wasn't great, distorted by truck headlights and handheld spotlights, and moving frame by frame meant I lost a lot of the already-poor clarity.

Come on, give me something, anything. Rank patch, combat patches, branch patch. A name would be like hitting the jackpot but that was perhaps a little too much to ask. After a few minutes of squinting, I had a Bingo! moment. It was a torso, and right in the middle of the chest was a familiar rank insignia. Or at least, I thought it was. Hard to tell with the blur, but I'd put a few dollars on it being the oak-leaf insignia of a lieutenant colonel. *Colonel.*

Who are you, you bastard? Scrubbing back and forth through a piece of video that was barely seconds long I could *just* make out some color on the left side of his chest—combat patches—and that there was *something* in the space on the right side of his chest where a military name patch belonged. Either a very short name, or… no, the angle meant it was the end of the name. I took my reading glasses off, put them back on, leaned closer to the screen, held it away. But I still couldn't make it out, except for the fact it wasn't many letters.

Why would he leave his rank insignia, combat patches and name badge on his official US Army uniform while engaging in a war crime? Arrogance was my number one guess. An arrogant Army officer. Well, that should be easy to find…

There was no way I could naked-eye this. Time for some AI enhancement. I loaded the video into the graphics software and skimmed the manual to find the idiot's guide to enhancing blurry frames. Having good software meant I was able to get slower framerates and slower framerates told me my vision wasn't as bad as it often felt like, and it was indeed a US Army uniform, in the latest camo pattern which was phased in a few years ago. I mentally placed a dotted line through "discharged or got uniform from surplus store" on my list. I mean it *was* possible, and I rarely ruled anything out, but it felt less likely than being active duty. Gross. I isolated some stills of the torso, and began playing around with them.

Being a graphics-manipulation novice meant everything took forever as I tried and then failed and then undid and redid each step to try a different thing. The worst part was that there was a graphic designer sitting across the room who could probably do what I was trying to in under five minutes. But I could never ask for her help. The greatest tease—a graphic designer and novice detective enthusiast was right here, and I couldn't utilize her.

Sharpen, brighten, brighten, no that's too bright, go back, contrast, and...is that...? I pulled my glasses off and rubbed my eyes then slipped the frames back on again. Holy shit. Actual letters! I'd done it! Kind of. It looked like shit and probably needed another twenty steps to make it clear enough to be used as actual evidence but that wasn't my job. I had my letters, and the last three letters of the American's last name were...

Drum roll, please. I drummed my hands on the sides of my thighs because I was so tired and delirious that I needed to pat myself on the back. Or pat myself on my fake drum roll drum thighs. Whatever. Sophia looked over at me from her position on the couch. When had she moved to the couch? Fuck. It was after midnight. "Are you all right?" she asked.

"I am more than all right. T. E. R, Sophia, my darling."

She grinned. "That means absolutely nothing to me."

"Even better." Because I really shouldn't have even said that. Ah, stress.

I turned back to the enhanced picture. TER. Well that narrowed it down to about forty bajillion people. Okay. Fine. There weren't that many people in the US Army. Ten bajillion. "TER," I whispered to myself.

TER was for ter-morrow. I knew myself well enough to know when I'd reached my functional limit. I was physically and emotionally drained, and anything I did now wouldn't be good work.

"You have the most adorable concentration face," Sophia observed once I pulled my earbuds out. I'd been done with the audio for a while and had been so engrossed with my image enhancement that I'd sat with soundless earbuds in my ears for hours without realizing. So smooth. Form an orderly line, ladies.

I curled the cord around my fingers. "Yeah? What's it look like?"

"Like you're confused and frustrated and amused and triumphant all in one."

"Wow, that sounds really bizarre." I tried to make all the faces then, laughing, gave up.

Sophia's answering laugh was quick and sharp, full of mirth. "When you do it like that, yeah it is."

I shut down then closed the laptops, took off my glasses, stretched, squeaked, and stood. "You mind some company while I decompress before bed? I'm done for the night, approaching migraine territory."

She patted the couch beside her. "Only if you don't make me change the channel."

"What're you watching?"

"*Top Chef* rerun."

Grinning, I stepped back to the table. "On second thought, giving myself a migraine seems like the better option."

She threw a couch cushion at me and I stretched to catch it. Tucking it against my chest I carried it to the couch with me and snuggled up to her, hugging the cushion to myself. Sophia slung an arm around me, pulling me even closer to her. She stroked my hair gently, kissed my forehead. "Saved the world yet, Not-Spy?"

"Not yet," I murmured, closing my eyes. "Maybe tomorrow."

Sophia kept stroking my hair, and when the ads started, she murmured, "I keep meaning to thank you, but it feels a little weird."

My eyebrows shot up at the gratitude non sequitur. "Thank me for what? How's that weird?"

"I want to thank you inviting me on this trip. For rescuing me… from myself. Being around you makes me feel more like *me* than I have in years."

I sat up, shuffling to face her. "What do you mean? How have you not felt like yourself?"

Sophia exhaled a breath, but it was a few long moments before she spoke, and when she did it was like she'd had a revelation. "I got so stuck, Lexie. Stuck in my routine, stuck in my life and my work, in making my business something that would last, something I was proud of. I didn't recognize myself. In my twenties I used to be…eeurgh, I hate this phrase, so 'carefree,' traveling as much as I could, doing adventurous stuff on a whim. And then it was like… four years ago, I just sat down and never got up again."

"What changed?" I quietly asked. "From carefree Sophia to sit-down Sophia?"

"I'm not really sure, just a snowball of things I guess. Aside from the new business? There were a couple of bad relationships, and my dad got sick and I moved back with my parents for six months because I'm the only one of my siblings without a family or a job in a fixed location." She shrugged. "And while I was living with them, all but a few of my friendships faded away. Everything just felt too hard and overwhelming and I got anxious about creating new friendships, so I didn't. You know, you were the first person I had the guts to try to connect with on that dating app and I was so nervous about meeting you."

"You were my first swipe, and I was nervous too," I admitted. More than nervous, given my own lack of outside-of-work human interaction.

"You didn't seem it. You were confident and controlled, but without being pushy."

I put on my best showbiz-whiz voice. "All for show, bay-bee." When she laughed, I kissed her. "And I get it. Sometimes I feel exactly the same way. It's so easy to get stuck, wondering if you can get yourself out of your life rut or if someone will come along and pull you out."

Her eyes softened. "So you needed a hand too?"

"I did." I cupped her face. "And you know, I think it's possible that maybe you'll end up rescuing me too."

CHAPTER THIRTEEN

Averting a disas-TER

I woke up startled and gasping from a nightmarish dream about carrying a faceless someone away from a monstrous tsunami. The person in my arms, clutched tight against my chest, was important. I didn't know who it was, I just *knew* I had to keep them safe. But no matter how fast I ran, the wall of water kept inching closer and closer until it pooled around my legs, trying to pull me under.

Not hard to figure out where that dream came from, right, Subconscious?

Sophia stirred when I untangled my body from hers. A morning-clumsy hand fumbled over my hip. "You okay?" she mumbled. "You're all sweaty."

"Just running marathons in my sleep, as my dad used to say." I sat up on the edge of the bed, twisting to look back at Sophia. The soft morning light washed over her, highlighting the reddish tints in her dark hair, the smoothness of her skin, the sleepy smile. The image of her lying in rumpled sheets was one I wanted to imprint into my memory. Gorgeous. Desire twisted my insides. If I was a regular person, and we were a regular couple, or even a couple, then I would have slipped back under the sheets and shown her that desire. Instead, I stuffed it down, and left her lying there. Intimacy was another delay I couldn't afford when there was work to do.

I tried to keep the morning as normal as I could. Normal for us... My regular yoga and workout, a "relaxing" walk hand-in-hand along the beach in the fresh morning air, a quick swim—Sophia in a bikini was a wonderous thing—then breakfast at a hipster café. I thought we'd been found, but it turned out to be a guy who couldn't find his girlfriend and once he did, they left in a cloud of young love.

Love. A silly wistful want that kept bobbing to the surface, driving home how nice it would be if this were real, you know, without me carrying a backpack full of laptops and hard drives around and constantly worrying that I'd been found, and that this might be my last moment of freedom, that I'd failed in the most basic task I'd been assigned by Halcyon. I longed for the realness where I could balance my work and a girlfriend, where I wasn't lying to her almost every minute. I wasn't lying outright to her face, but lies of omission were still lies.

I'd been steeling myself for a solid dose of persuasion to extract Sophia from the café, but once she'd finished her breakfast, she gulped down the last of her second coffee and reached across to take my hand. "Time to start our workday grind?"

Grind wasn't far from the truth. Sophia remained engrossed in her work, still dancing in her chair, this time with a set of chunky headphones on her head. And I...I struggled. An hour in and I was already so frustrated that I felt like tossing the laptops out the window. No Oolong makes Lexie grumpy-grumpy. At least we'd stocked up on Combos, so I had one of my two necessary problem-solving food items.

To make everything that much more frustrating, I couldn't get the Army personnel last name search function to work for more than one criteria, no matter how I changed my search terms or swore at the program. So, I could either isolate all lieutenant colonels in the Army but then manually check for my magic three letters, or I could filter by the last name of every person in the Army of all ranks whose last names included TER somewhere in them—not necessarily even at the end, where my TER was—and see which were Lt. Cols. And I had no time to import all these names manually into another low-tech but guaranteed-to-give-me-what-I-needed spreadsheet where I could search by multiple criteria, like both rank and the string of letters.

I mulled it over for a few seconds before choosing the better of two annoying options: sorting through the Lt. Cols. Luckily, narrowing it to one rank meant I only had a pool of about nine thousand to wade through. Easy.

Four hours after I'd first put butt to chair I'd finally wrangled the data, had a shortlist of lieutenant colonels, and was slowly scrolling through the alphabetical list to find my TER unicorn. So far I had fourteen possible unicorns on my short-shortlist, and was only about halfway through the B last names. It was slow, tedious work with a solid margin for me simply missing names. So I'd have to make at least two passes. Joy.

A knock at the door startled me, and I was even more startled when I realized Sophia had ordered us lunch. After an effusive thank-you, I settled back in front of the screens and ate vegetarian pho with one hand while scrolling through the names with my other. I was up to last names beginning with F. Progress... Hopefully, I'd have double-passed through the whole alphabet by tomorrow lunchtime and could move onto the next phase—staring at the short-shortlist and hoping something magically popped out at me.

At the moment, magic felt like my best bet. But until a spellcaster turned up, I just had to keep scrolling, keep staring at names, keep making my short-shortlist of Lt. Col. -TERs. God this was tedious. If it didn't amount to something, I might just throw my hands up and tell Lennon I was done. I shook myself out. If I was trying to unravel this mystery under my usual working conditions, I'd still have this same exact intelligence to work with, and I'd be expected to figure it out, and what it might mean for our interests both here and abroad. I shut down my grumbly internal monologue about all the resources I didn't have access to, and got back to it.

The ringing hotel phone almost made me leap clear out of my seat again, and when I checked the time, I was surprised yet unsurprised to see it was almost three thirty p.m. Time flies when you're not having fun. Sophia was already reaching for the handset. And I was mentally throwing all our things into bags and getting the fuck out of there. Great. I really liked this room. And now we had to leave. "We're not expecting a call, are we?" I asked, trying to keep the rush of panic from my voice.

"It's the front desk. The light labeled 'Front Desk' is flashing," Sophia explained patiently. "So, I'm going to answer it."

"Okay, if you're sure," I said, trying not to sound like I thought it wasn't a great idea. Short of tying her to the bed—which was appealing for another reason—I couldn't stop her doing what she wanted to. I could only hint that it made me uncomfortable, and the rest was up to her. She knew the stakes. Kind of.

Sophia snatched up the handset and after a quick greeting, nodded, and said, "Mhmm. Great. Thanks so much. I'll be right down." She popped up from the desk and I stood to meet her in the middle of the room. Resting a hand on my shoulder, she stretched up and kissed me. "I just have to duck down to the front desk." At my dubious look, she assured me, "The package I ordered yesterday, Lexie. Remember? It'll be fine and I'll be right back. I'll be careful."

"Right, gotcha," I agreed with as much calm as I could muster.

I didn't pace, but I sure felt like it. Instead, I settled for anxious couch sitting, thinking through all the scenarios—Sophia being spotted, Sophia being grabbed to force me out, Sophia running. I knew how long it took to get to the front desk and back, taking both the elevator and the stairs, and if she wasn't back in seven minutes, I was going to go charging after her. She came back up in under five minutes, smiling like she'd just found the meaning of life. I jumped up from the couch, suppressing my urge to ask if everything was all right. Of course it was. She was there, unharmed, and had the aforementioned package.

"That's not a Jet Ski," I said once she'd secured the door.

"You don't know that. It might be a toy Jet Ski..." She handed me the box, addressed to Mary B. Goode, care of our hotel and room number. And when I stared at it, not quite sure what to do with a package not addressed to me, she laughed and told me to, "Go on. Open it. It's not anthrax."

"What if I *wanted* anthrax?"

"Then you're shit out of luck."

After digging into the box like a kid at Christmas, I had to take a moment to compose myself when I realized what was inside. Two tins of high-quality Oolong tea, along with an adorable sloth infuser to hang over the edge of the handmade, hand-painted Sasquatch mug. I'd been a terrible traveling companion, even if I set aside all the Halcyon stuff, and she'd gone out of her way to make my life better. She was like Mother Teresa and Mary Poppins rolled into one beautiful package. And I couldn't say a goddamned thing about her gift because I was so gobsmacked by the fact she'd bought me something, just randomly, just because, just to make my life better.

"Shit, is it the wrong one?" Sophia mumbled, grabbing one of the tins from my hand, turning it over to read the label.

"No, it's exactly the right one. It's all perfect." I blinked hard, suddenly overwhelmed with a mix of emotions. Gratitude mostly, with a sprinkling of something deeper, something I was afraid to name. "I can't believe you got me these. Well, I can, because you're the most thoughtful person on the planet. You really didn't have to do this, but thank you, I'm so glad you did. It didn't even occur to me to get something delivered here with a fake name and billing address."

Sophia shrugged, but she was obviously pleased. "You're welcome. I'm so glad you like it."

"You may have saved my life." In more ways than one.

Endless TER and cups of excellent tea kept me occupied until Sophia's voice broke into my concentration. "Are you ready to think about dinner?" She'd abandoned her work sometime in the past few hours and moved to relax on the couch with the book, and I hadn't even noticed it.

I went through my now-familiar refrain of "I'm a terrible person but hey, I'm trying to avert a maybe world war, and I'm genuinely sorry" self-flagellation. Dinner hadn't even registered on my radar, but now she'd mentioned it, I realized I was starting to approach the wrong side of hungry. "What time is it?"

"Six thirty."

No wonder I felt like a pretzel. "Mhmm. Sounds good." I kept scrolling. Ah, a TER! I moved him to the short-shortlist. "What are you thinking? We should go out, right? We've been inside all day. What about the hotel restaurant?" I rambled as I scrolled, went too far, overshot my place and had to scroll back.

"Sure."

"Great. Let me...just...finish this...thing," I said slowly as I made my way through another page.

"Lexie?"

"Yeah?" I asked, without taking my focus from the screen. When there was nothing more, I looked up, turning my body fully toward her.

I could see the battle playing out on her face, and braced myself. She was calm, but matter-of-fact as she stated, "I don't want to tell you how to live your life, but this is not a sustainable way to exist. Working constantly, no breaks, is not good for anyone. If you work yourself to burnout then you won't be able to do anything at all, and what'll happen then?"

"Adrenaline's a wonderful thing," I said around a grin.

She rolled her eyes. "Yeah, until it's not."

"Hah," I coughed out. "You know, I've had that exact thought before."

"Lexie?" she said again.

"Mmm?"

"Come here, please," she said quietly. That quiet tone was as loud as a shout.

I closed both laptops, unfurled my cramped body, and joined her on the couch. Facing her, I dragged stiff legs up underneath myself. "I'm closer to saving the world," I said in a lame attempt to lighten the mood. Making a weak cheerleading motion, I added, "Super Lexie, yay."

"I'm glad." Sophia ran her hands up and down my thighs. Her eye contact was unwavering, but completely without aggression. "When you told me about this evaluation, you asked me to trust you. And I did. I do." She paused, inhaled. "But *this?* The way you're so hyperfocused to the detriment of just...living normally is starting to freak me out. And I don't know you well enough to know if you're just absorbed in what you're doing, or if this is how you work, or if it's something deeper. But either way, it just doesn't feel nice. It's worrying me."

"I'm sorry. I don't mean to worry you. And I'm sorry this is taking my entire focus." I pulled off my glasses and leaned over to set them on the coffee table. "I just...thought I'd have made more progress by now. That's all. I'm starting to feel like I'm running out of time. I've been thinking about this stuff for days and all I have is a bunch of absolute facts that I can't put into a logical picture. And I have more facts missing than I have facts in my possession, and no way to get those missing facts." I rubbed my eyes, pressing my fingers hard against them in the hope it might ease the grittiness.

"That must be frustrating."

"It is. And normally I wouldn't have such a time crunch, I'd be able to prioritize it and work through it steadily and logically, but now…" I frowned, trying to think of a nonspecific way to describe what I was up against. "Imagine you've got a jigsaw puzzle that you know is a picture of a dog, cat, and fish. But there's no box or picture to go by and like, the background is one uniform color. All you know is somewhere, somehow, these three animals are going to make a jigsaw puzzle picture. So you've got some of the border done, you've managed to do enough of the puzzle so you've got three complete animals. But no matter how hard you try, you can't work out how the completed animals go together in the jigsaw puzzle. That's what I'm working with."

Smiling, she made a conciliatory gesture. "Okay, that's a solid analogy. You're off the hook." Sophia brought her thumb and forefinger close together. "Just a little."

Despite my fatigue, I smiled. "Sometimes I'm good at explaining things. I just need to work it out, figure out how to fit the picture together. Or I need someone to walk past the table, see the puzzle and just say 'You idiot, it goes like this.'" I stretched my arms above my head, felt the muscles on either side of my spine rejoice.

She raised her eyebrows. "Is it really the end of the world if you don't solve this problem?"

I suppressed my laugh. It could well be. "It might be. If I don't find these connections, then I've failed. And if I fail this, what else might I fail? People's lives depend on me succeeding."

"I can't imagine how hard you must work if this is what you're like for just a training thing." Sophia thumbed the edge of my mouth, stroked down to my chin. "I have a feeling you're incredibly good at your job, and I have every confidence that you're going to figure out what you need to. I'm sure it'll be okay."

I didn't have the heart or energy to tell her that it probably wouldn't be okay. Carefully, I drew her closer and wrapped my arms around her waist, dropping my face to her shoulder. Her shirt smelled of fabric conditioner and I breathed it in, felt comfort suffuse me. "I hope so. Otherwise all this has been for nothing."

Sophia's thoughtful fingers massaged my neck. "I don't think all of it has been."

"No, you're right. Spending time with you has definitely been something. Something great." I pulled back and exhaled a long sigh. "I'm just sorry this hasn't been the fun-filled sightseeing adventure I said it'd be."

Sophia smiled gently. "Yeah, but if you'd told me what it really was, I probably wouldn't have come so readily. But I'm glad you did tell me. Glad you asked me to come with you." Her voice dropped, and I heard the truth in the words when she said, "I'm enjoying spending time with you."

"Me too." I burrowed down into her lap with my arms still around her waist, wanting to pretend I was safe at home with her for a minute. "I…just don't know how to not be like this while I'm here, in these circumstances. And I know it's not who you signed up to spend time with, but I— Can you hold on to the woman you first met? The kind of normal one instead of this kind of deranged workaholic?"

"I don't need to. This is just a facet of you, one I still like, one that sits alongside all the other facets that caught my attention when we first met." Laughing softly, she added, "But, FYI? I probably won't come along with you for your next evaluation thing."

The fact she was thinking about the next "evaluation" gave me a spark of hope. I sat up, feigning a nonchalant shrug. "I've already used hot-woman-as-cover so they'll be on to me for that one next time."

Sophia bent forward, took my face gently in her hands, and kissed me. "I'm sure that even without me, you'll pass your next evaluation with top marks, just like you're going to pass this one, and I'm going to gloat about how clever my girlfriend is."

Girlfriend.

Once we'd come back from dinner, I'd fallen asleep watching mindless television and chatting with her about nothing that I could remember now that it was two a.m., and I was in the bathroom working. I couldn't remember the conversation, not because I hadn't been engaged, or because it had been boring or anything like that—I couldn't remember because it was so mundane, so normal and easy that my brain had let it float blissfully in and out as I'd relaxed against her, with *girlfriend* wafting around my head. She hadn't snatched that word back from where it stood between us, hadn't explained that it was something she could see for us later. She'd just let it hang in the air as a possibility. And I grabbed it, holding it close as a *maybe*.

Maybe.

The unimaginative same-same layout of hotel bathrooms made for a decent makeshift office. But I was not a nocturnal person by a long shot and was battling to stay awake, unaided by these past few days of stress and not much sleep which had made me dull and honestly, a bit dumb. I heard the footsteps a few seconds before the bathroom door opened and couldn't register what was happening until it was too late. Well, if this had been a genuine intruder instead of the woman I was sleeping with, I'd have been dead. And she probably would have been too. Fuck. Add "situational awareness gone to shit" along with "dumb."

Sophia froze when she saw me. "What are you doing?"

I said the first stupid thing that came to mind which was of course, stupid. "Watching porn?"

"Ouch. My ego." Eyeing the laptop, she asked, "You always take notes while you're watching porn?"

"Mhmm. I'm very studious. Why do you think I'm so good at orgasm bestowment?"

"Funny." Sophia's eyes strayed to the sink. "Is that a gun?"

My sleep-deprived and stressed brain went again to idiocy and I almost said "No of course not," despite the fact it was a very obvious handgun resting on the sink beside me. Thankfully I found some lucidity to answer, "It is."

"Why do you have a gun?" It was asked quietly, almost as if she didn't really want to know the answer.

"Because I'm technically working. And to protect us should the situation arise. You never know when you might go through a bad part of an unfamiliar town." It might have sounded more convincing if I hadn't yawned halfway through. And let's not forget moments earlier when she'd come into the bathroom without me realizing until she was two feet in front of me.

She clearly didn't quite believe me on the "protect us," and I realized immediately that I'd overplayed my hand. Just a game, Sophia, there's no danger, but yeah, I've got a gun to protect us. Her fingertips came to rest against her thighs. "Have you been doing this every night?"

"No. Just some nights."

"Why? Is there an award for most hours worked? For putting yourself in a coma by working nonstop?"

I tried to smile, but my facial muscles felt paralyzed. "I'm really close to my next stage and I couldn't stop thinking about it. And I didn't want to wake you up by working out there while you're sleeping." I frowned as my brain finally caught up that she was there in the early-morning hours, looking adorable and sleep-mussed. "Why aren't you sleeping?"

"I need to pee."

"Ah." I slapped the laptop closed, gathered my things, and awkwardly removed myself from my office chair a.k.a., the toilet. As an afterthought, I took the gun too and slipped from the bathroom to give her some privacy.

Sophia came out a few minutes later. "Have you had that the whole time?" She crossed to where I'd settled on the end of the bed. Bed…bed…

"Yes. Actually, I have two. Mine, and another one I took from the guy who was following us on the burger day. Now that I think about it, it really is an excessive amount of handguns. I should really get rid of one of them." Why had I just rambled that to her? Fatigue, you suck. "Mine is legally owned and registered, if that's what you're worried about."

"That's not it. I'm just curious as to why you have it."

I was sure I'd told her why. "I'm working, remember?"

"Right," she said slowly. Her face held the same expression as before, like she'd caught a hint of something that didn't feel right.

"Do guns bother you?"

Her eyebrows scrunched together briefly before her face smoothed to neutrality. "When used by appropriate people in the appropriate manner, no."

"Okay then." I gestured to myself. "I am an appropriate person with an appropriate manner. Anything else you want to talk about?"

She shook her head. And I kept thinking about the hole I'd inadvertently started digging for myself.

Sophia nudged me gently. "Lexie?"

"Mm?"

She brushed her thumb over my cheek. "You must be really tired. I asked you a question."

"Little bit. Just thinking." I smiled. "And sorry, what was the question?"

"Are you going to come to bed, or do you have a few more hours of hiding in the bathroom to do?"

I gave her my best charming smile, though at this hour and with my level of fatigue it felt more like wobbly grimacing. "I'm not hiding."

She made a point of looking at the digital clock on one of the bedside tables. 2:47 a.m. "Good, then you won't mind staying at the table like a normal person. You won't keep me awake." Sophia kissed me then gave me a small shove. "Go, now, or I'm going to haul you under the covers to snuggle."

"Yes, ma'am." I bent down to kiss her again, letting myself linger. "I'll try not to be too long."

I lied, but not on purpose. Two hours later, I was still hunched over the laptop as I sorted through endless lines of names, trying to filter out my TER unicorns. As I passed V into W—Hello three Lt. Cols. Walter—I could see the end in sight.

As I slowly rolled through X, Y, and finally Z, I should have done a victory dance at completing this stage of my investigation. But instead, I sat in the darkness, staring at the glow of the laptop screen as I tried to shake the feeling of being watched, even though I knew that thought was ridiculous. Nobody was watching me. Not in person. Not through cyberspace. But I still couldn't shake the paranoia that maybe I was being tested somehow. By whom and for what reason, I didn't know. You don't know because thinking this is a test is delusional, Lexie. Nobody would go to these lengths to test me. Too much work and stress and not enough sleep makes Lexie paranoid.

Occam's Razor. The simplest answers are usually the right ones. And the answer was that I knew something incriminating that someone or someones with a lot to lose wanted to remain secret. Keeping dirty secrets was the very thread that made up the fabric of the corrupt, and to them I was nothing more than an obstacle. Not willingly. I was just following orders. All I wanted was to do my job and tell the truth—it was up to others what they did with that truth.

Occam's Razor.

The answer to the question of "What the hell happened in Kunduz Province ten days ago?" was going to be the simplest one. And I was going to find it.

CHAPTER FOURTEEN

An absolute truth

I took a few seconds to study the image in the steamed-up bathroom mirror. It was the first time I'd looked at myself beyond a cursory glance while brushing my teeth since I'd left my apartment in the middle of the night, and the reflected image wasn't surprising. I looked wan and really *really* tired. I wiped the glass with the side of my hand. Yep, still wan and tired. Not to mention the fact that with my hair down and damp, it was obvious I'd done a piss-poor job of cutting it myself. I'd totally forgotten Bink's admonishment about my hair—didn't they say something like "it looks like complete shit"? I wrapped myself in a towel, finger combing my hair as I left the bathroom.

Sophia glanced up from her borrowed book when I stopped in front of her. Her eyebrows went slowly north. "May I help you, naked woman?"

"You may." I tugged a strand of hair by my temple. "So...when you mentioned my haircut and that it looked great, you were just being polite, right?"

"What? No! It does. Shorter hair really suits you."

Laughing, I pulled pieces of hair on either side of my neck down to accentuate the disparity. "Do you need to borrow my reading glasses? I'm so lopsided I look like a Picasso."

"I thought it was like an edgy asymmetrical type thing."

"Yeah, not so much. It's a screw-up, is what it is. How do you feel about tidying it up? Clearly my haircutting skills have faded over the years."

She bookmarked her spot and tossed the book onto the couch. "You cut it yourself?"

I tried to remember what I'd said when she'd commented on it on Saturday morning. No mention of a hairdresser that I could recall. Lying or backpedaling was the fastest way to trip myself and arouse suspicion, so I nodded. "I sure did. No salons were open when I had my 'I must change my hair' moment of desperation. Judging by this, I probably should have waited until the next morning and a professional."

The best description for her expression would be alarmed, and her voice squeaked adorably when she said, "I've never cut anyone's hair before. I'm sure there's a salon around here that could fix it. Let's do that."

Being stuck in the hairdresser's chair without the option of being able to leave immediately was not my idea of a good idea. "I'm sure you can handle it, just a little snip here and there."

"What if I really fuck it up?"

I winked, and leaned down and kissed her. "Then I'll shave it." I already knew I looked fine with a shaved head. It was just hair. It grew back.

Sophia pushed herself up from the couch. "Sounds hot. Okay, I'll do it. Where?"

"Bathroom." I fetched the nail scissors from my bag and passed them to her. "Easier to clean up the mess."

She eyed me, her mouth forming slowly into a mischievous smile that sent a pleasant zing down my spine. "Good. Because I like making a mess."

Sophia watched a quick technique video on YouTube, and deemed herself ready to hack and slash. I sat on the edge of the bath and she stood behind me, in the tub where snipped hair would be safely contained. Sophia pulled my hair back, exposing my neck.

She crouched down until I felt her breath against my neck and when I shuddered, she kissed just below my ear then kept kissing her way down my neck until she reached my collarbone. "So," she murmured. "Where am I cutting?"

I swallowed, unable to think of anything except how much I wanted her to keep kissing my neck. "My hair?"

Sophia laughed, low and amused. "Yes, we've already established that." A tiny grazing nip of teeth on my shoulder. "But where exactly?"

"If you want me to be able to articulate, then you need to stop doing that."

But she didn't. Sophia's fingers kept lightly tickling up and down my neck as she pulled the ends of my hair down. I'd cut it to about an inch above my shoulders—on one side at least—and as she checked the length, her thumbs gently massaged the tops of my shoulders, the base of my neck. The movement only served to further fritz my brain on giving her an answer.

Sophia's fingers drew a line across the side of my neck. "How about here? I'll only need to take a little bit off the left side." She traced my jaw with the lightest touch.

I could barely think, let alone speak, and managed a "Mhmm."

Sophia moved to my left side, her thigh pressed to my arm. "Tilt your head so I can see better." When I moved my head to the right she ran her fingertip over my ear before combing my hair, then pulling it up and away from my neck diagonally. With careful snips she cut my hair, making me straighten my head constantly so she could check the length. The whole time she was working on my hair her fingertips played over the skin on my neck.

"What do you think?" she asked after ten minutes of trimming.

I stood and looked in the mirror. "I think you missed your calling. It seems very professional."

She laughed. "Yay, YouTube." Sophia used a dampened edge of a bath towel to wipe the cut hair from my neck with slow, gentle strokes. The sensation had my skin goose-pimpling, my nipples tightening. If she was trying to wind me up, she was doing a good job of it.

"Who knew getting my hair cut was such great foreplay?" I found her eyes in the mirror. "To be fair, my regular hairdresser isn't as hot as you, nor does she touch me quite as much."

"No? Probably a good thing. But I couldn't help myself." She pressed herself to my back, murmuring against my ear, "You're still very naked underneath that towel."

"Yes I am. I also don't have any way to pay you for the cut."

Sophia reached around to pull the end of the towel free from where I'd tucked it into my cleavage. "I can think of something."

I took her hands and placed them on my breasts, using her fingers to stroke my hardening nipples. "I think you should show me exactly what you mean."

And she did. As we caught our breath, Sophia's light touch traced the long surgical scar on my torso. She spider-walked her fingers across my belly until she'd touched each of the smaller scars, before resuming the slow caress of the larger scar. My skin was still hyperresponsive from her earlier attention, and the scar tissue sensitive compared with the surrounding skin. The twin sensitivities had me shuddering at the sensation. Sophia pulled the sheet up over us, then shifted on the bed so she lay on her side, facing me. "Will you tell me about this?"

"I thought I already did."

She smiled at me like a parent trying to coax a reluctant child. "You did, just the barest outline. It looks horrible and I hate that whatever it was happened to you." She sat up, gripping my hip. "If you don't want to, or can't, talk about it, then that's fine. But I'd like to know. I'd like to try to understand what you do, how you do it. I want to know these things about you."

"I don't mind talking about it, but it's not pleasant, Sophia." And she *was* pleasant. She was sweet and gentle and kind, and she deserved to be protected from the ugly things that happened while ordinary people slept, or went to work, or cooked dinner, or made love. And the ugly things we did to make sure that ordinary people *could* sleep or work or cook or make love.

Sophia's eyes softened into understanding. "Life isn't always pleasant. And if you and I are going to keep seeing each other after this little vacation, which I hope we are, then we'll have to accept the not-pleasant as well as the pleasant. That's what a relationship is about, right?"

"I hope we'll keep seeing each other," I said quietly. *Hope.* I'd had that word in my head so many times in this past week, but the frequency of it hadn't made me feel any more hopeful. Mostly, I just felt sad.

"Me too…" She settled back against the pillows, propping her head in her hand. Her face was kind, almost neutral, and I knew she'd sit patiently for as long as it took me to tell her this awful story.

I scratched my eyebrow to appease the nerve which had begun twitching. "Uhhh, basically, I was meeting with a contact and it went bad. The meet was in a semi-crowded place which I'd been watching for the hour prior, but I'd seen nothing, nobody. It was secure. But he was followed, and I missed it because I wasn't paying attention. I was…thinking about a woman I'd been sleeping with, upset because I'd had to end it."

I had to end it because I was about to have Elaheh's brother collected and questioned for his involvement in a local terrorist cell and I couldn't afford the distraction of her. I hadn't set out to talent-spot Elaheh. She was simply a woman I'd found attractive, courted, and we'd begun a secret dance, a—to sound old-fashioned—dalliance. But my relationship with her had led organically to information about her brother's role in the cell, and I'd had to act. I'd wanted desperately to help her somehow, but there was no way. So I'd left her, in every way imaginable.

I sat up, pulling my knees to my chest. "It was the rookiest of errors. I lost concentration for just a minute. But that's all it takes. And my partner was on the other side of the market, nothing he could do. My contact had assured me repeatedly that he knew what he was doing, but he was new and sloppy, so they knew who I was and that he was feeding me, and therefore American intelligence agencies, information."

"What was it like?" Sophia asked in a tentative whisper.

"Fast. Confusing. Noisy market, beat-up van, Kalashnikov rifles, shouting, hoods over our heads, shoved into a dark dank room."

"Did they talk to you at all? Feed you?" Her face remained impassive, leaving her voice to carry the weight of her emotion.

"Talk, yes. Food, no. They wanted to know who I was, and nothing I said convinced them that no person of theirs being held in US custody would be swapped for me. Because I was nobody, I was just a woman who'd come to buy a scarf at the market. I said it over and over and over again. Just buying a scarf, just buying a scarf, just…buying a scarf. I must have said it a hundred times or more, and every time I said it, they slapped me. But I kept saying it."

Just buying a scarf…

"Uh, there were two main guys and after about an hour they left, and a younger guy I hadn't seen before came in." Elaheh's brother. I still recalled the sick shiver that'd overcome me the first time I'd seen him. He looked younger in person than in his photos, photos I'd pored over for hours. A kid doing adult things. "He just stood there, staring at me like he could kill me with his gaze. I'd seen that look before, but never aimed at me. He spat on me. Kicked me to the ground. And I thought…I thought he'd rape me. But he laughed, like he'd realized that thought had crossed my mind. Told me, in his cracked English, that he wouldn't dirty himself with a Western whore like me." And oh god, the unfiltered part of my brain wanted to tell him his sister had done just that. Repeatedly.

"And I kind of just resigned myself to dying in there. I knew my partner would be looking for me, had hopefully seen what had happened, but it would take time to find information about where I was. My contact was basically dead. They'd shot him in the back when they'd put us in the room, like the traitor they said he was." I paused to lick my dry lips. "Sorry, is this okay?"

"Not really, no," she whispered. "It's not okay. I can't believe this happened to you." She stroked my face tenderly, pulled me closer to kiss my forehead, my temple, my cheekbones, and finally, my mouth in the softest, most intimate kiss I'd ever had. "You don't have to keep going if you don't want to."

"It's fine, Sophia, really. My therapist says I sometimes keep too much inside and I should try to open up more." I pulled a self-deprecating face, rolling my eyes. Understatement. "Honestly though, if you're squeamish or don't like it, I can stop." It was going to get a lot worse than me telling her about a man shot in the back and left to die.

"Does it help you to talk about it?"

Frowning, I considered it. "Oddly enough, yes. It used to be hard, uncomfortable and anxiety-inducing, but now it's almost… soothing. Like confronting it and remembering it gives me back the power."

Sophia inhaled deeply and settled herself more comfortably against me. "Then I want to hear the whole thing." She kept lightly stroking my torso, and I wasn't sure if she was trying to soothe me, or herself.

"Okay," I quietly agreed, shoving down my fear. Once she heard what I'd done, she might not be so comfortable. "It's mostly a bunch of weird, disjointed memories, almost more like...feelings? They shaved my hair off, right down to the scalp, because apparently they thought that would be one of the hardest things for an American woman to bear, losing her *beauty*. And the worst thing was all those little hairs were stuck to my neck, in my ears and in my collar, itching and prickly the whole time." I ran my hand up the back of my neck, expecting to feel the prickle, but Sophia had so lovingly wiped my skin clean after cutting my hair.

"They'd cuffed our hands and feet with these heavy old chains and metal shackles, like they'd found them in some museum, and I just sat there in the dim room for hours and hours. I was using my feet to put pressure on the gunshot wound but my contact died after about five hours, I think? They left me in there with him, just...dead on the floor. They never took him away. He was just... there. Dead. For days.

"I hadn't slept more than a few minutes at a time because I couldn't get comfortable, and didn't want to, um, let my guard down. In case the others didn't share the sentiments of my young friend who thought I was filthy. They'd given me water which stank of cow shit and I drank half of it, vomited it up, drank the rest of the water, kept it down. Nothing to eat. And all I could think about was I really had to survive because I knew things about these people, important things I needed to report. It was so vital and I was ultra-focused on that. On doing my job, completing that task, doing anything I needed to do to survive."

I paused at those words. Was that what I was doing now? That same stupid "do the job at all costs even to the detriment of yourself" mentality? Was I tunnel-visioning? So focused on one thing that I couldn't see everything falling down around me? It didn't matter. I had to keep going. I'd been told to keep going, and I would run until I dropped.

"I, uh, but then I realized they might break me somehow, that I might give up secrets. And I couldn't let that happen either.

Like…what do you do? Because the needs of the few are always outweighed by the needs of the many," I murmured absently.

"Sorry?"

"Do you know the ethical question that involves the trolley-slash-train problem?"

Sophia's forehead creased and she shook her head. "No."

"Okay. I mean, it's so illogical because it can never actually work, but the nuance is plain. There's an out-of-control train or old-timey trolley or tram or whatever hurtling toward a station, and when it hits the station it will certainly kill, say…a dozen people. But I can stop it by pushing a"—I air-quoted—"very fat man who will stop the train with his body and therefore save the dozen lives at the station, but of course, he'll be killed. So what do I do? Nothing, or push the fat man? What they're basically getting at is will you sacrifice one person to save many people?"

Her expression blanked and I could see she was working through the puzzle, trying to figure out what she'd do. I'd bet she'd push the fat man.

"They ask me that question every psych evaluation, sometimes with slight variations in the setup, but the meaning is always the same. Will I sacrifice one to save many? And what they are *really* asking is…will I sacrifice myself for the good of my country? And I always push the fat man. And I decided if that's what I had to do, then I was going to make sure I could never tell them things they could never know." I inhaled slowly. "I mean resistance-to-interrogation training is helpful, but I'd never been in a real-world scenario and I didn't know if could withstand actual…torture." I shuddered as I remembered that moment, the moment I made peace with killing myself to save the lives of everyone who lived safely inside my head. It was a last resort. But it was still on the table.

Sophia brushed her fingers over my bicep. "Hey, you still with me?" She squeezed gently. She took my hand, gently kissing the base of each of my fingers.

"Mhmm. Sorry, it's an uncomfortable thing to confront, the idea that you might have to…get rid of yourself when you really don't want to do that. Uh, so…I was staring at my feet and these stupid massive heavy metal cuffs around my ankles and I started laughing because I kept thinking that it was like being in the Middle Ages or something and that the whole situation was just utterly ludicrous.

"The young guy came back in to see what was going on, why I was laughing. And I couldn't speak because I was laughing so hard, like I'd just totally lost it, so he came over to me. And he dropped his guard for just a second. I hadn't planned anything, but I took the opportunity. I jumped as best I could and somehow managed to get my arm around his neck and pull the chain between my wrists tight to strangle him. I had to make that choice to kill him. And I didn't even hesitate. I did it knowing that was the end goal, to kill someone to save myself. He was on his back on top of me, crushing me and I was so exhausted and thirsty and weak and I just kept thinking *don't let go* but he was like, twisting his head, gnawing on my forearm to try to get me to release him. The whole time I could hear a helo off in the distance and it wouldn't come closer, wouldn't save me. A dog was barking, sounded like a big scary one."

I took a long, deep breath and let it out slowly. Deliberately not looking at Sophia, I let the words rush out of me. "He lost consciousness and sagged back onto me, and I lost my grip and slipped and he came to and started struggling again. So I had to start all over again. I had to make the choice again to kill him, or let him live. I got my feet on his back, using leverage to pull on the chain and I was so desperate, so weak. TV and movies make it seem like you can strangle someone to death in seconds, but I knew it takes minutes. *Minutes.* Constant, hard pressure. You can't let up or they come to, like this guy did. And I kept thinking, why isn't it working, why is it taking so long? I was crying the whole time, trying to not be loud so they wouldn't hear me. It was the worst five minutes of my life. I didn't let go. My arms were shaking so hard with the effort, and then he was just…dead.

"The oldest guy came back as I was trying to get the body off me so I could get his rifle. I don't know what I thought I could do, like shoot the shackles off or something and escape, and I'd have the rifle in case I needed to…fat man. I didn't even get a finger on it. I killed someone for nothing. The guy went ballistic. Beat the shit out of me. I thought he'd shoot me in the head right then and there." Inhaling a shuddering breath, I continued, "It wasn't just a body to him, it was his nephew, twenty-three years old and the family's greatest hope for a better future. Or so I learned between face slaps. Shooting was too good for an American bitch like me, so he decided one stab wound for every year of the boy's life, every fifteen minutes so I would *really* feel it right up until I died, but he doubted I'd make it until the twenty-third because I was just a weak American. I almost wished I didn't speak the language; it would have been much nicer to just get stabbed without all the drama of talking it up." I smiled wryly, and glanced over at Sophia, trying not to absorb her devastated expression. "Of course I couldn't help myself, told him if I'd known what my punishment would be then I'd have killed someone far younger. He broke my nose for that." I touched the bridge of my nose, tracing the now-familiar bump.

"I didn't think he really had the stomach for it because the wounds weren't all that deep. Deep enough to damage, but…yeah. I realized later that was the point, deep enough to be painful but not enough to kill me until he'd managed to inflict all of them. The coup de grâce was supposed to be the big one, right in my heart." I rushed out the end of my story on an exhale. "Thankfully he only got to six years of payback before a Special Operations team burst in, and that was that."

I ran my hands over my stomach, fingers splaying unconsciously. He'd spaced each of the stab wounds out, so that after two I simply didn't have enough hands or reach to keep pressure on all of them. And I'd almost maniacally moved my hands over the wounds like a sick version of Whac-A-Mole as blood soaked my shirt and seeped through my fingers. I'd stared at my blood, wondering if Elaheh knew I was there. If they'd tell her a blond American Intelligence woman had killed her brother. If she'd connect the dots and figure out it was me, and who I really was. If she'd ask to see my body once I'd died from the stab wounds.

Sophia had remained mostly silent during my monologue, and now she opened and closed her mouth repeatedly as if everything she thought of to say felt wrong. After twenty seconds, she finally got a breathy word out. "Fuck." She exhaled, and managed a few more shaky words. "Fuck, I'm so sorry. I don't know what to say. I'm sorry. You are fucking incredible. So brave. I'm so sorry."

Bravery. Never a concept I'd thought to apply to myself in any aspect of my life. I'd killed someone and even though I knew rationally that it was *justified*, I still hated it. In the years since, I'd learned that guilt comes in waves and it'd been months since it had last washed over me. I paused, waiting for the burn. But it never arrived. I smoothed my hand over my right arm and left it there, covering that white scar that was a perfect rendition of his bite mark. "Thanks," I whispered.

"When did it happen?" she asked.

"Early 2017."

"I can't even imagine how you, the general *you*, could do that. What it must have taken to be that strong."

"I don't know and honestly, I'm not sure I ever will. And I don't know if it's strength so much as…perseverance maybe? Like I said, movies make it look effortless and painless and fast. It's not. And it's all mental because even if you're evenly matched, physically, there is always going to be someone who has one more punch or knife thrust because they can overcome the fear and pain and fatigue. And you have to make sure that person is always you, even if they're biting you and squashing you and you're so tired and thirsty that you're almost delirious. You can never give up, otherwise it's over."

Sophia smiled sadly. "I wish I had that kind of fortitude." She lightly dragged her fingertips up and down my stomach, now studiously avoiding the scars. The touch made me shiver.

"I don't know that it's fortitude so much as a stubborn kind of stupidity. I just don't know how to quit, I've never known how. If I can see even the slightest hint I can keep going then I will." I laughed, though the situation wasn't exactly humorous. "Do you remember that motivational poster that was everywhere around like…the early 2010s? Maybe earlier, or later. I don't know. But anyway, it's the stork eating the frog and the frog's got its hands around the stork's throat. 'Never ever give up' I think it used to say. That's me. A frog against a flock of storks."

Her mouth twitched into a small smile. "Watching you work, I can see that."

"Mmm. I've given *everything* I have to my job, Sophia, because I believe I'm truly doing good, and keeping people and their way of life safe. I know it might seem over the top at times, but…" I shrugged. "This is who and how I am."

"I like how you are. Your integrity is admirable."

Admirable but also sometimes to my own detriment. The sound that came out was half laugh, half scoff. "I can't quit, I *won't* until I know I've reached a complete dead end. While I can still see backroads and little paths I can try then I have to do that. This is just how I am."

"If it makes you feel better, I don't like the danger, but I like knowing you've been out there doing your thing so I can be safe." She shrugged, a sheepish smile curling those full, soft lips. "I know it sounds trite and basic, but…"

"It does make me feel better." I rolled over and pressed myself to her, an arm wrapped tightly around her waist. I wanted to bury myself in the warm safety of her body and never emerge. I kissed her shoulder, the smooth, soft edge of her breast. "As does this. As do you…"

I stood beside the external door to the deserted hotel gym at four a.m. and app-dialed Derek. The call was against my better judgment but rehashing the incident that had led to my diced-up torso made me think of him. And though I was sure he knew I was alive, he deserved a check-in.

"Martin." My last name was a relieved exhalation. "You secure?"

"As I can be."

"Intact?"

"Aw, you're worried about me. How sweet. I'm fine, but annoyed. I had an uninvited guest a few days ago. Who are they?"

"They're who you think they are."

Yay, government. Suspicions confirmed. Hadim's intelligence had a big fish on the line. "I have someone with me. Someone who probably shouldn't be unwillingly involved in this, if you know what I mean." It was a pointless thing to tell him—they would know Sophia and I were still together. But reminding him of that fact couldn't hurt.

"I know. But what makes you think I can tell them anything about you?" he asked.

"Well they're clearly liaising with you, given how you bitched and moaned on Saturday morning about your weekend being ruined. Mine was ruined too, just so you know." I peered around the side of the dark building then shuffled back into the shadows. "Why is this suddenly bigger than WikiLeaks? What am I missing? This obviously goes far deeper than what it looks like on the surface."

"I have an idea, but I'm not willing to verbalize until I'm one hundred percent. And I'm definitely not sharing my thoughts over the air, even with app encryption." He sighed. "Look, I know a few things that might help explain what's happening, but I can't tell you unless you come in. I can't help you like this. The more you run, the worse it looks."

"Then I guess you won't be telling me. And maybe not helping me." I hung up, and used a thumbtack from the corkboard advertising local activities to open the small side panel on my iPhone and eject the SIM. I snapped the tiny plastic card in two and put the halves in my pocket. One of the bricks in the low wall edging the garden looked loose enough to pry free. Once I'd extracted it, I used it and the wall to mortar-and-pestle my phone into a few pieces. I collected all the smashed phone parts, shoved them in my pocket then put the wall back together.

Shit. Hope my auto-cloud backup was working as it should. I'd decommissioned the phone without thinking, and that action confirmed that this whole thing was starting to wear on me. One thing I'd always been was careful. Thoughtful. The events of the past five days had completely thrown my equilibrium out of whack.

I ran up the internal staircase to the hotel room, rehashing everything that'd happened since Hadim's call. About three feet from our door, I realized the only reason I hadn't completely cracked up was Sophia. The thing that'd kept me feeling somewhat grounded was her. Her dedication, her kindness, her sweetness, her normalcy.

Relying on someone else was such a dangerous thing.

CHAPTER FIFTEEN

Not all heroes wear capes; some wear nerdy T-shirts

The blue phone rang as Sophia and I were discussing what to do about lunch—so far, go out was the option at the top of the list. After my confession last night, she'd been tentative in our interactions, not scared but more...unsure, as if she just didn't know how to approach me. I empathized. It *would* be weird being told that a woman you barely know and who you've been sleeping with while on an impromptu road trip had killed someone with her bare hands. Bare hands, and a helpful medieval-esque chain.

I'd made a conscious effort to be more engaged with her through the morning, taking frequent—for me—short breaks from poring over the dossiers of all the TERs on my short-shortlist, where I'd been trying to find someone who stood out. But it was like they were all born in Normaltown, USA, and boasted the usual college/military/distinguished service records. Some married, some not. Nothing that said "This guy is in bed with the Russians and he's somehow connected to someone else you don't know about yet." Taking these breaks felt counterproductive—to Halcyon's agenda, but not to my agenda of having Sophia want to stay with me. Withdrawing into myself now would be disastrous, because

I needed her to stick with me, just a little longer. I didn't think I could make it without her.

After murmuring sorry to Sophia, I answered the call. "Yes?"

Lennon sounded relaxed. "Are you in a position to converse?"

"Give me a minute." I let my hand fall to my side, phone still clutched tightly in my fist as I walked to the door, now speaking to Sophia. "Sorry, hon. I've just got to take this."

"Sure." She stood, already moving to lock the door behind me. "I'll be here when you're done."

I nabbed the car key. "I'll just be down in the car. Won't be long."

She blew me a kiss through the gap in the door before she closed it. I waited, as always, to hear the chain slide into place before I left her. I kept my phone in hand as I walked, not bothering to raise it to my ear again and explain what I was doing. Even if Lennon hadn't heard me explaining to Sophia, he'd wait silently, as long as necessary until I was somewhere suitable for a conversation.

I jogged down to the car, checked around myself, and when I was satisfied nobody was around, slipped into the back seat and hunched down. "I'm here. Had to get to a quiet place."

"It's quite all right. How are you, Alexandra?"

"I've been better."

"I can imagine. And how is Ms. Flores?"

I was zero out of ten shocked that he knew who Sophia was. "She's fine."

"Very clever of you to bring her along with you."

"I thought so." But it had become so much more than what I'd intended. "She doesn't know anything she shouldn't, by the way. In case you were going to ask."

"I wasn't going to ask. I know you wouldn't divulge anything sensitive."

"The vote of confidence is nice." I examined my fingernails and noted I needed a manicure. Oh well. Not like they'd care about my nails in jail. "I haven't seen anyone else since our second day in Tampa. But I'm sure they're here."

"They are. You're doing an excellent job of remaining hidden."

"Gold star for me. This is really shitty, just FYI, being treated like I'm some sort of criminal by the people I work for, the people I'm trying to protect."

"I know. But in their eyes, you are a criminal. They don't know there's greater meaning behind your service." He sighed, sounding unusually weary. "You work for a *secret* branch of the government, Alexandra, one tasked with maintaining the stability and honor of our country, ensuring that our governmental system works in a way that ensures our continued strength. Think of it as a tree. The government and people of this country are the trunk. The branches are all the things needed to keep the trunk solid, like Halcyon. And you're a leaf. Small, but essential to the health of the tree."

"Yeah, until I fall off my little stem and die," I muttered petulantly.

Lennon ignored my analogous response to his analogy. "Just remember that no branch or twig or leaf can know about every other part of the tree." I caught the meaning—that obviously I didn't know everything that was going on. His tone turned sober. "I need you to keep trying to unearth the truth. Our investigation isn't yielding the results we were hoping for. How are you doing, by the way?"

"I've got more information than I had the day I started working on this, but nothing I'd put in an official report."

"What about an unofficial report?"

"Still not yet, but I anticipate soon." Even with the security of the app's call encryption, I still didn't feel comfortable saying it all out loud in what was essentially a public place. I cleared my throat. "What if I can't do it? What if I can't find the links you need? I can't do this forever."

"*If* that day comes, I will give you permission to relinquish this duty."

"And then?"

"And then it's up to you how you handle yourself. I will let you know when you're free to act independently."

"Do you know what's going to happen to me after this?" I asked quietly.

"Not explicitly, no."

His sidestep meant he had a pretty good idea but didn't want to verbalize it. Because we both knew I was probably screwed. "Is there anything you can do to make things a little...softer for me?"

"We have ideas and we can offer a certain amount of protection for you. It simply depends on whether or not we're able to implement those plans without showing our hand."

"Right. Guess I'd better get my résumé updated and my prison fight skills sharpened up."

"If they send you to the prison we know they will, you won't have to worry about fighting," he said matter-of-factly.

"That's so…comforting."

* * *

The vice president was on television, droning on in the background while I stared at military personnel files, looking for my unicorn. My unicorn seemed even more elusive than real unicorns. Given there was no such thing as a real unicorn, well… you get the idea. I still didn't know if this line of investigation was even relevant, if I'd just wasted days crawling down the wrong rabbit hole. But it was the only line I had.

My call with Lennon at lunchtime had left me feeling out of sorts and borderline upset, despite the fact I'd always known there would be no movie-happy ending for me. "You are the fat man," I murmured to myself. "Think of who you might save…"

From my short-shortlist of two hundred and sixty-eight lieutenant colonels, I'd further narrowed it down to twenty-two who had both the requisite last name ending in TER and had been awarded the combat patches-slash-awards I'd seen on the chest of that uniform after further noob photo manipulation. But there was nothing more to distinguish them. Nothing stood out in their dossiers. I just needed *something*. A beacon, a North Star, just… something to point me at the right guy, because all I had at the moment were twenty-two maybes. I had the American's accent— Boston area—but was he born and raised there, or did he move there young enough to acquire the accent? What the hell. It was as good a distinguishing point as any. I moved four of the twenty-two, either born or residing in the general Boston area, to another list titled, cleverly enough, "Boston."

Those four were still indistinguishable from each other. I supposed the next logical step would be to go back to Bink and ask if they could look into each of these men for me and see if any of them had anything tying them to Russia. Calls, flights, emails, shit…even looking at Russian porn. But, fuck, I didn't have time for that.

"Are you going to eat dinner?" Sophia asked from the couch, Reuben sandwich halfway to her mouth. She'd arranged my sandwich and some sides on a plate, then left it on the table behind the laptops, where I'd promptly not even touched it. "I got you extra pickles," she said brightly.

"Hmm? Oh, yeah." Smiling, I assured her, "It looks great." The roast-veggie-and-pesto sandwich smelled incredible but I really wasn't hungry. Still, ignoring Sophia in favor of work was a total dick move in a sea of dick moves I'd already made. "Thanks, babe." I crunched a pickle in half, closed the laptops, then picked up the plate with its teetering stack and went to sit with her on the couch.

The delighted look she gave me as I sat down confirmed being with her was the best thing. "Welcome to the slums," Sophia said, bumping me with her shoulder. The movement jostled sauerkraut from her sandwich onto her chest.

Delicately, I picked the morsel of food from where it rested on top of the cartoon rendition of R2-D2 from *Star Wars* across her breasts, and held it out to her.

She looked like she was considering eating it straight from my fingertips but instead, she carefully plucked it from my fingers and ate it. "Yum," she murmured before returning to her sandwich, her eyes glued to the television mounted on the wall. I brought my legs up to sit cross-legged on the couch, bending my head over my plate and biting into my dinner. It was really good. I leaned back and closed my eyes as I chewed. Sophia interrupted my foodgasm with a grumbled, "God I hate the way he talks."

"Mmm?" I managed around another too-big mouthful. The moment I'd swallowed the first bite, I'd realized I was actually starving and had started indelicately chowing down. "How's that?"

She gestured at the screen where the VP was continuing his bullshit rhetoric. Or at least I assumed it was bullshit rhetoric, because that's all he spouted. "The upper-class accent, with his thuggish bully slipping in all the time. 'Randy' Randolf Berenson," she mocked. "Like, I know he's rich, but he's got *no* class. He'd probably beat you up in an alley if you asked him a question he didn't like. He's so fake, so gross, and so mean. So is the president. Argh, I hate them both. *So much!*"

I used my elbow to point at the screen, while still looking at her. "You know, you could always turn it off. Disconnect yourself from the news cycle for a while?"

"No I can't," she whined. "It's like a sick compulsion. And it fuels my rage."

I laughed at the whine. "What do you need rage for?"

"For the resistance! One day we're getting rid of them. Two more years, Lexie. Two more years."

Still laughing, I glanced at the screen then back to Sophia. "What's this press conference about?"

"Foreign aid or something. Some trip he took somewhere to shore up the president's…oh, sorry, *our nation*'s support overseas. My taxpayer money, wasted on sending these clowns around the world. I hate that. How do you stand working for them?" she asked. Shared political ideals had been one of the things that'd first attracted me to her profile. "I mean, gross."

"Well, firstly, I've never met either of them. Thank fuck. So it's not like having them as my direct bosses. And secondly, Congress is made up of the sum total of its parts, the good and the bad. Thirdly, yeah I suppose *technically* I work for the president and vice president if you want to distill it down to who sits in the Oval Office. But no matter who's occupying the White House and how I personally feel about that, my job is the same." I kissed her quickly but not softly. "In my mind, I work for people like you. Keeping *you* safe."

Sophia gave me a sweet, eyelash-fluttering smile. "Now *that* is a usage of my tax dollars that I'm happy with. Keeping cute government employees employed."

I gave her a smile of my own then turned back to my sandwich. Sophia pressed against me, stroking my thigh as I ate the rest of my dinner while half-heartedly watching the vice president blathering. I'd never paid much attention to the way he spoke before, but now Sophia had mentioned it, he really did have a weird accent—a thug who'd been born with money. And of course, now I was tuned to it, I couldn't push it aside.

Something about the way he pronounced *funding* stuck in my brain and refused to budge. Boston accent. I let my mind blank until the thought burrowed in further. Too far to be pulled out. Thinking about Boston brought my four Boston Unicorns to mind, and I almost choked on the pickle I'd just put in my mouth as the face of one in particular nudged its way to the front. Staring at the TV screen where the vice president was still rambling, everything coalesced into a single clear point of fact. It was unmistakable.

"Excuse me a minute," I blurted as I set my plate on the coffee table. Scrambling over Sophia, I said, "You can finish my chips."

She gave me a curious look, shrugged, then grabbed the last handful of chips from the plate.

Heart pounding, I brought up each of my Boston unicorn dossiers again, and stared at the four faces. Discarding three, I zoomed in on the remaining photograph. I wasn't wrong. It was a logical conclusion, wasn't it? I stared intently at the face of Lieutenant Colonel Patrick Randolf Kannegieter. The middle name. The face. No. Oh no. No…yes.

My brain made a leap and I yanked it back before it leaped off the precipice. Assumptions could be dangerous. But this was *such* an obvious leap. Anyone with eyes would be able to see it. I looked at the television. Back to my laptop screen. Yes… Could it *really* be this easy? Something I hadn't even considered, something I hadn't even been looking for, and I'd just tripped over it.

Scrambling off the chair, I collected my dirty laptop from where it was charging on the floor near the bathroom door. Sophia's eyes followed me as I rushed back to the table. I opened up a private browser and typed *Randolf Berenson*. Top result. Wikipedia. Randolf Michael Berenson, 49th Vice President of the United States. I tabbed to Images and slid the two laptops close together.

Oh my fucking god. How had I not seen it earlier when I was looking at the dossiers, trying to find something *more*? This was definitely my more. Randolf M. Berenson, 49th Vice President of the United States and Lt. Col. Patrick Randolf Kannegieter shared a strong jaw and cleft chin that stretched lips thin, the same cool blue eyes and strong nose, the same pale complexion and red hair. I didn't need a face-matching program, nor would anyone who had eyes and a modicum of logic. I knew the moment I saw them side by side that they shared genetic material.

How had anyone who worked with Lt. Col. Kannegieter not noticed this before? I shook the thought out. Because they had no reason to see any connection. I hadn't seen it. The only reason it'd twigged was because I'd been poring over these photographs in close proximity to seeing the vice president.

Uncle and nephew? My gut turned over uneasily as I discarded the idea. This resemblance was *far* too strong—it was a closer blood tie than that. This was father and son. I'd bet my paycheck on it. An entire year's worth. And in case you're wondering how much certainty that translated to? I had a killer mortgage, I loved expensive wine, good food, and overseas travel.

I shoved my knuckles into my mouth to stop myself from blurting what I'd found, and instead mumbled, "Fuuuck" around my fist.

"What?" Sophia asked. She'd been quietly watching my manic display. The woman was an absolute goddess. For the millionth time I told myself I had to make this up to her when all of this was done. If I could, I mentally amended.

"Just found—" I almost forgot myself. Almost let it slip. After a pause to collect my thoughts, I added a vague, "Never mind." I looked up and smiled to try to soften the brush-off. "Something really good. I think. Maybe."

"That's great." Her expression was soft, understanding, and then she smiled and nodded and turned her attention back to her brownie dessert.

I turned my attention back to my revelation. Even though I was sure of the results, I typed in *Randolf Berenson children*. Yep, two daughters. But only two daughters listed doesn't mean he didn't sire other children. Okay, stop. Facts. Just facts. Well, why couldn't that be a fact? Just because something wasn't publicly known didn't make it any less true. Unless it's only true because you want it to be, Lexie. So let's work out the truth.

There was also the name—Randolf was *not* common and two men who looked like they were cast from the same mold having it as first name and middle name was more than coincidental. Okay, so the last names were different but that wasn't uncommon. Especially if someone, say one of the most powerful people in the country, was trying to hide the fact that this person was their son. Previous marriage? No, he'd only been married once, still married to the lovely Mrs. Berenson. So this was his illegitimate son. Maybe. Allegedly and all that.

Cool cool. No big deal, right? Just the VP's (alleged) hidden illegitimate son committing war crimes in cahoots with Russia. What a time to be alive.

There was only one thing left to do before moving on. I couldn't do facial matching, and I definitely wasn't going to ask Bink to do it, so I needed to verify the voices of the American and Kannegieter matched. Or as best I could using just my ears. With no access to our voice database, there was only one option. Googling Lt. Col. P.R. Kannegieter. There were a few vague mentions, mostly relating to Army this and that. Nothing about the fact he was possibly responsible for murdering hundreds of innocent people, of course.

On the third page I struck gold with a YouTube video for an Army promotion ceremony that listed Kannegieter among the names of the newly promoted. Headphones in. Bland chatter, line-up of soldiers, a few promotions and remarks. At 10:46 my boy Kannegieter stepped onto the stage to receive his new rank pins. Military talk. Then it was time for the new Major Kannegieter to make his remarks. I turned the volume up.

Fuck.

Fuck.

Oh. Fuck.

I didn't need voice matching software. I only needed ears. I didn't know if I wanted to let out a triumphant yell, puke, cry, or all three. This was…huge. Unconfirmed, but huge. I had basic information and now, I needed to find the golden ticket. A connection between Patrick Randolf Kannegieter's birth mother and our illustrious VP. Given the comparatively young age of VP compared to Lt. Col., the most obvious link was high school or college. Thankfully Kannegieter was a less common last name than something like Johnson. I searched frantically through the personnel file for the forms that showed emergency contacts. FATHER NAME Berenson, Randolf M. would be too easy, but I could dream.

In the box for MOTHER NAME was Kannegieter, Patricia A.

Patricia and Randolf. They may as well have left me a note in the file saying "Patrick Randolf is our child!" I brought up another browser and typed in *Patricia Kannegieter Randolf Berenson Boston*. After a few moments of deep thought and quick Googling, I added *Marks Academy or Harvard*. Bless the ease of finding things on the Internet, like the schools our members of Congress attended.

It took an hour of trawling through sites, archived school records and assorted random ex-student pages reminiscing about their time at school before I hit the jackpot. A low-res scanned photograph from a high-school yearbook dated 1978. Patricia Kannegieter and Randolf Berenson – Junior Prom King and Queen. Aww, they were high school sweethearts who had a murderous traitorous child.

How adorable. I studied the photograph. Lt. Col. Kannegieter had his mother's ears, the shape of her eyes.

Some more digging told me she missed graduation and the months before due to *illness*. 1979. I did some basic math. The year Lt. Col. Kannegieter was born. I made a mental leap, perhaps a judgmental one. Given the vice president's father was Governor of Massachusetts at the time, it wasn't beyond the realm of possibility that Governor Berenson wasn't overly pleased with the fact his teenage son had gotten a teenage girl pregnant.

Yet Patricia Kannegieter had remained in Boston and raised her child. With or without the help of teenaged Berenson? Given he left for Harvard in '79, I was going to put my money on *without*. Juicy, but not entirely relevant to what I was working on. Just more reasons to dislike Berenson. As if I needed another.

Fuck. This really was what it looked like. I set all the pieces out on the table—metaphorically—and started moving them around like a pretend chessboard. No matter how I set the board up, no matter what opener I used or followed with, I came up with the same basic answer. The illegitimate son of the current Vice President of the United States had been the military officer directly liaising with a foreign militia group to carry out a chemical weapon test on a group of innocent unsuspecting civilians in exchange for either weapons-slash-cash-slash-aid, or all of the above.

Take a breath. Go over it again. I did, twice, and arrived at the same conclusion. I didn't want premature closure—jumping to the most obvious answer without looking at all the facts—but based on everything I knew, there really was only one conclusion that followed logic. If I had more facts maybe I would think differently, but for now, this was what I had. Why would they be going to such lengths to keep it hidden from the Intelligence Community? Because this was a personal and political embarrassment on top of an international humanitarian disaster. I knew no chemical weapon test of this magnitude would come without the highest authorization, which meant the VP knew about it. But did he know that it was Lt. Col. Kannegieter? My gut said yes, though probably not until after the fact.

I almost laughed. No wonder everyone was all over this. No fucking wonder they were trying to keep this away from all eyes. And my eyes were all over it. A sudden wave of nausea made me realize the implications of everything I knew. This was not only a huge deal but also frightening, as the reasons for my current situation grew clearer and clearer. The people trying to smother me were working on direct orders from the White House.

And Halcyon was going to use this intel to remove Vice President Berenson from office. But why remove Berenson? What's the reason? It's not your business, Lexie. But it kind of was. I'd run through mini-hell for this. The vice president was disgusting—bigoted, racist, xenophobic, self-serving, cruel and uncaring to those in lower tax brackets than him—but just because he was a horrible human didn't mean he was dangerous to our country. Unless he actually was.

What would make him dangerous? Not him having an illegitimate son. Not his illegitimate son either having Russian allegiance, or spying for Russia, or helping Russia do horrible things—that was just disgusting and traitorous. I made another logic leap, smooshing Berenson and Russia closer together. That one really was speculation and I had absolutely no proof. Yet. But Russia just kept popping up.

I mean, it wasn't the first time a member of Congress had been seduced by the ruble. But the vice president? Occam tap-danced around the room with his razor. It *was* logical, right? Not just me? Fuck, I didn't have the time, or the resources, or the mental acuity, to get into forensic accounting, follow money trails, connect Berenson to the million threads that had started unraveling in this intelligence. That was for Halcyon to follow up, Halcyon with all their resources and all their nice offices. I was simply going to present Lennon what I'd found, hint at what I thought, and see if Halcyon could reach the same conclusions.

No wonder I'd been told to keep a copy of this information safe. Fuck. Enacting the Protocol indeed. Hopefully enacting the Protocol also meant going after whatever sick fuckers had manufactured the chemical weapon, and ensuring it could never be produced again. I leaned back in the chair, exhaling a long sigh. I just felt...sick. Sick at what had happened in Kunduz, sick that I'd been forced into this situation because of it, and sick because someone entrusted with the safety and prosperity of my fellow countrypeople might not actually have their best interests at heart.

It was time to see Derek. Face-to-face. I needed to find out what he knew. The nausea surged even harder, and I looked around for a distraction.

Found one. A very good one.

I stared intently at Sophia, who was now curled up on the couch, reading, with a glass of wine resting on the couch arm. I blinked hard. It was like living in a time warp—burying myself in work then surfacing to see something had changed like food, drink, book, television, clothing, location. Seeing her helped soothe some of my distress. "Sophia?"

She didn't lift her eyes from her book. She was almost done with the two-inch-thick paperback she'd borrowed from Bink. "Yes, hon?"

My mouth turned itself into a smile before I could think about it. "Firstly, you calling me hon is adorable. Secondly, you're a genius."

That got her attention. She peered over at me, her eyes questioning. "How so?"

"I think you might have just saved the world, not me. I've been looking at this so closely I hadn't even thought to go big *big* picture yet. I could kiss you."

"Then do," she said simply.

"I will, but quickly." Offering a sheepish smile, I added, "Because now I have more work to do." I stood and moved to the couch, holding out my hand to her. Sophia set down her book and let me pull her up. Snugging an arm around her waist, I kissed her like she'd just handed me the key to the place I'd been locked out of for the past week. Great kiss. "And there'll be more of that later."

"There'd better be." She thumbed the edge of my mouth, leaned in to grant me another quick kiss then went back to the couch, her book, and her little bubble of contentment. After opening the book again, she asked, "So why am I a genius?"

I flopped down onto the couch beside her, exhaling a long disbelieving breath. "I think you just walked past, and without even thinking about it, pointed out how to finish my jigsaw puzzle."

CHAPTER SIXTEEN

How easily it falls apart

When I woke without Sophia on top of or beneath me, I panicked. 5:42 a.m. The room was dim, any streetlights that might have illuminated the space hidden behind curtains. My eyes went immediately to the bathroom. Door open, light off. The room door was closed and chained. I sat up, looking around frantically for her, aware that it was taking me an embarrassingly long time to reboot my faculties.

I'd been asleep for maybe an hour after working late, trying to find more solid evidence of Berenson's ties to Russia, of him being directly responsible for the weapon test in Kunduz, of... anything really. But I was going around in circles because I just didn't have the resources and personnel I needed. So I wrote a report for Lennon, laying out every strand of the spiderweb I'd been tangled in, and had finally crawled into bed a little after four a.m. And Sophia had definitely been there.

"I'm here," came the quiet murmur from across the room.

I turned on the bedside lamp and found Sophia on the couch, her legs drawn up to her chest. "You okay?" I asked, clearing my throat to chase away the sleep hoarseness.

"Yes and no."

The answer, coupled with the fact she was not only awake, but out of bed way before me, had my radar pinging. "What's up?" I untangled myself from the sheets, flipping on the room light as I went to sit beside her.

Sophia had her phone in her hand, turning it around and around. "I couldn't sleep, so I thought I'd see what's going on with the world, check my emails." She met my eyes, the edges of hers crinkling with the hint of a smile. "And before you ask, yes, I used a VPN."

Holding up both hands, I jokingly rebutted, "I would never have asked or implied that you hadn't been cybersafe, but I'm glad you did." I took her hand, stilling the nervous phone spinning. "What's up?" I asked again, gently. "Did they cancel *Top Chef*?"

She shook her head.

"Okay, then what is it? Or don't you want to talk about it?"

Sophia's eyebrows knitted together as her teeth nervously played with her lower lip. "I do, just not sure how to bring it up."

Ominous. My stomach lurched, but my voice remained steady when I queried, "Ah, then I assume it's something about us?" When she nodded, I continued, "Is it something you think is going to hurt my feelings?"

"I'm not sure," she murmured. "I don't think so, but I also don't think you'll be happy about it."

I had a sickening feeling what she might be about to say and tried to look interested instead of like I was already trying to figure out how to talk myself out of it. "Okay, well, I'm an adult. Mostly." I squeezed her hand. "So why not just lay it on me and we'll see where we end up."

Sophia pulled her hand from underneath mine to free her phone. "Someone sent me a weird email." After thumbing her phone screen, she passed it to me.

"I can't read your email."

"I think you should." She shook the phone at me. "Please."

After a moment's consideration, I conceded, "Okay. But I literally can't read it." After kissing her temple I hopped up to grab my glasses before taking up my position beside her again. The sender of the email was Alexandra Martin. "This isn't from me," I said as soon as I read that part.

"I gathered that, based on the fact you were in bed beside me when it was sent half an hour ago. Not to mention it doesn't really seem like something you'd email me. Or even say."

I raised the phone again, skimming the text. It was interesting, to say the least. Interesting, and infuriating.

Ms. Flores,

You're in a dangerous situation with Alexandra Martin. She's a liar. She's a treasonous traitor who stole intelligence from the government and is now attempting to evade capture for this crime. She's using you and when you've outlived your usefulness she will discard you with no thought as to your safety or feelings. She's done it before, and she would do it again without hesitation in order to ensure her own freedom.

For your safety you should leave her as soon as you can, and advise where we can find her before she does any more damage.

Regards,

A Concerned Person

I ground my teeth. This was taking things too far. Clearly they were getting desperate about their inability to find me if they were resorting to this. "God, they make me sound like a fucking monster," I murmured as I read the email again. "Whoever they got to write this definitely doesn't have training in negotiation." I skimmed the line about *done it before*. "And this is *such* a lie."

"Which part?" Sophia asked flatly.

I looked up at her, surprised by the mistrust on her face. I could have lied again, told her it was just part of the evaluation, but...I didn't want to. "I am *not* a traitor." I passed her back the phone, wondering how exactly I could repair this. Maybe I couldn't. Maybe it was time to give up.

"Not a traitor? That's it? So you did the rest of the stuff they said?" Her eyebrows shot up. "You stole intelligence, like...like... that WikiLeaks thing?"

There was no way to answer that which wouldn't make this whole thing worse. So I stayed quiet.

Sophia's mouth fell open, and it was like her whole face fell along with it. "Oh my god. You did," she accused, her voice hard with anger and upset.

"No, I didn't."

But it was like I'd never spoken. Her entire body was rigid, as if she was forcing herself to remain on the couch. "This isn't an evaluation thing, is it? You're really on the run, aren't you? What the *hell* did you do?" Sophia's entire demeanor changed from cautiously curious to defensive, like she was putting up a hard shell against me to protect herself. "Oh my fucking god," she repeated disbelievingly. "You...you...you've basically been lying to me this whole time, from the moment we first met?"

"No," I said emphatically. "I haven't been lying to you from the moment we first met. This...this is new, just days old, but yes, there are some things I haven't told you, because I couldn't."

"Stop fucking around with words, Lexie. Call it what it is. Lying."

"Okay fine," I snapped. "I've lied about some things. But only when necessary, and not because I wanted to. Because I *had* to. Even if I knew how to explain it to you, I couldn't. But I'm doing it because lives and ways of life depend upon me doing what I'm doing right now."

"Doing what? What are you doing?"

"My job," I said quietly.

"Is this an evaluation?" she asked roughly.

"No."

"Are you on the run from the government or the CIA or NSA or FBI or some other fucking spy organization I don't know about?"

I didn't answer, didn't move. I didn't have to. My silence and stillness told her everything she needed to know.

Sophia stood up and crossed the room, practically jamming herself against the wall to get as far away from me as she could. "I can't believe it, this is insane. And I'm...part of it now. Fuck, am I going to get arrested because of this?" Each word was laced with panic, the syllables rising and falling unevenly.

"No, because you're *not* part of it. You don't know anything about what's really happening." They might question her, but if the agencies wanted my cooperation—which they would—they wouldn't touch Sophia. And if they tried anything, I'd threaten to release the information. Yay, blackmail... I stood, but she moved farther away from me. Holding both hands up in a gesture of surrender, I murmured soothingly, "Can we just calm down? Just... calm down and I'll explain what I can."

"Explain? You mean *lie* to me again. I need you to tell me the truth," she demanded, her hands curling into loose fists against her thighs.

"I can't tell you the truth. Not all of it."

"Is what they said in the email true?"

I made eye contact, willing her to believe me. It was clear she'd already made up her mind based on the email, and continuing to deny it would only fracture our relationship further, maybe beyond repair. "Not in the way they put it, no, but...also I suppose in a way, yes."

"I see." She studied her hands intently, as if she could stop the faint trembling through sheer willpower. "Why?"

"I can't tell you why. But I can tell you that I felt I had no other choice." Was given no other choice.

"What will happen if I email back and tell them where we are?"

"I'll be gone before you can hit send." I swallowed hard. It felt like a betrayal, even as I knew she didn't really owe me anything, even as I knew I'd betrayed her by dragging her into this, by lying to her. "You don't understand how important this is, Sophia. I need to find the answers, even though people don't want me to."

"Right." She came toward me, taking a wide berth around me to collect her phone from where she'd abandoned it with me on the couch. Before I could speak, she'd already crossed the room again to grab a room key from the kitchen counter.

My question came out cracked as I rushed to intercept her. "Where are you going?"

She held up both hands, a clear signal for me to keep my distance. "Away from you. Away from...this. I need some fucking air." Her face contorted as I opened my mouth to protest. "Don't worry, Lexie, I won't let them see me. Wouldn't want you to *fail* because of me."

"It's not even light out. It's dangerous alone. Sophia—"

But she angrily yanked the chain off and flung the door open, slamming it closed behind her. The sound echoed through the room. A fountain of emotion surged inside me. This wasn't my fault. I'd been ordered to do this. I had no choice. Halcyon's directive was more important than all of this. I felt a sudden, frightening urge to break something. Break everything. Do anything to get rid of the anger and despair and betrayal within me.

But I didn't.

Not because I had a sudden attack of sanity, but because I had to leave. As I started stuffing clothes into my duffel, I called Lennon. The moment he answered, I blurted, "I have a problem. Sophia Flores knows. Not all of it, but she knows."

There was a long pause, but his response was steady. "How?"

"Someone, three guesses who, emailed her with a lopsided version of the facts. She's not happy, to put it mildly. And they invited her to turn me in."

"I see," Lennon said carefully. "Do you think she will?"

"Right now? The way she just stormed out? It's highly possible."

"Do you still need her?"

"No…" I stalked into the bathroom to grab my toiletries.

"But you want her," he said neutrally.

"Yes." Want, need. The line was so blurred.

"Attachments are dangerous, Alexandra."

"I know," I whispered angrily. I'd never believed it until now.

"And if this attachment compromises your work, then it's doubly dangerous. You need to make a decision."

"I know," I repeated, yanking out power cords and throwing them into the backpack.

"You've been with her for less than a week. Known her for only a month. I urge you to stop and consider that this might simply be circumstantial attraction."

"Don't," I growled. "You're not here, you don't know what it's like. And you're not the one who's going to swing for this. I am. So let me have my fucking attraction because it's more than that, and it's not *circumstantial*."

Silence.

I leaned over the clean laptop and began moving files into a folder ready to encrypt and upload securely. "I'm going to send you what I have, in case I have to disappear again and can't make contact. I've written a report, but there's more to this that I can't figure out from where I am and with my lack of resources. But I'm sure you'll be able to connect the rest of the dots. And I'm moving, leaving, I don't know where I'm going." Fuck, but I couldn't leave until she came back safely. I was going to have to go out and find her.

"Okay. Be careful," he said.

I forced bravado into my voice. "Always am."

I'd sent Lennon what I had in the encrypted folder, finished packing, and was sorting through prepaid Visa cards to find one that would cover the airfare home for Sophia, when the room door opened. I tensed, my hand automatically going to the backpack where my gun resided in the outer pocket. But it was only Sophia who came in the room. I withdrew my hand as she calmly closed the door behind her and engaged the chain. When she turned back around, her red-rimmed eyes found mine.

"I didn't think you'd come back so soon," I said steadily. She'd only been gone ten minutes. Not enough time to sort through her feelings. But definitely enough time to email A Concerned Person with our location.

"Me either." She swallowed hard. "But...I realized I need to understand how someone who makes me feel the way you do can also lie to me the way you have."

"And what if I can't tell you? Not because I don't want to but because I literally can't share this with you."

She held my gaze. "Will you tell me what you can?"

"Yes," I breathed. "But it probably won't be enough to satisfy you. I don't want to lie, didn't want to lie, but it's necessary." I had no idea why I was even entertaining telling her. I had no idea if they were coming, and I needed to leave. I'd gone as far as I could with Hadim's intel, and it was now in Halcyon's hands. I no longer needed her, as much as I desperately wanted to be near her.

So why couldn't I make myself go?

Because I'd had a tiny glimpse of what life with her might be like if my other life wasn't in the way of everything. And I wanted that life with her so badly that the want felt like it was suffocating me.

Sophia collapsed onto one of the chairs at the table. Her entire body screamed defeat, and I wished I could comfort her, tell her I was sorry and that it'd be all right. But I couldn't. Not because I wasn't sorry, but because I didn't know if it would be all right. She sighed. "Then that's enough for now."

"Okay," I exhaled. "But I can't stay here. So, if you want to come with me then I need to be gone in five minutes."

"I didn't email them and tell them where we are," she said defensively.

"Okay. I still need to leave." I checked that the files had sent and slapped the laptops closed.

Sophia offered me her phone. "Do you want to check my sent emails?"

"No." She could have deleted the sent email from her phone entirely. I wanted to trust her, and if Halcyon wasn't at stake then I probably would have.

"You don't trust me, even after you asked me to trust you?" The question dripped hurt.

I paused pushing laptops into my backpack. "My trust is maybe the difference between a national and international security incident, maybe even a world war. Yours is about hurt feelings." She looked like I'd slapped her. Which I suppose I had, emotionally… I inhaled deeply through my nose. "I'm sorry," I said gently. "I'm a little short on time and patience right now."

Sophia carefully smoothed her expression, and without a word, stood up and dragged her suitcase from the closet. "Then let's go…"

It took her less than five minutes to pack, and as we left the room, she turned off her phone and wordlessly handed it to me.

CHAPTER SEVENTEEN

Light in the dark

I didn't know where I was going exactly, but my brain instinctively seemed to take us north. Back toward...I didn't even know what. Not home. Not yet. Sooner or later I was going to have to go in and face the consequences of what Halcyon had asked me to do, but not today. I wasn't ready.

Despite the uneasy truce that had settled between us, we didn't speak. But every now and then I felt her gaze on me. I couldn't look at her, couldn't bear to see the betrayal lurking in her eyes. As I listened to the rhythmical hum of tires on interstate, I fought with my duty and my desires, knowing that in the end my duty would win. This had always been a possibility, her finding out, me having to own up to using her and lying to her. It wasn't like I'd never done those two things before, so why did it hurt so much to admit what I'd done to Sophia? I knew the answer to that question as soon as I asked it of myself.

Because I'd never done it to anyone I'd actually cared about...

As miles passed, I wondered why she wanted to come with me again, why she didn't just go home, cursing my name. Maybe the connection we shared overrode her feelings of anger about what I'd done, how I'd lied to her. Maybe...maybe I just didn't know.

The most intrusive thought was suspicion that they were using her to trap me. Had they gotten to her earlier and she'd hidden it from me? I'd seen no sign. And why bring up *this* email but hide other contact? No. She was clean. She was a safe place. I had to believe that. And if she turned me in, then who cared—the intel was securely out of my hands now, if they caught me, they caught me. And at least then I'd know where I stood with Sophia.

Midmorning, I pulled off the interstate and into Jacksonville, and found us a hotel that didn't look like it was going to collapse on us during our sleep. I was certain we hadn't been followed, but I still checked the room and took my time with a visual sweep of the surroundings to be sure. I wanted to trust her, so badly, but...

After dumping my things on the table and floor, I asked, "Are you hungry?" We'd drive-through breakfasted not long ago, eating in the parking lot before continuing on, so it was a pointless question. But I needed a gentle opening.

Sophia shook her head.

I pulled her phone from my pocket and placed it on the tiny Formica table. An offering. A test. She didn't take it.

We'd settled at opposite ends of the room, like opposing teams, just staring at each other. Though I'd spent the entire drive from Tampa thinking about what to say, I hadn't settled on any route— the path I walked would depend on her reactions. I took a deep, calming breath. "This whole thing is so much bigger than our little bubble, Sophia. It's life and death for some people, a clear right and wrong. And I'm on the side of right, I always have been. I hope if you choose to believe only one thing I say, you believe that. I'm not the enemy."

"Okay," she said quietly. "I mean...I've spent the last three and a half hours in that car just...thinking about you. About this. About us. Just trying to figure it out." She seemed to have calmed down a little during the drive, or maybe she'd just come to terms with what I'd done and wanted all the information before she acted.

"And did you figure it out?" I asked.

"No. But I did realize that the woman I *think* I know isn't a monster. Because I can't believe I wouldn't see it in you. Not the way you touch me, not the way you look at me, not the way you make me feel."

I sagged, fighting against the crush of fatigue. "I'm not a monster. I'm just in a really awkward spot, trying to do the right thing."

"Seems like it…" she mused quietly. "So, what is it?"

I looked up and held eye contact with her. "On Friday morning, I found out a secret, a big one. A secret that has far-reaching implications, whether or not anyone else ever knows about it. I mean, I find out secrets every day, Sophia, it's nothing new. And keeping secrets is part of my job. But this one is…really bad, for so many reasons. I found out that some people did something horrific.

"And the people who did this thing don't want anyone to know about it, obviously, because it's bad. But it's something I think the appropriate people *should* know about, and it should never be allowed to happen ever again, and those who did it should be held accountable. But those people disagreed and threatened me if I didn't drop it. So yes, I ran, and yes, I decided to try and uncover the truth anyway because I couldn't live with myself if I didn't try to stop it happening again. And those people are unhappy with me for that and are trying to prevent me from doing my job."

"Who is it? Who did this thing? What is the thing?"

"I can't tell you that."

She nodded slowly, and I kept quiet while she worked through what I'd just said. She looked up, meeting my eyes again. "But what about me? How do I fit in?"

How I answered her would be the fulcrum upon which everything would balance. Truths and lies. If I wanted something after this, if there *was* an "after this" for me, then only the truth would do. If I didn't want that, if I wanted to walk away from her when this was done, then I could tell her whatever the hell I wanted to.

So what did I want? What did she want? Would she even want me after I told her what I'd been doing, even if I couldn't tell her the whole truth about Halcyon?

More than anything, I wanted to be truthful, because I felt something for her beyond simple attraction, beyond not wanting to hurt her. The self-admission was surprisingly difficult. I'd never had an issue with telling the truth, when the moment to tell the truth was right. But what I'd done to Sophia…? The truth wouldn't fix it. Because the truth was that I'd used her, even though it had been necessary, and even though I'd wanted her before all of this, separately from Halcyon's directive.

Her expectant gaze loosened my thoughts and unstuck my tongue. "You fit in exactly as I told you when you thought this was an 'evaluation,'" I said steadily. "I needed you with me to help throw those people off and to keep them from getting close, and I wanted to spend time with you because the thought of not seeing you for weeks or more was so painful I just couldn't do it." I laughed, surprising myself with the expulsion of mirth. "And then I realized it was actually *much* harder to hide with you, because you didn't really understand why it was so important to not be seen. But I still wanted you with me, even as I realized it wasn't working as I'd hoped, because I…" I couldn't get those words out. *I have feelings for you.* There. It should be so easy. But I just couldn't say them. I managed a simpler version. "And then when I didn't need you anymore, I knew I still did. But it was because I needed you for myself, instead of for the secret."

Her entire body seemed to collapse in on itself, as if I'd just confirmed her worst fears. "Right," she said flatly. "You used me."

I didn't deny it. I had used her for Halcyon. I nodded in confirmation. "Partly, yes."

That nod made her eyes dim and her voice harden. "When exactly did you decide you were going to do this? Use me, I mean. Like, from the moment we met? Before that?"

"Are you *serious*? I know what I did to you was wrong, but do you think so little of me that you actually think—" I couldn't keep that line of thought going, the continuation of her speculation that I'd planned this from the moment we'd connected. So I answered with a sharp, "No."

"Then when?" she asked quietly, so quietly it was almost childlike.

I didn't know if I should keep digging, or try to build a ladder. "When you called to ask me why I wasn't at the breakfast that I had actually forgotten about. I'd forgotten about it because the night before, the guy with the broken nose who approached us that morning broke into my apartment and threw around a whole lot of words and threats to try and make me go with him while waving his gun about. I'm sure you can imagine how that made me feel.

I escaped, and spent that night hiding in a hotel, trying to work through the information and figure out what the fuck I was going to do next with intelligence that was so important that they would threaten me just for *knowing* about it. I was tired, Sophia, mentally and emotionally and physically. And honestly, I was fucking scared. When you called me, I *was* going to brush you off, reschedule for another time though god knows when I could have made it work. Then it just hit me. A solution to my problem, and also something personal that I wanted."

"Personal?"

"You," I murmured. "I wanted to get to know you more. I wanted to be with you." I'd always been fairly solitary, never having felt the need to be surrounded by people. Sure, people were fine and if I was around them, then I was happy enough. If I was seeing a woman, I enjoyed it but my life, my job, had shaped me into someone who was content to move through life alone. But then there was Sophia, who'd stumbled into my life after I'd mistakenly swiped while trying to figure out how a dating app worked after I'd decided I needed to follow my therapist's instruction to get a social life. And now she felt so ingrained in it, so entwined with me that I couldn't imagine her not being there.

"You could have gotten to know me the regular way people get to know one another."

"No," I said instantly. "There was no time. I knew I might be gone once this was over and I just…I wanted to be selfish for one moment in my life." I stood up, pacing across the small, tattered room. I needed to move, to try and expel the emotion from my body. "I wanted someone to protect *me* for once instead of the other way around. I wanted to be not lonely for once. I wanted goodness, something nice in case I failed. I wanted time with someone who seemed to enjoy being with me. Because you are so beautiful, so warm and friendly and funny and…nice and kind, that when I thought about it, I wanted it to be you who was with me.

"Like I said, I thought having a support person, a companion would keep them away. There are certain lines they don't like to cross unless it's unavoidable, and I needed you to keep me safe while I found out the truth. You protected me just by being around… being a witness." My eyes prickled, and I rubbed at them to ease the sensation. I was so tired, so…just…done. "Then I realized the way you were keeping me safe wasn't the way I'd first thought you would."

Her expression had softened, but I still wasn't entirely sure she believed me. I knew it sounded like a bunch of lines, but it was the truth. "What way was it then?" she asked.

"I don't know, whatever you want to call it—emotional, spiritual, sexual, soulful. But it wasn't just a physical sort of protection. I've started to depend on you being here. Waking up with you, having a few moments of respite before it all crashes down on me again, those moments during the day when we're having a conversation, or trying to figure out what to have for a meal and I'm not thinking about keeping the world safe. I'm just thinking about how much I want to be with you."

"Sexual," she repeated tightly, her throat bobbing up and down. "Are you just sleeping with me because you want something from me? To keep me here?"

My fraying nerves snapped. "What do you think I am? Some kind of robot, fucking everyone I can, man or woman, even if I'm not attracted to them, just so I can get their secrets and make them do what I want before I chew them up and spit them out?" I sucked in a quick, ragged breath, having run out of air near the end of my rant. "Being with you intimately was because I *wanted* to, because you consented, because you wanted to. Every single time. Honestly, I think it might have been the thing that's helped me hold on to a little of my sanity during this insane thing."

I turned away from her, moving to stare out the window into the gravel parking lot. Her question had been a fair one, but it hurt deeply and I had to fight to calm myself, even as my inner voice told me I deserved every ounce of her outrage. I stared at passing cars, trucks, people out enjoying the sunshine, while I was trapped inside a prison I hadn't asked for. A prison…

Sophia's quiet question broke through my upset. "Am I in danger? Because I'm with you?"

I spun around and answered with an immediate, "No, I wouldn't let that happen. They're the train, you're the station full of people." I shrugged, trying to smile, but it wouldn't come to my lips. "And I'm the fat man." I sighed. "Have you ever felt like you were in danger? Even when we had our game of hide-and-seek with that guy after the burgers?"

She paused, her mouth partially open. After a few tense moments, she shook her head. "No. I've never felt like I was in danger."

Her admission gave me a small measure of relief. "Good. I've *really* tried to keep you safe, to keep you away from this, out of its path as much as I was able. And when this is done, I'll still keep you safe."

"How?"

"I can't tell you."

"Of course."

"I'm sorry I can't tell you. I'm so sorry that I used you," I said, injecting every ounce of sincerity I could into those two statements. "It was a horrible thing to do to you, and I don't deny that. A normal person would never have done it. But I'm not a normal person, Sophia, and sometimes my life is not a normal life."

She stared at me, blinking rapidly. Finally she asked, "Why can't you let it go? Is this secret really worth it? Can't someone else figure it out?"

I rubbed both hands over my face, hard, as if it might scrub away the layer of fatigue and guilt. It would be so much easier if I could tell her about Halcyon. Instead, I had to bend the truth again. "Because I can't," I said simply. "Because giving up and letting bad guys do bad things is not who I am. Because if I let it go, they would bury it and I cannot allow this thing to ever happen again. My integrity means everything to me, which means I have to keep this information safe, work out the truth, and give it to people who can do something about it."

"You can't let it go, even though it might mean...what? That they'll lock you up and throw away the key?"

"Yes. It's a character flaw. An annoying one." I forced a smile, relieved when she returned it, albeit shakily. "Look, the option is still there, the same one I've offered before—if you want to leave then I'll book you a flight right now and drive you to the airport and you can go home and forget all of this. Forget me if that's what you want. There's no guilt or hard feelings if you leave. I'm not forcing you to stay. I've never forced you, have I?" The question made my throat feel tight, and I fought back the sting of tears. I wanted to believe she was with me because she liked me, liked being with me the same way I did her, not that she'd ever felt coerced.

I'd led her, sure, made suggestions, but in the end the choices were always hers.

She went silent and I could see her working through that in her mind, checking off everything we'd done, all our interactions. After a sigh, she quietly agreed, "No, you haven't forced me and yes you've said plenty of times that I could go. And I never wanted to." Sophia shrugged helplessly. "And that's just it. I don't know if I want to go or if I don't. I know that you're not my responsibility and that what you're doing has nothing to do with me, but there's this stupid voice in my head that makes me want to stay. And I have all these feelings about this, but no idea what to do with them."

"What feelings are those exactly?"

"My anger at you and what you've done. My worry about you, about leaving you and what that might mean. My concern about this thing you won't tell me about. And my…shame and embarrassment at being gullible."

That one word pierced me. "You're not gullible." I swallowed. "It's just…me. It's my job. And I know this sounds horrible but sometimes part of my job is persuading people to do what I want, either overtly or subtly. And I'm good at that because I have to be."

"Right."

She looked utterly crestfallen and there was nothing I could do except offer another apology. "I really am so sorry, Sophia. I own what I did to you, and that it was a manipulative way to get what I needed, but I would *never* have done it if I'd been able to think of another way at the time. I would never have done it if the stakes weren't enormous."

Sophia stood and crossed the room to me. But she moved away again almost as soon as she came near, like she just couldn't make up her mind about where to be or what to do. After a few moments of staring helplessly at me, she turned away and began pacing slowly back and forth across the room, gesturing expansively as she tried to explain her thoughts. "I understand why you felt you had to do it, but it still hurts, so badly. And it makes me wonder what else you might have lied about, how I can trust you now."

I fought to breathe around the panic. She had every right to be angry, to hate me, to not trust me. But I still couldn't stand it. It took me a few moments to calm myself down enough to answer. "I only lied about things related to the secret. Everything else, the stuff between you and me, my family, my life, all true."

She raised her chin, staring me down as she came closer. "I want to leave you, even as I just want to kiss you and make you tell me it's going to work out fine. I want to stay, because this thing between us feels incredible, even though you've been preoccupied, because I keep thinking what if this wasn't in the way and we really had a shot to try something. And I don't know why those feelings are still there because I'm furious with you and I want to go. I don't understand how I can feel all these things at once." Her hands curled into loose fists then relaxed. "I'm so mad at you for lying to me, even though you say you had to and I'm trying to believe you." Her shoulders dropped along with her voice. "And I'm so scared that this might be all we ever have and it doesn't feel like enough."

I smiled sadly because it was all I could do. "I'm a complex person and this is a complex situation. There's no right or wrong feelings for you to have about this."

"Do you understand how you've made me feel?"

"Yes," I said instantly. "I understand perfectly because I knew what I was doing when I asked you to come with me, every time I didn't tell you the truth, and I knew what that would do to you if you found out. I knew it would hurt you, what price I'd pay for it, knew that I might be ruining any chance of there being more with us. But some things are bigger than my own desires. My whole life, I've been the fat man, putting myself in the firing line."

"Desires…" Sophia mused. She paused her pacing. "I used to make fun of my friends for the whole instant-love U-Haul thing, but now…now I think it might be real. I've never felt like this with anyone, Lexie, not ever. That on its own is fucking scary, but when you add all this other stuff, it's terrifying."

"I know," I murmured. "But I feel it too. I don't know if it's chemistry or compatibility or what, but I just feel like I want to be near you all the time. It's confusing for me too."

"What will you do if I go? What will happen if you go out alone?"

"Same as I've been doing now, but I'll just…be really lonely. And then eventually, once I've gone as far as I can, I'll have to give up, and turn myself in." I'd have to wait for Lennon to give me the okay, to confirm he had what he needed from me before I could relinquish my duty to Halcyon.

"You're not going to flee overseas or something?"

I laughed dryly. "No. Unfortunately, there's no Bahamian vacation in my future. This face is not getting out of the country. But you can still go, I can give you a prepaid credit card. All-expenses-paid vacation." The offer sounded deranged, like paying for a vacation would make up for what I'd done.

"I don't want to go to the fucking Bahamas, Lexie!" she exclaimed.

"Okay, sorry, I just—"

She steamrolled my explanation with a question. "What will happen if you have to give yourself up?"

Not if, when. "You probably won't ever see me again." I blew out a long breath, tried to disguise how shaky it felt.

"Really?" The word cracked on the second syllable.

"Not in person, no."

"Is that a certainty?"

"Yes. I mean…you've heard what happens to government whistleblowers, right?"

Her mouth fell open. "I—" That's all she got out. She dropped onto the faded couch.

"Yeah." I gave up and collapsed onto the soft bed. Telling the truth was far from cathartic, and the rush had left me feeling like I might fall over. "So…there's some of my absolute truth and it's not very nice, really. A lot of my truth isn't. But I'm not a robot, Sophia. I'm not someone who can turn their feelings off and be intimate with someone just because I need to be. I need you to understand that even with all of this going on around me, I was attracted to you, *am* attracted to you and that's why I"—my fingers fumbled in the air, trying to grasp the words—"initiated intimacy with you. The way I feel about you isn't part of this. It's separate from work and it's personal and it's *mine*."

The moment I'd said it I wanted to swallow the words back down, not wanting her to think I was trying to worm out of responsibility for my actions by sweet-talking her. Mercifully she didn't do what most people would—ask a question along the lines of "And how do you feel about me exactly?" because I had no idea how I would have answered, how I would have explained the complexities of lust and like and enjoyment and excitement and pleasure and protectiveness.

My eyes burned and I blinked rapidly to force the feeling away. "I just don't know what to do, where to go from here. I've figured out the first part of the problem, but the answer is almost as awful as the question." The burning turned into tears and I covered my face, utterly mortified to have broken down. "I feel like I'm so far into the tunnel that it's getting harder to see the light behind me and I can't see one in front of me yet. I'm just…stuck in the dark."

Sophia stood and moved toward me like she was going to hug me, but I stood too and stepped backward. Not because I didn't want the comfort—I did, desperately, but I couldn't stand the sweetness of it. Didn't feel like I deserved it.

I wrapped both arms around myself. "I don't know how else to say sorry, to show you that I am truly, deeply sorry for hurting you. But I had no other choice, because some things are just bigger than you or me."

"I think I understand that a little better now," she murmured. "But…"

"But you're still mad etcetera."

"Yes, definitely 'mad, etcetera.' To put it *really* simply."

Sniffling, I raised the bottom of my sweatshirt to wipe my eyes. "Good. You should be. I just want you to know it's easier for me to keep going because you're walking in the dark with me. And that makes me feel like maybe I might make it to the other end, where the light is."

CHAPTER EIGHTEEN

Hopefully the Beatles were right and we can work it out

Mad etcetera I could deal with. I could handle her upset, handle her—more than justified—feelings of betrayal, but I didn't think I'd be able to cope if she hated me. I wouldn't blame her if she did, but I got the feeling she didn't hate me, and if she did, Sophia was doing an excellent job of hiding her true feelings. The main vibes coming off her were anger, distress, and confusion. No hate in the mix that I could find.

We spent the day stepping carefully around each other, then coming together at times. A brief touch. A tentative smile. A shy laugh or a joke. And then the seriousness would overwhelm us again. It felt a little like a stage of grief, where everything was okay…and then we'd remember what I'd done and a blanket would be thrown over us and it was all dark again. Until one of us would lift a corner and tentatively peek out.

I still didn't know why I trusted that she wasn't going to give me up, but I did. Maybe for the same reason she still trusted me after my lies—because we both so desperately wanted this thing between us to be real. And what did it matter anyway if she decided to turn me in to A Concerned Person? She had every right. I'd sent my report to Halcyon, my work was technically done. I just had to wait for Lennon to confirm he'd read through what I'd uncovered, that it was enough, and that I could go no further from where I was. I'd done my job.

I'd done my job…

And now, I didn't know what to do. I'd invested my whole life, all my emotional and physical energy in this for a week and now that I'd figured it all—or mostly—out, I felt aimless, lost, uncertain. So I could either sit around and do nothing, which I had never done, or I could keep digging, see if there was anything else I could find out. It was pointless, and probably impossible to do from where I sat, but it was better than watching television and trying to appease the heavy discomfort in the room all day.

I wasn't afraid of rocking a boat that was already leaking water, but I didn't want to antagonize Sophia unnecessarily. Not because I was trying to stop her from leaving or turning me in, but because I wanted her to stay with me. Stay for me. So I made an effort to put away my pointless work around five p.m., and suggested we check out some dinner options. She agreed, smiled, said whatever I wanted was fine, and returned to her e-reader. Not hate. But there was definitely not love.

We made easy, light conversation over dinner. Watched a little television on the couch, sitting close-ish together. Talked about the show we were watching. Around nine, Sophia stood from the couch. "I think I'm going to go to bed. Today has been…"

"A tiring mess? Yeah, it has been."

Instead of sharing bathroom space for nightly teeth and skin routines as we usually did, I let her go ahead of me, not wanting to intrude in such a tiny space. The last thing I wanted was for her to somehow feel physically threatened after I'd obviously made her feel emotionally threatened. That she might somehow be afraid of me had crossed my mind, and I'd shoved the thought down where it wasn't so painful. I would do many things, but I would never put my hands on her in a way she hadn't asked me for.

My face in the bathroom mirror looked exactly the same. No matter what happened, no matter what I did, I was still the same person. It was both a comforting and upsetting thought, that my insides held so many facets. I was capable of both lies and love. When I emerged from the bathroom, I stood awkwardly in the middle of the room as Sophia pulled back the bedcovers. "I'll sleep on the couch," I said.

She paused. "Why?"

"I just…didn't know if you…wanted to sleep next to me."

I watched the understanding move over her face, followed quickly by a decision. "Has anything changed, really? It's just that I know about it now, right?"

"Right," I agreed cautiously.

She dropped the pillow she'd been fluffing and stood straighter, her eye contact burning into me. "Are you suddenly going to hurt me in my sleep, Lexie?"

"Of course not," I spluttered, tripping over my words in my desperation to get them out, to reassure her.

"Okay," she said quietly. "Then come to bed."

I settled stiffly on my side, half my body hanging off into nothingness. We lay quietly in the darkness, the steady sound of breathing undercutting the faint traffic noise filtering in from outside. Sophia rolled over, and I felt her hand moving across the bed until it found me. She fumbled until eventually her fingers lightly held the fabric of my tee at my shoulder. After an eternity, she asked, "Are you scared?"

"Yes."

"Of what?" she murmured, reaching up to stroke my neck softly before gripping my shirt again.

"Everything. Of not being believed. Of it all being for nothing. Of losing my freedom when what I did was for the freedom of others. Of losing what you and I have started to build. Of having screwed it all up when I wasn't given a choice."

She took a little while to answer—understandable given what I'd just dumped on her—and I could hear her quiet breathing. After what felt like an eternity, she quietly said, "I'm really trying to put myself in your shoes, imagine how you feel about it all. Because I think you're mostly cerebral, Lexie, but I'm…instinctual, I guess. Everything in my life has always been about what my metaphorical gut tells me to do. I don't think too deeply about decisions. If it feels right it's right and if it feels wrong then it's wrong. And what you did was wrong. But being with you feels right. And I'm really struggling now to reconcile those opposing feelings."

"Which feeling is stronger?"

"Neither," she said immediately. "So I don't know which way I'm supposed to go. And the thing is, I have this niggling thought that I shouldn't feel so betrayed, because you never promised me anything. It's not like we're in a relationship, had made a home together, and you've spent years lying to me about something, like a gambling habit or another woman. And your lies weren't personal lies, so...I just...I don't know."

"No," I agreed carefully, "there were no promises about *us*, but there is a standard of decent, normal human behavior which you'd expect from someone you might be dating. And then there's what I did." I inhaled deeply. "Sophia, if it wasn't for this intelligence, you'd have that decent, normal human behavior from me. For as long as you wanted it. Because I am a decent person."

"I know you are. And I knew from the first fifteen minutes of conversation over coffee that there was something between us." She exhaled loudly. "So, I'm going to hold on to that for a little while and see where it takes me."

"Okay," I whispered. "When you figure it out, I'll either be here for you or not. It's your call."

The silence lengthened, but it was contemplative rather than uncomfortable. And sure, there was still a fissure between us but it felt like we were each reaching out, building a bridge toward each other. As I fell asleep, still with her fingers tangled in my tee, her words from our argument that morning echoed in my mind.

I've never felt like this with anyone...

* * *

I dropped my head into my hands, massaging my temples and the back of my skull. The added pressure sent a lance of pain bouncing through my head to the backs of my eyes and I winced, trying to ignore the headache I'd been trying to ignore for the past hour. I'd been awake since before dawn, and after untangling myself from Sophia, I'd snuck outside to place an early-morning call to Lennon.

He'd confirmed that he'd received the files and my report, apologized for not being in contact yet, and explained that obviously my report had set the Halcyon offices—wherever the hell they were—ablaze, and everyone was scrambling to verify what I'd uncovered. He hadn't mentioned Sophia. And I hadn't offered anything about her. But he'd left me with another "Be careful, Alexandra" and I knew he meant not just with those who were trying to find me, but with my feelings.

My feelings… Aside from the ever-present attraction, lust, like, and desire, I mostly felt guilt and relief. Of *course* I felt guilty about lying to her, but the relief of her knowing, and me no longer having to fabricate so much of our day-to-day living felt like finally inhaling a breath. But there was a flipside. Setting aside hurting her with my actions, I had to question if having her more aware of what I was involved in, yet not knowing everything about it, was better or worse than her being pretty much clueless? That was yet another conundrum for which I had no answer.

The object of my thoughts had been mumbling to herself for the last ten minutes and I finally turned my attention away from my pointless, circular work and toward her. Sophia sat on the floor in front of the coffee table, her knees drawn up, her shins brushing the edge of the table. She was so hunched over in this position that my back almost screamed in sympathy. The mumbling grew clearer now that I was focused.

"Sure, let's add a bunch of shadow so it looks like a two-year-old designed it. That's a great idea. Never mind the fact last week you said you wanted everything light and inviting." Sophia threw her stylus down in disgust. "Idiot."

I swiveled fully on the chair to face her. "Not going so well?"

She pushed herself up so hard she nearly got airborne. "Clients," she said by way of explanation. Sophia smiled in my direction then continued to the bathroom.

I called after her, "While you're in there could you grab me some Tylenol or Advil, please? I think there's some in my toiletries case."

She paused and turned back to face me. "What's wrong?"

"Raging brain-ache."

Her expression softened. "Sure."

Sophia set the bottle of Advil and a glass of water on the table, and when I uncapped the bottle and tapped three pills into my hand, her mouth formed a thin line. Her voice was pure maternal disapproval when she said, "Three is more than two which is the max recommended dosage every four hours."

I downed the pills and half of the water. "That is true, for ordinary headaches. But this headache is not an ordinary headache, therefore I know from experience that it requires an extraordinary dosage of ibuprofen."

"Your liver must hate you."

"I think it does all right." I smiled wearily. "Every once in a while I treat it to superfood smoothies."

"I don't think superfood smoothies have anything to do with keeping your liver healthy."

"Okay, well…I drink a lot of tea. Proven liver benefit." I peered at my laptop screen again. Still blurry. Come *on*, it's been twenty seconds since I took something for my headache. Go away now.

"Lexie." The word was quiet, imploring rather than exasperated.

"Mmm?"

"Maybe it's time to take a break?"

I took a moment to absorb the statement, the soft plea nestled in it, and closed the laptops. "Only because you said it so nicely."

Her mouth quirked. "Ah, then I've found my new secret weapon. I'm going to use it against you all the time now."

I almost came back with a joking "You manipulator" before I realized how it would sound. Not good, and it would just draw attention to how I'd manipulated her. When I stood, Sophia gestured to the bed and told me to "Lie down. On your back." I did as I'd been told and she positioned herself behind me, pulling my head onto her lap. She carefully removed my glasses and set them on the bedside table before gentle thumbs began kneading my temples. "Close your eyes, try to relax."

"You know telling someone to relax usually has the exact opposite effect?" I tried to sound teasing. Tried to ignore the way her proximity had my nerves firing.

"I have heard that, yes," she mused. Her hands drifted to my neck, stroked gently up and down and then came up to my jaw.

"So that's why I'm not going to relax *just* because you said I—" I exhaled a long breath, unable to continue because her fingers were suddenly doing magic things to my cheekbones and temples and that weird spot that's at the back of your skull but is also kind of your neck. "Scratch that," I mumbled. "Relaxing now."

Sophia laughed quietly. "You were saying?"

"I'mma bottle you and take you everywhere with me."

"You'll need a big bottle. This headache thing happen often?"

With my eyes still closed, I smiled. "Only when I'm on the run from bad people who are doing bad things."

She tensed fractionally, her fingers stilling before she relaxed again and resumed her massage. "Funny."

Her magic fingers worked to ease my tension, but my mind wouldn't quiet down. We'd talked about it, come to a truce, seemed to be okay. But this…this was as if nothing had happened. I drew in a deep breath. "Do you hate me?"

Sophia paused a moment before answering, "If I hated you, would I be touching you like this?"

"Okay then. Fair point. Will you forgive me?" I was surprised by the desperation in my question.

The pause was longer this time. "Yes, I will. Once I've had some time to sort through my feelings, and to fully accept that your reason outweighs my reaction."

"You're entitled to that reaction, to your feelings," I protested.

"I know I am. But it's hard to be furious if it's really what you say it is—"

"It is," I interrupted.

"Then what right do I have if this thing is bigger than both of us?"

"You have every right."

"Yeah. But you saving the world is a pretty big deal." I felt her shrug. "And maybe I helped with that a little."

"You definitely made it easier," I mumbled. "All of it." I tried to twist around to look at her, and was gently encouraged to remain where I was. I looked up at her as best I could from where I was. "I'm sorry, Sophia, I really *really* am. I know I've said it before but I just really want…no, I *need* you to believe it, and believe that I was pushed into a place where I had no choice."

She shushed me, her thumbs moving to just in front of my ears, working at that tight jaw joint thing. "You don't need to keep groveling. It is what it is and we'll deal with it. Assuming you want to deal with it?" she added quietly.

"I do, yes. Very much."

"Good, me too. I just…can you give me a little time to get myself and my feelings in order?"

"Of course I will. And if there's anything I can do to help you figure it out…"

"Then I know where to find you," she finished.

"Thankfully only you do," I joked.

Our shared laughter broke some of the tension away. I reached up to hold her forearms as she massaged the tension from my skull. Her thumbs stroked my cheekbones, exerting firm pressure that made me feel like energy was flowing through me, carrying the headache away with it.

"What's your middle name?" she asked out of nowhere.

"Elizabeth. Alexandra Elizabeth. Talk about a mouthful."

"It suits you. Tell me something truthful."

I frowned, trying to think of something. Truth, truth, truth. But not something boring. After a minute I said, "I really love octopus."

"Wait." Her fingers paused. "To…eat?"

"No, of course not. I just love them as an animal. They're awesome creatures."

"Seriously?"

"Yes. They're incredibly smart, capable of problem solving and logic, masters of camouflage not just with their skin patterns but their body shapes, like they can disguise themselves as so many different things, and they can manipulate their bodies to get out of any tight spot." I looked back up at her.

Her eyebrow crease smoothed out, eyes crinkling as her mouth formed into a teasing smile. "Ah, not unlike you then."

I'd genuinely never thought of the comparison, but the moment she said it, I laughed. "Actually, you're not wrong. Though I'd put money on an octopus over me."

"I don't know, everything you've done since we left home? Smart, logical, camouflaged…" There was an edge of heaviness in the light teasing of her words.

I carefully sat up and squirmed to face her. "What's up?"

Sophia's face transformed as if she was trying to force herself to appear normal. "Look, I don't know exactly what's going on and obviously I can't." She took my hands and pulled them into her lap. "But from the moment we met, I felt like I wanted to know you, to spend time with you. You've made me feel seen. You've made it so easy to say yes. Yes to dates number two and three, yes to kissing you, to going to bed with you, to coming on this road trip."

I squeezed her hands, turning them over to study her fingers. "I've loved every yes you've given me, but you know you don't always have to say yes to me. You can say no to anything, at any time. Even being here. I know I've said that, but I want you to know it for sure, even though I really want you here."

"But I know I want to be here now. This is my choice. I want to stick this out with you because…" Her eyebrows drew together. "Because you said me being with you helps you, but it's also helping me."

Helping her… "Are you sure you're not suffering from Stockholm Syndrome?"

She was already in full laughter by the time she asked, "What? No. What do you mean?"

"Well, I know I'm all around wonderful, smart and charming, and a great bedmate. And don't get me wrong, having you here is everything I'd thought it would be. I *want* you to stay until…until I have to go." I paused, tried to find the words that I suddenly wasn't sure I wanted to say, in case I scared her off. "But this isn't…fun. I misled you. I kept the truth from you. How can you want to stay when it's just nonstop tension and worry?"

The laughter faded into seriousness. "Because it's not nonstop tension and worry for me. More like…occasional tension and worry." She moved closer and reached up to tuck some of my hair behind my ear. "Moments like when I'm watching you work, and you stop and look up, searching for me like you'd been thinking about me and just had to see me. The look on your face when you told me the truth. The way you make me coffee every morning, and the fact you bought a French press that first day when we stopped at the store, just so you could do that for me."

"Oh," I managed. "I see."

"Yeah. And when—" She stopped abruptly, seemed to think through what she wanted to say, then after a long pause, continued, "When we're making love, or having sex or fucking or whatever," she added in a rush. "I feel *wanted*. Like it's just you and me and nothing else matters. So yeah, it's helping me to be here with you. And being away from the Xbox definitely helps my work productivity."

"Well then, we should go on the lam more often. Think of all those shiny new websites you'll build while we're hopping from state to state, changing our names and appearances with every location. Totally worth all the stress."

"Maybe we should," she mused teasingly. "But I think my parents would get shitty if I missed too many dinners and weekend visits."

"Probably," I agreed.

"So uh, speaking of, I haven't talked to them in a few days, and I should probably call them. Are you okay with that?"

The idea of such a close relationship stunned me for a moment. I couldn't imagine having anyone in my life outside of work to talk to so frequently. Even my own parents had always felt more like acquaintances than parents, but the love and affection Sophia had for her family was obvious. What would that be like? Having people who wanted to know how you were doing, who wanted to share their lives with you too, parents who were excited to spend time with you. "I'm not your jailer, Sophia," I said gently. "But... maybe you could call them using WhatsApp or Signal? It's a little safer than a regular call."

"Sure. Mom has WhatsApp."

"Great, thank you. I'll go for a walk and see if I spot anyone who I shouldn't be spotting."

"No!" she said instantly. "I don't want you leaving because of me. Stay here and relax until you stop squinting like that. I won't be long." She leaned forward and kissed my forehead, then paused before tilting her head to kiss my mouth. Sophia lightly sucked my bottom lip then scrambled up, leaving me on the bed while she slipped out to the small smoker's patio. No hate detected.

For the next twenty minutes I dozed to the sound of her laughter filtering through the sliding glass door, the quiet intensity of indistinct conversation, and more laughter until the door slid open again. "Okay, will do. Love you, and yes I'll be careful. You too. Bye."

Yes I'll be careful... I stuck a smile on my face. "Everything okay?"

Sophia flopped back onto the bed, leaning against the headboard and draping her legs over mine. "All good. Mom's delphiniums are still flowering late in the season, and Dad's beloved Camaro bit the dust and he's trying to find a rare part for it. They've been wondering where I am and what I'm doing." Sophia paused for a moment and then explained, "I spoke to Dad for a bit. Apparently they've had some calls and even a house visit from some very polite people in very expensive suits."

My antennae shot straight up. "Calls and visits about what?"

"Asking about me, if they knew where I was. About my new girlfriend—that's you, and by the way, Mom's over the moon and they can't wait to meet you and I'm in trouble for not telling them—and just stuff that he thought sounded a little off and out of the blue. Dad said nothing to them, obviously, because he doesn't know anything." She bit her lower lip. "Is it...?"

Stuff that sounded off. Goddammit. "Probably, yes. I swear I didn't know they would do this. But I don't have any family or friends for them to...use. All I have is you." I caught her gaze. "Do you understand what I'm saying?" I kept a tight grip on my fury. Fury that they'd do this and fury that it hadn't even occurred to me that they would consider it. "They've failed to take me in, failed to find me again. The only thing they have to hold over me is you. I'm so sorry."

She shrugged, but the nonchalance felt forced. "Remember I said my dad was a Mexican American in the US Army in Vietnam? He can handle a little harassment. Especially if it's in service of the country. He'd probably enjoy the chance for a good fight, even if it's just mental sparring."

"Sweetheart," I said gently. "This isn't a game. I'm so sorry. I think..." I inhaled deeply. "I think maybe it's time to think about turning myself in, otherwise they're just going to keep coming at your family." I wouldn't risk them dragging her family into this mess. I'd reached my dead end. I just couldn't get over or around the massive fence surrounding me.

They'd beaten me. I'd always known I could never win, but it still stung.

"No..." she whispered. "I want more time. I'm not ready to say goodbye to you. Let me call my dad, I'll—"

"Sophia, stop," I murmured. "There are some lines I won't cross, some things I can't abide. And this is one of them. I won't let them harass your family." Or worse.

"So what will you do?"

I blew out a breath. "I really don't know." The idea of facing the consequences of what I'd done wasn't terrifying so much as upsetting. Action and consequence. No choice, just obedience. "I need to contact my boss and figure out what my next steps are, make sure you're protected and all that. Just a bunch of logistics really." Bosses. First Lennon, then Derek.

She gestured helplessly. "I wish we could forget everything and just travel and spend a lifetime relaxing and experiencing amazing things together."

"Oh, I'm still holding you to that vacation I promised you."

"I look forward to it," she whispered tightly.

"But for now, until I figure out what to do, why don't we enjoy our last few days of playing hooky from real life…" I pulled the neckline of her top aside to kiss her collarbone and when she didn't protest, I moved my kisses up her neck. I paused to ask, "Is this okay?"

Sophia nodded and pulled me up until our mouths met for a kiss that was so achingly sweet that I wanted nothing more than to lose myself in her. And for the rest of the night, I did.

Once Sophia had fallen deeply asleep, I slid from the bed with the stealth of a spy—ha!—and slipped the room key into my pocket and the gun into the waistband of my jeans like a massive cliché. If push came to shove, I doubted I'd actually use the firearm but having it with me made me feel marginally better. The small alcove outside the hotel's laundry was a perfect place for a private conversation, and at one a.m. it was even more so. I unlocked the blue phone and called the only number in the only app on the phone.

Ten seconds later I was rewarded with a groggy, "Lennon."

"Any progress?"

"Yes, good progress. You could have called in daylight hours to ask me this question."

"I know. I wanted to make someone else miserable with my insomnia. I have another problem. They're threatening Sophia Flores's family. Probably to get me to cooperate."

"That was always a risk. One you must have known could be on the table."

"No, it slipped my mind in amongst all the other stuff I was worrying about." I still couldn't believe how stupid I'd been to not even consider that possibility. "Can you stop it?"

"No. The best person to discuss this with would be Derek Wood. I know he's liaising with the White House. He might be able to leverage something for you."

"Okay. To borrow a phrase from the movies, because honestly that's what this whole thing has felt like, the net is closing around me. I think it's time to turn myself in."

"Yes," Lennon agreed. "You did excellent work, and there's nothing more you can do from where you are. Consider yourself relieved of this assignment, effective immediately."

"Okay, thank you," I breathed. I didn't feel relieved by the burden being taken from me. "I...might take a few days. Suck down as much free air as I can before I'm dungeonized."

"Good idea. Call me when you're ready to go in, and I'll do everything I can for you."

"Thank you."

"I'm proud of you, Alexandra. Think of the good you've done."

Good... That was going to be such a comfort in my cell. I hung up and slumped against the wall before swapping the blue phone for one of the throwaway cell phones. The conversation with Derek was going to be harder and I braced myself as I input his number from memory. He answered with a sleepy, "Wood."

I injected a little extra contriteness into my voice. "Oh I'm sorry, were you sleeping?"

"Remind me to fire you when you get back." There was a rustling sound of fabric moving, a dull thud of feet landing on the floor. "You're lucky Roberta's out of town or she'd probably fire you herself for waking us up."

"Oh? Is everything okay?" Derek's wife, Roberta, was sweetness personified but had a strict no-work-comes-home rule, and on the single occasion I'd broken the unspoken rule to call Derek at home after ten p.m. about something important, I'd received the full force of Roberta's ire when I'd next seen her. Four months after the fact.

"Her mother had a fall. She'll be fine," he added before I could ask about his mother-in-law. Though I wasn't friends with his family, we were amicable enough, and in his unguarded moments Derek had often spoken about his wife, kids, in-laws, and future grandchildren.

"Glad to hear it. And I really am sorry to interrupt your REM cycling."

"I was only dozing," he said finally, the admission gruff as if he hated admitting I hadn't inconvenienced him as much as I'd thought.

"Sophia Flores's family. The contact with them needs to stop."

"You know how to make it stop."

"Yes. But I'm not ready. I need a few more days."

"Delaying it is only going to make things worse."

"They've waited this long, another couple of days isn't going to change anything. Can you help me? I…don't know what to do."

"Not over the phone." His exhalation was audible. "I want you to look me in the eyes and tell me why. Then maybe we can figure out what to do."

Interesting. "Why should I trust you? How do I know you're not going to arrive with a takedown team or something?" I'd trusted him with my life before and knew him to be honorable. Was my trust going to be my downfall?

"Because I give you my word that I won't."

Derek and I often got together to shoot the breeze while slogging golf balls, both while stationed overseas and stateside. I could always use a nine-iron to whack anyone who looked suspicious. "Okay," I murmured. "Tomorrow. There's a place called Power Putts in Jacksonville. Ten a.m."

"I'll see you then."

"See you then," I agreed. As I hung up, I hoped I wasn't making the biggest mistake of my life.

CHAPTER NINETEEN

There's always time to work on your golf swing, even during a crisis

I dug through my bag, lamenting my on-the-run wardrobe and choices that were woefully inadequate for golf. The fact I had nothing suitable to wear, even if this was just a casual not-really-playing-golf-but-actually-discussing-national-security-and-my-imminent-incarceration session, was discomforting. I pulled on jeans and sneakers and decided I would stop by the pro shop to buy something more appropriate.

It wasn't my golf snobbery. Wearing not-golf attire would draw unwanted attention. The likelihood of any of my fellow players knowing Derek and I weren't really working on our game was slim to nil. But all it took was some stickler-for-the-unspoken-rules golfing housewife to tell the nice man in a nice suit that yes, she has seen something strange, that there's a blonde wearing jeans and a hoodie, playing with an older gent who looks like a younger, beefier Clint Eastwood and they're on the driving range just over there.

From the couch, Sophia watched me tie my laces. "What's going on? Are we going out?"

"I'm going to the golf course."

Her eyebrows shot up. "Seriously? You're taking a break to play golf? Alone? What happened to staying under the radar?"

"I need to practice or I'm not going to win next month's office Putt-Putt challenge."

"Why are you making a joke about this?" she asked incredulously.

"It's a coping mechanism."

"Ah, right." Sophia's expression relaxed. "You really are the antithesis of every secret agent I've ever encountered in movies and books."

"I'm not a secret agent." I leaned my butt against the couch arm, resting my hands against my thighs. "But don't worry, I don't think you're going to meet another person like me."

"I'm glad. I don't think I'd know what to do with two of you."

"Then it's lucky I'm one of a kind, baby." I leaned over and kissed her quickly. "I'm meeting my boss, just going to chat, in public, like two normal people. I don't think we'll draw any attention." Unless Derek wanted attention drawn to us. I desperately wanted to trust him and hoped I still could, but I wasn't going to take the chance. Tucked inside my backpack with the laptops was my handgun. I doubted we were going to have a shootout showdown on the golf course, but outside of that, who knew what was going on behind the scenes, and having it gave me a—probably false—sense of security.

Sophia worried her lower lip with her teeth. "Is it safe?"

"As safe as I can get." I debated elaborating, then decided to give her something. She deserved this honesty. "I think it'll be okay, but if I don't come back by two p.m., just pack up your things and go home. I'll leave you a prepaid Visa card."

"I don't like the sound of that." She huffed out a breath. "Actually, I really fucking hate it."

"Me too," I admitted. I took her face in my hands, thumbs caressing her cheeks, and pulled her forward to kiss her forehead. "I know this man and I trust him as much as I trust anyone outside of this room right now. I need to talk to him. I need to make sure you and your family are safe and separate from all of this. I can't leave you until I know that. And I promise, if anything ever happens, I will do my best to get a message to you."

"Okay." She smiled a smile that seemed as if she had to work to keep it on her face. "Just be careful."

"I always am," I said cheerfully. Except around her. With my feelings. Oh god. Did I really just think that? Was I catching feelings? But we'd hardly spent any time together and I'd been a manic idiot glued to my laptop for eighty percent of this trip and everything was so weirdly upside down and we'd had a fight like twenty-four hours ago. I took a moment to consider. Yep. I'd caught feelings for Sophia. Shit. She was right. The U-Haul joke was no joke. I glanced at the door, working hard to keep my voice steady and not sounding like I'd just had a massive personal revelation. "If you really need to go out, then just…be cautious, okay? If something feels off then it probably is." I passed her a small card with a cell phone number printed on it. "This is the phone I have on me. Use Signal to call me if anything feels wrong, even if it's just that you feel like a barista is being too friendly."

Sophia's fingers closed around the card I'd passed her. "Will do. I—" She cut herself off abruptly and smiling, shook her head. "Just, please be careful, and I'll see you soon?"

"That you will."

I hoped.

I tugged at the collar of my new polo shirt—to pop or not to pop, that is the question—as a shadow fell over me. Derek looked like he'd lost ten pounds and gained a bunch of blood pressure. "What are you doing down here?" he asked as he looked me up and down. "You always take golf clothes with you when you flee your house in the middle of the night?"

I stood from where I'd been sitting at the course café waiting for him, and watching for anything untoward, for the past hour. "I'm here checking out places to retire." I made a vague gesture. "And of course I do. Never know when the urge to practice your swing might strike." When I stood, my new golf shoes creaked loudly. "You're looking a little pale. Good thing you came down here to see me in the sun."

"It's stress. Over this whole fucking mess. You alone?"

After a moment's pause, I said, "I am." I'd just handed him everything he needed to throw me on the ground, cuff me and drag me home. No witnesses around that had any stake in my wellbeing. I swallowed my unease and tried not to think of SWAT teams and snipers. "You?"

"Yes. Nobody wanted to fly down with me. Apparently I'm not a good travel companion," he added dryly.

"That doesn't surprise me." Despite his assurance and the fact I'd been here for a while making sure everything was fine, I checked the surroundings again. Looked secure, but the people who could take me down wouldn't be seen until they were on top of me. I indicated one of the bags beside me. "Took the liberty of hiring you a set of clubs. Got you top-of-the-range gear, but doubt it'll help your game."

"Brat." Derek shouldered the bag. "Let's go. Start with some putts to warm up?"

"Sure." Once we'd walked onto the dedicated putting area and were away from ears, I calmly said, "I assume you're recording this conversation."

"No, I'm not. I thought this was a casual chat between friends. Are *you* recording?" he asked, eyebrows raised.

"No. I want no more records than I have to of this whole thing. And my memory is good enough for me." I grinned. "So, what's the gossip?"

Derek made a gesture of frustration, fist clenched, the muscles in his forearm straining like taut rope. "Where to start? I've basically done nothing but try to sort through this mess since you left, meeting after meeting, briefing after briefing. And I have so many questions, I don't know where to begin."

I gave him a saccharine-sweet smile. "Best not to begin at all then. Do you trust me?"

"I've always trusted your honesty, your integrity, and your work ethic. Which is why I don't understand why you've done this."

"It hasn't exactly been a barrel of laughs for me either." I unpacked two boxes of golf balls and dropped them to the green. "You want orange or yellow?"

"Orange."

I tapped all the orange balls over to him and indicated that he should make his first putt. We messed around, pretending we were just two people practicing our golf skills for a few minutes, him missing every second putt he attempted, until he'd finished all the orange balls. Once he'd moved them all away from the hole so I could begin, he murmured, "I've been authorized to make you an offer."

"Authorized by whom exactly?"

"Someone who has the authority."

I took my time with my first putt. The ball dropped neatly into the hole and I strode over to pull it out. "And what offer is that exactly?"

Derek leaned on his putter, legs crossed, the very picture of relaxation. Forced relaxation. "They're willing to make a concession, a small compromise."

I didn't bother to hide my disbelief. "Really? Like what? They'll stop trying to hunt me down and silence me in exchange for…what exactly? I mean, it's a bit late don't you think? Like trying to spoon all the toothpaste back into the tube after you've already squeezed it all out."

"The government will release a statement regarding the weapon test and in return, you will hand over every piece of intel you have, and remove all traces of same from any digital storage you might have backed it up to, and you will swear and sign a document that you will never mention it to anybody, ever. And you keep your freedom." No mention of my job.

"No deal," I said immediately, even though it was *so* tempting to not go to jail. "That's a bullshit concession and you know it. They think I'm just going to forget that our country was, *is*, testing a pretty fucked-up chemical weapon," I scoffed. "As if that wasn't bad enough, we're apparently bribing other countries, our enemies, to test them on another country's citizens. I don't give a shit how you frame it as protecting our interests or our citizens, it's repugnant. And let's not forget the other thing I found out."

"Which is?" His expression was impressively neutral.

"Come on, Derek. Surely *you've* figured it out by now if I managed to with hardly any resources. You've figured it out, or you've been told why it's so important that this never gets out, and that the reason has nothing to do with the actual chemical weapon test."

He didn't want to give away what he knew, in case I was bluffing. I'd have behaved the same way and we could have been at an impasse for the rest of time if one of us didn't shift. It had to be me. "Okay fine, have a carrot. Kannegieter."

"Kannegieter," Derek breathed. His shoulders dropped. "What a fucking nightmare. You know I'm probably going to get fired for this mess."

"I'm sorry. Really I am," I said sincerely. "But you've been counting down to your 'final' retirement for a year. I'm just sorry it might be early because of me."

"Retirement, not fired," he rebutted indignantly. "I'd like to keep my pension, thank you."

"Then I'll tell them it was all me when I go in."

He grunted out a sound that could have been "sure" or "it won't work."

"What will happen when I come in?" I asked quietly.

"Debriefing. An investigation. You'll be held in a secure facility until it's done. Whenever that might be. And after that…I don't know. But I think we can both guess what they'll do with you." Without looking at me, Derek used his club to tap some debris from the bottom of his shoe. "I hate to say it, considering what you did, but you've done good work. I just wish you'd done it *at* work."

"Thanks, boss. But we both know I wouldn't have been allowed to work on it. Nobody would have."

"Has it been worth it?" He gestured vaguely around us. "Your security clearance is gone. You'll *never* be able to get a job in government again, or maybe not any job that'll dig into your background. And that's if they don't toss you in jail, which we both know is a very strong possibility. The most likely possibility."

"Yes. Because now they know they can't get away with it, there's a chance they'll be held accountable, and a chance it won't happen again. And, you know what? I'm not sure I want to work for this government any longer. Who'd want to work for a group of people who'd harass and intimidate one of their loyal employees just for trying to uphold their moral duty?" I fought to control my rising anger. "I spent years cultivating my contacts, building relationships, learning about them and their families. The government might provide the money but my contacts come back, even after I've left fieldwork, because they trust *me*. The information from Kunduz came to light because of *me*."

"That's not how it works, and you know it." Derek sighed. "Martin, stop being so narrow-minded about this. We're all cogs, turning together to make the machine work. Big picture, remember. Just like I taught you."

"You also taught me about the greater good. That some things are more important than just *us*. This is my thing, and I'm not going to let it go, I can't. Even if I'm dead, I'm going to ensure this isn't buried with me."

"Then you may well be digging a grave for yourself."

My heart felt like it'd thudded itself into a brick wall. "Is that a threat?"

"Of course not," he hastened to correct himself. "Just a word of caution, metaphorical. You should know by now that if there's one thing the president hates, it's to be made to look foolish. And you're doing that to him."

"No, Derek. He's done it to himself." I half-heartedly tapped a ball toward the hole. "I didn't authorize the manufacture and test of this weapon. I didn't choose a vice president with questionable moral codes."

"I'll ask you again. Do you want to go to jail for this? Is getting the truth out worth all of this?"

"It is to me, and it's not just about me wanting people to know they did something bad. And no, of course I don't want to be imprisoned. I just—" I raised my hand, fist clenched as if clutching air might ease some of the frustrated tension in my body. It didn't. "I'm going to be branded a traitor and thrown in jail? Just for *knowing* something?"

"It's more than that, and you know it. Don't be obtuse. You worked intelligence outside of our secure walls. You went behind those secure walls to get it."

"After they hid it so they could hide their crime," I rebutted instantly. "Does that not tell you something? Does the offer of this deal not tell you there's more to this than you or I know?"

Derek held up a hand. "You can argue semantics all you want, but you broke the rules, and there are consequences for that."

No shit.

A long silence settled between us, and it was me who caved first. "I know I can't hide forever. And I don't intend to. I just need a few more days to get my affairs in order before I turn myself in."

"What affairs?" He smiled wryly. "I'm the executor of your will, remember?"

"The Flores family..."

"Go on."

"Sophia and her family are not part of this. And that's the truth. Sophia knows nothing, has seen nothing. And I've never even met her family."

"Martin." It was a sigh. "Yes, they are part of this. Because you made them part of this. Even if they know nothing, their association with you makes them currency, and they will be traded for you, whether you like it or not."

My jaw felt so tight I could barely unclamp my teeth. Sophia's parents who'd met in the ocean and who had three children and two grandchildren and who might be pulled apart because I'd dragged their daughter into something I shouldn't have. I shook the thought out of my brain. "No. That's not good enough. I need you to make them leave Sophia and her family alone. Now, and then later when this is over and done and I'm in chains. Otherwise I'm not cooperating." Not that they needed my cooperation, but it was a nice threat.

"I don't have the clout for that. They're frustrated that they can't find you, and they'll do whatever necessary to bring you in now. You really should have gone into undercover espionage work."

"Maybe. I'm great with languages and fake accents but fuck, I hate wigs." I snicked a ball and watched it sail to, then bounce over, the hole. Boo. "What if I promise to come in tomorrow, agree to all their demands, surrender myself to whatever they deem a suitable punishment, including imprisonment?"

"Will you really do that?"

"If you give me assurances that the Flores' will be left alone." Halcyon could handle the other stuff.

His jaw tightened. He really didn't have the clout. Fuck. "Listen," Derek said gently, grabbing my forearm. His grip was comforting rather than threatening. "It's already happening. If you want to keep playing this game with them, they will use whatever necessary to get you to play by their rules. You should know as well as anyone what's in their arsenal."

"I'm not playing a game. This is *not* fun, believe me."

Derek sighed and made an open-handed gesture of conciliation. "What's your end game here, Alex?" Alex, instead of his usual usage of my last name, threw me. He hadn't used my first name, or a variation of it, since 2017. And even then I'd always thought it'd just been stress and relief that I was alive—just—that'd made him blurt a teary "Alexandra…"

"Truth," I answered immediately, surprised he'd asked. "You know what? I really don't care that the VP knocked up his high school girlfriend before graduation. I'm not a political reporter.

I'm not a campaign manager. I'm a truth finder. And this is one truth that *cannot* get buried, because I think you suspect as I do that these roots go deeper than just Kannegieter. If I don't do everything I can to make sure this is brought to light, then every future death from that weapon is on my head. I have so little left, but I still have my integrity."

"Your integrity won't be worth anything if they discredit everything you've done. Which they *will* if you keep pushing this, and then it's over and everything will have been for nothing. We are not the decision makers, we're the information providers. And sometimes our government doesn't use our information the way we personally would have wanted it used, and we have to accept that."

"For fuck's sake! This is our government developing and utilizing a chemical weapon. A horrible one. You saw it. I wouldn't wish that death on my worst enemy." And then there was the whole Berenson plus Russia might equal true love. "And they tried to hide their involvement."

"I know that. I know this weapon is horrendous. I know what they did was wrong. But what I don't know is why you're doing this in this way."

"Because someone threatened me for it and I still don't know who exactly I can trust, and I need to keep this safe. Classified intel should remain classified, so that's what I'm doing. You've always known I have a ridiculous sense of what's right and wrong." I made another putt and watched my ball kiss the edge of the hole and skate past. Bastard thing. This conversation was starting to mess with my concentration.

He was quietly watchful, and made a *give me more* gesture.

I walked over and tapped the ball into the hole, then leaned down to collect it. "I know I can't hide forever. But I *won't* come in until I have assurances of the Flores' safety. I know I'm fucked, but not them. They've done nothing."

"Do you really want to test them?"

"Do they really want to test me?" I rebutted.

His mouth fell open, his entire body projecting disbelief. "You... wouldn't. I have to believe that no matter what you think this is, no matter how you feel, you wouldn't go that far."

Even bluffing about doing something as treasonous as going public with classified intelligence made me queasy. "Come on, Derek. It's a bluff. Don't tell them that though, please. But if bluffing is what I have to do to assure the Flores' remain protected, then I will say what I need to."

"It could make things worse for you."

"Honestly, I don't think it could get any worse for me. So I'm willing to take the chance and bargain with what I have, even if it's all talk."

He studied me intently, and I watched the cogs clicking into place. "You fell in love with her..."

"Maybe," I mumbled. "I don't know. But I do know she and her family are innocent and don't deserve this." Don't deserve me ruining their lives.

"I just don't think you have any bargaining power here."

"Maybe. Maybe not." I shrugged. "I won't know until I test that theory. At least tell them what I want. And in return, I will come quietly. I will tell them everything I know. I will show them how they fucked up. I will roll over. But not until I have assurances that the Flores' will be protected."

Squinting, he stared off into the distance. "I will. But I don't think it'll make any difference. I don't think this is going to end the way you want it to."

"Oh no. I know exactly how it's going to end."

Derek turned back toward me. "I'm so disappointed in you," he sighed.

"I'm sorry to disappoint you. You've disappointed me too." I studied him, searching for the man I thought I knew. "What happened to you? You used to be so...gung-ho. Truth at any cost, charge in and get the information, no matter what. And now you're just...I don't even know who you are. Not the Derek who muscled his way into an op to rescue his friend. I heard you punched one of the team, knocked him out, because they said no to you coming along. You were the first face I recognized and I can't tell you what that meant to me, seeing someone I trusted so much. It meant *everything* to me that day, having you be there, having you rescue me. And now I feel like I don't even know you."

"I have a job to do," he said stiffly.

I swallowed the sickening knowledge that this man was now a stranger to me. "Apparently so. Even if you're doing the wrong one." I walked over and collected all our balls, dropping them back into their cartons. "Here." I offered him both boxes. "You obviously need these balls more than I do."

CHAPTER TWENTY

When I asked how things could get worse—that was a rhetorical question, not an invitation

From my workout position on the floor, I could hear Sophia stirring awake. I was so antsy and desperate to go for a run but it really wasn't an option, hadn't been this whole trip, so I'd been hammering myself with calisthenics and bodyweight exercises in the hotel rooms, balanced with yoga whenever I'd been able to find a quiet space. I'd managed a half-hour run a few days ago in a hotel gym but it wasn't enough to quiet the building discomfort of having been mostly stationary for so long. The covers rustled, her pillow was thumped and then I heard a sleepy, "You down there?"

"Mhmm, yep," I huffed out between crab walks.

"How long have you been up?"

"A while. I'm almost done."

"'Kay. I'll make coffee in a minute." There was a dull clunk as she presumably fumbled her phone from the bedside table. "Dammit," Sophia muttered.

"What is it?" I dropped back to the floor and crawled over to her side of the bed.

"Another email. About you. Or about *us*, I suppose is more accurate." She offered the phone automatically.

Fuck. I hopped up and located my glasses. The email was from the same address pretending to be me.

Ms. Flores,

I see you haven't taken my previous email seriously. You should. Are you currently in danger? Do you fear for your safety in Alexandra Martin's presence? Is this why you haven't tried to leave? Are you being held against your will? If you're afraid, please be assured you may reply via this email and we will help you.

I do hope you reconsider your position. Association with Ms. Martin is dangerous for you and your family.

Regards,

A Concerned Person

I passed the phone back. The whole thing was so absurd, like a caricature of a villain. "Do you fear for your life or safety when you're with me? Blink twice if you need help," I said dryly.

"Well, you did roll over in the middle of the night to lie on top of me. It was rather smooshy." She grinned. "But what a way to go. Death by Lexie's body."

I started laughing, then it suddenly turned on me and before I knew it, I was crying. I dropped onto the bed, buried my face in my hands, and sobbed. And I had no idea why.

"Heyyy." Sophia's arms came around me, pulling me against her. She rocked me slowly, soothing me with quiet words and gentle strokes up and down my back. "It's okay," she murmured. "You're okay."

Tears. What the hell? I really wasn't the fall-into-a-heap-and-cry type, but the more I tried to get myself under control, to stop and rationalize, to explain why I thought I'd just lost my shit, the more I sobbed. And having Sophia there was beyond comforting but also made me all too aware of all my weaknesses. I wanted to pull away, move to a place where I could regain my composure before coming back to her, swaggering and full of bravado. But I couldn't shift myself from the safety of Sophia's embrace.

So I burrowed into her shoulder and cried until I felt like my tear ducts were burning. Even while crying I couldn't shut off my brain, and that ridiculous ever-analytical part of myself kept turning. An outpouring of emotion was probably natural after everything that'd happened since I'd received the call from Hadim. I was exhausted—physically, mentally, emotionally—and if I was really honest with myself, my self-confidence was pretty bruised.

Sure I'd managed to dig up some part of truth about the whole mess, and with a fraction of my usual resources. But where had it gotten me, really? Nowhere except deeper into a pile of shit, with knowledge that made me sick. And I childishly, selfishly, wished I'd never taken Hadim's call, that I'd never joined the agency, never recruited into Halcyon. Maybe then I'd have a normal life, a normal relationship. Me. Me. Me.

Me.

But what about everyone else who depended upon me, even if they never knew it?

Sophia pulled back, cupped my face in her hands, and tenderly used her thumbs to wipe underneath my eyes. "It's going to be okay, really."

It was a sweet sentiment, and I knew what she meant and that she wanted to be encouraging. But deep down I knew it wouldn't be *okay*. Maybe passable, eventually, but not okay. Still, I couldn't help asking, "How do you know?"

"Because it has to be. Because I don't want this to be all we ever have together." She smiled tremulously. "It can't be."

I had no answer, no witty comeback. So I pulled her close, kissed her and then dropped my face into her neck and tried not to fall apart again.

Freaked out about Sophia's latest email, I decided—once I'd stopped blubbering—that we should change hotels again, and she agreed unhesitatingly. We packed, again, and I took our key to the front desk, again, and gave them a bullshit story about plans changing. Another few hundred dollars wasted. Again. Sorry, Halcyon accountants.

This whole experience was reminiscent of my brief stint backpacking through Europe before I started college, and reminded me how much I'd hated not being settled in one place. In deference to Sophia's desire to have something homecooked, I agreed with her find of a studio apartment with a small kitchen. It was probably only going to be for a night or two, at most, and I wanted to give her what I could, while I could. Before I...left.

I claimed the shower first, and Sophia declared she'd order dinner. I paused midway through unlacing my shoes. "Weren't you saying something about cooking? Isn't that why we decided on an apartment with a kitchen?"

"Mhmm, and didn't you say something about cooking for me?" she rebutted playfully. "Or was that just to get me into bed?"

"I did say that, yes, and it had nothing to do with trying to sleep with you. Tomorrow we'll get some fresh groceries and I'm going to woo the shit out of you with my culinary prowess." I'd cook a last supper of sorts.

"Careful. You've already wooed the shit out of me with your personality and bed skills. Too much wooing and I might pass out."

"Too much ego boosting like that, and it might be me who passes out." I kissed her as I passed the closet where she was hanging clothes.

"Feel like Mexican?" she asked my departing back.

I glanced back at her, smiling. "Always."

Standing under the hot spray, something pleasant niggled at the back of my mind. It was just like our first night on the road when she'd chosen Mexican and dishes she'd remembered I'd liked. Maybe, sometime in the future, we might get to go to a nice restaurant and have an actual date night where I could dress up and put makeup on and we could act like a regular couple. I twisted the faucet to cold, gritted my teeth through the arctic blast for twenty seconds, then shut off the water. Maybes were nothing more than pointless wishes.

When I came out of the shower to dress, Sophia glanced up at me then back down at her phone, nervously chewing her lower lip. I didn't know how to ask what was going on, yet again, but I didn't have to.

"I just got a call from Mom," she said with forced calm. When she looked up, her expression was like someone had dragged her face downward. "Dad's been...taken."

For a moment, I forgot how to breathe. "What do you mean, *taken*?" My stomach lurched, and though I was sure I knew what she would say, I asked the question anyway. "Taken where? How? By whom?"

"She said a bunch of people in uniforms, waving badges and papers and shouting a whole bunch of stuff, came in and then handcuffed him and took him." She used her palms to wipe under her eyes. "They said something about his immigration status? What the fuck? He came here as a *kid*, Lexie. He's a naturalized citizen. He served in the US Army. He married an American woman. His accent is basically American, for fuck's sake. They can't deport him to Mexico, can they?"

"No." But they were sure as hell going to threaten it. "I'm so sorry. This is my fault."

She didn't acknowledge what I'd said, just started pacing around the room. "They came in the middle of his meal. Just grabbed him, didn't let him get any spare clothes or even his wallet. He's got a heart condition and they didn't let him take any medication. He's in his seventies." Sophia's voice broke up. "What if something happens and he doesn't have his pills?"

"Nothing's going to happen to him, I promise. I'm going to make a call right now and make it right, make sure he's okay."

"How can you make sure he's okay?"

"Because they want me, and I'm going to make them release him in exchange for me."

That stopped her short. "You're...what?"

"Yes. He's the perfect negotiation tool. Sorry, that sounds impersonal but that's how they would be viewing him. They've found my weak spot. You and, by extension, anyone who is associated with you." I watched her working through this new information. If she didn't already hate me... I sighed. "This is how negotiations work. Or, not *negotiations* in this case, but rather a bargaining chip." I offered a weak smile.

She sank onto the bed. "No. No..."

"Yes. *Think*, Sophia, not about me and what I'm doing. This is your *dad*." Nobody would choose me over their father, and I would never, ever ask that of her. "I'm so sorry. I told my boss yesterday that this was unacceptable, that I wouldn't cooperate if they didn't leave you and your family alone." I shrugged. "I broke rule one-eighty-six of spy camp—don't show your hand. By telling him that, I told them exactly how important you are to me, and showed them exactly what they needed to do to make me comply immediately."

"But...I...but...you've done so much, worked so hard, and... and...it's not right to just end like this. For them to force you into a corner. There has to be some other path, a little hidden tunnel or something. Isn't that what you said? That you go until you can't find another path?"

"There really isn't, sweetheart. *This* is the end of the road. No more sneaky pathways or tunnels or bridges. It's over." I felt sick at the realization, and no matter how I tried I couldn't squash my anxiety and acute disappointment that we really would never get a happily ever after. "It's me, or your dad. And I can't have tearing your family apart on my conscience. I just can't. I won't."

"Oh."

"Yes, oh." I blew out a long breath. "So, we're going home. Or rather, you'll be going home and I'm going to a facility to tell them what I've been up to this past week. Now, I need to make a call and see if I can't unravel one part of this mess. I'll just be outside. Back soon."

I'd just pulled the door open and glanced outside when Sophia quietly said, "Lexie?"

"Yeah?"

"Thank you."

"Of course." I made myself smile. "It wouldn't be a great start for our relationship if I let them keep your dad away from you and your family."

Shit. That word again. Relationship.

Sophia's eyes had widened the moment I said it, but she didn't say anything. And I slipped out of the door before I could put any more of my foot in my mouth.

Lennon answered after the second ring and I dove right in. "I'm sure you know what's happening."

"I do."

"I anticipate I have twelve hours max before I'll be in custody. A little sooner than I wanted, but turns out they're smart."

"I'll be following closely, and if we can assist, we will." Ice cubes clinked. "But don't let her make you soft, Alexandra. People will always use that to their advantage."

I bristled at the implication. Sophia wasn't like that. Wasn't like them. Wasn't like...me. "She doesn't. She makes me strong. I need to destroy this phone before they get access to it. I assume you'll have a new one sent to me when the time is right. *If*, I mean."

"We will. Everyone at Halcyon will know what you've given up."

"Right. You know, that almost makes me feel not-shit. I told Derek that my only condition for coming quietly is that I want the Flores' protected. I may have pretended I was going to leak the intel."

"Clever. Never give up everything in a negotiation."

"I don't think this is a negotiation so much as a surrender. But, whatever. I'm telling you because I need you to prioritize their safety, because I don't know if he can do it. Whisper in ears, do whatever you do. I've done everything you've asked me, and it's cost me something I wanted." Something that I didn't even know I'd wanted. I swallowed hard and forced the words out through a throat tight with emotion. "Promise me you'll try."

"I'll try."

"Try really hard. This is my last communication from this number." I hung up and powered down the blue phone. It only took a few minutes to break the SIM and give the phone a brick wall smashy-smashy treatment.

Despite the fact I was using another new throwaway cell phone, Derek answered after three rings. "Wood."

"I'm guessing they didn't read your report detailing my demands."

"I haven't filed it yet."

That made me pause. "Why?"

"Because I'm trying to see if there's another way for you."

"There isn't. You need to make a call to the White House the moment I hang up. Tell them what I told you yesterday to pass on about releasing Sophia Flores and her family from any perceived wrongdoing. Unless I get that assurance and Mr. Flores is released unharmed, I will not share my exact location. And I mean *unharmed*. If he so much as doesn't like the chair in his room or the food they're giving him, no deal. He has a medical condition and they didn't let him take medication when they grabbed him. I expect that they will provide him with whatever he needs the moment he needs it or I'm going to be very upset. And you can tell them that when I'm upset, I have a habit of forgetting to secure classified intel."

There was a pause. I sighed. "Imagine I'm tapping my nose," I said. "It's all I have, Derek. Tell them, make them think they have no choice but to do as I'm demanding. *Please*. If you're trying to find another way to help me, then help me with this. Please," I begged again.

It took him almost thirty seconds to respond with a barely audible, "Okay."

"The issue of his medication? I want that to be the first thing you tell them."

"I'll bring it up right away." Derek's voice softened. "And I don't know what they have in mind, but I'm not going to let you rot in a detention facility for the rest of your life."

An interesting change of direction. "Got another taste for rescue, sir?"

He chuckled. "I always do." The laughter in his voice died. "I'll do my best."

"That's always been good enough for me."

Quietly, Derek said, "I'm glad." He cleared his throat. "I estimate it will take them a few hours to arrange for Mr. Flores's release." He didn't even try to quibble the point, or tell me that they might not agree to it, which told me it was nothing more than a tool to break me. A big fucking sledgehammer.

"Okay then. I'll call you when I've confirmed he's free and unharmed, and we can proceed from there. I'll hold up my end of the bargain, if they hold up theirs. Talk soon." I ended the call and opened the phone to remove and break the SIM card. This trip was really adding to my environmental waste toll. I made a mental note to plant some trees and pay the carbon offset taxes next time I hired a car or took a flight. If I ever hired a car or took a flight again.

Leaning against the side of the building, I tried to relax. I was ashamed of the relief that flooded through me now that I'd finally unburdened myself of this. I had a plan. A plan I didn't like, but having some of the pressure relieved made me feel better than I had in weeks. I'd changed course and now all I had to do was ride out the rest of the journey and hope Lennon and Derek would come through for me.

Sophia sat on the bed, staring at the door, and had clearly been doing so since I left. She hopped up the moment I slid the chain home, and moved like she was going to come to me but had suddenly realized her feet were stuck to the floor. "Is everything okay?"

"I've been assured your dad will be released very soon, and that he's safe and okay. I also pointed out the issue of his medical condition and they're aware of it and on top of the situation." Letting Mr. Flores die in custody was not a good way to proceed, and they'd know that. "When you receive confirmation from someone you trust, either him or your mom, that he's home, then I'll call them, tell them where I am and they'll come get me." I exhaled, feeling so suddenly fatigued I wasn't sure I could keep standing. I let myself sink into one of the unforgiving chairs around the table. "I was told that it might take a few hours for them to arrange the paperwork and drive him home again."

"Do you trust them?"

"I don't really trust anyone."

"Not even me?" The hurt in the question was unmistakable.

"Trust…is hard. Trust can get you killed. I trust you to be honest with me. I trust you when we're intimate, more than I've ever trusted *anyone* in that situation. I trust you to not betray me here and now." I exhaled a long breath. "But real, deep, reciprocal, place my life in your hands under any circumstances type trust? That needs time to build."

She bit her lower lip. "Do you think we could ever have something like that?"

"Yes, I do. If we had time to build it. If that's what you wanted." The truth of that statement hurt so badly I almost doubled over. We never would have time.

"It's what I want." She said it so quietly that I had to take a few moments to parse the words.

"Me too." I forced a smile. "So, I don't trust them, but I *do* trust that they're going to do what I asked, because if they don't then they risk me disappearing for real and spreading everything I know far and wide and very publicly."

"Would you really do that?" Sophia looked like asking the question made her feel sick.

"No. I've discovered I don't really have the stomach for this constant run-and-hide business. And I would *never* leak classified intel, regardless of how I feel about the situation." I grinned, shrugged. "But they can't know that for sure, so…at the moment, I have a little leverage." It didn't feel like it, but when they finally got me, I was going to do my damnedest to tip the balance of power in my favor.

CHAPTER TWENTY-ONE

Sometimes your best isn't actually good enough—how's that for a motivational poster?

I'd exhausted myself with mindless pacing, packing up all my stuff, working out logistics with Sophia like returning the rental car and her taking my tea stuff and my dress, and pulling apart the laptops and destroying the internal drives so nothing could be traced back to Halcyon. Sophia sat beside me where I'd dropped onto the bed, rubbing soothing circles on my back. She didn't say anything, just sat with me while I slumped forward with my hands clasped in my lap. I squeezed my hands together until my knuckles felt like they were going to burst through my skin.

"Do you want to talk about it?" she quietly asked.

I shrugged. "Not much to say. I'm just tired. Tired of trying to figure out how this happened to me. Tired of running and hiding. Tired of being the one who has to sacrifice."

She reached around to cup my cheek so she could turn my face toward her. "You don't have to be Atlas, holding the whole weight of this."

"But who else will?" Not her or her family—I'd make sure of that. Not Derek, he had no power. Not Halcyon—they'd do what they were tasked with doing and remain unsullied. It was all on my shoulders.

She was quiet for long moments, her hand stroking the length of my back. "Whatever you need to do, I'll support that. I'm here for you however you might need me. What can I do? How can I help you?"

She couldn't. Not in the way she thought, by doing something. Rather, her help would be just *existing*, me knowing she was out in the world living safely, being able to remember our time together. "Tell the truth if they talk to you. I've told them you're not involved and they're not to do anything to you or your family. That was part of my deal for turning myself in." I swiped the back of my hand over my nose. "And please, *please* tell your family sorry from me. I really didn't mean for your dad to get involved."

Now she held my face in both her hands. "I know you didn't."

"I'd still like to meet them someday." It came out quiet, hopeful, like a kid asking someone to be their friend.

"I'd like that too. I bet Mom would fall over herself to make veggie pozole for you."

I coughed out a dry laugh. "For the woman who dragged her daughter into a national security incident and had her husband taken and held in detention? Pozole with extra arsenic."

Sophia's laugh was loud and long. "Oh god. If she decided you had to be taught a lesson, she'd never do something as underhanded as poison you." She tsked jokingly. "She'd just come right out and wallop you, then point at your place at our family table. If she satisfies herself that you're a good person, and if she knows I'm happy, then that's enough."

"Are you happy?" I whispered, afraid to hear her answer.

"Right now? Not so much because of what's about to happen. But you, generally speaking, make me happy. I just wish we had some more time to explore that now. But…" She shrugged. "Maybe later."

"Mmm, maybe later," I agreed, hoping that saying it aloud enough might make that wish come true. "You know, I had no idea on that first date that being with you would turn into something so—" Something so what? Life altering? Fulfilling? "I mean, I just thought we'd have a few casual dates, maybe some sex and then that would be it and you'd realize like everyone else before that my life doesn't mesh well with others."

"Dates! Ha! You *do* think they're dates."

"Fine." I rolled my eyes. "We're dating. But if we make it beyond this, then I hope you know it's not all chases and hiding and cool gadgets and doing super-secret investigation. I'm actually very boring, just busy."

"I can handle boring but busy."

"Well, all right then. If I go—" I stopped abruptly, shaking my head at my careless wording. Not if, when. This was happening, soon, and I wanted to be sure she really understood that this was it for us, that she likely wouldn't ever see me again. "*When* I go, then I don't know when I'll come back, if at all." At her expression of alarm, I clarified, "Not dead, just detained, probably for quite a while if they decide to go after me for everything and make sure I'm not a threat to national security. I'm not, of course, but they might be in a lesson-teaching mood." I smiled, but it was so tight it was as if my mouth was splitting at the edges. I tried to get more words out, but I couldn't make the thoughts form into something audible.

"Will they do that?" Her voice broke up an octave halfway through her question.

"I think so, yes." Dropping my voice to a stage whisper, I said, "They aren't very happy with me. But...you might see me on the news."

"I'd rather see you in person."

"I know. Me too." I sagged against her. "They'll lie about me, about what I did, because otherwise they'd have to tell the world what they did. But, if something big and unexpected happens in the next few months, that was me. That was...this. And I hope it'll help you understand why I did everything I did."

"What? How will I know what it is?"

Smiling, I assured her, "You'll know. Trust me."

"I do." She ran her hand down my arm until she'd taken my hand.

"Sophia?"

"Mmm?"

I knew what I was about to say was going to be laced with tears, but I said it anyway. "I've loved every moment of being with you."

"Same. Weirdly not-vacation-like and all. I'd do it all again in a heartbeat." She inhaled slowly, then let it out again. "How will it happen? You leaving?"

"Once you know your dad is home and safe, I open the door a crack and wave a white flag."

"So our national security isn't as high-tech as they have us believe."

"Not at all. I get most of my intel by carrier pigeon and write my reports with a feather dipped in ink I make myself from botanicals collected by moonlight."

Smiling, Sophia swatted at me and I captured her hand, kissing her palm. I brushed my lips over her skin, turned her hand over and kissed her knuckles. When I let her hand go, Sophia framed my face with her hands and kissed me. I lingered against her lips, absorbing comfort and love through her kiss. It was unhurried, sensual rather than frantic and when she pressed me backward, I pulled her to lie on top of me.

She undressed me slowly, like savoring a gift she was unwrapping. When I was finally naked and bared for her, Sophia shed her own clothing almost as an afterthought, as if she'd been so solely focused on me that she'd forgotten everything else. She made love to me like someone who knew this would be the last time. She inflamed me with one touch then soothed me with the next and when I begged for more, she gave it to me. Each kiss and caress was calculated, unerring, and my climax built in a slow roll of pleasure that I knew would end in a spine-tingling, bone-melting orgasm. And quickly.

But I didn't want quick. I wanted this to last, to embed itself in my brain so I could keep it there for later. For when I needed to remember things like this, this normalcy, this connection, this want and need. I would need to remember that someone wanted me, someone cared about me.

"Together," I pleaded, my voice strained and desperate.

And even though all I'd said was that one word, she knew exactly what I meant. Sophia climbed up my body, bestowing kisses and licks along the way. She turned around, straddling my shoulders, presenting herself to me. I buried my mouth in her heat and felt her moan against me. The sensation was incredible and I raised my hips to seek more from her mouth.

Sophia gave willingly, her fingers pressed against my inner thigh urging me onward, guiding me until her breathing quickened further and the movement of her tongue and lips against my clit became erratic. When she came, Sophia kept her mouth against me, and her deep satisfied groan sent a reciprocal shudder of heat and pleasure through me.

She carefully disengaged herself and turned back around to lie against me, her head on my shoulder. We didn't speak, simply existed together. I held her close, stroked her skin and tangled my fingers in her hair. And I thought that maybe things would be okay after all. There had been the tiniest moment in time, barely a heartbeat right before I climaxed, where I felt nothing except the pure simple pleasure of being with her. No anxiety, nothing in my brain except being present in the moment. And it was glorious.

I had something to hold on to.

I was dead asleep when Sophia's phone rang. Fighting grogginess and anxiety, I checked the time—a little after three p.m.—and tried to focus on her conversation. It could be about only one thing. Mostly I caught Sophia's relief and "mhmms" before she said her goodbyes and dropped the phone onto the bedside table.

"Is he back?" I mumbled, rubbing my eyes. Another ten hours of sleep would have been welcome. "Is he okay?"

"He is," she said around her tears. Sophia palmed her eyes. "He's fine. Seriously pissed off, but fine."

I exhaled. "Good. Did they say anything? Offer any explanations or apologies or anything?"

"I'm not sure," she hedged.

"You can tell me."

"I'm not sure I really got what Mom was saying, but I gathered they did apologize, said it was a 'misunderstanding' and then on the back of that made some veiled threats that trying to seek compensation or recognition would not only be pointless but could make things worse."

"Isn't that nice of them," I grumbled.

"They do worse things to other people every single day."

"I know. They suck."

She took a deep breath. "So…is this it?"

"It is," I confirmed steadily. I kissed her quickly then rolled out of bed. "I'm going to have a quick workout, take a shower and then

I...have to go." The more I delayed, the harder it would be for both of us.

Her eyes widened at the final statement, and she nodded, offering a quiet, "Sure, okay then." She looked as if she wanted to say more but just didn't know what. I knew that feeling.

Showered after I'd worked out some nervous energy, I packed my things, double-checked everything and made my call. Derek sounded like he'd just finished a marathon when he answered, "Wood."

"It's me. Thank you for the release of Javier Flores. What about my other conditions?"

His voice was steady. "I have written assurances that Sophia Flores and her family will be left alone, without exception. Legally, this cannot come back to them."

"Good." After a second, I remembered my manners. "Thank you." I gave him my address and asked, "Can you have them call me with an ETA and I'll go outside and meet them. I—I don't want her to see it, see me in handcuffs."

"Will do." He cleared his throat. "Be careful with what you say to them, Martin. Remember whose side you're really on."

"I will. I hope I get to talk to you again."

"You will. I promise."

The call came sooner than I'd expected, barely thirty minutes after I'd spoken with Derek. There was never enough time. But I'd already known that. I forced all my feelings down where they couldn't touch me, stood up, and calmly said, "It's time for me to go." I had to be calm, because I could see Sophia was about to fall apart.

"No..." she said, her voice breaking on a sob. "I'm not ready."

"Me either. But I have to go. We knew this was coming, right?" I took her face in my hands. "If you drive back, drive safely, please. Use all of that prepaid Visa, fuck them, spend it all. And just...take care of yourself, okay?"

She nodded, not bothering to wipe her face. "You too."

"I will, I promise. I...just...I don't know what to say." Shrugging, I whispered, "Except, thank you, Sophia. Thank you." I kissed her goodbye before I could say something that would further upset her, hugged her for as long as I dared before I knew I'd break down, then walked out of the hotel room and closed the door behind me. I'd never open a door to her again.

There was so much more that I wanted to say to her but there was no point. Telling her those things was cruel. She needed to be able to forget about me, to move on from this. And me telling her that I thought I was falling in love with her would stick in her mind like a stubborn weed. It was unfair to her, and also to me, to verbalize that, to let it out in the world. Instead, I'd just have it inside my head to think about for the rest of time, but at least it was only mine to carry.

Falling in love with her. It was a strange thing to confront at this point in my life, let alone this exact moment when everything was about to get really, really tough for me. In all my forty-one years on the planet, I'd never been in love. I'd loved women, sure, but I'd never felt that extra thing, the thing I felt with Sophia. That thing that made me desperate to spend time with her, made me long to touch her, just...be near her. That thing, whatever it was, that made me trust her utterly. The thing that made me feel like I might shatter into a million pieces, because the reality was that I would never see her again.

CHAPTER TWENTY-TWO

Ever had two guys watching you pee?

I sat with my bags on the low brick wall fencing the front of the hotel, waiting for them to arrive and trying to think of what would happen, how I would handle it, handle myself. Preparation is king, or…queen. But every time I thought about it, I couldn't quite imagine the follow-through. It's hard to picture a debrief. Even harder to picture a detention.

In the end it was pretty boring and simple. Two guys, holstered weapons visible, and a black SUV with tinted windows—how unsurprising they'd use *that* vehicle. They took my bags and, hidden from view of the hotel by the open rear door, I was given the most perfunctory pat-down on the planet. Once it was done, I asked, "What, no squat-and-cough?"

The shorter guy said, "We already have your devices. And if you wanted to smuggle something into the facility to hurt yourself with then that's your prerogative."

Nice to know they cared. Once I was inside the vehicle, they handcuffed me and attached the cuffs to a chain bolted to an anchor point on the floor in the back seat. "Thank you," I murmured as I shuffled to get comfortable.

"For what?" the taller guy asked neutrally.

"For not letting my girlfriend see you handcuffing me." I couldn't stand the thought of her thinking of me as a criminal.

Then that was it. There was no more talking. We drove through the night, the day, and into the following evening, stopping like clockwork every three hours to stretch legs, eat, drink, pee if needed. They even shook me awake to make me get out of the car for this charade of hospitality, and one of them came into the bathroom to stay with me while I peed—badges could get you everywhere, apparently. At least they turned around while they made me open-stall-door pee. And I spent the entire drive fighting panic at being restrained like this again.

We drove through a security checkpoint a little after two a.m. the next morning, if the darkness and the dashboard clock were anything to go by. The building was one I didn't recognize, but even in the dark, lit only by sporadic security lights, I knew it was a government facility. It was like they'd gotten a great deal on bland, boring buildings. There was no preamble, no break or changing clothes. They asked if I needed to use the bathroom before they began. Yes, please, and by myself this time if you don't mind. I had a feeling this debrief was going to take a while and needing to pee the whole time would mess with my concentration.

I did not get to pee by myself.

The disorientation of the early-morning hour was likely deliberate, and I fought valiantly against exhaustion. One cat, two cat, black cat, blue cat. State capitals are: Albany, Annapolis, Atlanta, Augusta, Austin, Baton Rouge, Bismarck...

Boring.

US Presidents are: George Washington, John Adams, Thomas Jefferson, James Madison, James Monroe, John Quincy Adams, Andrew Jackson...

Even boringer.

If nothing else, I supposed, a zillion years in jail would give me time to write the erotic sci-fi novel I'd always thought I had in me. I will not tell them about Halcyon, no matter what they do. I will not tell them about Halcyon. I'd spent the drive hoarding pleasant thoughts about Sophia, something to disappear into in case I needed it. I didn't think they'd actually torture me, but they weren't going to make things pleasant. I really hated when things weren't pleasant. Hopefully Halcyon would provide me with a shit-hot lawyer.

Thankfully I was saved from my own brain when I was herded into a twenty-by-twenty room with two men waiting for me. One I knew, one I did not. I spoke up, directing my words toward the younger man. "Thanks for the McDonald's shake. It really hit the spot. You get your stuff back from the cashiers?"

He gave me the same pinched expression he had when I'd snuck up behind him and taken his gun in Tampa.

The other man, early fifties, medium height and build, so swarthy he should have been swashbuckling, gave me a look that would have withered most. I was never one for withering, and I was well beyond such reactions now.

I focused on Swarthy Man, who seemed to be the in-charge guy. "Where am I? What city? You're required to tell me."

We had a staring contest for a minute or so, and I'm pleased to say I didn't lose. But I didn't win either.

"No, Dr. Martin," he finally answered. His voice was unusually high-pitched for his manly man appearance. Tenor instead of baritone. "I don't have to tell you anything. You should know that there are no rules except the rules we decide upon. We can keep you as long as we need or want, or we can put you anywhere we want, forever if that's what we need to do."

"I know." And I did. But I'd hoped it wasn't going to be like that.

He smiled, surprisingly gently considering the circumstances. "So it's in your interests to cooperate."

I only just managed to keep the bite of exasperation from my words. "Yes I know how it works." With immense effort I also managed to stop myself from adding a facetious "I've seen those movies too." I squared my shoulders. "I'd like a lawyer."

"One is on the way. I'm not sure when they'll arrive."

They could do whatever they wanted, basically, if they spun it as anti-terrorism or whatever Homeland Security clause they felt like. "Are restraints really necessary? I'm not some super-spy or criminal. I work for the government too." I had to assume these were our people in some national security and investigations branch. If they weren't then I was totally fucked. Maybe even dead.

"Yes, I'm aware that you're not a spy and as to your criminal status, that's for us to decide."

Wow. Okay then. Just doing my sworn duty and following orders to ensure a stable and well-run government free from foreign influence. This guy wouldn't know about Halcyon. He'd probably sat behind a desk his whole career. Bet I've got higher security clearance than you, Swarthy Man. *Had* higher security clearance. Had…

"Sit there please." With a chin tilt he indicated the high-backed metal chair on the opposite side of the desk.

I did as I was told, and McDonald's brushed the side of my breast as he fastened the strap around my chest. The deliberate tentativeness of the touch told me he didn't want to, but he did it on purpose because they'd told him to. They wanted a reaction, to get me off-balance before they began. It wouldn't work, and it was laughable that they'd try it on one of their people who they'd trained to be unaffected by such games. My brain ran at a million miles a minute. Unless it was a reversal and they were using something hidden in my subconscious for this exact situation. Maybe they had protocols for agents they've deemed have gone rogue.

Stop it, Lexie. Ridiculous freaked-out fatigue thoughts. You're not a rogue agent, you're not even an agent, you're an analyst, and as if they'd be so forward-thinking as to implement a safety switch into the training of every intelligence analyst on the off-chance they needed to bring us back into line.

I smiled up at McDonald's. "I'm surprised you're still employed after what happened in Tampa." I made a tsking sound. "Such a rookie mistake. Seriously." Leaning as close as I could while strapped to a solid object, I lowered my voice. "I'd be happy to teach you some things. Well, some *more* things. Do you want your gun back? It's in the backpack they took when they picked me up."

He ignored me but wasn't able to stop the tips of his ears reddening as he looped a chain through my handcuffs and secured my hands to a loop around my waist. Once he'd made sure that I was Hannibal-Lecter restrained to the chair, he moved to the corner behind me to my left. I could see him in the reflective two-way glass in front of me.

I looked at both men as best I could. "So, just want to bring this up and double-check—is this legal? I'm an American citizen and I'm being questioned without a lawyer. No Miranda rights?" I raised my voice for the video camera pointing at me from over Swarthy Man's left shoulder. "Because I would like to state for the record that I have *not* been Mirandized or formally offered a lawyer, and I *would* like a lawyer please and thank you."

"You haven't been arrested. We're simply talking." Swarthy Man opened a leather-bound notepad and extracted a Mont Blanc pen. "Let's start from the beginning. On the fourteenth of October this year, at approximately oh-nine hundred, you received a call from an asset of yours who you refer to as Hadim. Correct?"

Okay then. That's how it was going to be. I ran through all my options. I didn't have many. Be silent and stay here for an indefinite amount of time, strapped to a chair, or tell the truth and hope I was smart enough not to incriminate myself, or Halcyon. I decided on the second option for now. "Yes."

"And what did that conversation consist of?"

"Words." Okay, so telling the truth didn't mean I had to be forthcoming.

He sighed. "Dr. Martin. I'm going to be frank with you. I've been here for fourteen hours already, my back is killing me, and I *really* don't want to sit here with you for the next eight hours while we play runaround. We both know that I already know what happened and simply need to get it on-record. So, why don't you stop playing intelligence analyst and give me the facts so we can both go home." A smirk. "Well, so I can go home and you can go to what's going to be your new home for the foreseeable future."

His attempt to soften me did anything but. A cardinal mistake, admitting he had something to lose, or wanted something other than information—even if it was just a fake-out to try and establish rapport. The only thing in my future was a secure facility so why wouldn't I try to bargain?

I sat up straighter. Well, kind of. It was difficult with the restraints. "I *am* an intelligence analyst, so isn't it logical that's what I'm behaving like? Not sharing information unless I'm certain is in my DNA." I stretched forward as far as I could, ignoring the strap tightening around my chest. "How do I know that you deserve to know what I know? You've shown me no real identification, so how can I trust that you have the security clearance to receive this information?"

"You can trust it because you're strapped to a chair and I'm not. And I know you discussed this with your direct superior, Derek Wood, so I believe that's proof enough that I have clearance."

Nice play. But he could have learned that without being a good guy. "Right. Well, you know what I believe? I believe in a flow of information. I tell you something, you tell me something. It's how I've operated for the past decade and I have to say it's worked pretty well for me so far. Where am I to be held after you're done with me here?"

"In a facility. Why did you take the intelligence you'd received from your contact and…go on the run?" The way he said it was like it pained him to use such a basic phrase for what I'd done. "I have to believe that someone of your supposed intelligence would know that goes against every rule we have."

"I didn't take the intelligence. I left work that day thinking it was just ordinary information. Why, and how, would I have taken anything?"

"I'll rephrase. Why did you use human resources, after the fact, to access secured areas of an agency server to take the intelligence for yourself?"

"Because a massive asshole broke into my apartment demanding everything I had pertaining to this. Given the information was from a legitimate source and something I needed to pursue in an official capacity, I'm sure you can imagine I was more than a little freaked out, thinking a foreign agent was trying to infiltrate the agency."

"I see." He made notes. Pointless notes given this was being videoed. "Why not bring up your concern with your superior?"

"Because…" My nose itched furiously, but with my hands stuck to the chain at my waist I couldn't do anything. I bent my head to scratch the itch on my shoulder. "Because I didn't know if I could trust him, given he was one of only three people who were directly aware of what I'd learned." The triangle of trust. Any more points and the shape is too big. Too many places to leak.

"Trust in your colleagues is important."

"It is."

"I suppose my big question is, what exactly were you hoping to accomplish?"

This would be so much easier if I could tell him all about Halcyon and the Protocol at play behind the scenes. Time for the Lie. I was so sick of the Lie. The Lie made me look like a traitorous idiot, two things I was not. "My job, primarily, which is to get to the bottom of the information and put as clear a picture together as I could so I could give it to those people in a position to act on it. Accountability for those who did wrong. And to stop this from *ever* happening again."

"By what means?"

"Whatever means I needed to use."

"Would you have leaked the information as you threatened?"

I said nothing. No way, not leading myself down that path of incrimination. I was already far enough along the path. But inside I was screaming, "No fucking way!"

"You're an intelligence analyst, not a journalist, Dr. Martin. It's not your place to decide what gets released or when. By definition, your job is to *analyze* and take that analysis to people who have the authority to act. Frankly, your behavior is disgusting."

"I didn't *want* to release it," I admitted quietly, ashamed that I was even giving him that bit of information. "I took an oath, and I would never betray that. I wanted answers and for the people responsible to be accountable. I wanted to save lives."

"Foreign lives?"

"*All* lives, American or otherwise," I said emphatically. "This, this...thing is horrific. No human should ever be exposed to it. It's criminal."

"Again, that's not for you to decide."

This guy was clearly cyborg, not human. "Have you seen the video?"

"I don't know what you're referring to," he said neutrally.

My hands strained at the restraints. "Bull-fucking-shit! We're both here so you have to know. You have to have seen it. That test isn't a threat, like look at what we have so don't go starting wars with us. It's fucking murder. And it's wrong on so many levels, legal and humanitarian, that it makes me sick. And my government ordered it." It felt good to get it all out, to finally let myself rage at what I'd seen. It was actually kind of nice to know Halcyon would take care of things—remove Berenson, stop the chemical manufacture—and I could just do and say what I wanted because I was fucked anyway. "Do you keep track of news and current events, Mr., um..."

"Smith," he supplied.

"Of course." I turned my attention to McDonald's. "And let me guess, you're Mr. Jones?"

There was the faintest smile twitching the edge of his mouth but he said nothing.

Back to Smith. "Do you? Pay attention to the news? Given what I assume to be your job, I'd be surprised if you answered in the negative."

"Yes."

"Great. One point for staying abreast of current events. You're not as dumb as I thought. So you would know about all the really horrible fucking things going on in the world, most of it to people who don't deserve it but are caught in the crossfire, so to speak. But this…this wasn't even a war crime. There was no war where this happened. It was murder. I listened to the audio recording of the conversation, watched the body cam video of the chemical weapon *test*, heard the audio of people screaming, or trying to as they choked on blood and their lungs came out of their mouths and their skin peeled from their flesh." I didn't bother to hide my emotion. They could call me weak, sentimental, a *woman* or whatever else, I didn't care. I owed it to those people to be horrified, outraged, appalled, and to not disguise it.

He said nothing. I tried again. "It's a crime. Our government committed a crime."

"I'd be careful if I were you, Dr. Martin," he said conversationally.

"And why is that, Mr. Smith?"

He turned the pen around in his hands, casually, as if bored and needing to fidget. "What you're saying skirts dangerously close to treason. Accusations like that are dangerous. We've tried to help you but it seems you're not interested in that. You're only interested in this little crusade you've decided to pursue."

"It's not a crusade," I rebutted testily. After a second I toned myself down. "I was simply doing my job. And I'm curious about what it is about that you don't like. The fact I found out our government manufactured an illegal chemical weapon and tested it on humans? The fact our government basically bribed a foreign entity to do this testing on civilians, presumably to create some illusion of keeping our hands clean? Or the fact I discovered the military officer who was the front man for this transaction is the vice president's illegitimate son?"

To his credit, he displayed no reaction. The guy was good. I could admire his professional skills, even as he was using them against me. I waited for exactly thirty seconds and when he still didn't answer, I kept talking. "I disclosed this information to *nobody* who didn't have clearance. The only person I spoke with about it already knew. Derek Wood. So why exactly am I in this position? Because I found out this dirty government secret? Because I embarrassed the president by uncovering the fact his choice for VP isn't as upstanding as he made him out to be?" I would have loved to do a thoughtful chin tap but alas, the chains prevented that. "Someone else would have found this out, if not me. Would you be treating them the same way?"

"You're in this position because you went against *everything* our intelligence community stands for. And I highly doubt anyone with a modicum of integrity or intelligence would do what you did."

"Bullllllshit." I leaned back in the chair, trying hard to appear confident and nonchalant. Tricky when you're strapped to a chair. "I was doing my job. Getting to the root of information. I'm incredibly good at it, if you'll check my performance evaluations."

He ignored me. "I think some time to think about how you want to proceed might be beneficial." Smith stood, smiling like a shark. "While you're thinking, we might have a chat with Sophia Flores."

If I could have punched him, I would have. I tried to leap from the chair, but hit the restraint strap around my chest, and would have tumbled to the floor if the chair hadn't been bolted to it. "You sonofabitch," I snarled at him. "That wasn't part of the deal."

He eyed me with disdain, and I caught a touch of condescending pity in the expression. "You stupid *stupid* woman. You of all people should know how this works. You don't get to deal. You have no power here. The only thing you have is your hubris."

"How do you know I didn't anticipate you wouldn't uphold your end of the bargain I made? How do you know I didn't film a video detailing everything, showing everything? How do you know I haven't done that and scheduled it to release in three days, unless I cancel the command, which I won't unless you do what I asked. Leave. The. Flores. Family. Alone."

"I know you haven't because you're not that smart. Or that stupid."

Ouch. Not true. I am smart. Really.

"You're also terrible at bluffing."

Am not. I raised my chin and looked right into his cold blue eyes. "I hope they test that chemical weapon on you next."

Smith graced me with a sardonic smile. "Have a nice evening, Dr. Martin."

* * *

The pattern was easy to discern. And also *really* fucking rude. I'd been put in a dark room, but every hour, someone would disturb me, either by banging on the metal door or turning on the light or coming in the room to shake me. A bastard technique but an effective one. I'd be useless with fatigue by the time they were ready to talk to me again.

Predawn wake up. I think? I couldn't tell what time it was anymore. Fucking assholes. In between the constant wake-up calls, I *had* managed to snatch snippets of sleep. I probably would have been better off not sleeping at all. After a bland breakfast of cereal, undercooked toast, overripe fruit, and watery coffee, they left me alone in the claustrophobic room. They left the lights on, the bright fluorescents searing my brain.

My day was broken only by calisthenics and yoga, and meals delivered by a faceless person who knocked on my door then shoved the tray through a slot. Fruit and crackers snack. Sandwich and fruit lunch with weak tea. Popcorn and fruit snack. Sandwich and soup and chocolate pudding cup dinner. When you're bored, things like food become very interesting. They'd even apologized after giving me a roast beef sandwich, and had promptly replaced it with a vegetarian option. But they seemed to take perverse pleasure in interrupting my yoga with noise. I'd spent a lot of time in Child's Pose.

The room they were keeping me in was of reasonable size and the toilet even had a privacy partition to give me some dignity from the camera in the corner. Deluxe. It was nothing like the tiny, dark, dirt-floored room I'd been held in during my captivity in 2017, but the thought of being held against my will still had a constant shudder of discomfort running down my back.

Sophia had presumably arrived home and was now resuming her normal life without me. Good. Normal was good. She deserved normal. Maybe I could be normal? One day. Then we could date and move in together and live like a regular couple with a cat. Excitement mixed with dread in my stomach until I felt queasy. No. My life would never be *normal*. I lay down on the narrow bed and rolled over to face the wall.

Another night of hourly disturbances leading into a predawn wake up for the day. Fucking assholes. Same breakfast as the previous day, and the moment I was done eating, the remnants of my meal were removed. The door opened again, no knock. Unremarkable man in cargos and a polo. "Against the wall, legs spread, hands flat against the wall. I have a Taser."

"Lucky you." I assumed the requested position as he reinstalled restraints around my wrists and attached them to the chain he fastened firmly around my waist. With a hand on my elbow he escorted me back to the room where I'd been interrogated, er... debriefed the previous evening. Or, was it the evening before? Yes, two nights ago. Yesterday was a day of nothing. Wasn't it? My pals Smith and Jones were there in the same positions as before, and I made myself smile as I was strapped to my other pal, the chair. The cuffs were left on, but this time they unfastened them from the chain around my waist so I could move my hands. Kind of. "Good morning, friends. I'd like my phone call now please."

Smith's thick dark eyebrow twitched up. "You're not under arrest." He leaned forward and I heard the creak of leather. "This isn't jail, nor is it television. The rules that you seem to think apply here do not."

"Oh? Really? I'm not? So I can go then? My bad, I thought being detained under one of the zillion Patriot or Homeland Security acts meant I was stuck here until you decided to let me go."

"How have you been sleeping?"

"Like a log. Great mattress."

"Enjoying the food?"

"It's delightful. Please send my compliments to the chef."

He leaned back in the chair and set his pen down. "Ms. Flores was very helpful. Very cooperative."

A muscle in my jaw twitched and I cursed myself for my reaction. "Did you tell her I said hi?"

"No. I forgot."

"You guyyyyys," I whined. "Dammit. Now she's going to think I'm ghosting her. Do you know how hard it is to date at my age when you work the hours I do? I finally found someone I'm attracted to, who didn't seem like they were going to throw a tantrum about the fact I miss dinners and movie dates and planned outings, who's also fabulous in bed, and you've ruined it for me. After your visit she probably thinks I'm a creepy weirdo and also a traitor to my country. Thanks."

Nothing from either of them. Time to dial it up.

I blew out a breath and fanned myself. "Speaking of the sex, phew. Out of this world. I mean, I'm talking best-of-my-life stuff, the kind of fucking that gets you through the cold lonely nights, if you know what I mean. This one time, she—"

"That's enough, Dr. Martin," said Smith, not bothering to hide his bored distaste. Scratch him. I probably could have stripped naked and not gotten a rise out of him. Metaphorically speaking.

Jones tried to hide it, but a flush rose above his starched collar. Bingo. His ineptitude in Tampa had given me the idea and this exchange cemented it. If there was any chance, then he was the one I could use for leverage and to get information. I winked at the younger man.

Smith cleared his throat. "Now. Let's start at the beginning."

"A very good place to start," I deadpanned. Dammit. I should have sung it like Maria from *The Sound of Music*. Next time.

"On the fourteenth of October this year you received a call from an asset of yours you refer to as Hadim. Correct?"

Aw shit. It was going to be like that, was it. "I feel like I've just stepped into a time machine. We've established that already."

"Why did you pursue something outside of your official duties? Why did you seek outside help? Why did you run?"

"We've been over this," I drawled, dragging the words out. "But I'll go through it again in case you're a little slow. I sought outside help because I was locked out of using my usual work channels. I sought outside help because half the things I learn every day come from outside help. How do you think we come by intelligence? Magic?" The annoyance at the stupidity and pointlessness of it all rose up again. "And I pursued it because some thug, maybe foreign, broke into my house demanding the intel, which was a huge hint that it was important. As for running, see my previous answer." Because Halcyon told me to, you dimwit.

"Did you stop to think, Dr. Martin, that someone demanding the intelligence in the middle of the night was a sign you *shouldn't* pursue it?" The way he accentuated *Doctor* as if to mock me was really getting under my skin.

"Briefly, yes. But I had no idea who wanted it. Government or private or even another country. I wanted to do my job because clearly this was important and I considered it my duty to keep the intel safe and figure it out while I figured out what and who was behind it." Try to accuse me of being unpatriotic now, you fucking asshole. "So maybe I overreacted, but tell me honestly—if what happened to me happened to you, would you not...I don't know, freak out a little bit? Be afraid someone was trying to kill you and steal something you'd classified as priority and shouldn't be seen by those without clearance?"

"No," he said dryly. "Because I'm not an idiot."

He was clearly trying to goad me into losing control of my self-control. Classic technique, but I had nothing to lose, so I answered the best way I knew how. With a sneering, "Fuck you." I unclenched my fists, spread my fingers wide. "I don't know what else to say. I did nothing wrong. I leaked nothing. I shared no intelligence with anyone outside of my immediate work chain, I didn't use an unsecured computer or server. As far as I can tell, the only *crime*"—I air-quoted that word—"I've committed was knowing something that people didn't want anyone to know. And given who is involved, I have to think the reason I'm in this position now is because this has the potential to be a political nightmare." I raised an eyebrow.

No answer.

"I mean, the White House covering up an illegal usage of a chemical weapon is bad enough. Doing it because they're embarrassed at *who* did it, and don't want a political scandal isn't concerning...at...all." I gave an exaggerated eye roll. The fact I'd been hounded, harassed and now incarcerated because of this put a sour taste in my mouth, and I wanted to spit it out. "Just to be clear, it's not the politics that's pissing me off. I care about national security and human rights."

"I think we're done." Smith closed his leather-bound notebook and tucked the pen in the seam. "You'll be moved to a new facility soon, one better suited to...long-term housing while you await trial. Perhaps you'll feel more cooperative and less snide there."

"Unlikely," I called at his departing back.

CHAPTER TWENTY-THREE

I really should have paid more attention to action movies

Left to stew in my own juices—metaphorically, because I was allowed to shower every day—I turned my two sessions with Smith over and over in my mind. There was no logic to the conversations because I'd laid out the truth repeatedly, and if they were investigating as they should then they'd know that my truth was actually truthful. And if he'd spoken to Sophia... I took a deep breath to calm the bone-melting fury I felt at that thought. If he'd spoken to Sophia then he'd know that she was truly unaware of what was going on.

So the only conclusion I could come up with for this charade was that someone was trying to intimidate me into dropping the whole thing and never ever speaking of it again. Given I was probably spending years in a secure facility, dropping it and not speaking of it again were guaranteed.

Some young guy, apparently my lawyer and definitely not shit-hot, had been to visit and nervously explained the charges. I didn't listen, just nodded, and said whatever, okay, yep, mhmm, sure, a dozen times. There was no point in absorbing it. I couldn't defend myself properly because doing so would mean pointing my finger at Halcyon. Opening statement: "I was just trying to do my job, Mr. President, sorry it upset your fragile ego, you disgusting monster."

I picked my nose, smiling up at the camera in the corner of the room.

A few hours after I finished my dinner of a microwave-meal-size teriyaki tofu and rice, a juicy sweet orange, and a banana pudding cup, the door swung open. Jones, in the door-visit uniform of cargos and polo. I smiled at him from my position on the bed. "Come to play cards with me, Jones?" A joke didn't ease my sudden surge of nervousness. He was here because it was time for me to be transferred. Halcyon wasn't going to intervene. Derek hadn't been able to do anything. They could be taking me anywhere and nobody on the outside would know about it. Sophia's upset rang through my head. The day of our third date, in her apartment, before we'd first made love when she'd seen my scars, what had she said? Think.

"So you might have been killed and I might never have met you?"

Something like that. Sorry, Sophia. Hopefully someone will let you know. Not dead, but not around anymore. I'm glad I met you and I really wish we'd had more time. A lot more. I tried not to think about how much I missed her. How comfortable and safe I felt with her. Comfort and safety…how sexy. But isn't feeling safe and comfortable the foundation for sexiness? I'd opened myself up to her and been completely vulnerable with her during intimacy. If that wasn't the ultimate trust, then I didn't know what was. I'd been worried about her developing Stockholm Syndrome by staying with me, but I realized then that maybe it was me who'd been inadvertently Stockholm Syndromed by Sophia.

Jones cleared his throat, interrupting my reverie. "Dr. Martin?" No longer in his cheap suit and clumsily knotted tie, Jones actually looked rather capable. His posture was confident and if I didn't know better I'd think he was military. I studied him closer. Maybe I didn't know better. He held up the handcuffs. "Stand against the wall, legs spread apart and put your hands flat against the wall."

All the fight left me. All my snark, my sense of humor, my bravado, my whatever you want to call it. Just gone. I let it go and didn't bother fretting over it. I didn't need it right now, but I would need it in the future to deal with everything they threw at me. If my coping ability needed a break to recharge then so be it. I swung my feet to the floor and moved to the wall farthest from the door. Good, cooperative prisoner. Detainee. Whatever. This time I was cuffed by both wrists and ankles, all attached to the chain around my waist.

Even though I knew it was pointless, that being transferred meant I was done, I still had to ask, "Where am I right now?"

Nothing.

"Where am I being transferred to? I'd like to call someone when I get there." When he still didn't answer, I offered a weak smile. "You're allowed to talk now. We're not playing the same game as we did in Tampa. Permission to speak granted, aaanndddd, go!"

He didn't even look at me. It was the *perfect* opportunity to make some snide remarks or rub in just how much the tables had turned or something. But he didn't say a word. If I were him, I'd have been blathering about it nonstop. Psychological warfare is very effective. But Jones was just…silent, self-contained. I'd made so many wrong assessments and apparently my impression of Jones as an easy mark for information, or someone soft, was way off. And it gave me the uneasy sensation that maybe I'd been totally off the mark about a lot of things recently. Halcyon wasn't going to help me.

I shuffle-walked as Jones led me through the winding corridors, down a flight of stairs, until we were in the underground garage where I'd been unloaded…some days ago. A nondescript gray van was parked right by the door, the kind without rear windows that always made me think it was a total creep-wagon. Definitely no candy in this van. The rear doors were already open, showing a stripped-out interior with two simple solid benches along each side and what I recognized as shackle anchor points on the floor and walls.

I wiggled my fingers. "Is this really necessary? It's not like I can pick the lock and escape out the back of this very clichéd van." More than that, the feeling of being shackled by both hands and feet was bringing familiar panic to the surface. On its own where I could move my legs, I'd been coping. But thinking about being stuck in one place this way, and in the dark, was terrifying. They'd know my history, know what cuffing me in this way would do, and they'd done it anyway. Fucking assholes and their psychological warfare.

"Protocol," was all Jones said.

I exhaled a long breath, trying not to sound shaky. "I see. Can you at least put my seat belt on, please?"

"Why?"

"In case the driver isn't good at slowing down around corners. I'd rather stay on this bench." I moved my hands as far as I could, which was about an inch from my waist and with about two inches of give side to side. "My balance isn't at its prime right now."

"There are no seat belts. In case you hadn't noticed, this isn't exactly a limousine."

"Perfect. You all really know how to make a girl feel special."

He attached the chain of my ankle shackles to a bolt on the floor, giving me about a foot of leeway with my legs. Jones gave everything a few tugs to test it was secure then closed the rear doors on me. No handles on the inside of the doors. Well, there goes my grand plan of MacGyver-ing the chains and escaping out the back. Two loud bangs on the side, a short pause, some conversation, and we were moving.

Apparently my request for a seat belt had given them ideas on how to be assholes and before every corner, they gunned the engine and whipped around the curve like they were pretending this was a rally car. After the third time of sliding around the back of the van like they'd greased the seat, I slid from my perch and shuffled awkwardly around the floor until my back was wedged against the opposite bench with my legs outstretched to accommodate being anchored to the bolt with my feet.

At least this way I could brace myself. Kind of. I let my head fall forward, and closed my eyes. Nothing to do but nap. Away from the looming threat of interrogation I was able to think more clearly. I should be able to wrangle some privilege for myself at the new facility. The first thing I'd ask for was communication of some sort, if only through my baby-faced lawyer.

Dear Sophia,

I'm fine and they are treating me well. I hope your dad is okay after they kidnapped him because of me. I miss the way you taste and how you fuck me until I forget about everything except you.

Wouldn't that be a fun letter for my counsel to dictate.

At least I could pass the time with memories. Our short time together had given me enough to think about to make personal time enjoyable, but also some nice, not-sexy memories. Just everyday thoughts of my enjoyment at being with someone, like in a relationship. I forced the melancholy aside. They wouldn't keep me locked away forever and maybe she'd want to meet up again when I was out. If she could get past all this, and me maybe having some sort of criminal record. And if she hadn't married someone and had kids or something.

I didn't deserve her, not after what I'd done. And you know what? She really deserved better than me, deserved more than my constant secrecy. She should find someone who could give her what she needed. That was what was best for her. Despite my pep talk, I didn't feel better. I felt like shit. Sure, we hadn't known each other long, but spending eight days in close and near-constant proximity while you're running at peak pace is bonding. I bent my head as close to my hands as I could and despite them being chained in place, managed to rub my face. Flexibility for the win.

Sophia – PS: You're super flexible.

Oh, and PPS: I hope you still have my tea stuff, and my dress. Please keep it safe in case I ever get out of custody. I'll wear it one night when I take you out for drinks on an island resort somewhere. The dress, not the tea.

Maybe Derek would visit me. Maybe Lennon would—exciting, I'd finally get to see what he looked like. Or maybe I was going to spend twenty years alone. God I hoped this was really worth it. After a way to communicate with people, I'd ask for a television so I could watch Vice President Berenson being arrested for being a Russian lackey. There's your traitor, Smith.

The driver braked hard and I was jolted to my right. "Oh, fuck you!" I yelled at the metal wall separating me from the van cab, trying to raise my elbow to bang on it. Before I could shuffle back into a position that wasn't straining the ankle cuffs to their max, there was a loud thud and bang from behind me. A squeal of tires. A metallic crunch. Another softer crunch. And then everything flipped. Repeatedly.

Metal shrieked and groaned as I was flung around the interior like a ragdoll, stuck to the floor with my feet as the anchor point. Pain everywhere as my body made contact with the walls, the floor, the roof of the van. The shackles on my ankles bit and cut in as my body whipped around. I couldn't even bring my hands up to try to protect my head and I cracked it against something that really fucking hurt.

I finally settled on my back, painfully jammed against the bench as the van settled on its side. The sound of metal grating along asphalt was deafening and as we skidded, I bent my knees to brace my feet on the floor. The movement sent an electric shock of pain from my right ankle all the way up my leg into my hip, but the alternative of being flung around even more felt worse.

Then everything was so still. The creak of settling metal, steam hissing, an engine pinging and ticking. My ragged breathing. The panicked rapid thudding of my heart in my ears. That wasn't them being assholes. That was a fucking traffic accident. Excuse me, helpful bystander? Hi, just wondering if you know how to pick locks? Oh, these shackles? Don't worry about them.

I took stock of myself. Alive but injured about summed it up. My entire body hurt, a mix of dull and sharp aches and raw stings. My limbs seemed to work but judging by the angle of the digits on my hands, I'd broken my right pinky and ring finger, and maybe my ankle. My head felt like someone had hit me with a baseball bat and cracked my forehead open, and all my ribs felt like they'd snapped. I tried to call out, to remind them I was in there but all I managed was a choking squeak. If they were unconscious and fuel ignited, well…things were going to get unpleasant very quickly. Oh fuck. I did not want to die burning in the back of a van. Oh fuck, please not that. I banged as best I could against the interior, but the sound just echoed around the space.

I heard the muffled sound of car doors opening, then two loud gunshots before the rear van doors flung open, the top one held so it couldn't bang back down. Five people. Combat clothing. Black balaclavas. Assault rifles. Sidearms. Serious business. The adrenaline that'd focused my brain went south and I had to draw on every ounce of my pelvic floor strength. I really did not think they'd end it this way. Seems being patriotic is its own kind of punishment. I closed my eyes.

"Martin!" Familiar, caring. Derek?

The tension around my ankles released and I was dragged out of the van and to my feet. Hot liquid ran into my shoes, onto my hands, down my cheek. Blood, not pee. Probably. One of the figures let the van door fall and it slammed back against the frame, the sharp sound startling me so much I almost peed for real.

The masked Derek-sounding figure held on to me around the waist. "Can you stand on your own? Walk?"

I tested both theories and nodded. I could stand, albeit somewhat shakily and ohmyfuckinggoddd, my right leg. The pain was out of this world, but I could put weight on my foot, just. Okay, probably not a broken ankle then, just very unhappy. I leaned against the closed van door, keeping weight on my left side as the cuffs at my wrists were released, the chain dropped from my waist. As soon as the pressure eased, heat flooded into my limbs, making them heavy and useless.

He fished something from his pocket and held it to my forehead. "Put your hand on this, you're dripping." Once I'd pressed my left hand to the fabric, he asked, "Can you drive?"

I had no idea, but I nodded anyway.

Maybe-Derek pointed down the street. "There's a gray Lexus over there, key's in the ignition. Everything you need to get to the safehouse is in the car. The address is already in the satnav ready to go."

"Why?" I choked out, wincing as my tongue moved. I spat a mouthful of blood onto the ground. It joined other spatters of my blood dripping onto the asphalt.

"Lennon sends his regards. He's sorry it took so long." Maybe-Derek grinned.

A fresh rush of heat filled me and I didn't know if I was shocked, surprised, angry, or incredulous. Probably all of those and a few other emotions I couldn't quite reach. "You...you...you are fucking shitting me."

"Not at all."

"Could he not have just...collected me from the facility instead of doing this? Much less painful. Fuck. I have questions. Like, a lot of them."

"I'm sure you do." He turned away to take a manila envelope from a camo-clad figure who'd just come running up to us from the front of the van, and shoved it into my hand. "Go, *now*, before we have a bunch of eyes. I'll contact you." He pressed me forward and I tripped on wobbling legs and hit the deck, instinctively trying to keep my injured hand from being injured more and only succeeding in making my left hand hurt as well. Under my palms I felt asphalt, gravel, grass. He hauled me up again, repositioned the cloth on my forehead and put my hand back on it, patted my shoulder and pushed me gently forward again.

I stumbled away from the van, glancing back at it as I tripped and fumbled and dragged and limped my way along the deserted street in the dark, toward the fog lights of what I could only assume to be my gray Lexus. My entire body felt like one great big bruised wound and it took all my focus and willpower to keep moving. No time to process right now. Only time to get away.

The driver's side door was already open and I threw the envelope onto the passenger's seat, eased into the driver's seat, and belted myself in. Wear a seat belt, kids. It'll save you a lot of pain. Trust me. I slipped the car into drive and gunned the accelerator. Or tried to. The moment I moved my leg, pain bit my ankle and shot straight up into my hip. I admit it—I screamed and fell forward onto the steering wheel. A few deep breaths helped settle the pain enough that I could try again, albeit this time with less enthusiasm. I crept up to forty and quickly passed the wreckage of the van and a second vehicle I hadn't noticed.

I didn't look in the rearview mirror. I just kept driving.

Blood ran from my hairline onto my eyelid again and I wiped impatiently at it as I drove, then wiped my hand on my thigh. The piece of fabric Maybe-Derek had pressed to my forehead had fallen onto my lap and I fumbled for it. The monogram in the corner caught my eye. His wife monogrammed all his handkerchiefs, which made him ripe for teasing in the office. DW, clear as day. Maybe-Derek really was Derek. He was on my side. He was on every side that I was on, and I was on a few.

I'd driven for ten minutes when it occurred to me that I had no fucking idea where I was or where I could go that was safe. Derek's words looped back into my brain. Punching the navigation system with my forefinger brought it online and a text query caught my attention.

Resume Route?

Seemed like a good plan.

The safehouse was nestled on the outskirts of Stone Ridge. So I'd been near Virginia this whole time. I drove around the block a second time to check the house, which had lights on and looked for all intents and purposes just like a regular family home. The double garage door rolled up as I approached and then when I'd parked, it rolled down again. Thank you, smart home system.

First, I peeked inside the envelope I'd been handed as I was being shoved away from the van. My actual real passport and other IDs, all my bank cards, and my house and car keys. How sweet, they were sending some personal effects to the dungeon with me. In the duffel resting on the back seat were clothes, including underwear and bras in my size—Derek, you sneaky perve—money, a brand-new phone, tablet and laptop, and a Glock 26 subcompact pistol in an ankle holster as well as a larger Glock 19. I laughed despite the seriousness of the situation. Derek was a Glock fanboy, and these two weapons plus his handkerchief confirmed that he had certainly orchestrated my escape, and not a Derek sound-a-like.

I took the 19 in my less-useless left hand and, exiting the garage, did a very slow limpy sweep of the two levels. Once I'd satisfied myself that there were no bogeymen hiding in the closets, I collected the bag from the Lexus, double-checked all the locks and trudged up to the second-floor bathroom. The wounded-bruise feeling had intensified into full body pain so bad that each step made me exhale a groan.

The person staring back at me in the mirror looked like someone working in a fright house. My face was bloodied, smeared from where I'd kept wiping it away as it'd run down my forehead, over my closed eye and down my cheek. Dried blood matted my hair, making it stick up from my forehead. I leaned closer, studying the bruising that was beginning to darken either side of my nose. Double shiners, both eyes starting to swell. Tentatively I touched my hairline, wincing at the sharp bite of pain. Parting my hair, I could see a gash about an inch and a half long, an eighth of an inch wide and deep enough to be gory without showing my skull. Probably needed stitches. Ah well, too bad. Leaving this safehouse was not an option.

I stripped out of the gray jumpsuit and left it in the bath. Further examination revealed no more major wounds—a miracle—but my torso looked like I'd gone ten rounds with the world heavyweight boxing champion. I'd look like a tree in the middle of fall in a few days, with bruises of all colors. My ribs felt a little better, almost okay. Okay as in not broken, maybe cracked but manageable. My ankle looked like a plum on steroids, but I could carefully weight-bear on it. A bit of bandaging and ice would take care of it.

And then there were my fingers. Definitely broken or dislocated or something not right. Don't think about it, take a deep breath and on the count of five you'll pull them back into their right place. One...two—yank. Fuuuuuuuuck. The trick is to trick yourself. Leaning against the sink, I sucked in some deep breaths until I no longer felt like I was about to pass out. I opened cabinets until I found a first aid kit under the sink, and with a shaking left hand, I taped the fingers of my shaking right hand together, splinting them. Then I puked in the sink. I was acquiring quite the habit.

Priority one—shower and deal with the rest of my injuries. Swearing helped when I rinsed my hair and then used antiseptic liquid to clean the cut on my forehead. The skin was taut with swelling, tight and uncomfortable, and coupled with the raw stinging from the open wound it was a pretty unpleasant experience. Once I'd used one of the nice ultra-fluffy white towels to dry myself, and left part of it red with blood—sorry, housekeeper—I gritted my teeth, pushed the edges of the cut together and stuck skin closure tape over it as best I could around my hair. It'd have to do. I declared myself all put back together.

Priority two—food and a metaphorical fistful of painkillers. Ibuprofen would have to do. I could almost hear Sophia's disapproval, and for a moment the sensation of missing her was so strong I had to lean against the wall until it passed. If she were here, she'd have cleaned me up, dressed and wrapped all my injuries, griped about me taking too much ibuprofen, then lovingly ordered food for me before bundling me into bed. I'd have to do it on my own.

The fridge and pantry were stocked with an assortment of premade meals, ingredients, Oolong tea, and snacks which consisted overwhelmingly of Combos. Bless you, Derek, and your knowledge of my tea and snack addiction. I tore open a bag of Cheddar Cheese Pretzel Combos and shoveled a handful into my mouth. Chewing my dry, crumby mouthful, I nabbed a bottle of Blue Moon from the fridge.

Priority three—process what the actual fuck had happened. Every attempt was basically me running into a mental brick wall. And spray-painted all over the wall was that Derek had been behind all this shit, and had then busted me out of a secure transport before they could lock me away, breaking who knew how many laws. *And* he was part of Halcyon Division? So it seemed he was safe, and I might be safe.

Safe…

Was Sophia safe? Did she tell her family what had happened or did she not mention it? Was she finished with the self-help website design job? Had she thought about me at all? And if she had, did she know how much I'd thought about her while alone in that room?

I hadn't cried at all since I'd broken down while sitting on that hotel bed with her arms wrapped around me and her face pressed to my shoulder. Not while they'd had me in that debrief room. While they'd been waking me every hour on the hour. While they'd been questioning me. Not through every second of being alone in the room they'd kept me in for days.

But I cried now, sitting on the plush carpet in this affluent safehouse, thinking about her. And I couldn't stop. I let myself fall sideways until I lay on the floor, curled in on myself, and I sobbed until I felt like my eyes were raw and my throat was bleeding from howling. After what felt like a few hours, my breathing finally steadied, my tears dried and I felt like I might be able to move without having another breakdown, as had happened when I'd thought I was okay and tried to sit up about half an hour before.

On my way back from washing my face at the kitchen sink, carrying a fresh bag of ice for my ankle, the phone Derek had left for me starting ringing. I glanced at it on the coffee table, noting *Derek* on the screen. Thanks for programming in some apps, friend.

I dropped onto the couch, propped my leg up and dropped the bag of ice onto my ankle. "Yes?"

No greeting, simply the comforting confirmation of Derek assuring me, "The safehouse is secure. And so are these phones."

"Well that's a relief," I drawled. "Because I'm really not up for visitors right now."

"Are you badly injured?"

I cleared my throat, trying to clear the hoarseness that remained from my meltdown. "Better than 2017. I'll live. I thought my ankle was broken but turns out it's just really fucked up." Grimacing, I wiggled my toes. Just. Can you wiggle your toes with a broken ankle? A question for Dr. Google later.

A long pause. The look on his face when he'd first seen me in that dirt-floored room was seared into my admittedly pain-hazy memory. Horrified. Distraught. He exhaled audibly. "Sorry, my driver got a little aggressive with his bump maneuver."

"Mmm." I swallowed a mouthful of beer and felt the sudden need to ask, "How are the guys who were transporting me? I… heard shots."

"Nothing but headaches. We couldn't get the rear doors open, had to use a little ballistic force."

Ah. Well that explained…well, not much really. I exhaled and regretted it as my ribs protested vehemently about the movement. "Sooo…what the fuck is going on? This seems like it just got a whole lot worse. Especially for me who is now technically classed as a fugitive, am I right?"

"Many things are going on, too many to talk about here. Take some time to recuperate. I need you back in the office in a few weeks and I'll lay it all on the table for you then."

Apparently I'd hit my head harder than I'd thought and was hearing things. "Back in the office. You have *got* to be shitting me. So, I'm apparently a fugitive criminal, but aside from all of that, hasn't my security clearance been yanked?"

"No. Halcyon has taken care of it. You're going to walk into the office like nothing happened and that's what everyone will assume because they know no different. You've had a bad dose of Covid, that's all. These events have been bleached." His voice lowered, softened. "Do you trust me? Do you trust the people you work for?"

A good question. He seemed to be on my side. And apparently had some friends in high places. I hedged, "Mostly."

Derek laughed. "Good enough for me."

I drank a long swallow of beer, tried not to burp in Derek's ear. "I…don't really understand what just happened. And what's going to happen."

"You're no good to the government locked up, and they needed to be reminded of that. The president was set on punishing you because he doesn't realize your value. Because he's angry about you finding out his secrets. Because he thinks everyone acts as dishonorably as he does, he assumed you spilled intelligence. So Halcyon had to intervene and set him straight. In some respects, their power is greater than the White House's."

Their power? My value? "What do you mean?"

But he wouldn't say. Great. Another puzzle piece. I was too tired to put this one anywhere, so I shoved it aside to deal with later. "I wish I'd known you were part of Halcyon earlier. It would have reduced my anxiety, knowing I could trust you."

"No. You did the right thing." He cleared his throat and the next words were gruff with emotion. "You did real good. Better than we could have hoped. You did exactly what was asked of you."

"Employee of the month for me. At one workplace at least."

He laughed, loud and long. "I'll back the recommendation."

"Thanks. I've been wondering about that first day, when I got the intel. Why were you so meh about it? It was like you thought I'd just heard a rumor and were trying to get me out of your office."

Derek sighed. "Yeah, sorry. Lennon had been in my ear for days about Berenson's suspected ties to Russia and I guess I was focused on that, on trying to get Halcyon the proof they needed. Would have alleviated my stress if I'd made that connection then and there."

"Fair. Can I just ask one more thing?" Without waiting for him to agree, I asked, "Why the middle-of-the-night snatch and grab?"

"Pure drama value."

"Funny. If I could laugh without it hurting, I would. I hope it was worth it to get to play action hero again."

"It was," Derek assured me. "Lennon was negotiating, with varied success, for your release. He received word you were being moved to an underground location and wanted to intercept before that happened. It would have been much harder to secure your release once you went off the grid."

"Good timing. I'm going to get my period soon and I really wasn't looking forward to dealing with that in captivity."

"That was our main concern," Derek deadpanned.

"I hope you're prepared for my bombardment of questions when I'm feeling better. This whole thing is fucking movie-plot bonkers. And I thought it was bonkers when it was just the Halcyon directive. Now it's off the chain."

"I know." Derek laughed. "Okay, we can debrief when you get back to work. Another Halcyon phone will be provided in due course. But for now you need to rest and relax. You're safe now. Take a few weeks. Go and see Sophia Flores."

I paused, taking in what he'd just said. Sophia. "I don't think that's a good idea," I said slowly. "I'm pretty sure I'm the last person she wants to see."

"I'm pretty sure you're the first person she wants to see." Then he quickly added, "Trust me on that if nothing else. You told me you love her. Don't let that get away."

I made a musing sound of not agreement but not disagreement. "I don't know if I love her or if it was just the situation and I was trying to justify what I'd done."

"What does it feel like?" he quietly asked.

"I...don't know. I'm not sure what any kind of love really feels like." I cleared my throat.

"A good way to find out would be to spend some time with her. Don't think about this for a bit, let your brain reset." His tone sharpened back to business. "I'll see you in the office on Monday, two weeks from now. I need you at your best when you come back, maybe go to the ER and get checked out. Don't let me down, Martin."

"Mmm. I might. But I promise it won't be intentional." I hung up, groaningly pushed myself up from the couch and went to the kitchen for more salty snacks and beer. ER tomorrow.

CHAPTER TWENTY-FOUR

Safety looks like a cute brunette in a Princess Leia T-shirt

I stayed at the safehouse for four days, periodically peeking through the curtains to assure myself I was still alone. Unless they were inside a tree costume or watching me through walls with thermal cams, nobody was there. Television. *Very* gentle yoga. Eating. Drinking. Napping. Having cathartic crying breakdowns. By the third night I'd finished the freshly prepared meals and as I crawled gingerly into the extremely comfortable bed, decided it was time to leave. Go home, see what my apartment looked like, then go to Sophia.

Sophia.

Derek's assurances that she'd missed me—fuck knows how he knew, but I didn't question the fact because he'd have no reason to lie about that—made the decision to go see her easier. But I couldn't ignore the massive lump of unease that it wasn't a good idea. Maybe now she had removed herself from our time together, she'd reconsidered how she felt about me, about us. I mean, I'd given her over a week of running and hiding and lying and subterfuge. But we'd also had over a week of connecting, talking, laughing, intimacy and getting to know one another. Over a week of...maybe falling in love.

Without my own phone or laptop, I didn't have easy access to Sophia's contact details. I could have searched for her business number or email, then contacted her through either of those, but that felt kind of icky. Email subject: *Hi, I'm not dead or incarcerated.* Straight to spam. In person was the best, though scary, way. The idea of seeing her again after…how many days had it been? Four? Five? I opened the calendar app in the phone Derek had given me. I'd turned myself in on the twenty-second and it was the fourth? No… I counted back again, couldn't believe it and did another count, using fingers this time.

It was true. They'd had me for ten days. Only seemed like three-ish. Right, so that made it two weeks since I'd seen her. I rolled into the middle of the bed and carefully stretched my sore body. Of course, lying in this huge bed alone made me think of her again. The way she slept like each of her limbs were compass points, all in different directions. Her love of snuggling, and how when I'd crawl back into our hotel bed after staring at my laptops 'til the stupid hours in the morning, she'd find me and wrap me up as if she wanted to keep me safe.

Then the sex. Incredible. Mind-boggling. Addictive. Safe. But also, when I really stopped to think about it, not the thing I missed the most about being with her. Being with her was the thing I missed most about being with her.

After a hot water-wasting shower I packed up my belongings that weren't really my belongings, sent Derek a message to tell him I was leaving so they could prep the house for the next person needing a safe space, and directed my borrowed Lexus toward home. Nothing I had was mine, hadn't really been for a while, and I felt an odd apprehension about returning to my apartment and having no idea of what I'd find.

I unlocked the door with the 19 trained in front of me, praying I wouldn't have to use it. I was so not in the mood, mind or body, for a fight. My apartment was dim, the only light from the windows which had curtains open all the way. Slowly, I checked every room and closet, and behind all doors in case bogeymen were there. Nothing.

My bedroom carpet, where Broken Nose had bled, had been shampooed and looked just as good as when I'd first bought the place. My wall had been patched and repainted, just like new, and whoever had cleaned up had also made my bed with fresh linens. Thoughtful. They'd even put basics in my fridge and refilled my ice trays. Geez, I should get involved in secret government conspiracies more often.

At two p.m. on the dot, I put a few things in a backpack and went to where I'd parked the Lexus on the street. I was going to have to message Derek again to come and collect it. But while it still had gas, I was damned well going to use it.

Sophia lived about fifteen minutes from my place, and I parked a few blocks away, stowed a few essentials in pockets and took a walk. On my second pass by her building, I saw movement up in her apartment. Could go up there. Should. But something made me feel weird about it. Made me scared. So I didn't.

I knew she played pickleball on Friday night, and knew the gym from her keychain. She'd probably leave sometime around five thirty which gave me a few hours to work up the nerve to approach her. I bought a sandwich, ate it sitting on a bench that was out of her window line of sight and then brought the Lexus around and parked down the street where I had a good view of the parking garage.

At 5:36 p.m. when Sophia pulled out and turned east, I started the car and slipped behind her. If she'd noticed me tailing her, she gave no indication. She was easy enough to follow, even with her typical speeding and constant lane changes as she'd done when she'd driven during our trip. Our trip. I swallowed and pushed the thought of it from my head.

When she pulled into the gym's parking lot, I parked in the Shake Shack parking lot next door. A burger place next to a gym. Cruelty. Sophia reversed into a spot with a clear line to the exit, and the fact she'd started parking her car facing outward and in such a tactical position made a small surge of pride flare alongside the discomfort that her time with me had been so affecting. I wondered what other things she now did that before knowing me she'd never even considered. That sense of inadequacy flared again. Maybe this wasn't a good idea. Maybe the best thing for her, for us, would be for me to stay away. But that thought was so distressing I had to shove it out of my head.

Sophia leaned over to pull a bag from the back seat then slipped out of her car, turning back to check it was locked. Oh geez. How could I stay away from that when she was dressed for her game of pickleball in the hottest gym outfit I'd ever seen. As she turned to walk to the entrance I spotted the front of her tee. Princess Leia. Tiny short shorts and a Princess Leia shirt? She may as well have just asked me to marry her.

Once she'd gone into the building, I waited another ten minutes to be sure she wasn't going to come back for something forgotten, then jammed a ball cap on my head, slipped from the shadows and walked across the parking lot. Though this gym and sport-court center was near my apartment, I'd never been inside, preferring to work out at the office. Inside were a bunch of courts I recognized and a couple I didn't. I spotted Sophia on one of the spaces that looked like a mini-tennis court, and wandered casually around to a viewing area where she wouldn't see me unless she had a sudden urge to contort herself in the middle of the game.

I settled a few seats away from a middle-aged couple who were intently watching one of the basketball courts where a group of teens appeared to be training. They eyed me curiously, not surprising given my appearance. The last thing I wanted was to draw attention to this part of the stands by having the two of them get up and move away. Deciding to put them out of their misery, I removed the cap, smiled and leaned in. "Stuck on the sidelines watching my team. I took a blinder in pickleball last week."

The woman nodded. "Looks like it. I didn't realize it was a contact sport."

"It's not supposed to be," I said conspiratorially, "but stick a bunch of adults who missed out on being college sports stars on a court and things get competitive real fast." I gingerly touched the bridge of my nose then gestured to the basketball court where the teens were still pretending to be the Lakers. "You've got someone playing?"

"Our son," offered the man, pride evident in those two words. He pointed. "Number twelve."

Number twelve went for a layup and completely fumbled it. The couple chuckled. "He's not great at it, but damn if he doesn't have fun."

I leaned back against the seat, trying to appear relaxed when my body was screaming at me from the position. "Well, that's what it's about. Right?"

Apparently I'd said the right thing. The woman beamed and we chatted about nothing important for the rest of their kid's training session, while I kept one eye on Sophia's game. Partly for recon, but mostly because watching her was pleasurable. And not just the whole running and hitting and jumping thing. She looked like she was having so much fun playing her sport, and the image was such an interesting contrasting dynamic to the time we'd spent together, another layer of Sophia Flores that rounded out what I already knew about her. I wanted to round her out fully, learn everything I could about her. The good and the bad, the confusing, the surprising. All of it.

When the couple got up, I stood too and walked down the stairs behind them, hidden from the pickleball courts. I'd looked up the rules and knew I had another twenty minutes before she'd be done with the game. And though I'd have loved to stay and watch Sophia for the rest of her sports, I had to prepare. I put the cap back on, ignoring the scream from the gash in my hairline, and ducked out the side door to the parking lot.

Using the fob I'd stolen from Sophia's junk drawer the first day I'd been in her house—sorrynotsorry—I unlocked her car and placed the items I'd brought with me on top of the steering column. After a quick glance around, I blended into the shadows at the edge of the parking lot by the dense row of tall shrubs. Unless someone with a flashlight was really looking for me, I would be next to invisible.

Once in position, I resigned myself to waiting. Not for long, unless she was going to have a post-match get-together or watch another game. Standing, especially pressed against coarse foliage, quickly became uncomfortable with the remnants of the crash making my body sore and tight. My ribs complained constantly and I tried to shuffle into a more comfortable position and only succeeded in making myself more uncomfortable.

After fifteen minutes, footsteps approached. Tension tightened my body, raced my heart. If it wasn't her, I was screwed. If it was her and I'd totally misjudged things, I was screwed.

The smell of Sophia's distinctive fabric conditioner mixed with the smell of healthy sweat was comforting. First hurdle cleared. She was here. Sophia unlocked the car and settled in the driver's seat. Then nothing.

I could see the side of her face, the movement as she reached for the rubber octopus and short note I'd set on her steering wheel. She turned both over in her hands and I could imagine her deciphering their meaning. The note wasn't deep or meaningful, just telling her I was nearby and a number she could call me on if she wanted to talk face-to-face right now.

Sophia turned on the interior light and scrambled for something on the passenger seat. Seconds later, my Signal app alerted. Relief and gratitude made my greeting a tight, "Hey, you."

Her voice was a hoarse whisper, the disbelief palpable. "Are you really *here*?"

"Yes."

She turned around, looking left, right, behind. "Where?"

"Right here in the parking lot. You can't see me. Not unless you want to?" My voice rose hopefully with the question.

"I do." A quiet exhalation. "Are you okay? Are you safe?" she asked.

"I will be. Are you okay?"

"Yes, I am."

"How's your dad?"

"He's fine too."

"Good. Fuck, it's so good to hear your voice. So good to see you. I...can I come closer?"

"Yes," she choked out.

"Okay...I'm going to approach the car now, from the passenger side."

I saw her nod, then a second later she seemed to catch herself and consented with, "Mhmm, right, okay."

I stepped from the shadows and walked slowly toward her car, wanting to be sure she saw me. The moment she did, Sophia raised her hand in a weak wave, which I returned. The sense of relief, of comfort, of rightness, was so overwhelming that I felt tears threaten. Blinking hard, I opened the door and slid into the front passenger seat. I ended the call, slipping the phone into my front pocket. "Hey," I said gently.

"Hey," Sophia croaked out in response. "I, um...what should I do?" she whispered.

"Just drive, darling." The endearment had fallen so naturally off my tongue that I'd had no time to think about it.

She flung her arms around me, holding me tight, her fingers digging into my back. I ignored the pain and hugged her, pressing my face against her neck. I felt her deep inhalation before she relaxed her grip. Sophia kissed me with such exquisite sweetness that I melted into the kiss. "Where should I go?" she asked.

I kissed her again, cupping her face, wet with tears, between my hands. "Anywhere."

Sophia paused and when she spoke, her voice was tight with emotion. "My place?"

"Yes. Please. Take me home."

Bella Books, Inc.

Women. Books. Even Better Together.

P.O. Box 10543
Tallahassee, FL 32302
Phone: (800) 729-4992
www.BellaBooks.com

More Titles from Bella Books